Unfollow Me

Judith Cuffe xx

Judith Cuffe

POOLBEG
CRIMSON

Published 2022 by Crimson
an imprint of Poolbeg Press Ltd.
123 Grange Hill, Baldoyle,
Dublin 13, Ireland
Email: poolbeg@poolbeg.com

© Judith Cuffe 2022

The moral right of the author has been asserted.

A catalogue record for this book is available from the British Library.

ISBN 978178199-703-1

www.poolbeg.com

About the Author

Judith Cuffe lives in Enniskerry, Co. Wicklow, with her husband, three children and two dogs. When she's not writing, you'll find her at the gym, walking the dogs, ferrying the kids, filling then emptying her online Zara shopping basket and dabbling in social media which she believes should be, first and foremost, social! *Unfollow Me* is her fifth book. She has also written *When Destiny Sings, Sing Me Home, Lying with Truth* and *Unexpected Events,* all published on Amazon.

For Yvonne. Through school, UCD, motherhood, and beyond. Try as I might, I can't seem to shake you and, for that, I'll be grateful until the day I'm wearing sunglasses in a coffin, and you're standing over me singing Dido's "White Flag". (You promised.)

This one is for you.

If you don't like what you see,
Please be kind and unfollow me.

#unfollowme

PROLOGUE

1999

There was a fly in the room, buzzing as frantically as Eve Kelly's thoughts, shifting from place to place. Eve's gaze followed as it circled above her head, looping backwards and forwards before pausing above the photo collage on the wall of the bedroom she shared with her boyfriend, Conor.

Her eyes flitted from frame to frame. The photos were mainly of her – her long blonde hair hanging past her shoulders, peering back at the lens or directly at Conor behind it. One of her perched on the concrete steps outside the UCD Arts building, French-inhaling cigarette smoke, Conor's leather jacket thrown over her shoulders, other students blurred in the background as they rushed past. It was like something you'd see in a magazine, making her appear older than her twenty years. Some of the other photos were taken here in this house, sitting on this bed, or while she stared out the window – her hair piled on top of her head, willowy arms behind her back.

1

They'd been renting the house for the past three years with Eve's best friend, Ronnie. Eve's eyes settled on the photo where her arm was hooked around Ronnie's neck as she kissed her cheek. Ronnie's nose was wrinkled in mock disgust, her boy-short hair standing on end. They'd met on the first day of college and had been thick as thieves ever since.

Another was of the two of them dancing in the kitchen, Ronnie even taller than Eve. Another by UCD lake, the two girls lying back, watching the day slowly drift past. In reality, the years had sped so quickly that Eve felt wholly unprepared for what was next – too young to face what was ahead although there was no other choice. Trying not to think of it, she averted her attention to a picture of her and Conor on one of the countless nights spent partying. There were more of those than Eve cared to recall.

Conor had made it look like the perfect college experience from this vantage: youthful, carefree, alive – the most incredible years of their lives. Now that it was almost over, perhaps she would choose to remember it this way, exactly how Conor told it in photos. After all, a picture never lies.

Downstairs, the front door of the house opened. Ronnie was back from the college library where she'd gone earlier to use the internet. Eve listened as she bounded upstairs, straight into her bedroom, shutting the door. Inside, she was probably lying on her bed, eyes moving from side to side, scheming, planning, preparing for whatever was next. As friends, they couldn't be more different.

As if on cue, the fly moved off again, this time landing on the dress that hung on the back of the door – layers of chiffon, intricately twisted straps, fitted bust, flowing to the floor. The red dress looked more ready for later than Eve felt. Staring at it, she swallowed the lump of nerves in her throat.

Sighing, she frowned. It was as if all their futures somehow depended on how she performed later in it when Conor took her photo. It was something he'd done a thousand times before, but this evening felt different – this evening it was about more than just her. It was for his portfolio.

The door to Ronnie's room flung open at the same time as Conor began to climb the stairs. Clamping her eyes shut, Eve listened to the exchange outside on the landing.

"How's Eve?" Even when she was trying to be quiet, Ronnie's voice boomed.

"She's resting." Conor's Northern Irish whisper sounded like silk in comparison. There was a hesitation. "Are you sure about this, Ronnie? Is it not too soon?"

Eve heard Ronnie tut. "She wants to do it, Conor, so let her. Besides, this is as much for her as it is for you. She needs something to fall back on too."

From behind the door, Eve grimaced. In case she failed her exams is what Ronnie meant. Despite desperately trying, she knew she'd left it late to cram in everything. Ronnie knew it too.

Eve had never considered pursuing modelling as a profession until Ronnie came up with "the plan" weeks before – a mass exodus to London where Ronnie would manage all their careers. In truth, it couldn't have come at a better time, giving them something to focus on, a goal to meet. If anyone could make it happen in such a short space of time, Ronnie could.

"I found a few places in London online that might suit," Ronnie said. "I'll show you both later on when we get back."

"Shouldn't we wait and see how the photos work out first?" Conor sounded cautious.

"We both know the photos will be great. Have a little faith. And, in the circumstances, I think it's better we have somewhere ready for when we arrive, don't you?"

There was another pause. Eve could imagine Conor nodding in agreement, leaning against the wall, flicking his dark fringe from his face.

"You'd better wake her," Ronnie said. "It's almost time to leave. I'll wait downstairs."

#

Ronnie drove in silence while Conor and Eve sat close together in the back seat of her car. Conor checked his camera, looking through the lens now and again while Eve sat quietly with her arms crossed, staring out the window.

Ronnie glanced in the rear-view mirror at Eve, who looked as beautiful as ever with her long hair loosely waved as if she'd spent the day on a beach instead of in bed. She was wearing an old grey hoodie over the red dress, runners on her feet in preparation for the short hike up to the cliff where Conor intended to shoot his vision, high in the Dublin mountains. Aside from a lick of mascara, a dab of concealer, Eve wore no other make-up but, even without it, there was colour visible on her cheeks for the first time in a long time. She looked like herself again.

Staring straight ahead, Ronnie focused her thoughts. It had been her idea to contact agencies in London about Conor's photos. Conor had talent, a keen eye for beauty, a way of capturing people and situations in a manner Ronnie had never seen before. Thankfully, a prominent London fashion agency had agreed. As long as Conor could complete his portfolio, they were interested. They wanted to be wowed, they'd told Ronnie, who'd assured them Conor knew how to do just that. His photos were raw, they'd said, edgy. Unsurprisingly,

Eve too had seized their attention as a model. After this evening, Ronnie would be able to offer them both as a package deal – two for the price of one. They'd be well and truly on their way.

Looking in the mirror once more, Ronnie glimpsed Conor reach his hand towards Eve to cup her face. Eve turned to him, smiled and mouthed, "I love you." The couple stared into each other's eyes with such intensity that Ronnie had to look away. In truth, not for one moment had Ronnie considered that the relationship would go the distance. Conor and Eve were the cool couple on campus: the grungy creative and his beautiful muse, so passionately in love that surely it couldn't last. Now, it looked as though it would.

Feeling a sudden lightness after months of enduring tension, a time where they'd all felt old before their time, Ronnie reached forward to switch on the radio. The corner of her mouth lifted as the beat of Alanis Morisette's, "You Learn" came on. Keeping one hand on the wheel, she let down the window and stuck her free hand outside, allowing it to whip back against the wind on the dual-carriageway. As Alanis sang all the ways to live and learn, Ronnie considered how much they'd all learned in UCD. Perhaps not what they'd intended, but an education all the same, a journey. Now, with any luck, this was their time to live.

Getting out of the car, Conor put his head back to survey the evening light. It was late. When they got to the cliff, it would be almost dusk. Of course, he'd planned it this way so the red dress would contrast against the natural backdrop. The result would be striking. At least, he hoped so. The last thing he wanted to do was put Eve under more pressure and exhaust her further, but she was adamant she could do it. Her sheer determination was a good sign, he supposed – promising.

Still, the future weighed heavily on his shoulders. Eve's mind was set on London. It was up to him to make it happen. Reaching back, he offered her his hand to help her from the car. She took it, stepped out and swallowed visibly.

Conor noticed. "What is it? Are you okay?"

"Stop," Eve chided. "I'm fine. My ears just popped on the way up that road. Right, where are we off to?"

She sounded chirpy, but she looked terrified.

"Over the barrier there." Conor pointed. "Then up that trail. It's not far."

They grabbed what they needed from the car and made their way towards the path, walking in line with Conor leading the way. The late spring weather had been dry so that the hardened muddy path was ideal underfoot.

The ground morphed to rock as Conor turned to help Eve and Ronnie up the final steps.

Once standing on the slab of rock at the top, they stared out across the Dublin landscape, so stunning it didn't look real, like a giant postcard suspended before them.

"It's beautiful," Eve whispered, taking it in, peering at the river below.

"It's high, is what it is." Ronnie wore a sudden look of trepidation.

"Right. I'm going down." Conor was going to shoot from below, next to the river. "You know what to do, Ronnie."

Once Conor was in position below, Eve pulled her hoodie off over her head and kicked off her runners until she was standing only in the red dress, impossibly close to the edge of the stage-like surface.

Conor gasped. It was indeed higher than he'd first thought – high enough that he had to shout to be heard, high enough that he reached inside his bag for a longer lens.

6

Eve stepped back and dropped to her knees, then lay back onto the slab of rock.

"*Hold her, Ronnie!*" Conor shouted up as Ronnie stooped down, out of sight.

Clutching Eve's legs, she called, "*You better make this bloody fast, Conor! Start snapping!*"

"*Okay, Eve! I want you to edge back slowly!*"

Eve inched backwards so that her hair flowed behind her and the top half of her body was curved over the edge of the rock face.

"*Now, your arms, Eve!*" Conor shouted. "*Just like we said! Just relax!*" He sounded anything but.

Keeping her eyes firmly shut, Eve allowed her arms to float back until they hung past her head. Her breath felt ragged as she did, what-ifs swimming through her mind – fear of the future cinching her body.

Ronnie tightened her grip.

"*Now, open your eyes, Eve! Look at me!*" Conor placed his hand on his heart as her gaze locked on his.

With every click, of his camera Eve could feel the future changing. They could all feel it. The plan was going to work. Taking a breath, relief flooded her veins. No matter what happened from there on in, Conor and Ronnie would always be there to catch her. She felt suddenly free, invincible, loved, leaning back further and further until it was almost as though she were falling.

CHAPTER ONE

#browncoat #irishblogger #freshstart #drownedrat #blood

@beli'EVE
Public Figure
Mama. Wife. Model. Content Creator. Collabs. Beauty. Fashion
Interiors.

5,698	1M	212
Posts	Followers	Following

**Hi Eve! I hope you don't mind me contacting you, but I've just
started a new business, and I was hoping ...**

I read the first line of the message, roll my eyes, then set my phone
face down on the step. Elbows on my knees, I cup my face and attempt
to re-centre. I love sitting here on the old stone steps, built into the
natural slope of the garden – or *gardens* as Mum insists on calling them.
Today, I'm distracted. Worse still, now I'm thinking of my mother. I
roll my eyes a second time, adding an irritated head-shake.

Mum grew up here, in this very house, in what she claims is the
most exclusive address in Annaford – a landmark property. It's mine
now. I pick up my coffee cup, cradling its last suggestion of warmth,
and force myself to savour the peace. I work alone but, as soon as I

log on, I'm virtually surrounded by thousands of people all wanting a piece of me. I've learned to take these few minutes for myself each morning to sit and breathe like yoga without moving an inch. After that, everything I do, say, wear, eat, drink, buy becomes public property.

Coming outside earlier, I'd grabbed my husband's ancient wax coat off his hook in the boot room. There's a chill in the April air as I adjust the fabric to cover my bare legs. As I do, I grimace. As well as the raincoat, my legs need a good layer of wax. I look down at my feet and grin. This morning, I've teamed Dex's coat with a grubby old charity T-shirt and work boots in a combo that screams vagrant-chic. You'd imagine that no one in their right mind would dare recreate this look. I beg to differ. If I put it on my feed, someone would attempt it.

I get the strangest requests: frantic pleas asking where to purchase the almost-invisible hair-tie I wore on my wrist before an exercise class or where I'd bought the nude bra I was wearing under a jumper in a picture posted two years before. It's all part of being a Blogger, Influencer or Content Creator as is now the widely used term. It reminds me of when late-eighties housewives began calling themselves Domestic Technicians. We all know it's the same thing. Not that I'd be brave enough to come out and say that online. A few years back, I made the mistake of having an opinion. My life has never been the same since.

I was one of the first in Ireland to make a career out of sharing my life online – manufactured by my management team as down-to-earth shrewdly mixed with unattainable. A haphazard mother with perfect hair @goldlockextensions, dazzlingly white teeth (see below for discount code), perfect clothes (#sponsoredadvert), and a model figure. Work hard, I mean really hard, @postionedpilates and you can achieve the same. Cars, holidays, clothes, jewellery, all on tap – sounds easy, doesn't it? It is if you're willing to let strangers peer through the front door of your house, follow your every move, share your inner thoughts. That's the job. Of course, it's never that simple.

I set my coffee down next to my phone and tuck my hands into the pockets of the coat, half expecting to find an old ticket stub or a mass of flaky tissues inside. Then again, it's a long time since Dex has worn it. When we lived in Dublin, Dex, along with every other man, would produce the brown expanse a couple of times a year for rugby matches in the Aviva Stadium. If you've ever driven through Ballsbridge on match day, it looks like a swarm of man-sized middle-aged turds gathering for pints in the rain. After its bi-annual excursion, the coat would return to the back of the toilet door, under the stairs of our Ranelagh (red-brick, blue door, zero space, cost-more-than-I'd-ever-like-to-disclose) terrace, making it smell like a wet dog until it dried out. I constantly threatened to hurl it into the recycling bin only to be reminded how much Dex had paid for it and that coats like it improve with age.

Behind me, a car door closes. My nose brushes the coat's collar as I glance over my shoulder. I inhale. Oddly, I've grown fond of its somewhat musty smell. I turn back towards the garden. Here, in the heart of Wicklow, the coat fits better than it had in Dublin. It belongs here. I suppose, like I do.

The sound of Dex's easy gait across the gravel makes me smile, even before he places his big, calloused hand on the back of my neck. He squeezes gently, then bends to kiss the top of my head. "I'm off," he announces. This morning, we'd made love, rolled towards each other in a still sleep-inebriated state. "Great way to get the steps in before breakfast," he had joked afterwards. Then added, "Mid-week no less."

I'd rested my head on his chest and smiled. It felt normal.

"Kids okay?" I ask now, looking up.

"Yep. All sorted."

I make to stand. "I'll go say bye."

11

"Don't bother." He puts his hand on my shoulder and gently pushes me back down. "They're in the car already, staring at their phones. It would ruin your morning."

I wrinkle my nose. I'm not exactly one to lecture when it comes to phone usage. Mine is my life.

Since moving here, both of us now work from home. The biggest perk is getting to spend time with Faye and Milo – time I missed out on when they were younger. They're both teenagers now. Milo is thirteen, and Faye is seventeen. Lately, I have this insatiable urge not to waste a single moment I have left with them. I think about it a lot, more than I should. Just the other day, I tried to describe to Dex how I'd begun to feel time accelerate, could almost hear the seconds ticking past one by one. The thought that the sand might someday run out often keeps me awake at night.

"That's called happiness, Eve," he'd responded. "You're happy."

Dex can be so American sometimes, but he's probably right. Or maybe it's guilt. I spent a lot of years far too focused on work, proving myself, building a following, nurturing meaningless relationships with brands and people who won't matter in the greater scheme. Then again, what choice did I have? In our marriage, I was the one with the ability to earn more, capitalise on who I am – "famous for absolutely nothing", as Mum would claim. It was what it was. It is what it is.

When my following ballooned, so too did the social aspect of the "job" – being out, being seen, being "on". I'd found it all too easy to be cajoled into drinks after a product launch, a late dinner, a club. I don't miss it. I thought I would, but I'd much rather be at home. I also now have the excuse that I live too far out to get caught up in extra-curricular activities. Not that I disclosed where we moved to after Dublin. I blanket-labelled it "relocating", getting out the of the rat race, slowing down.

Thankfully, Annaford remains one of my best-kept secrets. It's a good thirty minutes of straight motorway past suburbia, and what most people would find a stretch. I've heard countless auctioneers refer to it as a commuter's paradise. It isn't. Like most things in life, you can't have your cake and eat it. As beautiful as it is, you won't survive here by attempting to continue your Dublin life. Unless your pelvic floor is made of steel or you drive a bus kitted out with a toilet, it won't work. That's why when we relocated, we altered everything, schools, work, hairdressers, doctors, the lot.

Admittedly, the roads are better now than when I was a child. Back then, the journey from Dalkey to visit for the day felt like an expedition. "It's not that far," Mum would placate me as my two *much* older siblings (I was an extreme afterthought, a gift from heaven, a mistaken menopause) used the winding bends of the country road to body-slam into me in the back seat.

"Far enough for them to have a different mindset, Gwen," my father would say to Mum. "Let's face it. It may as well be another continent."

For me, what Dad meant as an insult is the best thing about Annaford. Not many know or care who I am here. It means it's a million times safer for someone like me.

My face must darken because Dex crouches down next to me. "Hey. You okay?"

"Fine," I lie. I'm not actually okay, not when something is playing heavily on my mind. I have a decision to make – a potentially life-changing one except I'm too afraid to face it.

"I'd better go," Dex says. "What's the bet they don't even say goodbye when I drop them off? Teenagers, huh? Such *assholes!*" My husband over-pronounces the last word in his still fresh New York accent.

I grin. "But they're my assholes. Tell them I'll see them later."

Dex stands. "Will do. You busy today?"

"Always."

"Lunch later?"

"I can't. I really am swamped, and I told Joanne I'd meet her for a quick walk this afternoon." Joanne is one of our neighbours – the only one I know. We've struck up a friendship – I won't call it an unlikely friendship, but we met under unusual circumstances. She was Faye's counsellor for a couple of follow-up sessions after we first moved to Wicklow. Although I do often meet Joanne, I've just lied to Dex a second time to buy myself time to think.

"Dex?" I ask suddenly. Maybe I should tell him.

"That's me."

"Nothing, sorry." I change my mind as fast.

He tilts his head and smiles, crinkling the outer edges of his eyes. "She's okay if that's what's up with you lately. Faye is fine." He pauses. "But if you're worried you could always chat to Joanne about it on your walk, ask her advice. I'm sure she wouldn't mind."

It isn't what's up with me, but I shake my head. And, understandably, Joanne doesn't like mixing business with pleasure. "I can't, Dex. It would compromise our relationship. Anyway she has a different job now." Joanne had taken a job with the Health Services shortly after she moved into one of the new houses.

Dex nods. "I suppose you're right, but I'm telling you Faye is fine so stop, okay? It was a blip. Everything is okay."

He's right, but I still worry despite how much Faye has come on since we moved here two years ago. Sometimes I still glimpse a tiny shard of volatility within her that I fear might someday multiply. Or maybe that's just me. At times, I catch myself staring at her like I'm looking directly at my seventeen-year-old self, but Faye isn't me. She's stronger than I ever was.

It makes my stomach turn to think I was so caught up in my life that I almost missed what was happening in Faye's. For as long as I live, I'll never forget walking into her bedroom in Dublin and seeing her that way: skin and bone, a blade in her hand, blood pouring from a self-inflicted incision on her thigh, eyes determined. After that, everything needed to change.

She'll be finished school in a few months, heading off to college to begin her journey, as I once had. It frightens me. If I could articulate it, I'd tell her the truth about my college experience, warn her, but I can't. Short of locking her into one of the vacant rooms on the third floor of the house, I must let her forge her own path.

"I'll see you later!" I call as Dex walks away.

My husband is a good man. Since we met, his sole goal has been my happiness.

Before he rounds the corner, he turns. "Let's go out later for a bite. Just the two of us, yeah? And mind my shit-brown coat, won't you?"

I laugh. "It's mine now. Don't forget the 250,000 likes. That's a lot of love for a shit-brown coat."

"It was a cute photo. I can be an Insta-hubby when I need to be." Dex shakes his head in dismay as he disappears.

He took the photo the summer we moved in. In it, I'm standing in this garden in the pouring rain, wearing this same coat. You can't see the house, only me, against a backdrop of woodland, staring up, hands splayed, my blonde hair so drenched that it looks brown, an exasperated smile on my face. That summer, the heavy rain made the roof spring a leak in a different place almost every day as though we were living under a giant colander. I'd never felt cold like it. To combat it, I'd started wearing the coat.

One morning, Dex came downstairs to tell me that part of the ceiling had collapsed in our bedroom. Unable to take much more, I'd fled through the back door to the garden, sobbing for having to uproot our lives. Moments later, I noticed that it was warmer outside than it was inside our utterly dilapidated home, and the tears suddenly morphed into hysterical laughter. Unbeknownst to me, Dex captured the moment on his phone.

It was the first thing I'd posted online after a noticeable absence and having parted ways with my management team. I'd coupled it with a tongue-in-cheek caption – something about a fresh start, washing away the past, realising my worth, embracing change. I hadn't planned to do it. I'd sworn to Dex that I was done with that phase in my life but, being back online, being in control felt good – like I was making a statement. To this day, of everything posted to my page that photo received the most likes.

My good old friend, Ronnie, my ex-manager, probably squirmed when she saw it and realised that I was back. Under her thumb, I'd never have been permitted to post a photo where I resembled a drowned rat. It wasn't "our" image. The messages of encouragement and support that flooded in like rain made me believe that I could continue my career without Ronnie. It was as though people saw the relief on my face before I felt it myself.

Yes, I'm happy here, locked inside our own little world, closed off by tall trees and bushes, securely behind electric gates. At least I think I'm happy. Dex believes I am. Maybe that's enough. Only happiness scares me. Sometimes, I listen to the sound of nothingness outside the window while Dex sleeps soundly next to me, and I wonder if something or someone is waiting to disrupt my life again.

I jump suddenly when a drop of rain falls onto my face. I whisper Dex's earlier words. "Everything is okay." The problem is, he doesn't know the half of it. No one does. I used Faye needing a fresh start and falling-out with Ronnie as excuses to get the hell away from Dublin. I had to. The whole truth wasn't an option. When you've spent a lifetime lying, it rarely is.

I swallow hard, pressing my nails into the heels of my hands until it stings. At the time, I hadn't needed to ask Faye why she was cutting herself. I understood only too well that she was trying to numb her pain. Yes, everything is okay, just as long as I can keep it that way. As long as I can continue to forget, but I'm good at that. I've had plenty of practice.

CHAPTER TWO

**#mylittlestudio #inthecountrynowmissus
#runrunasfastasyoucan #panicbutton #vanish**

@beli'EVE

Public Figure

Mama. Wife. Model. Content Creator. Collabs. Beauty. Fashion
Interiors.

5,698	1M	212
Posts	Followers	Following

With the fast-descending grey clouds, my mood has changed. I pick
up my coffee cup, grab my phone and stand. The rain won't matter
when I'm back inside, tucked away in my little studio. In reality, it's far
from small, but it's how I refer to it online. It takes up one side of the
third floor, looking out over the Sugarloaf Mountain through dual-
aspect windows. But no one sees that part, but me.

Dex and the kids endlessly tease me for calling it a studio in the
first place as if I'm an artist, up there creating masterpieces instead
of umpteen ways to style a pair of staple black trousers or wing your
eyeliner. Then again, if I were an actual artist with any talent beyond
knowing how to put outfits together, how to stand, take good pictures,
plug brands, I doubt anyone would care as much.

Before going back inside, I walk towards the tiered stone fountain at the centre of the lawn. Like the steps, it's as old as the house. It never worked until Dex decided to fix it shortly after moving in. I felt intensely irritated that he was hell-bent on conjuring more water when the entire house already felt like one big fountain. Once he got it going, I'd scrubbed the green-tinged stone until my hands ached, removing the moss that had gathered while the house stood empty and even longer before that. I remember thinking that if I could return the blasted fountain to its former glory, I could surely do the same with the crumbling house. And if I could fix the house, I could possibly mend my life. Naively, I thought the gleaming fountain might impress Mum when she paid us an impromptu visit – make her see that we'd be as good for the house as it would be for us.

#

"It's going to take more than fixing a fountain, Eve." Mum had sounded apathetic. "I can't believe how selfish you've been. This wasn't the plan. You must see that. My poor father would turn in his grave if he knew how you'd chosen to sell out. And Lily ..." Her voice caught on her dead sister's name.

"Can't you just be happy for us?" My voice wobbled at the rejection. "I like it here. The children are happy."

Curiously, Mum turned to glare at Dex, opening her mouth to say something more. She stopped when Milo ran over, straight for the fountain, sticking his hands under the flow.

"I thought I could let this go, Eve, but I can't," she whispered then. "You should be ashamed of yourself – both of you!" She threw Dex a final disapproving look, then stomped across the lawn in the direction of the newly erected gate.

As I stared after her, I felt Dex behind me. Allowing my body to deflate against his, I'd asked, "What's her problem with you now?"

I felt him shrug.

"Who knows? Guilty by association, maybe, but you have nothing to be ashamed of, Eve." He'd clamped his arms around me when I took a step to go after her. "Let her go. I keep telling you she's not worth it. Maybe someday you'll listen."

I did listen after that. I haven't exactly cut Mum out of my life, but I've distanced myself even more if that's possible – accepted that Mum and I don't get along. We never have, and we never will. As soon as this house became an option, it only further frayed our relationship. Mostly because she did nothing to conceal the fact that she didn't want me to own it. She hasn't been back since that day. There have been one or two very stilted phone conversations, but neither of us has brought up the subject again. It pains me to admit that Mum and I are alike in that way. We'd both rather ignore a problem than solve it.

Looking into the stagnant water, I pick out some stray leaves, recoiling when I notice a dead mouse floating under them. Barely hesitating, I scoop its defenceless body into my empty coffee cup, walk towards the end of the garden, and fling the mouse into the bushes. I used to be afraid of mice, rats, creepy crawlies. Not anymore. Not when there are far more frightening things that lurk.

That summer we moved in, I'd innocently called a pest-control man when I noticed a couple of rats frolicking in the garden as if they owned the place. He took a good look around the house, set some traps, blocked some of the hundreds of holes before seeking me out in the kitchen.

Hands stuffed into his pockets, he'd said, "Way I look at it, you're in the country now, Missus, and if you don't mind me saying in a big old place like this, get used to company."

It wasn't what I'd wanted to hear.

"Was this place a church or something?" He gestured up at the Gothic-style stained window over the hall door on his way out, then angled his head up the dark mahogany staircase towards the top floor.

"It was the rectory. Dates to the 1800s apparently." I gave my standard rehearsed answer. It was an easy mistake to make, considering the arched front door and the building's sharply angled pitched roof.

He tapped his forehead with his index finger. "Shoulda guessed by the name – The Old Rectory!" He chuckled, then raised his eyebrows. "Don't fancy the heating bills nor that roof. I noticed it on the way in. The brother is a roofer. I could get him to flick you a quote if you like."

"Thanks. I'll let you know as soon as we have the money." I'd shrugged good-naturedly, hoping it was already on its way.

"Keep playing the Lotto. I'll take a break to give you a shot, huh? Looks like you need it more than me," he'd said with a wink over his shoulder.

###

I turn back towards the house now. Despite where my thoughts have drifted this morning, I can't help but smile. It's still not perfect. I suspect with a 6,000 square foot, two-hundred-year-old house, it never will be. Still, what a difference nearly two years and a much-needed injection of funds made. No, we hadn't won the Lotto. We'd found a different way. It enabled us to fix the roof, insulate, install a new kitchen, do some badly needed structural work, kit out my studio. But, most importantly, to build a state-of-the-art workshop so Dex could finally pursue his furniture-making business.

I've no regrets over "selling out", as Mum labelled it, though at the time selling four acres of the land almost broke my heart. In one swoop, we lost the tennis court, the stables, much of the woodland. But we retained two acres and gained a habitable house. Contrary to what she believes, I'd never have done it unless I was sure Aunt Lily would have approved.

Being the sole benefactor of a property valued at close to a million, I'd soon learned I'd have to pay the guts of €300,000 for the pleasure. It might have been a darn sight more if Lily hadn't let the place fall to rack and ruin, devaluing it in the process. Oddly, I should be grateful that she did. That Lily left it to me, not Mum, carried a far greater penalty than the crippling inheritance tax. Of everything I've ever done to Mum, this was the most unforgivable offence yet.

"'And to my beloved niece, Eve ...'"

I'd glanced at Mum when the local Annaford Solicitor read out my name three years ago, following Lily's passing. While he spoke, Mum screwed her lips together in anticipation. It's a wonder her sickly pink lipstick didn't turn red when he declared Lily's final wishes. After the initial blow, he continued that Lily had bequeathed Mum her entire, very dubious art collection – primarily self-produced oil paintings of nudes with disproportionate bodies. I almost exploded with nervous laughter at how Lily had found a way to take a final pop at Mum from beyond. Then again, Mum had never hidden her disapproval of Lily. It was probably why Lily chose to bypass Mum, leaving the house to me. In a million years, I never expected it. It was as much of a shock to me as to Mum.

There was no money in the estate. Lily had never married and had no children. Instead, she'd dedicated her life to running an artists' and writers' sanctuary from the house or "hippie commune", as Mum labelled it. They'd pay (minimally) to stay with her and have their souls nourished with her wisdom and encouragement. At one time, I, too, had taken refuge with Lily for a spell – another crime in Mum's eyes.

In later years, Lily lived off the State Pension, moved all her belongings to the house's ground floor, and resided in just a few rooms. To anyone else, it might have sounded miserable, only Lily had been one of the happiest people I'd had the pleasure of knowing. She'd barely left Annaford or The Old Rectory, yet was far more open-minded than my mother, who'd gone to study medicine in Dublin and rarely returned.

"Did you put her up to this?" Mum hissed in the car afterwards. "You were always out here in her ear, letting her talk all sorts of nonsense into you. Remember how you ran off to New York without telling me, all because Lily told you to, Christ above!" She put her hands to her face.

"How dare you even suggest that!" I hissed back, then stared straight ahead, shaking my head and clutching the steering wheel. "Did you ever stop to think that maybe the reason Lily thought of me was that I did visit her?"

"And I wonder who else visited? *Hmm?* Why don't you ask yourself that? This isn't what I agreed with her. Lily promised."

Mum wasn't making sense.

"You'll have to sell it, or I'll buy it back," she suggested suddenly.

But we both knew she didn't have the money without selling her own home in Dalkey, and she'd never do that. "Besides, how could you live in a house like that? It would take hundreds of thousands to renovate it. Neither Dex nor you, God help your children, have proper jobs."

My knuckles turned white around the steering wheel as I tried not to react to the relentless jibe about my work.

"As it is, your family never see you. What will happen now? And your husband clearly doesn't like to pull his weight, sure I know that only too –"

"What I do *is* a proper job," I interrupted, swivelling my body towards her. "And stop going on about Dex, will you? This isn't the Dark Ages."

Mum tutted loudly. "Showing yourself off like that. It's immoral."

"Oh, for Christ's sake. I'm not a stripper."

"Telling the world your business. Having all sorts of kooks watching you. What sort of example is that to Faye and Milo? And all because of that stupid photo of you spilling off a cliff. Sure, it could be anyone in that photo. Anyone!" She threw her hands up. "If people knew what really ..." She trailed off as my stomach dropped.

I often forgot that Mum knew far more than I'd like her to. She'd never tell another living soul, but she liked to remind me every so often.

"And what am I supposed to tell your brother and sister?" Mum quickly changed tack. I knew she'd go there – try and bring Miriam and Hugh, the older siblings I barely knew, in on it. They'd both lived in America since I was a child. Both were doctors like Mum and Dad, both equally dismissive of my career and me. "They're entitled to their share of that house, Eve. It was my childhood home, after all."

"It was Lily's house, Mum. She bought you out when your parents died. You didn't want anything to do with it then."

"I practically gave it to her. You know that, but I knew it would come back someday. That's what we agreed. Something or someone changed her mind." Mum narrowed her eyes at me again.

"No one changed her mind except maybe herself," I said.

"Still, selling it and divvying it fairly is the right thing to do. I know you know that. And it's not as if you're going to move there, are you? Don't let me down now. Sure, you won't?" There'd been a dramatic pause. "Not again. You owe me that much."

I did consider doing what Mum asked, sharing my good fortune with my estranged siblings, or selling it back to her. There'd been so much else going on that I sat on it for months before receiving the courtesy call from the solicitor to remind me that I'd had only six months from Lily's death to pay the tax due. When I went to see him alone to discuss options, as soon I mentioned selling he excitedly produced an envelope with my name scrawled across it in Lily's hand. When I opened it, it contained typed instructions, along with details of a developer who'd approached her a few years before.

Don't let your mother talk you into selling. Sell some of the land, Eve. It will enable you to keep the house. I know you have fond memories of your time here. Consider it a lucky break. You belong here. You might need it someday, and if you do, it's here. *Lily.*

Back inside, I double-bolt the back door behind me and remove my coat and boots in preparation for entirely different attire. I glance at the monitors mounted in the boot room on my way to the kitchen. As usual, nothing stirs on them. It rarely does. Still, I'd insisted on installing the high-tech security system when we got the other work done. Dex hadn't needed much convincing. As a former New Yorker, he's crime-conscious. I told him it was because the house was so isolated, set so far back. It's a lonely road, even with the four new homes now built in the old garden. Our house is now behind two gates: the original ones which we share with the new development and a newer set installed by the developer. It's essentially Fort Knox.

I place my mug into the dishwasher in the kitchen, push the button, and listen as it whirrs to life. It's hard to believe it's the same space that I'd stared at with dismay when we were waiting for the money to come through from the developers. In the end, the someday that Aunt Lily predicted in her note came far sooner than I could ever have imagined. Just a matter of weeks after visiting the solicitor, my perceived perfect life, which had already begun to unravel, came entirely undone.

It turns out there's a big difference between being followed and being targeted. Instead of gifting me a lucky break, Aunt Lily unknowingly presented me with a panic button that I was forced to push. Sometimes it upsets me that she predicted I might need a place to vanish to as I had done after college. Only this time, I hadn't been running from my life. I'd been running for it.

CHAPTER THREE

#gifted #affiliatelink #fivegoldrings #youoweme #overshare
#risetofall #deceit

@beli'EVE
Public Figure
Mama. Wife. Model. Content Creator. Collabs. Beauty. Fashion
Interiors.

5,698	1M	212
Posts	Followers	Following

In preparation for the day ahead, I fix my phone into the tripod in
my studio and angle it towards the hot-pink velvet sofa in the centre
of the room. The light here is incredible. I could probably do away
with the ring-light I use when filming if I wanted to. It's designed to
reduce shadows but, I swear, it can wipe ten years off any face at the
flick of a switch. At forty, I can do with it.

Still, people speculate. Recently, some woman paired a revolting
old photo of me bearing a striking resemblance to Gollum from *The
Lord of the Rings* alongside a more recent one, then posted it to the
comments section of a video I'd uploaded about my skincare routine.
A fully fledged debate – that's putting it mildly – broke out as to what
I have and haven't had done. Apparently, Gollum had undergone

rhinoplasty, a facelift and a chin implant before morphing into me.

None of it is true. Reading it, there was a part of me that wanted to defend myself, respond that I was sure there was a disgusting photo of them somewhere out there that they'd rather burn than let anyone see. I'd resisted. I've learned it only makes things worse. Instead, I made a video with a skincare clinic, explaining that I get baby Botox twice a year along with hyaluronic-acid facials. The response was so high that the clinic gave me free treatments to give away to my followers, of which over one hundred thousand people entered to win. The three women who did sent me the loveliest thank-you messages. To me, it felt better than any petty response might have done.

I plump the scatter cushions, straighten the magazines on the side table and light some candles. This area is decked out as if you're sitting in my living room next to me. The studio has other sections too. A full-length mirror and clothes rail sit on a cream carpet next to a high-backed armchair, like a bedroom without a bed. There's an office space, a kitchen area, and a bathroom to demonstrate beauty products and skincare. I put a lot of thought into it after parting ways with Ronnie. I didn't like the idea of my followers feeling short-changed. I wanted it to seem as though I was still welcoming them into my home, only behind these doors I could be anywhere – still in Dublin, the wilds of Galway or in Timbuctoo.

There'd been no resistance from Dex about me having my own dedicated workspace. If he's noticed significant changes to how I work lately, he hasn't commented. Secretly, I think he's happy that I'm contained up here, so he's no longer tripping over boxes, and our personal living space remains just that. Nowadays, I record everything ahead of time, especially if what I'm putting out isn't in the studio, so it's impossible to place my exact whereabouts from what I share. Not unless you can time-travel. It's time-consuming but worth it.

Practically everything here has been gifted to me or is a collaboration with a brand hoping to get a feature on my feed or in my daily stories. In layman's terms, I either get a gift, promote it for payment, or do an affiliate link where I get paid a commission – or a combination of all three. In recent years, everything has been regulated, so I must call out what type of promotion it is in each post unless I want to be torn apart again like Gollum.

A lot of people like to think that this business is a scam. It isn't. What I am is advertising space, a form of marketing, evolved product-placement, a way to communicate with a brand's potential customers.

Walking towards the full-length mirror to the left of the sofa, I make a face at what stares back. Believe me, no one wakes up like what you see on camera. Even a just-out-of-bed look or "I've just done a workout" has been somewhat curated or filtered.

Moving towards the clothing rails, I make sure everything is ready for today's try-on. As well as talking to myself in an empty room, playing dress-up before stopping recording and getting back into pyjama-like attire is also a massive part of my everyday life. Truthfully, I'm never off out to a boozy lunch. I haven't been to a wedding in years, and "Girls' night" is a thing of the past. When I say I'm going "out-out", I'm most likely staying in-in. I'm not trying to trick people. It's just more straightforward than the truth – a way to give the brands I work with one hundred per cent. To them, I'm a method to instantly boost sales. "Eve is a no-brainer!" Ronnie would often joke after slapping prospective customers with her very healthy fee structure.

At the thought of Ronnie, I unconsciously circle the outline of the infinity tattoo on my inner wrist. I had it touched up a few years back, adding my children's initials inside the two loops. It was so faded that I'd considered getting it removed altogether, but I couldn't do it. Instead, I gave it a makeover. A few weeks later, the tattoo parlour I tagged informed me that they'd been asked more than a hundred times to recreate it. It makes me sad to think that people are walking around with Ronnie and my symbol of eternal friendship on their wrists. Especially since it didn't last.

When the plan to move to London after college fell through, we went our separate ways for about six months until the day Ronnie unexpectedly showed up at Lily's house, where I'd been taking some time out. Apparently, under duress, my mother had told her where I was. It had been nice to see her again until she produced Conor's photos of me in the red dress. I'd tried to look away, but Ronnie only shoved them further under my nose. Despite the heartache they represented, even I could see how striking they were.

"I know, Eve, I do." Ronnie patted my hand when she saw my face contort in still raw pain. "But look at you! Think of these photos as compensation – a second chance. This is who you are! Better still, this is who *we* could be, together."

That time, Ronnie had taken it upon herself to bypass London and send the photos to several modelling agencies in New York under the guise of being my manager. They wanted to meet me; one even claimed to have a buyer for the images. It was late 1999 and, seemingly, I had the right look – waiflike, vulnerable, haunted. It wasn't an act.

"But what about …" I still couldn't bring myself to say his name after how our relationship had abruptly ended.

"Conor gave them to me … to you. They're ours."

"You spoke to him?" I couldn't hide my surprise.

Ronnie nodded sheepishly.

"Where is he?"

30

"London," she answered fast, ripping off the plaster.

It hit like a punch in the gut. He'd gone anyway.

"He said we could have them. He signed a waiver if …"

"If what?"

"If neither of us contacted him ever again."

My chest caved at his callous words. When I lifted my gaze, Lily, who'd been sitting quietly throughout the exchange, was holding the photos.

"Uncanny." She looked over at me. "You're not a bit like either of your parents," she said with a grin. "Nor your siblings, nor me for that matter." She paused for effect, turning serious. "Doesn't that say something, Eve? Maybe how you look is your gift no matter what your mother says."

When I was a child, Mum constantly scolded Lily for praising my appearance.

"Gwen is just bitter that you bypassed the pig's snout that she and your sister got." Lily jokingly pushed the tip of her nose up with her index finger. "You made mistakes, Eve. You got lost. Bad things happened. You've suffered, but don't waste the rest of your life being afraid."

"But I want to stay here," I'd tried. "With you."

"I know you do, but I don't want you using this place as a crutch. Do you hear me? If you end up here like me, then I've failed you. I didn't make you see that you're destined for more. Sure, look at you! This place isn't for you, Eve. It never will be. It's too small. And remember what I said? Find someone who'll jump off that cliff with you or go without. No man is worth giving up on life. Go to New York and never look back." Then she'd tapped the photos. "These photos are a sign. *Jump, Eve.*"

So, I had.

When Ronnie heard it was the American rock band, Timeline, who wanted to use the photos for their upcoming album, *We Fall*, she almost lost her life. Of course, there was no way either of us could have foreseen how iconic the image would become. If I had, I might have thought twice. If Ronnie had, she'd have negotiated a greater fee instead of signing away the rights for next to nothing. It remained one of her greatest regrets. Especially since the photo refuses to go away even after all these years, ending up on posters, mugs, emblazoned across T-shirts, baseball caps. People claim it speaks to them. Some say it's the lighting, the muted colour save the flash of red. How real it looks. Others claim it's my face, my stunned eyes. Some say it represents hope, refusing to fall. I've heard it all. I'd certainly felt optimistic the day it was taken, ignorant that my heart was about to shatter into a million pieces. When asked, I've settled on saying that it was a fluke.

In the same way that Timeline's drummer seeing it was a fluke. He was dating a model. She dropped by her New York agency with him. The photos were out on a desk … fluke. As a result, I got signed with the agency, instantly thrown into catwalk and editorial. I hit the jackpot when Calvin Klein booked me for their jeans campaign. It would make me one of Ireland's biggest exports.

It never happened. Instead, I returned home to Ireland less than a year later as the girl on the cover of a world-famous album, an excellent dinner-party story under my belt, and able to pick up modelling work in Ireland at the drop of a hat. I also came home with Dex.

Off the back of it, Ronnie opened a Dublin modelling agency. She never shied from the fact that she saw me as a means to make money. Her barefaced honesty used to be what I loved about her, with her short, spiky, peroxide hair. Ronnie Delaney didn't think like a woman, and I found it refreshing. Whenever I was interviewed, she made sure I always credited Conor as the photographer of the original photos. Despite how it ended, she'd say, fair was fair. It must have worked because Conor realised his dream in London by becoming a highly sought-after fashion photographer. In a way, it defined us all, but my real break came seven years later in the form of social media.

I honestly never considered the risks or that there might be people out there who'd want to scratch even further below the surface of what I already shared which was *everything*. In truth, I was surprised anyone wanted to look in the first place. After all, I was only a girl falling in a photo, still waiting to hit the ground.

When the number of followers began to soar, so too did my confidence – seeing the amount of people viewing my stories became a drug of sorts – sharing my every move, a strange addiction. The idea that people liked me shocked me, that is, until they didn't, and I realised that I was being lied to, shielded from the truth: there were people out there who not only didn't like me but despised me.

It shouldn't have come as a surprise. I always knew someone like me didn't deserve admiration or a voice, and certainly not a pedestal. If I'd had nothing to hide, I'd have had nothing to fear. Perhaps that's the reason it stung so much. The truth always does. I should have guessed that my big break would eventually break a person like me. Then again, Ronnie should have known it too. The idea that she must have still haunts me.

2006

The panic on Ronnie's face was palpable after Eve gingerly revealed from behind a bunch of flowers that little Faye was going to be a big sister. Eve soon wore a similar expression.

"What exactly do you mean, share the experience?" she asked, frowning deeply as Ronnie's usually deadpan face began to twitch, her eyes darting from side to side. It was a positive progression from her initial reaction: "*Shit, Eve. Really? Pregnant? Again? Christ!*" Ronnie was never one to mince her words. Despite having plenty of other Irish models on her books, Eve was still the most prominent name, and it was still Ireland. To her, Eve having another baby while she was trying to grow her business was a problem.

"What do most people want?" Ronnie started pacing the floor of her tiny flat, which doubled as her office. They'd met there this morning to discuss Eve's schedule for the week. Now, they seemed to be talking about something else entirely.

"Money?" Eve raised her eyebrows hopefully.

"Aside from money."

"Love?"

"And ..." Ronnie rolled her hand like she was playing a game of charades.

"Hope?"

"And?"

"Health?"

"Keep going."

"Babies?" Eve suggested with a grimace. "Understanding friends?"

"Very funny." Ronnie turned her nose up. "Okay. Aside from all the obvious ones – world peace, fortune, fame, love, *blah, blah ... think*, Eve!"

"I'm trying, but this is hard."

Ronnie pointed at Eve so fast that she almost fell backwards. "That's right. Life *is* hard. So, what do people want instead?"

Eve cowered before saying, "Ease?"

Ronnie clapped her hands together. "*Bingo!* People want ease. They want someone to tell them what to do and how to do it."

She nodded wildly. "What to buy, where to shop, how to dress, style their hair. They want someone to make the big decisions for them. They want someone to tell them what it feels like to go through life, marriage, babies, raising children, doing up a house ... someone to assure them that they're normal. Someone like you." She clapped her hands together a second time. "They want to see you do it first, and then they want to copy it and let everyone think they came up with the idea themselves. And they want it online. I think this pregnancy is an opportunity, Eve. A huge one."

Eve scrunched her face in terror, imagining Ronnie following her for the duration of the pregnancy, then angling a video camera at her vagina for the finale. "Only I don't do life with ease, Ron. I never have. You know that! You must be joking." She jerked her head back and then exaggeratedly shook it from side to side. "Me? Come on. I'm twenty-five years old, and we're struggling, and now I'm pregnant, like you said, *again*. Dex and I barely make enough to cover rent and childcare for Faye. That's what I wanted to talk to you about today. I think I need to be more realistic, Ronnie. Get a proper job. Maybe Mum is right?"

Eve didn't need to explain to Ronnie that the modelling opportunities in Ireland consisted of the odd magazine shoot, modelling clothes your granny wouldn't be caught dead in on television, wedding fairs, or holding placards in a bikini advertising student loans on Grafton Street.

Ronnie gave a dismissive wave. "But this *is* realistic. I'm telling you, Eve. Social media is the future. Facebook is where it's at. Everything is about to change, and we need to be the first to do it in Ireland. Businesses are already signing up to have social media pages. I'm getting mine together for The Agency."

Ronnie had named her company, *The Agency*, anticipating that someday she'd be *The* agency in Ireland. As yet, it hadn't happened.

"People will love it. It'll be like being pregnant alongside your best friend. Wouldn't you have liked that when you were expecting Faye?"

Eve had often spoken about how lonely she'd felt during her pregnancy.

Eve thought for a moment. It would sound clever if it wasn't her Ronnie was planning to exploit. "I'm not sure I'm the right sort of person for it. What if –"

Ronnie cut across her. "And what's the alternative, Eve? Get a couple of gigs modelling dowdy maternity wear for catalogues, and then what? After the baby, the work will dry up for at least six months. Okay, so you've already proved that you can get your figure back after a baby, but you'll be twenty-seven by then. You need to future-proof your career now." She'd paused for a moment. "Besides, you owe me."

Eve looked away. It seemed owing people was to be the theme of her life.

"I'll try it, okay? But I'm not promising anything. And swear to me that this will just be fashion, parenting, nice things. I don't want anyone knowing my … private life." She raised an eyebrow in warning.

"This is about the future. Not the past. You trust me, don't you?" Ronnie took her hand.

Eve shrugged. "Yeah."

Ronnie stared into the distance. "As soon as I leak that Eve Kelly, Ireland's First Supermodel, is expecting her second baby and plans to bring the nation along for the journey, brands will be throwing money at us to promote them. Screw that! We'll become our own brand!" She grinned, then stopped when she saw Eve's worried face. "Relax. This is business. Besides, you're good at more than just modelling. You're a great mum, a hard worker … a survivor. Let people hear your voice."

CHAPTER FOUR

#staticskirt #toddlerhate #honesty #deletecomments
#ambermessedup #Jabber.ie #hated #whatdidevedo?

_._

@beli'EVE
Public Figure
Mama. Wife. Model. Content Creator. Collabs. Beauty. Fashion
Interiors.

_._

5,698	1M	212
Posts	Followers	Following

"A slip skirt will owe you nothing, girls. It's trans-seasonal, perfect for day to night and, best of all, most waistbands are elasticated." I wink at my reflection. "This one looked great on the hanger – but, I have to be honest, it's not working in real life." Holding my phone up, I stand back to demonstrate how the skirt should fall but, in this instance, doesn't.

I look different from how I had earlier. Since then, I've showered, dressed, applied make-up – careful to keep aside all the products so I can answer the slew of questions that will accompany this video when I post it. I've waved my hair using a styler I was sent last week – one of those ones that suck your hair into a vortex, spin it violently, then spit it out like you've spent the morning at a salon. It's slightly terrifying, but it gets my seal of approval. As does anything that speeds up getting done up to the nines to go nowhere. As soon as I give out my personalised discount code, I expect it will fly off the shelves. This business is fast.

I continue my spiel. "As you can see, the skirt is a little on the static side." I raise my eyebrows at the understatement. "It's hugging my legs tighter than a toddler being dropped to preschool." I laugh. "Remember those days, girls! The guilt! Honestly, though, if you're at that stage, as soon as you're around the corner, they stop crying, or so they tell you anyway." I laugh again, pulling the satin skirt out from where it's rammed between my legs. "If anyone has a solution for static, let me know, and I'll share it. Did I hear something about standing barefoot on grass?" I shrug into the mirror. "Or is it hairspray?" My voice echoes in the empty room. "Anyway, I'll put up some more styling ideas for slip skirts later and link all the looks so you can buy." I'm almost out of breath. "Next up is spring jackets and the all-anticipated wedding-guest attire. Be sure to let me know about that static." I flash a final smile at myself, stop recording, exhale loudly, then reprimand myself for finishing on a request. Now I'll have to reply to all the messages on how to prevent static: **"Great suggestion." "Thanks for sharing." "Why didn't I think of that!"** Followers like interaction, sharing their opinion, knowing something I don't.

I drop the phone to my side and step closer to the mirror. With my forehead practically touching the glass, I look beyond myself. Never knowing who is watching is the strangest feeling. At night, sitting watching TV, I often scroll through the list of daily viewers on Instagram, wondering if the faces in the tiny circular icons are real. Even when a profile picture is a family snap with a nice standard name, I still wonder. Mind you, the smiling photos are far more comforting than the ominous grey, faceless, nameless profiles – with handles like @fangurl, @blondeforlife, @truthordare or the one that still irks me most of all. I stop myself before I even think of the name for fear of summoning them back from wherever they vanished like a horror movie.

Instead, I try to focus on the piece I've just recorded. I probably shouldn't have said what I did about toddlers. I could imagine the thread on Jabber.ie: #beli'Eve *toddler hate, static skirt up-her-hole fate.* The titles of the threads are never the worst parts. It's what's written after the juvenile rhymes, growing increasingly vicious as each person adds their tuppence-worth. Throwaway comments, meaningless remarks, tend to incite outrage on the website that tears apart social-media accounts. Or as they put it in their mission statement, call out people who chose to monetise their personal life as a business.

It's so different from how it all started or what I expected it to be like.

After Ronnie drummed up plenty of publicity around my pregnancy, she conceived the idea for @beli'EVE. It was born well before my son, Milo. First, as a website and Facebook page, a blog where I'd share products I found helpful during pregnancy, pictures of clothes I liked, outfit ideas, what to wear to an event. I'd add thoughts about motherhood, marriage, friendship. It was intended to be light, airy, positive.

When Instagram launched in 2010, followed by Snapchat, Ronnie jumped straight on the bandwagon again. We doubled our following when they launched the function to share "stories" – snapshots and videos into everyday life. Ronnie encouraged me to show people everything – "Get Faye involved – think teenage fashion! Your house, your day, the kids, Dex, your life ..."

Without thinking, I did. That is until I discovered Jabber.ie three years ago. Almost the moment I did, everything changed. I was as oblivious to what lay ahead as I was on the day I lay on a rock and Conor photographed me in my red dress.

After almost a decade online, I learned that I had no voice at all, not where it mattered anyway. Worse still, I began to understand how intrigued people were about every aspect of my life. All because I made a living from apparently living the high life. If they only knew.

I step back from the mirror, sigh loudly at the memory, throw my phone onto the armchair next to it and glance at my watch. I'm already behind schedule. I'm finding it impossible to concentrate today. I still have two fashion slots to film, which I'd be wise to do now while my hair and make-up are still intact. As if on cue, my phone shrills and I jump. Stepping closer, I turn it over to look at the screen, then close my eyes and shake my head, choosing to ignore the relentless caller. When it stops, I glance around the room, deciding to film the next part near the sofa just three feet away, for a change of scene.

How I now work, mostly holed up here, goes against everything Ronnie believed in. At her insistence, I would allow the world to know my every move, my whereabouts, my plans, but after the day I discovered Jabber.ie, I stopped. I grew nervous. My sudden reluctance to comply drove a wedge between Ronnie and me, as did what I decided to do next. But then fear can make you do stupid things – give you a false sense of power. I lashed out, attempted to fight back. It was a mistake. After all, if I were guilty of nothing, I'd have had nothing to say.

Years before, Ronnie had been bang on the money when she said that people wanted to be told what to do – that they craved guidance – but not everyone, it seemed, wanted guidance from someone like me. I still wonder where I'd be now if I'd taken Ronnie's advice that day and ignored the online negativity. If Amber from the office wasn't on holiday, posting pictures of a straw hat carefully positioned next to rattan slides instead of sitting at her desk doing her job. Would the white noise have faded in time?

What hurts most is that Ronnie became someone who wanted to take me down a peg too. "Self-righteousness and hypocrisy go together worse than socks and crocs," she'd told me towards the end of our relationship.

Now, I work alone, no longer surrounded by a team of people who'd once been like family to me. There are no photo shoots in St. Stephen's Green, strutting down Grafton Street, sitting outside trendy cafés, laughing our way through the working day. I miss it. Despite how it ended and everything that happened, I still miss Ronnie. But could I be willing to forgive and forget, move on? It's the burning question, the reason I'm caught in the past today, and it requires an answer soon.

A sound outside distracts me, and I walk towards the window. Below, Dex is unloading his truck. My eyes dart towards the trees surrounding the house that now guard me. I'm safer here than I ever was under Ronnie's protection. Her line of defence had left me vulnerable. I was right to worry about what I uncovered that day on Jabber.ie, but Ronnie was right too. I couldn't handle the truth that some people despised me. Yes. I should have ignored it, but not when, in my eyes, all I was doing was styling clothes, hair, make-up, smiling brightly at the camera. Not when, in their eyes, I'd never done anything to harm anyone.

As I stare out the window at my husband, I'm reminded of something our neighbour, Joanne, said after she first assessed Faye. Still wearing her counsellor's hat, she'd told me that no matter how much you think you might, you never know what's going on inside someone else's mind. In some ways, I hope she's right. I certainly wouldn't like her, or even Dex, to take a peek inside mine.

2006

"*Look!*" Eve burst into Ronnie's basement office on Leeson Street, brandishing her phone like she was holding up a bank before thrusting it in front of Ronnie's face.

Calmly, Ronnie adjusted her ice-blonde fringe and narrowed her eyes at the screen. "Yes. I know." She returned her gaze to her laptop.

"You knew about this?"

Ronnie finished what she was typing, sucked her cheeks in as she scanned back over it, then tilted her chin upwards. "Yep. I suggest you ignore it like I do."

Eve's mouth gaped open.

Ronnie exhaled impatiently. "It's been around for a while, okay? Like the name, it is mindless jabber, tattle, gossip, trash, whatever you want to call it. Bullshit is what I like best."

"It's a bit more than that, Ron." Eve blinked at her indifference. "Why didn't you tell me about it?"

Ronnie stood, walked towards her, and plonked down on her desk, fur-lined Gucci loafers stretched out in front. Ronnie was tall – broad-shouldered, strong. Over the years, she'd learned to dress for her shape. Instead of hiding it, as she'd tried to in college, she now highlighted it in tailored clothes and powerful silhouettes. She was no shrinking violet in the fashion stakes. Often, you'd be forgiven for thinking that she, and not Eve, was the influencer. As usual, she was impeccably dressed: leather trousers, black silk high-neck blouse, signature wide gold cuff-bracelets encasing both wrists like Wonder Woman. Whatever the weather, she was never without the bracelets. Then again, for what she'd paid for them, it was no surprise. Everything Ronnie owned was high-end. Eve would often tease that it was Ronnie who got to wear the designer gear while she was stuck with whatever was seen as accessible to the masses. Anything above shopping in Zara and she was getting above her station.

"Sit." Ronnie gestured at the chair opposite, looking Eve up and down, frowning. "Are you even wearing a bra?"

Eve had crossed her arms over her sweatshirt as she sat, to hide the fact that she wasn't. "No, actually. I barely slept after seeing this. Breast support was the least of my worries. Although I can see I'm not going to get much other support here either."

"There are crazy people out there, Eve – jealous, bitter, not happy in their lives, trolls. That's what this is – jealousy." Ronnie made to stand then sat back down when she saw Eve's face.

"*Jealous?*" Eve screeched. "*You're going to pull the jealousy card?*"

It had been Ronnie's go-to response for every upsetting situation since the day they'd met. Eve uncrossed her arms, opened her phone, and flicked through the threads she'd found the night before on the website dedicated solely, it seemed, to attacking everything about her or catching her out. "*#Eve rakes it in with sweatshop clothes fit for the bin,*" she read aloud. "And that's just the title. You should read what's in each thread."

Ronnie tutted. "It's *all* bullshit. How did you find it anyway?"

"Some woman complaining about said clothes on Facebook called it out, telling everyone to go and take a good look at Jabber.ie. That it was the funniest thing she'd read in ages. There are hundreds of responses." She took a deep troubled breath. "We shouldn't have got involved in that clothing range."

Ronnie aggressively tapped her red nail-extensions on her

desk at the mention. They'd already argued several times about the collaboration with the athleisurewear brand whose performance, Eve felt, wasn't up to scratch.

Eve continued, "Stuff people have ordered and paid for is already out of stock, and they can't get answers from the company. And the quality is terrible. I told you, Ronnie!"

Ronnie ceased drumming. As she crossed her arms, her gold cuffs banged together. "And I told you it was too big an offer to refuse. There are staff to pay here, remember. Lest you forget, this is a business. Sometimes we go where the money is."

Eve shook her head, groaning inwardly. "Oh, I know it's a business. You've been telling me for years, but I don't want people saying we're ripping them off! That's *not* good business, Ronnie."

"Oh, come on, Eve. Some people are never happy. Like, how bad can the clothes honestly be? And the reason everything sold out is that you looked amazing in them."

Eve rolled her eyes. "Anyone would look good in a fully styled shoot, but I'd say after one wash they would be fit for the bin. I could tell." She paused. "I know you know it too."

Ronnie's eyes flashed to her feet before meeting her eyes. "I'll make some calls, okay? Release a statement about the clothes if we must. No big deal. I'll sort it. I'll accept the responsibility on this one if it makes you happy."

"It wasn't just about the clothes, though. They called me a whore, shallow, a money-grabber. They were talking about where my house is. The kids' school. Whatever about talking about my whiny voice or my horsey teeth, and that's not the worst of it, there was an entire one about pimping out my children –"

"Just forget about it," Ronnie cut in, then softened. "Look, I'm sorry you saw it. Those Facebook comments should have been deleted, but they must have slipped the loop with Amber away. People are only too happy to jump on any bandwagon and have a go." She stood and made her way back around the desk to her chair, then attempted to dismiss Eve with her hand like a headmistress. "You better get home and get ready. We have that product launch later today, and you're going to need more than a bra."

For a moment, Eve looked as though she'd given up then something dawned on her. "Hang on. What do you mean that with Amber away they 'slipped through the loop'?"

Amber was one of the @bel'EVE team whose job, as far as Eve was concerned, was to take the pressure off her by answering questions, messages, queries. @beli'EVE made it their business to engage. It wasn't meant to be a trick. When she had time, Eve loved chatting online with followers. Many of them had become friends over the years, but it wasn't always possible to answer the sometimes thousands of messages alone.

"And what do you mean *deleted*?" She narrowed her gaze.

Ronnie looked lost for words, then put her palms up to calm her. "From time to time, Amber removes certain ..." Ronnie struggled to find the word, "opinions."

"What opinions?"

Silence.

"Ronnie?"

"Negativity," she said at last. "Amber stops things escalating or making it onto those stupid threads – so that you can concentrate on what matters – the followers who adore you."

Eve looked confused. "For the record, what's on that website isn't negativity. It's ..." She couldn't find a way to describe it. It was so personal, so cutting.

46

"It is what it is!"

Eve gritted her teeth at another of Ronnie's usual dismissive responses. If Ronnie had a tagline, that would be it.

"No, Ronnie. It isn't what it is. You've been lying to me. I should know what's being said about me."

"Fine." She threw her palms up again. "You want the truth?"

"Yes, I do."

"Are you sure?"

"For Christ's sake!" Eve shook her head impatiently. "This sounds like a bad Jack Nicholson impression. Are you about to tell me I can't handle it?"

"Well, can you?" Ronnie glowered. "Because if I tell you the truth, it makes me the bad guy."

"I can handle it."

"Okay. You can't stand it when people don't like you. There!"

Eve flinched as if she'd just been poked in the chest.

"You've always been the same."

"That is not true!"

"I'll put it another way. We have well over a million followers. A million! And because a few don't like what we do, you freak out. That's why I didn't tell you about Jabber.ie. Not everyone can love us. With those high numbers comes —"

"*What? Verbal abuse? Online bullying?*" Eve's voice wobbled dangerously. "Those comments aren't about *us*, Ronnie. They're about *me*, *my* life, *my* family. I'm the one on the stage, while you've kept your life private. Put yourself in my shoes for a minute."

"So, what do you want to do? Call them out individually? Moan about it? Try and make them like you?" Ronnie laughed sarcastically.

"I know not everyone likes me." Eve scowled with a mixture

47

of frustration and hurt. "But what if Faye saw those things about me?"

At the mention of her goddaughter's name, Ronnie's back straightened. "And did she?"

Eve shook her head. "No. I mean, I don't think so, but that's not the point. She could have. She might. Imagine her reading …" Once more, she opened her phone. "Ah yes, here it is . . . *'If Eve was wedged between two cars and I was driving one, I'd press the accelerator – hard.'* Followed by several laughing faces and an ambulance emoji. Or how about, *'Eve couldn't give a shite about her kids. She'd probably sell them at one of her pop-up shops if she could'.*" She glanced up briefly, frowning as a new comment caught her eye. She read it, her expression instantly altering.

"Eve?" Ronnie watched curiously.

Eve passed her the phone. As Ronnie read, an uneasy look flashed across her face, but she composed herself fast. Before she spoke, she handed back the phone. "Empty words," she said at last, but this time she didn't seem so sure. She tried again. "I promise you, it's just some nutter pretending to have some dirt on you – dirt that doesn't even exist."

"How do you know?" Eve looked at the page again, silently rereading the message, hoping she'd read it wrong the first time.

Sooner or later, Eve will fall, and I'll have front-row seats. She's not so squeaky clean. I have plenty of gossip about her from back in college when no one knew who she was … what she liked to do, how she'd do whatever it took to make it to the top.

It was followed with a string of enthusiastic replies pleading for more gossip, begging for it to be true, teamed with plenty of cruel speculation.

When Eve looked up again, Ronnie was staring straight ahead. Struggling to meet Eve's eyes, she smiled. "It's a coincidence," she said. "Eve, how long have I been protecting you?" There were certain things the two friends didn't speak about, but that didn't mean they didn't exist. "I'm hardly going to stop now, am I? I'll keep an eye on it, okay?"

Eve acquiesced with a nod.

"If I have to, I'll make it go away," Ronnie went on. "And you know what they say?"

Eve looked up, desperate for comfort.

"Any publicity is —"

"*Don't*, Ronnie, please." Eve put her hand up in warning. This wasn't good publicity. It was also ran deeper than not being liked. They both knew it. A message from @anoldfriendfromcollege was Eve's greatest fear. It was enough for bile to inch jaggedly up her throat until she could taste it on her tongue — enough to awaken the pent-up self-hatred she'd tried to banish.

CHAPTER FIVE

#princessinatower #watcher #itchyback #unfollow
#indeliablepen #adamandeve #whatsyoursecretdex

— · — · — · — · — · — · — · — · — · — · — · — · — · — · — · — · — · — · —

@wood4lifedesign

— · — · — · — · — · — · — · — · — · — · — · — · — · — · — · — · — · — · —

65	3,545	598
Posts	Followers	Following

Dex briefly lifts his hand to wave when he sees Eve in the window above. She doesn't look down. He pulls a reclaimed floorboard from the truck, hoists it onto his shoulder then heads inside the workshop. When he comes back out, she's gone. By the look of the sky, he doesn't have much time to get the rest inside before it lashes rain. Taking a moment to catch his breath, he wipes the beads of sweat from his brow before counting how many boards are left, sighing when he realises there are at least ten more. Despite weighing a ton, the hardwood planks will be ideal for the dining table, recently commissioned by some eye-wateringly wealthy couple in Dublin.

He'd salvaged the boards from a church renovation that his old boss had given him the heads-up on. He's glad they'd stayed in touch.

It's proved invaluable since going out on his own. He enjoys being part of the "scratch my back, and I'll scratch yours" culture – considering that a few years back, he never had anything that required itching. It used to make him feel worthless. As soon as he had something to offer, he'd outstretched hands in a gesture that guaranteed it was returned, bounteously.

With what he's saving on materials on this piece alone, he'll make a tidy profit. When they got in touch, the couple in town boasted about having their finger firmly on the pulse regarding up-and-coming designers. Dex had liked that, except the label made him concerned about quoting too high, ready with the spiel about treating the wood, the intricate varnishing process. He needn't have worried. They'd barely flinched, assuring him that as soon as their friends saw the table, they'd want bespoke pieces too. The Irish are like that – terrified of anyone having one up on them.

It's probably why Eve has been so successful. Only, with her, it's not just friends, it's everyone. Then again, he can hardly blame them – the parts they see anyway. Confidence, humour, natural beauty, impeccable taste, killer body, enough coats to warm an army if she found herself unexpectedly transported back to the Ice Age. Yet still she steals his! He smiles. Not to mention the shoe collection, sparkling social life, darling children, model husband (literally) … perfect marriage. This time, he issues a hollow laugh. Is anything ever as it seems?

Although he'd better get a move on, he doesn't move. Instead, he sits on the back of the truck, leaning back until his shoulders are resting against the planks. Earlier, when he'd gone to collect them, his old boss had offered him half a dozen church benches too. "It's the least I can do, mate. After the tip-off you gave me." The boss had pumped Dex's right hand like he'd just won a lifetime achievement award. Dex could see the other lads watching, wondering how "Pretty

Boy" as they'd once called him, had managed to jump rank. Dex didn't care. He'd spent long enough waiting for his moment.

When he first arrived in Ireland, working on building sites became necessary after discovering that male modelling jobs here were thin on the ground. It was a mighty fall from Tom Ford's New York catwalk to modelling acrylic sweaters slung over checked shirts on breakfast television. He'd had no idea that Ireland was so different. He won't use the word *behind*. He'd made that mistake once before with Ronnie. It hadn't gone down well. Ronnie did her best as his agent: an indigestion medication advert, an extra on *Fair City*, Ireland's answer to *The Young and the Restless*, only exhausted and downtrodden. The feedback was always the same. Dex was too good-looking for the Irish market. People couldn't relate.

He hadn't liked working as a labourer. It wasn't enough money, but it was in his blood. His father had been a carpenter in New York. When Eve's star began to rise, Dex became a stay-at-home dad. There'd been nothing wrong with it per se – he loved his kids – but it felt like he and Eve were on different trajectories: one down, one up. It bothered him.

Dex chews the inside of his mouth, thinking of it, then removes his phone from his pocket, pivots and snaps a "before" picture of the remaining floorboards. People like to see the transformation. It works well with the ethos of his business, Wood4Life Designs – reusing wood and other unwanted materials to design furniture to last a lifetime. Once he's finished here, he'll head back in to collect those benches. Despite not fancying the lunch-hour drive into Dublin, it'll be worth it, and it's nice to get out and about. Much as he loves it around here, unlike Eve who barely leaves the house, sometimes he needs a change of scene.

Glancing back at the phone, he opens an email, grateful that it's another enquiry. It's now a daily occurrence. Not so long ago, he'd been terrified the business would never get off the ground. He might have packed it in before now if it wasn't for Eve telling him to be patient, that he had nothing to prove. Only he does, to himself, at least.

"Give it time," she'd encouraged. "It can take two to three years for a business to become profitable."

It hadn't taken @beli'EVE that long. Eve claims that it was down to her and Ronnie being in the right place at the right time. *Fluke* was one of her favourite words. For once, Dex hopes he's in the right place. After all, sustainability is current. A few weeks ago, he won a significant contract to produce furniture and design outdoor eating areas for the Gallagher Group – a hotel chain branching into sustainable holiday villages around Ireland and the UK. It was a turning point for him, a massive confidence boost that his name is now out there. Then again, he'd been ready to do whatever it took to have his chance. It reminds him of something his father used to say to him, growing up in New York. He'd say that life was written in an indelible pen – that you don't get to undo what you've done, so to always make sure you can live with your actions.

Jumping down from the truck, Dex purposefully pulls a plank onto his shoulder and strides back into the workshop. He repeats the process until the truck is empty. When he finishes, he leans against the doorframe of the workshop and looks up at the dizzyingly tall trees which practically obscure the sky. Eve loves those trees. Then again, they're the only privacy she has from the watchers.

In the early days, Dex used to watch too, finding it strangely addictive until he began to feel like he was lurking in his own life. Without even seeing her in person or speaking a word, he'd know what Eve would be wearing, where she'd been, what was for dinner.

Online, Eve was a souped-up version of herself – someone who looked and sounded like his wife, but somehow wasn't her. It made him think of the person she might have been if they'd never met. If Eve had stayed on in New York, she'd probably be married to some famous musician or actor instead of him, appearing on far more than one album cover. Eve must know it too because she can't bear to look at that photo of her falling in the red dress. It doesn't take a genius to figure out that it acts as a reminder of what she'd given up for him. Watching Eve dazzle online, growing more famous by the day, began to trouble Dex so much that he'd deliberately clicked *unfollow* one day. Knowing it was only a matter of time before the constraints of a smartphone, or him, became too small for her.

Eve never even noticed he was gone. By then, there were so many other people in their lives. Perhaps they saw the cracks in their marriage before he did.

When Eve told him that they needed to talk two years ago, Dex instantly feared the worst. Instead, she'd said precisely what he'd been waiting patiently to hear.

#

"I can't do it anymore. It's become too … intrusive. Let's start again, please." Eve had sounded desperate. "Just us, the kids, a house in the country. I didn't know what to do with the house in Annaford until right now, but I know Lily wanted us to live in it. She left it to me so I'd have options."

It had been over a year since Eve had been left the house. Six months since she'd discovered the note urging her not to sell.

"You can finally start your business. I can be with the kids. Take up golf." She'd laughed before turning serious. "It's over with Ronnie, but this," she'd gestured at the ever-increasing gap between them, "we can mend this, Dex. I know things have been strained for a while, but it's work. I see it now. I want to stop."

After they moved, Eve had stopped, but the break ended after Dex took that photo of her in the rain. His jaw clenches now at the thought. Eve claimed they needed the money, but he's certain that wasn't the only reason. Though Eve carries her fame like a cross, Dex believes it feeds her deep down like nothing else can – certainly not him. What other choice does he have but to accept it? Eve was always destined to be someone. He'd known it from the moment they met on a New York shoot. The problem was, Ronnie knew it too. It seemed the only person who didn't realise it was Eve.

"I hope to hell you don't dress like that on a Saturday night." Eve had raised both eyebrows when Dex walked into the New York studio the day they met.

"Are you kidding? This is dressed down. For the weekend, I go large," he'd said with a smirk.

"I'd like to see that."

"That can be arranged." He raised an eyebrow back, blinking furiously when his marabou-feather lash-extension went into his eye. "Sorry, I should have trimmed my feathers."

"Do you know what it's like?" She crossed her arms. "Like a bird flew at you and got stuck."

"I thought more Boy George mixed with Julius Caesar."

Eve gestured at his toga. "Either way, you wouldn't want to get caught in a gust of wind."

His mouth twitched. "Especially since all I'm wearing underneath are silk panties."

Eve grimaced.

"I'm kidding, obviously," he said with a smile, then added, "I've absolutely nothing on."

Surprisingly, she blushed. "I'll be careful to keep my hands tucked into this so." She rubbed her hands down her shiny tinfoil gown.

"I have one like that at home," Dex said, pointing. "I wore it after I finished the New York marathon."

"Yes! That's exactly it." She grinned before extending her hand. "I'm Eve."

"And I'm Adam." Again, he laughed at her shocked expression. "Okay. Okay, I'm Dex."

"Now, there's a name you don't hear too often back home."

"And where's that?" He feigned ignorance. His agent had already told him about the unknown Irish girl with the plucky manager, taking the fashion scene by storm, bypassing starter jobs, and heading for editorial. She'd asked Dex to find out the manager's name – that she'd consider offering her a job.

"Ireland."

"Hey, my surname is Ryan. That makes me Irish too, right?"

"Not another one!" She rolled her eyes dramatically. "Kelly and Ryan. We're quite the pair, but I'm sorry to tell you with a name like Dex, a toga, and those eyelashes, you're not Irish."

He stopped laughing when he saw the photographer and stylist approach to issue instructions. "I hate this part," he groaned.

"We'll be grand," she'd said with a wink.

Eve was more than grand. Dex was blown away by how she was in front of the camera. His agent had been right: "Word is Calvin Klein want her for their next campaign, and she's going to be on the cover of Timeline's latest album. Looks like the girl from Ireland is going places if it all goes to plan."

56

###

Things hadn't gone to plan. Still, back in Ireland, Ronnie and Eve managed to weave a different path to the top before it fell apart. When Dex first noticed it crumbling, secretly he'd been pleased. From what Eve told him at the time, which wasn't much, she and Ronnie had been arguing over online negativity and how to handle it. Eve wanted to fight back. Ronnie wanted to ignore it. They finally came to blows when Eve went rogue, speaking publicly about her perceived hardships. Ronnie claimed that the "rant" made Eve sound like a victim, "a poor little rich girl".

Dex only listened to it after it went viral and got a certain amount of coverage for the wrong reasons. In reality, it wasn't bad. Eve made fair points, but the severity of her emotions didn't quite equate to the topic. To him, it felt as though she was upset about something more than trolls and hate pages. He had to watch it a few times before he realised what Eve was really speaking about – all the things she'd never told him. All the things she thought he didn't know.

The plea to other influencers to join her in the fight failed to impact after someone made an unflattering, yet somewhat amusing, crying gif of Eve that ended up in every conceivable *WhatsApp* group known to man, leaving Eve mortified and Ronnie smug.

Afterwards came deafening silence. Not having Ronnie's support hit Eve hard. Dex watched Eve withdraw from the side-line, grow sullen, depressed, jumpy, and even more distant if that was possible. Holding his tongue, saying nothing, proved difficult for Dex, but silence was the only weapon he had until Faye became unwell. He hadn't meant to, but when Eve questioned him as to how they'd missed what was happening with Faye, he had answered, "Because

57

what Faye needs is a mother. Not me. Your daughter needs you. Maybe it's time you were here for her more." It was cruel of him, he knows, and not entirely true, but it had the desired effect. A few weeks later, Eve came to him, suggesting the move.

And now, here they are. He got what he wanted.

Dex walks back inside and runs his hand over the surface of another piece he's working on, wincing when a large splinter pierces his skin. Without hesitating, he turns his hand over, pulls at it with his teeth, and spits it out. Nothing good ever comes from things left to fester.

Eve misses Ronnie, he knows, but they're better off without her. Ronnie was a sacrifice that needed to be made for the greater good. Like Princess Diana, Dex had grown tired of having three people in their marriage. Things are good again. They still have their secrets from each other but, having accidentally discovered Eve's, Dex feels that bit less remorseful about his.

A few weeks back, Eve was featured in "Loves of Your Life" in the Sunday supplement, where she was asked to reveal things about herself: favourite food, smell, person, time of day, biggest weakness.

Lying next to her in bed, Dex had read through her answers. "Good start. I'm your favourite person. Biggest weakness … chocolate? Really?" He'd peered over the magazine. "You hardly eat it."

"What else can you say when you're perfect?" she'd joked. "What would you say?"

"I'd say you. You're my vice." It wasn't a lie.

Afterwards, he wondered how Eve would answer with a gun to her head. She has no idea he knows, but Eve has two significant weaknesses, neither of which is him. Then again, no one is perfect. Not him, and indeed not Eve. Both have held that indelible pen. Both have done things that aren't easy to erase. Only one of them can live with themselves afterwards.

Dex sometimes wonders if Eve knows that the door to her tower is unlocked – that it isn't a prison. He'd thought her self-imposed sentence might have ended by now. Or perhaps there are further crimes Eve has committed that he's yet to discover. His thoughts disperse when his phone pings, alerting him to an email. Dex reads it and mouths a curse. It's another enquiry, but that's not the problem. The problem is the first line.

I got your name from Ronnie Delaney.

Something is coming.

CHAPTER SIX

@beli'EVE

Public Figure

Mama. Wife. Model. Content Creator. Collabs. Beauty. Fashion Interiors.

5,698	1M	212
Posts	Followers	Following

I've finally managed to get some work done. I've spent the past couple of hours editing, sharing stats and insights with some of the brands I'm working with, invoicing. I'm about to start filming my next slot when I hear the door of the workshop bang shut. Walking back to the window, I see Dex pat the dust off his hands and climb into his beloved truck. It's one of those American-looking utility jeeps that a high-school football-team captain might drive. "*Back to the Future*, eat your heart out!" Dex had proclaimed, proudly banging the bonnet when he first brought it home with the *Wood4Life* logo along the side.

Milo thought it was the coolest thing he'd ever seen. Faye said it looked like something a serial killer might drive and that if he suggested dropping them to their new school in it, she'd die on the spot. "We're going in Mum's car."

I hadn't bothered to point out that my car actually isn't my car. I don't own it. I'm a brand ambassador for Mercedes Ireland and, like most things in my life, my car has been specially selected for me and my needs by a marketing team. To be fair, it's a gorgeous car and a great perk. After moving from the city and breaking away from Ronnie, I was convinced they'd want to go elsewhere. Instead, they'd swapped my city run-around for a four-wheel-drive fit for country life, and I recorded one of those embarrassing, *"Hi. I'm Eve, and I'd be lost without …"* endorsements. They also encourage that I record content whilst sitting in the car, show my latest manicure against the logo of the steering wheel, take a few fashion shots leaning against it nonchalantly – that sort of thing. Apparently, it works. In this case, who am I to argue?

Below, Dex grabs his Wayfarers from the dash, puts them on, then manually rolls down the truck's window. Something else I can't argue with is that Dex looks the part in his ever-so-slightly bashed-up old truck, utility trousers, scruffy T-shirt, tool belt. So much so that if he mistakenly walked into a rowdy 50th, he might not make it out alive.

Then again, there aren't many guises that don't work on Dex with his chiselled good looks, deep-brown eyes, sandy hair, sallow skin: preppy, soccer dad, confident groom adjusting his cufflinks, high fashion in a skirt! Despite what he says, Dex was a great model. If he'd stayed in New York instead of following me home, he'd have made it big. It makes me feel a little less guilty when he claims it was never really what he wanted to do.

Lately, I've never seen him so driven to succeed. It's as though he's becoming the person he might have been if we'd never met. I still feel responsible for forcing him into a supporting role in what often felt like *The Eve Show*. Appreciating this dusty, sunny, creative version of him makes me realise how unhappy he must have been for so long.

Thinking of it, my stomach twists with unease. Dex would never say it, but he must have resented me – how his career came second, how I stopped seeing who he was. To add insult to injury, I was so busy with everything else that I'd neglected our marriage. It became dormant. In the end, it was up to me to wake it. I'm happy that I could give Dex the chance to pursue his dream. It's his turn to thrive now.

Dex reverses down the forest path next to his workshop before turning onto the tarmac drive towards the main gate. He stops, allowing the electric gates to jerk open, then drives through. Craning my neck after him, I can just make out the top of the new houses. Seeing them somehow makes me think of Ronnie yet again. I now understand her regret after selling my photo for so little. I made the same mistake when I took the developer's first, wholly inadequate offer on the land attached to The Old Rectory. When I'd phoned him to finally accept, he told me that he'd already had provisional plans drawn up and was keen to submit them. His eagerness should have sounded alarm bells, but then he'd gone on and on that there were no guarantees he'd get permission. "It's a big old risk, love. The market has changed since I spoke with your aunt, God rest her. I could be left with a field, good for nothing but a few sheep and a donkey. But I'm willing to take a gamble. I'll probably live to regret it but, as my old man would say, nothing ventured, nothing gained. I'd say there'll be very little gained in this case."

Turns out, he was a good liar. In the end, he got permission for the four houses in an unprecedented amount of time. They flew up like Lego in less than a year, far surpassing our pathetic attempts at renovation, and then sold for an amount that I can't bring myself to utter aloud without my stomach turning. Joanne understands that part only too well. She ended up buying one of them. She often teases that it's my fault she's permanently broke from her crippling mortgage repayments since I was the one who told her about the new houses in the first place. At the time, Joanne had been working in the Wicklow branch of the therapy clinic Faye had attended in Dublin. A few months after we moved, I'd found their business card in one of the boxes and phoned to see if anyone could provide a house visit, a follow-up for Faye, after the move. Joanne came. I'd met her once before at the Dublin clinic and thought she'd had a nice way about her. Turns out I was right. She was far more amiable than the original therapist, Dr Robin, who'd always left me feeling bewildered with her elusive answers.

I was never happier than when after a few visits Joanne and I went into the garden to discuss Faye's progress, and she told me she was discharging her.

"She's reached her treatment goals, Eve. Look, I can keep seeing her if you want, but she's doing well. She's thrilled with the fresh start you've given her here, excited for the future, and loving her new school. Not every parent gets to do that for their child. You should feel really proud." She smiled broadly.

I'd exhaled as though I'd been holding my breath for a year.

Joanne put her hand on my arm and looked up at me. "She's doing great. And if anything changes, I'm at the end of the phone, but I'm not going to keep taking your money when Faye is thriving."

I appreciated her honesty so much that I'd wanted to hug her there and then. Instead, we ended up talking about the garden and the history of the house.

"And what about that part?" Joanne pointed at the sectioned-off bit beyond the gate, peppered with diggers and machinery.

"Long story," I began, rolling my eyes.

Joanne listened while I explained that we'd sold some of the land to a developer and that there'd be four new houses there soon. I couldn't help but notice her ears perk up as I said it.

"Sorry," she apologised after a brief pause. "You see, I've been renting in Wicklow Town for the past few years since moving from Belfast. I've been on the lookout to buy ever since. So whenever I hear of somewhere, I can't help but wonder, is this it? So far, no luck. There's nothing out there at the minute."

I later learned that her marriage had broken down in Belfast. When it ended, she'd wanted a dramatic change.

"Anyway, woe is me," she said. "I'd best get on. It was lovely to see you again, Eve. Just remember, if you –"

"I could put you in contact with the developer if you like," I'd interrupted before checking myself. "Sorry, that was forward of me. Would that be weird? Only you're not technically Faye's counsellor anymore, and the developer might be able to bump you up the list." My eyes twinkled, knowing there could be far worse people than someone like Joanne on your doorstep.

She has proved to be a great neighbour and, over time, a good friend – discreet to a fault, non-judgmental, not pushy – someone to have a walk and a coffee with. We've never spoken further about Faye's troubles, and I'm happy to keep it that way, but I know she'd come to me if she thought something was wrong again. There's a level of security to having her nearby if we ever needed her. There's no agenda with Joanne. If only I could say the same about everyone else.

Resting my hands on the windowsill, I sigh. I'm irked. It's all down to the email I received a few weeks ago. Before opening it, I'd gone into settings and switched off **"read receipt"** so the sender couldn't tell if I'd read it or not. After I had, I'd rested my elbows on the desk and put my hands to my face, dread building within. Since then, I've been trying and failing to ignore it.

Before I can dwell on it any longer, I turn my attention to the calming view outside. The surrounding trees are so tall that I feel dwarfed even up here on the third floor. Dex says they make the place dark, but it doesn't bother me. I'd quite like the branches to merge further, so our little world is within a cage. It probably still wouldn't be enough. Some things always find a way in. Or maybe it's me who invites them in.

It certainly felt that way when I allowed @anoldfriendfromcollege to preoccupy my thoughts three years before. In hindsight, I became obsessed with waiting for them to reappear. Back then, I began scrutinising the online activity on Facebook and Instagram like a hawk, scouring negative comments. Although they amounted to practically nothing in comparison to the usual heartfelt positivity, they were all I could see.

At my request, Ronnie had placed Amber elsewhere, relieving her of answering and deleting comments so I could deal with them myself. Whenever I came across something negative, with anticipation swirling in my stomach, I'd developed the unhealthy habit of clicking on the contributor's profile picture. To my surprise, they were primarily women hugging precious little girls in Communion dresses or proudly standing next to a daughter in a graduation gown. The same women who thought it was okay to criticise everything from how I dressed, my make-up, eyebrows, nose, hair, or tell me that I was underweight, that my children's names were pretentious, or I was a "stupid thick cow".

In turn, I'd flick through their public pictures, examining them, wondering how they'd feel if they knew I was watching back. If I was brave enough to tell them to "bin that dress" or "get a decent haircut", would it make me feel better? Did it make them feel better? After all, they were putting themselves on a public platform too. Did it give me the right to have a public opinion on them?

I pored over narrow-minded views and discussions about me as if I didn't exist. I read how I begged for clothes, how it was scandalous that one person could own that many pairs of jeans, jackets, whatever. "*Because it's my job*," I'd mutter endlessly at the screen like a woman possessed. "I don't keep them all. I don't even ask for them. It's to help all of you who keep telling me you don't know what to wear!"

I flinched over how I'd allegedly refused to help specific charities. How I took freebies from small businesses that could ill-afford it. I should be ashamed of myself. I itched to respond – to tell them that I helped practically everyone I could, most of the time, without telling Ronnie, who'd undoubtedly look for a fee.

And all this was from people who were perfectly happy for me to know who they were. Then, there were the others – those who hid behind fake names on Jabber.ie where the rumours grew darker. One claimed I abused my children. There was talk of affairs, a battle with anorexia. I was an alcoholic, a narcissist. I was fatphobic, homophobic, racist, I was rude. I was demanding.

Then they came after Faye.

When they did, it stung that my daughter needed someone like Ronnie or Joanne in her corner, who'd deal with it calmly instead of reacting like I had, making everything worse. Only by then, Ronnie was so angry with me that I couldn't tell her. My marriage was down the pan. Joanne and this sanctuary in Wicklow were yet to happen. I was alone, drowning. Like a fool I clung to the most unexpected person who threw me a lifeline. But then, isn't one bad decision often followed by another?

#

I look down now at where my fingers are gripping the window ledge, my knuckles white. "Damn you, Ronnie," I whisper aloud.

I wish I'd never come up with that stupid campaign to speak out against trolls. I was oblivious to what I was about to do to my life or who I'd aggravate further. It planted a seed of anarchy in someone who didn't like being told what not to do. Very soon, I was being followed so closely that I could almost sense their breath on the back of my neck – warm at first, then icy cold. Even when I couldn't see them, I knew they were with me. Or perhaps they always had been. Once again, my mind drifts to the email that awaits an answer. By replying, would I be making the same mistake again? Letting the past back in.

2016

Several weeks after Eve confronted Ronnie in her office about Jabber.ie they agreed to meet for Friday lunch at The Ivy, followed by drinks. Ronnie made her swear not to talk about work – that they were heading out just as friends. Eve might have believed her if she hadn't told her to get dressed up, then booked the best table to make sure everyone who passed saw them in the trendy Dublin restaurant.

"Christ, Eve, you're obsessed. Let it go!" Ronnie implored, dismissively taking a sip from her Pinot Grigio when Eve asked if she'd had a chance to look at the proposal she'd sent her concerning online bullying.

"Well, have you read it?"

"No."

"I want to address this, Ronnie," Eve said, lowering her voice as she noticed a woman at another table clock her, then turn to whisper to her fellow diners.

One by one, they turned to look, then pivoted back to comment to each other. "Have you read the latest attacks?" Eve went on, trying to ignore their stares.

"No!" Ronnie rolled her eyes, exhaling impatiently when Eve picked up her phone to show her.

Eve scrolled back through the screenshots she'd taken, then read some aloud before looking up.

Ronnie pursed her lips.

"You know they congratulate each other for coming up with clever titles like this one?" Eve read from her phone again. "These ones are mild. '#*Eve drinks wine so she can have another whine.*' Or '#*If Eve doesn't want Dex, send him here for the sex.*'" That time, when she glanced up, Ronnie was pressing her lips together so as not to laugh. "It's not funny, Ronnie. They think I'm having an affair."

"And are you?" Ronnie challenged.

"No!"

"Well, then why the hell do you care?" She shrugged. "Seriously, Eve. Grow a thicker skin. This is ridiculous! These women are no-ones!" She shooed the air. "I'm tired of wasting my breath on them. I'm going to tell Amber to start deleting comments again." She took a more purposeful slug of her wine, swallowed, then continued. "Regardless of what you say, it keeps stupid pricks from bouncing stupid opinions off each other. It shuts them down. It worked before, and it will work again. Then I want you to block anyone who sends you abusive

DM's and never look at Jabber again. Do you hear me? I'll get Amber to keep an eye on it, and if any one of those trolls breaks a rule, I'll contact the website myself. Okay?" She clapped her hands together and picked up her menu. "If you're so intent on talking business today, where are we with the new make-up line?"

Eve exhaled slowly. "Please stop dismissing this, Ronnie. They've already broken rules. They put my address up there. What if all this was happening to Faye? Would you do something then?"

"No." Ronnie looked at her over the menu. "I'd tell her the same as I've just told you – to stay offline. Seriously, Eve, let me take care of things again, so you can concentrate on fabulous content, beautiful pics, competitions, inspiring quotes –"

"Why should I stay offline on my own accounts? It's not enough to delete comments or block fake accounts, Ronnie. It shouldn't be happening at all. These people should take ownership of their words."

Ronnie began drumming her nails on the table. "I've said it before – some people are never happy. It says more about them than it does about you. And back to what you said earlier, this isn't happening to Faye. She's a child. If it was happening to her, I'd seek further advice."

"But not for me?" Eve eyeballed her.

"Believe me, Eve. I *am* protecting you. You're just so caught up you can't see it. This needs to stop." For the first time, she looked concerned. "Is there something else going on, Eve? Am I missing something? If I am, just tell me. Are you feeling okay?"

"I'm fine. It was that message about college." Eve shook her head. "I can't help thinking about it, Ronnie. What if someone

… what if … " She couldn't finish. Her heart was hammering in her chest.

"*Breathe*," Ronnie ordered. "Has there been anything more from them?"

Eve took a few breaths. "No."

"See, it was nothing."

"Even still, those people should be shut down. For everyone's sake," Eve continued, changing tack. "What about the younger influencers? If I'm getting this level of hate, they must be getting it too. I'm old enough to take it, but –"

"*Are* you? And yes, of course, they get it too. Do you see them complaining? No. Because they won't win, and neither will you. Christ, Eve, next you'll be saying you have a responsibility to fix this, which makes me believe that this is about something else."

"And what if I do? I should at least try." Eve leaned forward eagerly. She'd thought about nothing else for days but speaking out. "If you look at what I sent you, it explains it more. I was thinking of getting a group of bloggers together calling for accounts to be linked to a verified form of identification in order to banish fake ones – make people accountable for what they say online. You can't just walk down the street shouting what you like. So why is it okay online? I even thought of a name – #unfollow me – and –"

"You are joking!" Ronnie guffawed before Eve could finish. "First of all, this isn't Live Aid and – 'unfollow me'? I've heard it all now." Her tone dripped sarcasm. "When our entire purpose is to gain followers, not bloody well lose them."

"Yes, but it's to encourage people following only who they like. People who make them feel good. It's okay not to like someone, but it doesn't make it okay to attack them."

"That's very *Disney* of you. And then what? The world will be a better place? Is it going to make us money?"

Eve shook her head.

"But what?"

She clenched her jaw, frustrated, trying not to let Ronnie talk her down. "This isn't about making money, Ronnie. You once told me to use my voice. This is important to me. Do you have any idea what it feels like to read that stuff about yourself?"

"Stop reading it."

"I don't need your permission to do something I feel strongly about."

"Yes, you do. We're partners, remember?" Ronnie crossed her arms.

"It's my name, my face. Doesn't that count for something?"

"My brains," she said with a smirk. "Besides, people don't like it when people like you get self-righteous."

"People like me?" Eve frowned.

"That's right. The emotional ones who have it all, then complain about it. I can see it now. *#Eve is packed full of shite, with the latest unfollow-me tripe.*"

Her words pierced like venom. For a moment, Eve sat still, trying to think of a clever response. Instead, she spoke from her heart. "I don't have it all, Ronnie. You know that better than anyone. I never did, and I never set out to give that impression. That was your visual."

"This business isn't about honesty."

"Well, maybe it should be. Or maybe someone *emotional* like me isn't the right person for this job!" Eve pushed back her chair, turned on her heel and practically ran out of the restaurant.

When she was safely outside, around the corner, the tears came. She felt like an idiot. Standing there, hurt welled. Deep inside, she knew she deserved the hatred. What would those trolls do to her if they ever found out the real reason? Or that someone like her didn't always get to be honest.

CHAPTER SEVEN

#oompaloompa #bloggerbitch #loversleap #jumptoyourdeath
#followme #somethingiscoming

@beli'EVE
Public Figure
Mama. Wife. Model. Content Creator. Collabs. Beauty. Fashion
Interiors.

5,698	1M	212
Posts	Followers	Following

"You're still at it!" Dex stands at the studio door, arms folded, dismayed look on his face.

It's after six. Aside from running downstairs to grab something to eat, I've been here all day. From my Instagram stories, it looks like I've been for a walk along Dún Laoghaire pier before getting a quick T-bar of highlights in The Gallery – my new favourite hair salon. That was two days ago.

"I'm done, I swear." I retract my hands from the keyboard, holding them up in surrender.

"Did you meet Joanne?"

I shake my head. "She got stuck at work." The lie rolls off my tongue as easily it had earlier this morning. "And I got sucked in here."

In reality, I've spent the majority of the day pondering the email, the dilemma it contains, and how Dex will react when I finally tell him.

"These big, long days aren't good for you. You swore you'd pull back." Dex frowns as he walks over and sits on the edge of the desk.

Right now, I don't need a lecture. I'm so tired, my eyes sting. "I know. I know, but you know how it is."

Dex doesn't know how it is, or why I can't take time off at the drop of a hat. I am the job. Unless you work in it, no one understands the relentless burden to stay relevant, produce content, prove your worth, engage. If I drop the baton, someone is always waiting to pick it up and run with it. Perhaps that makes it sound more cutthroat than it is. There's actually a nice group of influencers in Ireland who, contrary to popular belief, don't pull each other's hair extensions out with their gel nails but, like any business, it is competitive.

Something else Dex can't grasp is that despite working harder than ever, I'm not earning as much as I had when I was with Ronnie. After restarting @beli'EVE alone, I'd had to renegotiate contracts. I'd also lost followers. In the same way that I'd doubted myself with the developer, I'd sold myself short. Now, I'm paying for it.

"You look tired," Dex says.

I nod.

"But very glamorous." He raises his eyebrows at my full-length gown. "A bit much for pub grub in the local, but I could slip-on black tie if you wanted to really go for it."

There's a pause. My blank expression must give me away.

"You forgot about dinner, didn't you?" he sighs.

I pretend to hide behind my hands. I'm hoping he lets me off easily. I've so much on my mind that I'm not really in the mood to go out.

"Where are the kids?" I push back my chair and head towards the clothes rail to remove the orange atrocity of a gown I'm sporting.

"Milo went to meet his friends in the village. Faye is studying. What's with the dress anyway?" His eyes follow me.

"Terrible, isn't it?" I pull down the straps and shimmy out of it. "It's for a feature next week. I got a few emails from people about wedding-guest ideas and high-street options for bridesmaids. A few places sent me samples." I hook the straps onto a hanger. "These have to be back tomorrow, so I got the pictures done today. Thanks for collecting the guys, by the way." He had texted earlier to say he could get the children on the way back from Dublin.

I glance up.

Dex is grinning.

"What?" I ask.

His smile spreads to my face.

"Just you."

"Just me what?"

"Just what would everyone do without you to solve the problems of the universe?"

"Hardly." I make a face.

From the little things he sometimes says, I get the impression that Dex thinks I can't live without being "someone". It's why he believes I restarted @beli'EVE after I swore I was giving it up. The truth is, we'd needed the money. Until recently, my husband hasn't had to think about money or where it comes from, so maybe it's not his fault that he often appears oblivious. The renovations annihilated every cent we made from the sale of the land and then some. Since I'd made the faux pas with the developer, it was up to me to find a solution to make it work here in Annaford. I did what I knew, restarted my social platform. Believe me, it was the last thing I wanted.

I regularly have to stop myself from asking Dex how he thinks we'd survive if I "pulled back". Mind you, he is a little savvier now that he's working again. The recent deal with the Gallagher Group is certainly raising his profile, so much so that perhaps soon I will be able to do what he so often suggests. But for now, we still have to finish the house and get Faye and Milo through school and college. Despite sometimes feeling so afraid that it's difficult to breathe, I plough on in sacrifice … or is it atonement?

"There's my wife," Dex says after I pull on a pair of leggings, a T-shirt and slip my feet into a pair of Birkenstocks. "I thought I'd be heading for dinner with the Oompa Loompa bridesmaid who'd spend the evening badgering me for sex."

"I could put the dress back on?" I suggest.

"Please, Eve." He makes towards me, his expression so deadpan that for one moment I'm fearful of what he might say. "We already did it this morning. I'm not a machine, you know?" He mimics flicking his hair.

"*Hah, hah.* What I was actually going to say was that we could –"

"Stay home?"

"Could we?" My face collapses with relief. "I haven't seen the kids yet, and the thought of changing again … " I shiver in aversion. "I'd just like to wash my face, get some fresh air and flop." I put my arms around his neck.

"Fine." He sucks his cheeks in, pretending to be annoyed. "What can we cook here instead?"

"Actually," I remember, "I bought this really great homemade pizza kit the other day for the kids. I was going to do it for them before we went out, but there's enough for all of us. It's in the fridge."

"Okay. Sounds good."

My face lights up. "There was a promotion on, and the girl who makes them was there. She was such a sweetheart. She kept offering to give it me for free, but I insisted on paying."

"Because she wanted you to plug it, Eve," Dex says, sounding like Ronnie.

"No. I think she was just really nervous about it all going well and she recognised me. That's all." I ignore his cynical look. "I said I'd do a quick pic or video or something to give her a little boost."

"Eve!" he chides.

"What? She was nice. I offered."

It was something Ronnie never allowed. "Nothing for nothing" became her mantra when we surpassed a quarter of a million followers. By the time we got to a million, she was even more stringent.

"You never stop, do you?" Dex said. "You're clearly exhausted, and you're still going."

"Come on, Dex! Everyone needs a bounce of the ball sometimes and if we're making pizza anyway . . ." I beam until I'm showing my teeth. "It will literally take one minute to do a quick story. Come on," I repeat. "You know what it's like now with your business. Starting out is tough."

His face softens as he wraps his arms around my waist. "Did anyone ever tell you that you're a good person?"

"Actually, no." I laugh mirthlessly. "Most people say I'm a fickle, money-hungry, fake, blogger-bitch who promotes an unattainable lifestyle, exploits brands, shops all day every day, wearing couture, eating caviar for breakfast!" I bob my head as I finish my spiel.

"You do that so seamlessly. Could it be true?" Dex jeers. "Particularly the unattainable lifestyle. Personally, I'm sick of caviar in my Coco Pops."

"If they only knew the truth." I feel a shadow crossing my face.

"Hey," he rests his forehead against mine, "you've always told the truth, haven't you?"

"Yes," I lie for the umpteenth time today.

"You know what?" He leans back. "If anyone can do this nice girl's business justice, I can. Why don't you go for a walk, clear your head and I'll take some pictures on my rusty old phone. Insta-husband at your service!" He salutes.

"Really?" I kick off my sandals.

"Go. I'll round up the kids and cook the dinner. And I got two more orders earlier. It's busy, Eve." He nods. "With the hotel contract, I'll probably need another pair of hands soon."

"Wow! That's amazing, Dex."

He leans in and kisses me, gently biting my bottom lip. "That stuff is in the fridge, right?"

"Yes. You can't miss it. Don't forget to take a pic before you open the box too."

"*O ye of little faith!* I've been watching you closely all these years, Eve." He heads for the door. "I know far more than you think I do!"

My stomach lurches suddenly at the thought it could be true, then I jump when my phone rings again from my desk. I already know who it is. They've been calling all day. I have the number saved under **Do Not Answer**. I'm not sure how much longer I can hold out before doing what the screen keeps telling me not to. That's the thing about me. I'm no rebel. I usually do what I'm told, but I have a strong tendency to repeat mistakes.

#

Beyond the rows of trees at the end of the garden, I head to the arched wooden door in the boundary wall. I retrieve the old wrought-iron key from under a rock and insert it into the lock. Like Aunt Lily before me, I pull the handle and wiggle the key until it opens to reveal the leafy walkway that borders the back of our land – my secret place. That's not strictly true. Nowadays, it's a walker's right of way, but it's still relatively obscure. I can count on one hand the number of times I've happened upon another living soul here.

There's a sharp drop to the Dargle river on the other side of the path. In places, if you were to veer too close or lose your footing, it wouldn't end well. When we first moved in, I considered blocking the door permanently as a safety precaution. I couldn't do it. It's part of the history of the house. Instead, I keep the key hidden for personal use. Dex and the kids know about the walk. I'd brought them on it – shown them the place that held such relevance for me. They hadn't appeared that interested.

Serenity hits as soon as I cross the threshold. I inhale deeply, tuck the key into the side pocket of my leggings and set off. To this day, awe washes over me in the same manner it had done when Lily first led me by the hand to reveal the mystery beyond the trees, speaking in a loud, lulling whisper.

"*I'm the gatekeeper,*" she'd told me. "*You can be one too. As long as you promise to believe.*"

"In what?" I'd looked up, bug-eyed, immersed in the fantasy.

"In love." She tapped the end of my nose with her finger then patted my head. "It's called Lover's Leap."

I follow the same narrow path now under a tunnel of greenery until I reach an opening in the foliage. "*Go on!*" Lily's words echo as I pass under the natural archway. The clay track morphs to rock as I step up onto the enormous boulder at the edge of the cliff until I'm standing on the stage-like surface, looking out at an expanse of open air. Below, the river murmurs. It's like being in another world –

breathtakingly and unexpectedly high, exceeding the treetops in the deep-cut valley below. "A place to come if you're hell-bent on self-destruction," Lily had echoed my exact feelings when we'd come here again when I was much older, after college.

Gingerly, I peer over the crag. I'm not afraid of heights. I certainly wasn't when I posed on a similar rock years before. Back then, it was everything else in life that frightened me.

"Makes you feel insignificant, doesn't it?" Lily had looked up at the sky that day.

While she spoke, emptiness reverberated in my hollow heart, so loud that I wondered could she hear it.

"We're only tiny molecules in the grand scheme of life, you know?" Then she'd turned to me. "It's the same with problems. In the bigger picture, they're just moments, specs of dust that will float away if you let them, when you're ready." She'd put her hand on mine where we sat.

I sit now, hugging my knees with my eyes closed, imagining her next to me, telling me the story again.

The legend goes, I hear Lily's whisper, *that hundreds of years ago there was a couple so in love that they preferred to jump to their death together than be forced to live apart.*

Dex suddenly appears in my mind as I open my eyes to look out over the valley. Chewing the inside of my cheek, I try to imagine having the clout to hurl myself off a cliff rather than live without the person I love. If push came to shove, could I jump? Or could I live without Dex?

I coax our first encounter from the recesses of my memory.

#

We'd flirted the entire day at a photo shoot in New York. Later, we wound up sitting opposite each other in a dimly lit bar.

"So, what's the life plan?" he'd asked in that all-American way.

"World domination."

"Good. Start small," he grinned, then squinted. "You serious?"

"No." I smiled back. He was so easy to talk to that without meaning to, I said, "It's more to never feel how I did before I came here."

He lifted his chin. "Oh, yeah? And what way was that?"

"Sorry." I shook my head skittishly and dropped my gaze. "That was very deep. Must be the whiskey." I raised my glass, swirling the barely touched amber liquid.

When I looked up, he was staring at me expectantly.

"Just sad," I admitted. "Really, really sad."

"I might have something for that. It will make you feel instantly better." His eyes twinkled.

Frowning, I watched him reach into his jeans pocket, then place his closed fist on the table in front of me.

"Want it?" His eyes bored into mine.

"I … I don't … I …" I made to stand.

"Hey, wait." He looked confused.

My gaze flashed to his hand as he opened his fist to reveal a rather squished eyelash extension. "I saved it for you. I'm willing to wear it for the rest of my life if you promise never to feel sad again."

"I thought it was … I thought you were going to offer me …" I'd exhaled slowly, then laughed as he shook his head.

"No. Never. But the eyelash, yes." He winked, understanding.

I'd been warned about the "scene" in New York. Clearly, Dex wasn't a part of it.

"You'd really do that for me?"

"I would." That time, Dex was serious. "Whatever you need."

In truth, I'd needed Dex to help me wipe away the specs of dust that relentlessly clung to me. I was tired of waiting for them to float away like Lily said they would.

Standing, I force myself to look over the edge. Without question, Dex would jump for me. He already did the day I told him I was pregnant with Faye just three months after that first photo shoot. I'd prepared a spiel as to why not having the baby wasn't an option for me and why I had to have it at home. He barely let me finish before telling me that he'd follow me to the end of the earth rather than be apart. He gave up his life in New York, his life-plan, at the drop of a hat.

Even Ronnie, who'd been furious over how I'd ruined everything days before signing with Calvin Klein, was impressed by his devotion.

"It pains me to say it, but Dex is a good guy," she admitted begrudgingly. "Stable, decent, calm." Without verbalising it, she'd meant he was everything I'd been missing with Conor.

"Will you stay on without me?" I'd asked her. She'd already tried to convince me to have the baby in New York, but I wouldn't be swayed.

Ronnie shook her head. "Nah. We're partners, remember? And we'll come back from this blip. Besides, we did what we came to do, right?" She already sounded like a native. "You're famous now!"

I could see her cogs turning.

"Even better, back home, we'll be big fish in a small pond. Just don't get fat and ugly," she'd said.

I threw my arms around her, hugging her so tightly that I almost missed what she muttered next.

###

Before heading back, I bend to pick up a stone, throw it over the edge and watch it vanish into thin air. I owe Dex everything for what he gave up back then and ever since. Deep down, I know my family hate what I do, how absent I am, how I'm never entirely at ease, present. It's better since we moved here, but it's not enough. Maybe it is time to go the final mile – give everyone what they want.

Walking along the path, it strikes me that perhaps what that email contains is my ticket to freedom – a way for me to assure that the dust from the past never settles again. Back in the garden, I lock up, replace the key, and lean against the door. "The goal," Aunt Lily would say, "is to find someone who loves you as much as you love them. If you jump, jump together. Or go without. Love yourself instead."

The sentiment fuses with Ronnie's muffled words back in New York – the ones I'd pretended not to hear. She'd said, "At least this time, you found someone who loves you more than you'll ever love them. At some point, we're all addicted to something that ruins us, aren't we?"

For one moment, standing here, everything feels eerily quiet in the same way life has lately. I hear branches snap, rustling, footsteps on the other side of the door. It's probably a bird or an animal, yet the blood rushes in my ears. I stride away, fast. Even before I got the email, I could sense that something is coming – that the silence is about to break.

CHAPTER EIGHT

#stoptellinglies #eavesdropping #ragingdebate #littlepiggy
#whosefaultisitanyway #thetruthwillout

@beli'EVE
Public Figure
Mama. Wife. Model. Content Creator. Collabs. Beauty. Fashion
Interiors.

5,698.	1M	212
Posts	Followers	Following

I kick off my shoes inside the back door and freeze upon hearing a voice I don't instantly recognise. My eyes dart to the security monitors, scanning them cautiously. It's only when I see Joanne on the screen that I realise I'm holding my breath. Blowing out, I suddenly remember my earlier lie to Dex about meeting her. Joanne doesn't often pop by unannounced, but I should have been more careful.

Trying to think of what to say if Dex brings it up, I peer around the kitchen door. Joanne has her back to me, sitting on a high stool at the island next to Faye. Opposite, Dex is slicing pizza. True to his word, he picks up his phone, snaps a photo, stands back, adds a sprinkling of rocket, then snaps another. Beyond, Milo is on the sofa, headphones on, shouting at some online game on the TV. When no one looks up, I edge back into the boot room.

"So we had this debate at school about social media, and I thought of you," Faye says to Joanne. "I still can't believe you have no online presence."

On the screen, I watch Joanne shake her head. She told me before that people would be less shocked if she said she used to be a man.

"I completely understand not being on Instagram or Facebook. I hate them so much I deleted my accounts – but not even Twitter?" Faye asks as if Twitter is more acceptable than the rest.

Oddly, it's the one platform I've never explored, too frightened to dip my toe in the pool of wit.

"Not even Twitter," Joanne confirms.

"I mean there's loads to hate, but social media is also about advancement."

Faye is clearly arguing with herself since Joanne isn't one bit forceful when it comes to her opinion. I learned soon after meeting her that she isn't part of the world I inhabit. It's what I like most about her.

"If you don't move with the times, you get left behind," my daughter continues.

"Only I'm happy to be left behind, poppet!" Joanne laughs. "I'm too busy with my own life to get sucked into looking at other people."

"I agree, unhealthy usage is a problem, but it's a great vehicle for businesses and a super platform to talk about beliefs. Look at the LBGTQIA community and how they've used it in their fight for equality. It should be more than people-watching. And it should be safer …" Faye trails off.

Even though she can't see me, I nod along. Making it safer for Faye and other people was what I'd been attempting to do when I'd concocted #unfollowme.

"I do get it, Faye," Joanne says. "But I can't help thinking of the poor wee girls at home with chests flatter than that pizza there, spending all day looking at bloggers with big hair and even bigger boobies."

From behind the door, I bite my lip to stop laughing at how her rebuttal sounds in her Northern Irish accent.

"God love them. They've no break from it. At least I can accept that I'll never look that way. And thank God. Have you seen those eyelash extensions as thick as roadblocks they all wear? Not to mention the tans. Jesus, Mary, and Joseph, it's like they've been dipped in creosote. Maybe that's the reason they banned it. To save the teenagers and the environment."

Dex laughs as Joanne continues.

"The other day, I saw a young couple in the village in what I'll label a passionate embrace. When he pulled away, he was all orange around his mouth from her tan like he'd eaten a bowl of chicken wings."

Faye howls too. *"But that's my point!"* she shrieks. *"It shouldn't just be meaningless tan, clothes, and what way to wear your hair like Mum's fashion games!"*

My heart sinks at the slight. I suppose that's what I get for eavesdropping.

"That sounds more teenage feels than Holiday Feels," Dex muses, referring to my tanning range.

The mood is light. I take a deep breath and make my entrance.

Dex turns, smiling broadly. "You're back."

"I am. Hi, guys." I walk towards them. "This is a nice surprise." I place my hand on Joanne's shoulder. "Did I hear someone slagging off my tanning range?"

"Not me!" Joanne holds up her hands. "I was sitting here innocently and got dragged into a heated debate with this little politician!" She gestures at Faye, who is munching on pizza and checking her phone. "I just popped in to say hi. Sorry I had to cancel earlier." She glances up and widens her eyes at me subtly when Dex isn't looking. "Dex was asking what happened to our walk? I was up to my eyes at work. Trying to pay the big mortgage." She laughs.

After buying her house, Joanne took a better-paid role as a counsellor in Health Services, so talking about work still isn't an option. It's something I find refreshing about her. She lives in the moment – leaves work at work. She claims it's the only way in what can be an emotional job.

I smile gratefully at her diplomacy. I've told Joanne before that Dex tends to go on about me working too hard. She must have assumed this was the case today.

As soon as he places a wooden board laden with pizza in front of us, hunger hits. I pull up a stool, call over my shoulder for Milo to grab some pizza and take a slice myself.

"What did I miss?" I ask between bites.

"I was just telling Joanne about a debate today at school," Faye says.

Faye is comfortable around Joanne. The idea that Joanne must know some of what she went through a few years back doesn't appear to faze her in the slightest. It's a good sign and testament to Joanne's skills as a counsellor.

"And you thought you could take her on?" I tease, making a face at Joanne.

Faye shoves my arm playfully, then reaches past me to grab another slice of pizza.

"There's not a chance I'm taking Faye on in any debate – I know I won't win," Joanne says through a mouthful of pizza.

I can't help but grin. Seeing Faye chatty and eating away without a care in the world is a joy. This way, it's hard to imagine that there was ever a time when she was self-harming and refusing to eat – punishing her body for not being small enough.

Although I'd found Faye's psychologist, Dr Robin, somewhat aloof, I can't deny that because of her Faye is a different person from the frightened fifteen-year-old she once was. Then again, I didn't need to like Dr Robin. Whatever she had done for Faye worked. I still struggle about not knowing what they discussed during their weekly sessions. I remember feeling short-changed when Dr Robin revealed she wasn't obliged to tell me unless she considered Faye a danger to herself or others and then encouraged me not to push Faye to tell me what they talked about.

"But she's my daughter!" I'd been genuinely taken aback.

"And, mark my words, if there's anything you need to know, I'll inform you, but Faye has a right to private thoughts. Think about when you were her age. Did you tell your mother everything?"

I didn't bother disclosing that I'd tried, but Mum hadn't wanted to hear. Instead, I'd begged Dr Robin to "Please, make it stop!". I'd been talking about Faye, but it could have been applied to almost every aspect of my life.

To this day, I don't know what Faye told Dr Robin about hurting herself, although I suspect it had to do with what she must have read online. During her sessions, I'd wait outside, feeling my ears burn bright, confident they were in there discussing me and how I'd placed Faye in the firing line by sharing too much online. When I discovered what they were saying about her on Jabber.ie, for the first time in my life I'd wanted to physically hurt someone. I despised them almost as much as I blamed myself.

#Eve must pout at her poor daughter, who's stout. #Eve's kiddy is a little piggy. #Why not cook a decent meal instead of showing us every fashion deal. #Charity begins at home. Bring your child for a walk, stay off your phone.

As always, what was contained within each thread was far worse than the caption. One person even had pictures to demonstrate how ugly they thought Faye was in comparison to Dex and me – that she couldn't possibly be our child. It was heart-breaking, ludicrous, cruel.

Unable to address it directly, I'd tried to coax Faye into telling me if she'd seen any of it. Whenever I attempted to raise it, she'd clam up. Worse still, I couldn't bring myself to tell Dex what I'd found online, too afraid it would shine a spotlight on everything else that was bent out of shape in my life. At extreme loggerheads with Ronnie, I was too proud to seek her help.

Instead, I contacted the website to remove it and then called a meeting with the school to uncover whether Faye was being bullied. The principal lectured me for over an hour about the dangers of social media, then asked what I'd expected to happen by putting her in the public eye. I'd wanted to die of shame. I honestly thought things couldn't get any worse until they did. The incident at Milo's school was the last straw. It was time to act.

At Faye's final session, I told Dr Robin that we'd decided to make significant changes to our lives – move from Dublin to Wicklow, change schools, work on our marriage, rethink our careers. She'd nodded precisely four times, acknowledging each individual suggestion, then she'd held my gaze longer than necessary and said, "I think that would be best for everyone.", making me feel like a complete failure as a parent.

Thankfully, that was the same day I met Joanne at the clinic. She'd handed me the card from their sister office in Wicklow and advised me to contact them should I require a follow-up appointment, if Dublin was too far. After the move, I'd found the card at the bottom of one of the boxes and decided to give them a call to make sure Faye was doing okay. For more than one reason, I'm glad now that I did.

###

"This pizza is great," Joanne says. "You'll have to give me the name."

"If you followed me, you'd have the details by tomorrow," I goad her.

"*Hah!*" Joanne laughs. "I don't need to follow you. Sure, I can just ask in person."

I'm distracted by a pile of packages on the kitchen table that I hadn't noticed before. "What are *they?*"

"They're yours," Joanne says. "That's another reason I called up. I met the delivery man on my way to work earlier. He said there was no one home, so I took them in for you."

I frown. "But I was here. Gosh, sorry. He's done that a few times now. He mustn't be arsed coming as far as the second gate. I'll have to give the company a call about him." Because I no longer give out my address, I'd set up a P.O. Box and an account with a small delivery company. I was stringent that they never give out my details or leave packages with anyone but me. I know it's only Joanne, but that isn't the point.

Joanne bats the air again. "Ah, don't. I don't mind one bit. The driver is a wee pet. They just had their first baby, and she doesn't sleep a wink. I can't bear the thought of him getting into trouble, and it's an excuse to pop into you every now and again."

I've only been in Joanne's house twice. Usually, she comes to us. She'd told me a while back that living on her own can be lonely, so she likes the hustle-bustle of our house.

"You're far too nice," I say and smile.

I haven't told Joanne much about my experience in Dublin, only to say that I wanted to keep my private life private for Faye and Milo's sake too. She'd accepted it without prying. I'm lucky to have her. Contrary to what people think, I don't have many close friends. Perhaps it looked another way online, but it was only Ronnie and my work colleagues when it boiled down to it.

After losing Ronnie, I'd felt at sea until I met Joanne, though they

90

couldn't be more different. For a start, Joanne wasn't interested in outward appearances and, better still, she didn't follow me or anyone else on social media.

"Right, as much as I'd love to finish this raging debate, Faye, I'm going to leave you all." Joanne reaches over, squeezes Faye's knee then stands.

"*Sit the hell down, lady!*" Dex calls in an exaggerated New York accent over his shoulder. He's taking another pizza out of the oven. "As usual, my good wife, the wonderfully talented consumer, has bought far too much, and we need assistance."

"Yes. Stay." I push Joanne back down onto the stool and turn to Faye. "Besides, I'd like to hear more. I thought I heard you say something about my fashion games." I raise my eyebrows.

Faye flashes her big brown eyes at me. "*Oops!*" She giggles before tossing her mane of chocolate hair over her shoulder. If she chose to, Faye could be a phenomenally successful model. Despite some blips in her journey, she has something I never had – confidence on both sides of the camera – but she's adamant about what she wants to do with her life.

"You know I think you're fab, Mum, obviously. I just think social media should be about more than appearances."

"*Hah!*" I laugh. "You don't say that when I give you reams of free clothes! Not to mention having the guts of a cosmetics store in the attic!"

"I know. It's cool, but I just want my life to be . . ." Faye chews her bottom lip. "Don't take offence – but to be more meaningful. I want to help people, especially kids. You know, make a difference."

Faye wants to study psychology. A sense of direction is one good thing that has come out of a bad time in my daughter's life. Although, I wish none of it had happened at all.

I lean over and kiss the top of her head. I understand only too well. "And you will," I assure her. "It's what we all want starting out, but sometimes our lives veer in a different direction." I glance over at Dex, who smiles at me as he places another wooden board of pizza on the island. "Not to mention that life is expensive and my fashion games, as you call them, pay bills, school fees, cars, holidays, everything. Even that pizza!" I look back at Dex who has pulled up a stool and sat. I expected him to join in, but his mouth is set in a thin line this time. There's an awkward silence before I blurt, "Did Dex tell you the great news, Joanne?"

"What news is this?" she asks, hopefully.

Dex smiles again. "I won a contract with the Gallagher Hotel Group. I'm still a bit shocked, to be honest. I have no idea how they even knew about me, but I must be doing something right."

Joanne claps her hands together. "That's fantastic, Dex! Congratulations!"

I get up, run to the fridge, and grab a bottle of champagne, then take three glasses off the shelf. "Shall we?" I say, beaming.

"I'm in!" Joanne giggles, running her fingers through her shoulder-length hair. She had it lightened recently. It's taken years off her. As she crosses her legs, I notice her shoes – little gold pointed pumps. She has them on with skinny jeans and a fitted leopard-print blouse. "You look fantastic, by the way," I say to her. She smiles appreciatively. "Just trying something new," she says with a wink, "now that I'm free!"

"People will be asking where you get your influence." I raise my eyebrows as she tuts good-naturedly.

Milo ambles over after finishing his game and takes some pizza. I reach out and ruffle his hair. "Can you please stay offline for a while?" He grunts a response I don't catch. Milo is a miniature Dex, albeit at that awkward stage where it looks like his eyebrows and nose have invaded his face. "Did you hear me, Milo?"

"If you do the same," he says with a cheeky smile. "You're on your phone and online more than everyone."

I stick out my tongue at him. "Okay. I won't touch my phone for as long as you stay off that game." I take my phone from my leggings pocket and set it down on the counter.

"*Whoa!*" Dex teases. "*Steady on!*"

"See!" Joanne is off again. "You don't get these real moments online. I only know your lovely mum as my neighbour and dear friend, but if I'd known who she was before we met, I might have already formed an opinion. This way, I draw my own conclusions."

"Do I want to hear what those conclusions are?" I lean away and grimace.

"Actually, I get why the whole bloody world loves you. You're gorgeous. Inside and out."

"Would you go away!" I swat the air.

"Annoying, isn't it?" Dex says.

"But is it true? Or is it all a ruse?" Faye tilts her head, stares at me dead-pan.

"What doesn't she let people see?" Dex adds.

"Everyone has something to hide. Isn't that right, Dad?" My daughter's eyes narrow.

I omit a high-pitched laugh, unconsciously closing my fists and tapping my fingers in the palms of my hands. I blink repeatedly.

"That's right, Faye, and you know what they say? The truth will out." Dex isn't smiling.

They're joking, I'm sure, but it feels so real that even Joanne looks unsure. Dex glares at me as he eases the cork out of the bottle of champagne. My heart thumps in my chest so hard that I'm sure everyone must hear it. They say fear is a false emotion, but mine is very real. As the cork releases, my hand flies to my chest, and the golden liquid fizzes free. Dex fills the glasses while I wonder whether the truth would liberate me. Or further destroy everything.

Faye's eyes flash from Dex to me while Joanne shifts uncomfortably, averting her gaze.

It's probably only seconds, but it feels longer before Dex speaks. "Sooner or later, people will learn how Eve's baby toe is permanently folded over her other one." His mouth twitches in amusement.

"And let's not forget the snoring," Faye adds. "And sleeping with her mouth wide open, drooling."

"*And the farts!*" Milo calls from where he's slunk back to the sofa.

"*Good one, man!*" Dex says. "So loud, they're tricky to edit them from her videos."

Everyone laughs. I do, too – mostly in relief.

"You're hilarious, all of you!" I roll my eyes with mock exasperation. Inside, I try to stop my heart from racing and tell myself that today isn't the day that the truth comes out. For now, I can relax.

Dex places a glass of champagne in front of each of us.

"Right! Let's drink to Dex's success!" I say.

We all lift our glasses, click and drink.

Then, to my dismay, Joanne returns to the previous subject.

"My God, your poor wee face there, Eve," she says. "There was me thinking that you'd murdered someone."

"Hah. Not yet, anyway, and I'm used to the abuse. Kids will hang you with the things they say. Faye, remember the time you told the teacher you were late because I was hungover!"

"Oh, Lord, you did not?" Joanne throws her head back. "And your mother hardly even drinks!"

"*Exactly!*" I shriek. Joanne is right. I rarely have more than one glass of anything. It doesn't agree with me, but Ronnie and I got carried away on this occasion.

Faye grimaces. "Guilty! But you *were* hungover."

"I was," I admit. "To be fair, we'd just won *Blogger of the Year* for the first time, but you didn't have to go and tell the teacher!"

"It was okay! She said she voted for you."

Once again, everyone laughs. It sounds funny now, but it was another time in my life that I was swiftly brought back down to earth after a high.

"I'm still getting over those sandwiches you put in my lunch," Faye reminds me.

I shake my head. "I'd win no award for them, that's for sure."

#

It was, in fact, Ronnie who'd made the sandwiches. We were so happy to win that's we'd stayed out with the entire @beli'EVE team celebrating all night. When I looked at my watch, remembering that Dex had an early call for a modelling job on breakfast television and I had to drop the kids to school, I grabbed Ronnie and pushed her into a taxi. It must have been close to 6 a.m. when I stumbled over the threshold, Ronnie in tow, giggling like excited schoolgirls.

Dex lost it when he saw us. "You're a mess!" He'd stood at the bottom of the stairs, not bothering to congratulate me. "Luckily, the award wasn't for Mother of the Year!"

With that, he'd stormed out, leaving me staring after him, upset swirling.

"Come on," Ronnie patted my back, sticking her two fingers up at the recently slammed door. "In my eyes, Mother of the Year is the one who wins awards *and* gets her children to school on time."

Ronnie made black coffee thick as treacle and forced me to eat something, then set about making the kids' lunches while I got them up and dressed and changed out of my dress. I never laughed so much at what she produced, still wearing a black tuxedo suit and for the first time ever sky-high patent heels. The bread had kept tearing when she tried to smear it with rock-hard butter straight from the fridge, resulting in ham sandwiches that looked like she'd chewed them up then spat them into tinfoil.

Then, of course, neither of us could drive for fear of being over the limit. Ronnie phoned a taxi and sat in the front, directing the driver while I sat in the back with Faye and Milo, frantically chewing gum. As soon as we pulled up outside the school and I got out, only slightly late, I clocked a group of mothers turning to watch, nudging each other, laughing and whispering.

I knew I looked ridiculously conspicuous in my tracksuit, still sporting last night's hair and almost theatrical make-up. When Ronnie saw the other women and my embarrassment, she got out herself and shoved me back into the taxi. She handed Faye and Milo their schoolbags and waved them off, but not before throwing the women a glare. Right then, after one of the biggest successes of my life, I felt awful – even more of an outsider. The other mothers barely spoke to me as it was. I was never included in their coffee mornings or bake sales.

I talked to Ronnie about it afterwards. "Take it as a compliment," she'd said. "They can't cope with you because they follow you, Eve. They copy what you wear, your hair, everything. They envy you."

I didn't bother saying that I envied them back. I wanted what they had: a real life. That day was only the beginning. The bigger we got, the more scrutinised I became, the more I was shoved out and judged by far more than my husband and the mothers at school.

#

"And how many times have you won since?" Joanne asks.

Faye interjects. "She wins almost every single year."

"Except the last two," I say. "Maybe people did find out about my gammy toe," I joke.

Dex laughs. "I'd say if people knew about the toe, they'd copy that too!"

"That's true," Joanne says. "Remember I was here last week for coffee and you were wearing that lovely Zara dress – the beige one. You had it on with a T-shirt underneath, runners and a blazer. Well, since then, and I'm not joking you, I've seen about ten women in that exact outfit. I had to do a double-take!" She shakes her head.

Again, I shrug. "To be honest, I like hearing that. I get so many messages from women telling me that they walk into shops and haven't a clue where to start. If nothing else, I can help with that."

"But it doesn't stop there," Faye chimes in. "People don't just watch you for styling. They want dirt. Thank God you don't share our every move anymore, Mum. *Morto!* You practically used to tail us with your phone."

"Slight exaggeration, Faye." I bristle, uneasy. "Maybe it seemed like that. I didn't mean to. Sharing was a new thing." I try to justify it. "It takes a while to find out what's right and wrong. Anyway –"

"Deep down, we're all voyeurs," Faye says, refusing to move on. "It's wired into us. Checking out other people fulfils some social need to justify our own lives – something like that anyway."

"Like the modern-day curtain-twitcher," Joanne says.

"Exactly!" Dex says.

"Except instead of peeking through the blinds at neighbours, we do it on social media," Faye continues.

Much as I want this conversation to end, she's right. It isn't just about fashion. People want to know everything.

"Also, a real-life curtain-twitcher is unlikely to open the window and shout something at you," Faye says, "but online people don't hold back on giving their opinions. Isn't that right, Mum?"

I nod. Please stop, Faye, I internally whisper. It's too close to the bone. I've told Joanne before how I often get messages from people who've accidentally replied to my stories, thinking they've sent the messages to their friends.

Cannot stand her! That photo is edited. She doesn't look like that in real life. Would you say she's bulimic? Anorexic? Look at the way she pats her leg when she talks? OMG. Her voice? Her son never gets a look-in. So sick of her going on about her tanning range. More freebies. Like, WTF? LMAO at this bullshit. Who cares?

"What do you expect when you overshare?" Faye says nonchalantly.

Dex pours more champagne. "It's still the young folk I feel sorry for in this age of social media," he says. "Having all their mistakes plastered online. I'll be back in a sec. Just heading to the loo." He leaves the room.

I nod absently. This conversation feels relentless.

"I'm only glad it wasn't around when I was at Uni," Joanne giggles. "No one needs to be reminded of my curly mop of hair, no eyebrows, enough brown lipliner to line every pair of lips on earth. Let's not forget hipster jeans with severe muffin tops, bandana tops, platforms – strutting around Belfast. No, thank you!"

"I'd say you were wild!" I tease.

"Oh, I was."

"Not like Mum," Faye says. "The wildest thing she ever did back then was get a tattoo."

As she says it, I self-consciously cover my wrist.

Joanne's eyes follow the movement. "I thought you said you got that for the kids?"

I shake my head. "I added them later." I smile wanly. "It's a bit older than them." I don't elaborate.

"Mum never talks about college," Faye persists, continuing to shine a spotlight directly at my face.

"Which one did you say you went to again? UCD or Trinity?" Joanne asks.

"UCD. Then straight into modelling."

"Ah, yes. The album cover." Joanne smiles wistfully, and turns to Faye. "I can remember buying that Timeline CD in HMV in Belfast many moons ago." She looks back at me. "It's such a great shot. I still can't believe you don't have it up anywhere in the house. If it was me, I'd get it blown up and plaster it everywhere."

I smile back. When Joanne first asked why I didn't have it hanging pride of place above the fireplace, I'd told her it was because I was sick of the sight of it. But the truth is, still, every time I lay eyes on it, I relive what came next, just weeks afterwards.

"You never told me how you ended up getting that job?" Joanne asks.

I shake my head. "It wasn't a job per se." I lower my voice. "My ex-boyfriend took it." I take a sip from my champagne then reach for my water bottle which is under the counter. Internally, I'm sinking.

"He's famous now, too," Faye adds. "Have you ever heard of Conor Malone – the fashion photographer?"

Joanne thinks. "I don't think so."

"Well, that's who Mum dated, but she doesn't like to talk about him either."

I tut loudly. "Because it was a college fling, that's all."

When Faye starts clicking away on her phone, I lean closer to Joanne.

"It ended badly," I say quietly before she can ask more.

Joanne nods. "Well, you landed on your feet with Dex. He's one of the good ones. Easy on the eye too." She giggles, taking a sip of champagne. "You're lucky." Her smile fades.

Joanne doesn't talk about her marriage often, but she did say once that it had often felt like a prison. Seems he hadn't been one of the good ones.

Faye looks up again. "It's literally the only picture I've ever seen of Mum in college. There's nothing online from back then. I tried googling it once."

"Did you?" I jerk my head in surprise. "Why?" If Faye had wanted to see photos, she could have asked. Of course, I don't have them anymore. I assume they were thrown out when we vacated the house we'd rented in college.

"Come on! Haven't you ever googled yourself?" she asks then turns to Joanne. "I wanted to see what Mum looked like normally, not falling off a cliff. I've only ever seen modelling shots, but it's like she didn't exist before 2001."

"Maybe I didn't," I say. "Maybe I was transported here from another planet." I make my eyes round and suck in my cheeks. Faye makes a face back. "Honestly, Faye, there was nothing to see. My life started when I met your dad, and then we had you. And remember, we had no cameras phones when I was your age. It was different all the way back in the olden days."

"Mum?" Thankfully, Milo interrupts as Dex reappears and sits back down. "Can I play one more game ... please"? He is waving the TV remote at me.

"Oh, go on!" I exhale, grateful for the distraction. It frees me from my promise not to use my phone, too. I turn it over to check the screen. For once, there are no messages.

"So, you're past-less," Faye surmises.

"I suppose I am. Everyone is until they make a past, and mine started with you." I pat her leg lovingly.

Faye goes to say something, but Milo calls out *"Mum, look!"*

100

I turn to where he has switched on the TV, but instead of his war game Ronnie's face fills the screen. My stomach lurches.

Simultaneously, everyone swivels in the direction of her voice. She's being interviewed outside the Leeson Street offices of The Agency.

"We're incredibly excited. The Netflix documentary about the rise of the social-media star will be a huge deal for the lucky participant," Ronnie says.

"And why Ireland?"

"Ireland is an attractive movie location, as we all know. It's no different for other productions, and we have a wealth of people making a healthy living as content producers. I manage most of them at The Agency. You won't have long to wait to find out who the star of the show will be. It's a tight schedule. Filming needs to be finished by the end of June. I should be announcing who it is imminently." She grins.

"I think if we're talking social media stars, there's only one name on everyone's lips ..." The entertainment correspondent raises her eyebrows.

I dart my eyes towards Dex, but his eyes are fixed on the screen. I know exactly what's coming. He must sense it too.

"Is there any truth in the rumour that you and Eve Kelly will be joining forces once more on this project?"

Ronnie stares right at the camera, directly at me. If I know Ronnie, she planted that rumour herself. In my peripheral vision, I can see everyone watching me.

"Now, now," she says, smirking. *"Never believe rumours – but speaking off the cuff, it should be her. I'd be thrilled to revisit the past with Eve – tell the world what she was like before she was famous."* Ronnie dangles her words like an axe.

I gasp inwardly then tuck my hand under my leg, noticing I'm unconsciously tapping my thigh while Ronnie speaks.

Once again, Ronnie grins beyond the camera, her chin jutted forward in what looks like victory.

"*So, all is well in Ireland's entertainment world?*" the presenter asks.

"*It couldn't be better. This is a great news story for Ireland. I'm also working closely with a major hotel chain which is going from strength to strength. We'll be shooting many documentaries on their grounds, and I'm happy to say I've already introduced the Gallagher Group to some other brand-new Irish businesses. Wood4Life being one. I'm a big believer in doing everything I can for start-ups. This really is an opportunity for us all.*"

Ronnie nods definitively at the screen before the segment moves on.

Silence envelopes the room.

Dex is the first to break it, "Well, that solves the mystery of how I won the contract. That's just great." He shakes his head in frustration and turns to me accusingly. "Did you know she was working with them? Did you know about all this?"

"No," I lie.

He doesn't look convinced. "This is so typical of Ronnie. This is her way of making sure you do what she wants," he growls at the television before swivelling his stool back to face the kitchen island.

He's right. Throwing in that Gallagher Group comment was clever. I genuinely didn't know Ronnie was working with them. Now that she is, she'll be reckoning that this contract is worth so much to Dex that he'd do anything not to risk losing it – even go so far as convincing me to do the documentary. It's what I get for blanking her calls, pretending she doesn't exist. It was only a matter of time before she found a way to make me listen. Ronnie had outlined everything involved in her original email. For good measure, she'd even mentioned our college days and "owing" her "one last time".

If I do it, I'll have enough money to finally move on with my life – pull the plug on @beli'EVE once and for all, so I can focus solely on Dex and my family. I can revert to being a no-one, just like before

I met Ronnie. Somewhere deep inside, it feels as though @beli'EVE is coming to an end anyway. Followers are down. It's slight, but it's still cause for concern. My passion for the job isn't what it was. How could it be after what I've been subjected to? I'm no longer making enough money to warrant the time I plough into it.

Beside me, Faye is unusually quiet. After dominating much of the evening, she now appears speechless.

Joanne coughs uncomfortably, stands and puts her coat on. "I'd better get on," she whispers.

I nod absently. I can feel apprehension spreading across my face like heat.

"I'll walk you out." I stand too.

As I reach for my phone, it buzzes, lighting up with the words **Do Not Answer**. Too late, Dex sees it and shoots me a death stare. I stuff the phone into my back pocket.

When Joanne is gone, I stand with my back to the front door, and take my phone out again. This time, there's a new message. I shiver as I read the familiar words – **I have a proposition for you**. Ronnie knows I'll get the reference. It's how it all began in the first place. I'm about to make a deal with the devil. Then again, if I don't, people might discover that I already belong in hell.

1996

The first time they spoke was in late September 1996, standing in the never-ending registration queue in UCD. Ronnie stood behind Eve, watching her fidget restlessly with her documents, taking them in and out of a brown envelope, checking her watch, fixing her hair. When Ronnie tapped her on the shoulder,

Eve almost jumped out of her skin but relaxed quickly when Ronnie started chatting, asking Eve about herself.

"Where do you live?" Eve asked eventually.

"Kildare. Arsehole of nowhere."

"Isn't that where the horsey people come from?"

"That's the one."

"Are you going to be living on campus?"

Ronnie rolled her eyes. "Supposed to be. It's too far to come up and down every day, but the rooms look horrible. I'm dreading it."

"Me too. At least you *have* to live here. I only live about twenty minutes away, but my parents are forcing me out– said it will be good for me." Eve made a face. "I'm the youngest. The mistake. Like explain how a doctor doesn't know that she can still get pregnant in her forties?"

"First explain why your parents were still *doing it* in their forties?" Ronnie countered with a chuckle.

Eve put her hand over her mouth as if she was going to be sick.

"Well, they're not anymore." Eve hesitated, lowering her voice. "They're getting a divorce." There was another brief pause. "Dad is banging one of his patients. He's also a doctor."

"Oh." Ronnie's eyes widened in surprise. "Juicy."

"Mortifying. He and Mum share a practice. It's a mess."

"Are you gonna be a doctor too?"

This time, Eve laughed. "No way! I just about got enough points in the second round of offers for Arts. Otherwise, it would be theology in Trinity."

Ronnie burst out laughing. "You could be a priest!"

"They would have made me do it too. It's all my mother ever says. Get a degree. She never stops."

"What subjects did you pick?" Ronnie asked.

"English, French." Eve made a gagging noise. "Information Studies. Whatever the hell that is."

"Computers. The future, apparently." Ronnie nodded.

"I barely know how to turn one on. What about you?"

"Commerce." As an afterthought, Ronnie said, "Your mother is right, you know. You *do* need a degree. Once you have it, you can do whatever the hell you want. I'm going to be my own boss."

"Doing what?"

Ronnie shrugged. "Dunno. I'll know when I see it." She smiled broadly.

Eve looked at her feet. "I haven't a clue what I want to do. Maybe you're not meant to know at seventeen."

"You're seventeen? Well, that's a huge problem."

"Why? Am I in the wrong queue?" Eve was instantly terrified.

"No!" Ronnie laughed again. "Worse. If you're seventeen, they'll print your date of birth on your student card. You won't be able to get into the bar – but I can help you." She patted Eve's arm.

After registering, they'd ambled out the back gate of campus to the chemist's where they bought what they needed, then headed back towards the lake.

Like a surgeon, Ronnie used a Q-tip and nail-varnish remover to erase Eve's date of birth from the plastic card.

"Thanks," Eve was impressed. "Like I turn eighteen in December, but vodka might be the only thing to get me through living in residence, knowing absolutely no one."

"You don't know no one. You know me," Ronnie said, grinning, handing back the doctored card.

Ronnie had already been tailing Eve that entire morning when she'd followed her into the registration building. She'd stepped in front of several disgruntled students to make sure she ended up behind her. Though classes weren't due to start for a week, on advice from an acquaintance back home Ronnie had been familiarising herself with the campus, the main lecture theatres, getting to know where people converged to chat, drink coffee, smoke. Student residence wasn't going to be an option for someone like her – the fellow from home had told her that too, so she'd been keeping an eye out for something suitable.

Although it was out of her price range, she'd gone to see a house near campus on Fosters Avenue that morning – a two-bed, originally built in the garden of a bigger house for a wayward son who'd eventually gone away. It was ideal. All Ronnie needed was the right people to share with and the money for the deposit.

She'd been wondering how to get it when she noticed the statue-like girl sitting on a bench, a thick brown envelope on her lap. She was stunning – perfect face, blonde hair heavily layered around her face, rail-thin, wearing a denim skirt, white T-shirt with a black lacy Wonderbra clearly visible underneath, wedge sandals on tanned feet, an expensive bag next to her. Ronnie sat on a low concrete wall, picking at bark chippings, avoiding the cigarette butts mixed throughout, quietly observing. Ronnie wasn't the only one watching.

A group of lads in *Russell Athletic* sweatshirts and grey tracksuit pants gathered a bit away, nudging and goading each other. Despite their being clearly visible through the cloth of their pants, not one of them had the balls to go near her, eventually moving off. Moments later, Ronnie overheard a couple of girls further along the wall questioning how any lad would fall at their feet when there were girls like *her* on campus. Looking them over, Ronnie tended to agree. They'd disappear next to someone like her. Ronnie would too, but that's what she wanted.

Unlike the plain girls sitting up from her, Ronnie Delaney hadn't come to UCD to find herself a man; she'd come to make herself a life – one as far from Kildare as she could manage, where the only horsey set she'd been part of was chasing a loose piebald off the football pitches next to the council estate. There were no wealthy parents to back her. If she wanted a better life, she had to get it herself. There was always a way. Now, all she had to do was form the right connections with the right sort of people: people like Eve.

When Eve got up from the bench, to walk through campus, Ronnie followed, noticing how people stopped to stare, step out of her way. Eve moved with grace, but there was a visible unease to her minor actions – a tremor when she pulled out a gold pack of Marlboro Lights on the steps of the Arts block. When some guy next to her flipped a zippo at her cigarette – possibly the coolest thing about him – Eve nearly died before sucking hard, then exhaling with a shudder. His face fell when she floated away, oblivious.

Eve would do perfectly.

Ronnie squinted over at Eve, who was picking up pebbles, rolling them in her palm, then one by one throwing them in the lake. The early evening sun had started to fade, yet neither made any move to leave.

"I have a proposition for you," Ronnie said, sitting up suddenly.

Eve stopped what she was doing and pivoted her head.

"Let's ditch student residence. I saw a place just out the back gates."

Eve glanced over her shoulder in the direction, gave a humourless laugh and went back to throwing stones.

"I'm not joking," Ronnie continued.

Eve laughed again. "Yeah, right."

"It's not as fancy as it sounds. Actually, it's sort of gross, but we could make it nice. We'd need one more. I might know someone. He's a friend of a friend from back home. It's two bedrooms, but we could share, and he could have the other –"

"He?" Eve turned her entire body this time.

"Yeah."

"Why me?"

"Why not?" Ronnie flashed a smile, lifting her eyebrows. "It'd be a great way to piss your parents off. We can go find the other guy now, if you want. He's in the bar, I think. All we'd need is a deposit … and roommates."

Eve shook her head. "I can't. I was meant to pay for the village hall today. Mum said it was up to Dad to sort out where I live. Clearly, he doesn't give a shit." She rolled her eyes. "I was supposed to do it at registration, but I keep hoping Mum will change her mind and let me stay at home. I'm not good at …" She stared at the ground, "I don't know … being around other people … I get …" She stopped and shook her head. "Anyway, now, I'll have to come back tomorrow. Dad gave me a blank cheque to pay the year upfront. He was that keen to get 'it' sorted. It being me."

Eve threw the entire handful of stones into the water and patted the dust off her hands.

"I'd better go," she said, defeated.

Ronnie leapt to her feet. "Did you just say you have a blank cheque, and your dad doesn't give a shit where you live?"

Eve nodded. "Yeah, but I can't spend more than residence will cost. It wouldn't be enough, and my allowance won't cover the rest. Besides, if my own mother doesn't want to live with me, you won't either."

"But I *do* want to live with you. Do you trust me?"

Eve looked up at her in earnest. "Yeah."

"Well, come on." Ronnie put out her hand and dragged Eve to her feet. "I want to introduce you to someone."

Twenty minutes later, Eve Kelly would feel as though she took her first breath and that her life had just begun.

CHAPTER NINE

#threaten #strangle #theronnieshow #puppetmaster
#nochoice #controlfreak

@beli'EVE

Public Figure

Mama. Wife. Model. Content Creator. Collabs. Beauty. Fashion
Interiors.

5,698	1.1M	212
Posts	Followers	Following

After seeing Joanne out, I go straight up to our bedroom and walk
towards the window to stare out. The evening had taken a sudden
turn for the worse. I'd felt jittery, robotic, even before Milo switched
on the entertainment show and Ronnie appeared. From the moment
I'd arrived in from my walk, it felt as though Faye was poking at me,
testing me somehow. With all that talk about social media, then college
… being past-less, I'd already felt uneasy.

A thought strikes. Lifting my phone, I open Safari and type my own
name followed with UCD into the search bar. I hold my breath. Just
like Faye said, nothing appears. I exhale before tilting my head. Why
had Faye googled it in the first place? It seemed odd, but then her
reason was plausible. She'd wanted to see what I'd looked like back

then. I suppose, with her about to head off to college herself, maybe it isn't so odd after all. I wonder if Joanne noticed anything about Faye this evening. Much as I wouldn't like to put Joanne on the spot, perhaps I'll ask her about it when I see her. With any luck, I was being paranoid.

It's precisely how I'd felt when Faye brought up Conor too. Thank God, Dex had been out of the room at the time. I'd done my best to brush it off as a fling, hoping no one would clock it had once been far more.

Without being able to stop, myself, I type **Conor Malone** into the search on my phone. Hundreds of images of models and magazine shoots populate the screen. I click on his website, open it and press **"About Conor"**. A close-up appears against a solid black background. It's so starkly lit that it looks three-dimensional. Every line, crevice, imperfection on his face stand out as though he wants you to see them. His dark hair is shaved tight to his head. He looks haunted, flawed, as if life has been tough. In spite of myself, my heart twists. Instinctively, my fingers travel towards his face, as if by touching the photo I'll be able to feel his stubble brush my fingertips.

Seeing Dex behind me in the window's reflection, I blink suddenly, exit the page and stuff my phone into my pocket. I snap the bedroom curtains shut, then walk around him to close the bedroom door.

I sit on the bed, my shoulders slumped. I steal a glance at him. His hands are stuffed in his pockets, jaw moving side to side. The soft beige tones I'd worked so hard to achieve in our bedroom belie the emotion between us.

Dex is furious.

"This time, I want the truth. Did you know?" he asks.

My body tenses. "There was an email," I admit, eyes on the ground. "Ronnie sent it a few weeks ago. So, yes. I knew she wanted me to do the documentary."

His mouth opens, then closes in disbelief.

I splay my hands. "I'm sorry, Dex." I look up. "I had no idea she'd go public before I had a chance to respond. I was going to tell you today as soon as I got back from my walk, but then Joanne was here and —"

"Why didn't you tell me earlier when I was up in your studio? Or before that. Why wait?"

"I needed time to think before …"

This time, he throws his head back. "Oh, my God! You're planning to do it, aren't you?"

I swallow. "I don't think I have a choice." Earlier this evening, when I told Faye my life had begun with her, I'd said what I'd wished were true. In reality, my life started with Conor Malone and has been directed by Ronnie ever since.

"You cannot be serious." Dex begins pacing the floor. "How so?"

"Because I don't want to be me anymore."

He stops.

"What I mean is I don't want to be @beli'EVE. This can be my way out – our way out. I —"

He laughs sarcastically. "This feels strangely familiar." He steps in front of me. "I thought our way out was moving here?"

"It was. It is." I can't find the words to explain. It happens when I'm being dishonest. Dex must realise it too.

"Why do I always get the feeling that you're holding something back? What haven't you told me, Eve? What else is to come?" He throws his hands up, exasperated. "And this is what happens as soon as Ronnie joins the party. I got an enquiry earlier about a dining set. At the end of it, they said Ronnie recommended me. I just knew it. I just knew she was up to something."

I don't know how to respond.

"You don't have to do this, Eve. You *do* have a choice. What about us? For once, we're on the same page, and you want to throw it all away *again*," he spits the word. "You know what I think? I think you're addicted to fame. Hungry for more." He recommences pacing. "I watched it for years, and trust me," he pounds his chest, "this won't be the end of things with Ronnie. What this will be is the end of everything we've created here. Read into that what you will. I turned a blind eye when you wanted to restart @beli'EVE on your own when we moved here after *you* took your eye off our family for so long, but this is too much now."

Dex is taking the opportunity to vocalise all the things I assumed he'd felt.

It looks like I was right about everything. I suppose it was bound to happen — when you suppress your emotions for long enough, it's only a matter of time before it bubbles to the surface.

"And if mentioning the Gallagher Group was meant to be some sort of twisted threat thrown at me to get me onside, Ronnie can go fuck herself. I'll tell her that myself. Man," he groans, grasping his hair with both hands, "I thought you finally understood that Ronnie used to control you! Looks like I was wrong."

I close my eyes for a moment. This is precisely why I was nervous about telling him. Before I get a chance to speak, he's off again.

"And don't even think about saying you're doing this for me, Eve — for the kids." Pause. "If you do it, it is solely for you."

He couldn't be more wrong.

"That's not fair. It's worth a lot of money, Dex. We could finish the house. We could –"

"Bullshit. This isn't about the money."

I exhale loudly. This time I throw my hands up. "And what if it is? I know that you have the potential to make great money, but you're not there, just yet – this could give you more time to –"

He interrupts with a laugh that sounds like he's gasping for air. "I was waiting for you to throw it in my face that I can't provide. You sound just like your mother."

This time, I stand and walk towards him. He backs away.

We've obviously hit a sore spot.

"I've never said that, Dex, not once. I just want to give you the same dig-out with your business that you gave me."

"Is that what you call it? A dig-out?" This time, his expression is colder than ice. "I was your skivvy. Waiting at home while you were out living your life – wondering if mine would ever begin."

"Dex! Where is all this coming from?" I reach for his hand, but he pulls it away. "Can't we just talk about the future instead of dragging up the past? That's what's important. Your business, us. I'm prepared to do whatever it takes to make Ronnie happy and then be rid of her for good. I won't allow her to threaten your contract. You deserve it. You wouldn't have won it if you weren't good enough. Regardless of where they got your name."

He sniffs loudly. I try to take his hand again. He stuffs it in his pocket.

"All you are to her, Eve, is a puppet. The front because you look like that." He gestures at me with his free hand. "And she doesn't." Then he narrows his eyes. "Why don't you tell me what this hold is that she has over you. *Hmm?* Tell me, will you? Once and for all, what are you so afraid of?"

He walks towards the door, opens it, and stops when I don't answer.

With his back to me, he says. "If you've something to hide, Eve, doing this thing won't help."

He closes the door behind me, leaving me alone. His words and the decision I must make strangle me.

#

There's a pedestrianised section in Annaford around a monument at the centre. It's where I'm sitting at a table the next day when I spot Joanne outside the fruit and veg shop. She doesn't see me. Hardly surprising since I'm dressed in a grey hoodie, a pair of workout leggings, sunglasses, and my hair tucked under a baseball cap. I watch enviously as she chats to another customer then heads across the road to the convenience store. She'd texted me both last night and this morning to ask to meet for a walk and to check if I was okay. I still haven't answered. Mostly because I don't know how.

The village is surprisingly busy. I can't remember the last time I was here.

I used to love taking a walk down with Lily, who'd stop and talk to almost every person she passed so that by the time we made it to the shop, it would be time to go home. Lily always made Annaford seem larger than it is. Even though Lily labelled it "a vast community," it isn't big. Aside from driving through the village to collect Milo from the football pitches on the other side, usually when I leave the house I turn right in the direction of the motorway towards Dublin. Today, I'd turned left.

On the table in front of me, there's a frothy cappuccino and an untouched fruit scone. Despite taking the time to half it and spread butter right to the outer edges, I can't will myself to take a bite. My mouth is too dry. Instead, I watch the Saturday activity around me – my eyes darting from table to table of couples, parents with young kids, groups of friends, cyclists kitted out as if they're heading for Tour de France. There's enough to look at it, distract me from thoughts of Ronnie and Dex.

115

Next to me, a little girl throws her juice carton to the ground, then precociously scrunches her face up. Her mother grabs her tiny arm and mutters something through gritted teeth before glancing over her shoulder to check if anyone saw. I avert my gaze. *#badparenting*. At another table, a young couple sits so close that it's difficult to make out where one ends and the other begins. The girl who looks even younger than Faye, lifts her eyes seductively towards the boy, removes her hand from her pocket, and snakes it towards his crotch. *#notinpublic #badexample*.

A group of women howl loudly as one holds up their phone. Turning, I glimpse the Instagram logo above a photo of a woman. Thankfully, it's not me. There's a rush of words. "State of her." "Like, what is she wearing?" "I don't get her at all." *#bekind #ifyouvenothingnicetosay*

Lastly, an older couple with a grandson of about six or seven. They're drinking hot chocolate, chatting happily. *#life #love #specialmoments*.

Sitting here, observing, I can appreciate how easy it is to judge others. Perhaps it's no different with my followers. To them, I'm an image on a screen. None of them really know me. Maybe that's the problem.

"I thought it was you! Are you in disguise?" I squint up at Joanne, who stands over me, looking me up and down.

"Hi. Sit down," I gesture at the chair opposite. "Sorry, I must look a state."

"Not at all. I just had to do a double take. How are you?" She sets her shopping bag down and pulls up a chair.

I consider how best to answer. I'm not really in the mood for small talk, and the entire story is too arduous. "Not great," I settle on. "A lot on my mind. I'm sorry again about last night."

"Is everything okay, Eve?" Joanne leans closer. "It was just … I don't want to overstep the mark, but it was all quite tense last night. I don't mean to pry, but I wanted to ask."

I bite my lip and nod. "So, you noticed. It's fine, Jo, honest. In short, Dex doesn't want me involved with Ronnie again."

Joanne nods and sits back.

I exhale, fed up. "It's such a complicated relationship – me and Ronnie. Although it went wrong, I suppose I still care about her. I'm not really sure why she wants me to do this thing with her," I lie. "I don't want her in my life again, but I suppose she thinks I must owe her." I use Ronnie's term. "And with Ronnie, she mostly gets what she wants."

Joanne looks concerned.

"I told you it was complicated." I smile sadly. "We were close. She became family really, especially in college and after." I shrug. "But she did something horrible in the end." I blow out slowly. "Bet you're glad you ran into me." I muster a pitiful laugh.

"Losing family is hard. No matter what the relationship."

I nod and smile warmly. Joanne has a sister in Belfast that she sometimes mentions, but other than that, it's just her. She must be lonely. I take a breath. "Joanne, I hope you don't mind me asking, but I wondered if you thought Faye was … I don't know … off last night? You know how I worry about her, and she seemed … " I struggle to find the word.

"Confrontational?" Joanne offers.

I grimace.

Joanne smiles. "I think what I saw last night was a normal teenager, Eve."

"Really?" I exhale.

Joanne nods. "Absolutely. She was sparking off you. Asserting her opinion. Finding her voice. Teenagers test boundaries at home. What I saw was a healthy debate. She's also about to go to college. She's

117

probably nervous, which is why she was talking about your experience. The best thing is to try not to react."

My shoulders deflate. "You're so good at this. I was awake all night thinking I'd have to call Dr Robin again." I make a face. "I can't use you now that we're neighbours."

"Honestly, I don't think there's any need to call anyone unless you want to. I can give you a name but, just like you said last night, children and teens will hang you sometimes with the things they say, but it all goes towards their development. Faye is better than ever."

I nod along, relieved, and then bite my lip. "If you ever thought otherwise … if you ever thought there was something wrong, as a friend, you'd tell me, wouldn't you?"

Joanne laughs and places her hand on mine. "Yes. I'd offer some clever counselling tips in a nice way, but Faye is fine, Eve." She pauses. "But are you?"

This time I laugh. "Who knows?"

Joanne tilts her head. "Whatever about Dex, do *you* want to get involved with Ronnie again? Could you fix what happened between you?"

I look away, trying to think of a way to explain it all. Ronnie's refusal to support me against trolls was only the tip of the iceberg. What she did next, uploading a questionable photo of me to my online accounts, was genuinely unforgivable.

"I'm not sure," I say.

Joanne is silent for a moment. "Maybe you should meet up with her. Hear her out. Is the *Netflix* thing something you'd like to do?"

"I'm not sure," I repeat. "Sort of. I don't know. It would certainly allow me to cut back on my daily work in the long run, but Dex is adamant, and what about the kids? It would be close to Faye's exams. Milo would be on school holidays for some of it. Dex is up to his eyes with work." I put my head in my hands. "It's a mess. Anyway." I look up. "Distract me from it, please."

For a while, we sit mindlessly chatting about anything but my burning reality – the shops, our neighbours. Aside from the small bits Joanne has told me, I know virtually nothing about any of the other residents in the cul-de-sac. Aside from sharing a small stretch of road, we're a bit away from them, so I've never bothered to introduce myself. Then again, neither have they. I listen wistfully as she tells me about them – the older couple who spend half of each week preparing for an onslaught of adult children and grandchildren for Sunday lunch and the other half recovering. The younger couple with two toddlers leave the house at the crack of dawn each day, returning in time to put the children to bed. The couple in the last place: Charles and Eoghan, mid-forties, no kids, two ginormous Rhodesian Ridgebacks who have their own upstairs bedroom. Charles has a job in the city, and Eoghan is an author. Seemingly, they moved out of Dublin so Eoghan could find inspiration in the countryside. Instead, he told Joanne, he spends long periods of time holed up inside, working.

As she describes it, I have an insatiable urge to know more. For too long, I've been so caught in everything that I've failed to recognise that there's a ready-made community outside my gate.

When there's a lull in the conversation, Joanne asks, "So, where are Dex and the kids now?"

"At home. There's a cold front sweeping through the house." I try to make light of it. Earlier, I'd tried to smooth things over with Dex. I'd stuck my head around the door of his workshop to ask if he wanted to do something "normal" like go for a walk to the village to grab a coffee. He'd circled his hand over his workbench to indicate that he was busy, then given an over-exaggerated thumbs down.

Joanne nods then leans forward. "Can I offer you some advice?"

119

"Please."

"Do what's right for you, Eve. You're a great mum. Your family will be okay for a few weeks if you do the show. And if afterwards it allows you spend more time with them, then it's win, win. Dex will get over it. Not to mention what an honour it would be to get to tell your story. Look back over your life like one big therapy session. It's a big deal."

I try to smile. The real story certainly wouldn't be received well, but she's right about the rest. I consider telling her more for an instant, but she starts speaking again. I nod absently, hopefully agreeing in the right places, but I'm not listening. Instead, my mind drifts to three years before in Dublin, where I'd allowed someone to terrorise me – mess with my head until I thought I was going mad.

Going to the Guards hadn't been an option. Not unless I wanted to destroy my entire life in one fell swoop, especially since, at the time, I'd been doing something I shouldn't. Whoever was trying to scare me knew it. They knew about my past too – things very few people are privy to – things I've even hidden from Dex. I've had a lot of time to think about it since, and what I've come up with is this: of the four people who know my secrets, one is dead, one is my mother, one would never hurt me … one is Ronnie. She had access to my online accounts. It doesn't take a genius to figure out the rest.

Because of everything, I was forced to build a new life. Now, I'm not prepared to let anyone threaten to take it away. For the last few years, I've deprived myself of everything I need to live – company, human connection, support, so much that I yearn for it.

"Eve?"

I startle when Joanne says my name.

"Did you hear what I was saying?"

"Yes." I nod. I hadn't.

She doesn't look convinced. "So, I could give Dex a dig-out with the kids if you do the show. Keep an eye on Faye and Milo. I'm going on holiday at the end of June with my sister, but I'm here before that if that's any use to you. Sure, what else am I doing? I can help with the lifts. Dinners. Whatever. Open house!"

I'm taken aback by her generosity. "I couldn't ask you to do that." *Could I?*

Joanne laughs. "You could. You know I get lonely. You'd actually be doing me a good turn. If this is something you want to do, let me help."

"I don't know . . ."

"Meet Ronnie. At least then you'll have all the information to make an informed decision. That's what life is all about ... options."

If only. There's no option here. Ronnie holds things on me, but I have something on her, too, if I need it. When this is over, I can be myself again – not who I was in college, not the person Ronnie curated, then tried to destroy. There's a real-life ahead, so close I can almost touch it, and oh God, I want it. I want to live it so badly it hurts and, unbeknownst to Joanne, she may just have given me the freedom to grasp it.

CHAPTER TEN

#invisible #allbecauseofme #carnage #UCD #1998
#wonderbra #notsoinnocent #russelathletic

- -

@theagency

- -

147	6,590	89
Posts	Followers	Following

Ronnie chews the outer corner of her lip until it's almost raw, picks up her phone, glances at it, then flings it next to her on the sofa of her Ballsbridge apartment. To distract herself, she's spent all of Saturday tidying, moving things about then back again. It's a pointless exercise, considering nothing is ever out of place in her utterly modern three-bed penthouse overlooking Herbert Park. Now, she's getting impatient. Waiting isn't something she's good at. Why hasn't she heard from Eve yet? If the interview hadn't alarmed her, the text that followed should have catapulted Eve right back to a time she'd do anything to forget.

Getting up, Ronnie pads towards her bedroom. There, she flops onto the bed, sighing loudly, exhausted from persistent rage. It's as fresh as the day Eve scarpered in a blaze of self-righteous glory, abandoning everything they'd built together, leaving Ronnie to explain to their business partners why @beli'EVE was suddenly no more, forced to plant rumours of contract disputes. In reality, the original contracts weren't worth the paper they were written on. Ronnie had typed them up herself years before from a template she'd found online. Having them amended was something she'd never got around to. Besides, she and Eve were like family. They'd never fall out. Not for one moment did she think Eve would actually go. She had never seen Eve so angry. That said, it had been building for a long time, beginning when Eve discovered that she had been deleting comments, worsening when she refused to support Eve's #unfollowme campaign, and spiralling out of control when Eve accused her of uploading that damn photo to the @bel'iEVE page.

Now, Ronnie is back in the driving seat. Taking a breath, a glint of a smile appears as she musters a positive. Throwing in that loaded comment on air about the Gallagher Group had been a last-minute decision. Dex would be shaking in his work boots if he thought she had the power to pull the plug on his big contract. She doesn't, of course, but he won't know that. Her role with them is solely to manage their online presence, an area into which she'd been forced after Eve vanished into thin air, then reappeared to pinch most of her clients right from under her nose.

Another flash of fury strikes. Ronnie sits up suddenly, fiercely pulling off her black-suede ankle boots, and hurling them at the wall. She quickly regrets it – they cost more than an average monthly wage. She lies back again.

She almost feels sorry for steadfast Dex, faithful as a Labrador, perpetually following Eve about like a puppy. He'd always been the same – talking about giving up his life in New York for Eve when in reality he'd been going nowhere fast in New York either.

When Ronnie heard Dex's name bandied about at a Gallagher meeting, she'd actually been happy for him. He'd never had much luck earning a crust, not that he'd tried very hard. When @beli'EVE first began to grow, Dex was only too happy to bow out of work to look after the kids, then sit at home complaining that Eve was always out at work. There was no denying he was a great father, but he was too weak a person for Ronnie's liking. Over the years, she witnessed him pass snide comments here and there, even in front of Faye and Milo, about Mummy "always" being busy. What did he expect when Eve had to hold the fort alone because he harboured some American dream of making furniture? To her mind, if he'd really wanted to start a business all those years, he'd have found a way before now like she had. She makes a face when the thought that she'd used Eve to front a business crosses her mind, then pushes it aside fast. This was different, surely. Yes, she nods to herself, completely different.

Her thoughts return to Dex. She supposed his stuff was nice if you liked that rustic, hippy sort of thing, which she didn't, but she certainly wasn't going to stand in his way of finally making a decent living and jumping off his wife's coattails. Still, the worry that she might should help him sway Eve. Not that it ever took much to convince Eve to do anything.

What most people don't realise is that Eve is savagely ambitious, almost as much as she is, although, unlike her, Eve cares too much about what other people think. It's her greatest downfall. Her biggest strength is that she's an insanely talented actress.

Feeling jittery, Ronnie decides to take a shower. Standing, she catches a glimpse of her reflection in the full-length mirror and inches nearer. She'd looked good on-screen yesterday, enjoyed letting the world know that *she* was the secret behind Eve Kelly's success. *She* was who they should have been following all along. She'd remembered to speak slowly so as not to let her diction falter. The odd word still caught her, ringing flatter than the rest, but mostly Ronnie could walk the walk, talk the talk, play the game.

It was she who'd called the entertainment show to tip them off that she'd be working with Reel Time Productions, who'd already pitched to Netflix. Assuming that Ronnie was still Eve's manager, a documentary-maker named Heather, a plain-looking, rather serious girl, had made contact with Ronnie a year before, looking to pitch the idea about Eve. Ronnie had played along, allowing Heather to give the full sales spiel before saying she'd get back to her. At the time, things were still too raw to consider it, but time is a great healer, as is money. When the time was right, namely, as Ronnie's profits plummeted to an all-time low, she'd met with Heather again. When she heard the numbers, Ronnie wanted in. She'd promised them Eve. Now, she had to deliver.

Ronnie twists sideways, lifts her black shirt, and sucks in her stomach. She's lost weight – unintentionally this time. Not that she was ever fat, more "sturdy" or "manly" to use her father's choice words. As though being gifted with a man's name had somehow made her grow tall with a somewhat square jaw, beyond statuesque shoulders. It used to make her wish she were invisible. She was always happy to fade into the background, allow Eve to provide the outward image. Only someone as striking as Eve could make someone as big as Ronnie vanish. It's why Ronnie chose her in the first place. Being invisible carried far more advantages than being beautiful.

For a moment she stares into space, thinking about the first day they met in the registration queue in UCD. It was almost as if her life began right then. Now, looking at herself in the mirror, the memory barely seems real. Back then, she had needed Eve to get going, but Eve ended up needing her just as much during college, if not more.

They'd been so young, so impetuous, that the very next day Eve had filled out the cheque for the deposit and first two months' rent for the house Ronnie had found. The landlady was so suitably impressed with Dr Kelly's name on the cheque that she never batted an eyelid. Ronnie swore that she'd take care of the rest of the rent. Not once did Eve ask where she would get the money from, nor, it seemed, did she care.

Eve soon became otherwise occupied, or maybe the word was *obsessed*. Eve fell in love – twice.

Ronnie moves from the mirror, shimmies out of her leather trousers, unbuttons her shirt and removes her gold-cuff bracelets. Pulling the left one off, she stares at her wrist. If she squints, she imagines she can still make out the tattoo she'd got in college. Afterwards, in New York, she'd suggested that Eve get a matching one as a symbol of their friendship, everything they'd been through together. Ronnie had hers lasered off when things began to go wrong between them. She'd no longer wanted to be eternally linked to Eve.

Going to the bathroom, Ronnie carefully removes her make-up. While she cleanses her skin, her mind ticks backwards once more.

The moment Ronnie introduced Eve to Conor Malone in the student bar, something shifted within Eve, far more than dilating pupils or dopamine rushing to her brain. To this day, Ronnie regrets it. Between them: Conor as a photographer, Eve as a model, they possessed endless talent, charisma, star quality. It was carnage, destruction, doomed before it even began. Granted, there'd been a short, glowing spell around the time the photos were taken when Ronnie believed they might actually last but, in the end, as she'd always suspected it would, the relationship had splintered.

Another regret is developing the roll of film that Conor gave her before leaving for London. She should have destroyed it like he'd advised. When she saw all thirty-six exposures, the reality of what

126

happened with Conor and how he'd captured it was too much to bear. She'd felt appalled, deeply distraught. Immediately, she recognised she could never un-see the contents, yet she also knew that the photos of Eve held the key to her future. Could she forget the rest? She'd been trying to ever since.

Hearing a sound, she dries her face and rushes to the living room. Grabbing her phone from the sofa, she holds it to her chest. *You need Eve. You need Eve. You need Eve.* The voice is relentless, but it speaks the truth. Yes, she still needs Eve, but when this is over, she'll never need her again. Ronnie will make sure of that. For two people who share the same history, there's a gaping expanse between their recollections of the past and what they'd both like erased. Lowering the phone, Ronnie reads the words – **I'll do it. One last time** – then omits a strangled sound.

Ronnie doesn't have to like it, but she knows what she has to do. She's spent her life protecting Eve. Now, it's time to look out for herself. This time, she'll do whatever it takes.

CHAPTER ELEVEN

#slay #thighboots #youhavewhattheywant #whatpicture
#princessdiana #yourserve #whatsinthatphoto #andcut

@beli'EVE
Public Figure
Mama. Wife. Model. Content Creator. Collabs. Beauty. Fashion
Interiors.

5,698	1M	212
Posts	Followers	Following

It's Thursday. I'm early, so I remain in the car in the underground
hotel car park until I'm confident Ronnie will be at the restaurant.
Sitting waiting, I plan my route. It's a short walk from the hotel down
Dublin's up-market shopping throughway before I'll cut across to
where we've arranged to meet at Ronnie's favourite haunt, The Ivy. It
will be enough. Today, Grafton Street will be my catwalk. I want as
many people to notice me as possible. Dressed in an impossibly high-
end outfit, I'll certainly stand out. Pale-pink over-the-knee boots,
tan-suede shorts, bright-green oversized mohair sweater with a
designer tote swinging on my arm isn't my usual Thursday-afternoon
attire, but attention-grabbing is what I'd asked the head stylist
of Brown Thomas to send. The bag alone cost so much that each time

I look at it my insides clench. He'd sent a note that the clothes were complimentary, but they'd be grateful for a feature on my page. I promised to do my best.

In reality, if today goes as I suspect, my picture will be splashed across every newspaper and online magazine by Friday morning. If Ronnie wants drama, then that's exactly what I'll give her. I need her to know the ball is in my court, remind her I'm in control. I'd stopped in Dun Laoghaire to have my hair done on the way here. According to my stylist Roy, everyone in the industry saw the news slot and were talking about how the documentary will relaunch my career and springboard me to the very top. The sudden surge of new followers to my page suggests he might be right. I hadn't bothered to reveal that, to me, it was more a retirement party, a way to bow out with a seven-figure sum tucked into my back pocket. I'd already tried that tack with Dex. Since Ronnie's TV debut last Friday night, there's been utter silence all week from him.

My mother texted too. Having not heard from her in months, she sent me a message asking me if I thought I was Princess Diana and reminded me how that tell-all ended. Even Joanne seems too busy to chat this week. Mind you, she'd still managed to send me plenty of encouraging texts to let me know she was thinking of me and to remind me that she's there to help if I need her.

Before dropping the kids at school this morning, Dex had paused at the back door. Expressionless, he'd turned and said, "Break a leg. I'm sure your performance will be Oscar-worthy."

I close my eyes now, trying to summon how I feel when I'm in front of a camera or striding down a catwalk when I get to be someone else entirely. Dex is right. In a way, it is an act. But he was wrong when he said getting involved with Ronnie would destroy everything we've built in Annaford. It would be ruined if I didn't. If

I want a life, I must face my fears – stop being afraid. Ronnie may have me in a vice-grip, but I'm not going to make this easy on her. I have conditions. I also need her to admit what she did to me. If I know Ronnie, to her this is about money. If I'm right, then first she must pay the fine.

At ten minutes past one, I get out of the car, glance around cautiously, adjust myself in the car window and set off. I encounter two men in business suits at the door leading into the hotel from the underground car park. One of them holds the door while the other smirks, raising his eyebrows at my thigh-boots. I thank him and stride past. It's a good start.

Once inside the lift, I stare at myself in the gold-tinged mirror. Taking a deep breath, I nod at my reflection and tell myself I can do this. Instinctively, my hand reaches inside my bag for my sunglasses before I recall purposely leaving them at home. Today, I'm not hiding behind anything. I harness the words I was continuously told back in New York. *"You have what they want, and you're happy about it, but not too happy,"* the show coordinators would coach before pushing you onto the runway.

With a trembling hand, I press the button. From experience, it takes less than ten seconds until I hear a chime, and the door will open. I close my eyes as I count backwards, three, two, one … *slay*.

###

"Nice touch," I say, slightly out of breath as I take my seat opposite Ronnie, a smile still plastered on my face from the onslaught outside.

"And what a surprise – you're dressed as if you knew the photographers would be there waiting." Ronnie nods back wryly. "Hello, Eve."

"Hello, Ronnie." The tension is palpable.

"That was quite the show," she says.

As soon as I'd rounded the corner from Grafton Street onto South Anne Street, I'd spotted the press photographers huddled together, waiting for me to arrive. It almost threw me until I recognised one of them from my days of standing half-naked outside shops holding up plaques in the hope of press coverage.

"Alright, Eve, darling. Give us a few nice ones, and we'll be on our way." He'd grinned broadly, already clicking away. "Don't think I've ever seen you with so many clothes on."

Despite myself, I'd laughed. "You know how it is. At our age, you start to feel the cold. Let's make this snappy. Pardon the pun. I've a lunch to get to, but I assume you already know that."

"Aye, aye. Not just a pretty face."

"Thousands would argue!" I laughed, then gave them what they wanted – front pose, angle leg, hand on hip, glance over the shoulder, lean forward, laugh, head-tilt, hip-pop, smile. Passersby stopped to watch, taking out their phones to capture it too. It was over in seconds.

"Beautiful, Eve. And that's why you are who you are. I'll take one last one through the window when you're inside with herself, and then you won't see us 'til Christmas."

Now, Ronnie lifts her glass of champagne, instructing me to do the same as the photographers snap away. The entire restaurant is watching, peering out from between the leaves of the tall plants dotted throughout. I try to ignore the feeling of being hunted and raise my glass, endeavouring to think of an appropriate toast.

"To –" I begin, lost for words. It's been more than two years since I've laid eyes on her. There's so much to say, too much that's already been said.

"Friendship?" Ronnie offers.

I lift my eyebrows. "Is that what you'd call it?"

We smile at each other like ventriloquist dummies as we lean in, lightly touch glasses and take a sip. Ronnie turns to the window where the photographers check the screens on their digital cameras. They glance up, give her the thumbs-up, wave at me, then they're gone.

My smile drops. "I need the loo. I'll be right back." I push my chair back and head in the direction of the bathroom, ignoring the glances from other diners. The aftermath of the sudden adrenaline rush has left me jumpy, and I need to gather myself together. It's how I used to feel after hosting those lady's fashion lunches for years. I'd wear a roving mic, working the stage like Britney Spears. Afterwards, I'd have to throw on my runners and jump on a treadmill or go for a speed-walk to burn off the excess energy I'd created.

Inside the bathroom, I'm alone. The heavily patterned wallpaper and the overpowering floral fragrance make the space airless, especially since my senses are already on high alert. I vigorously shake my hands, pacing up and down, willing my alter ego – the quick-witted, collected person I'd been moments before with the photographers – to return. Where does she go when I need her most? Often, the expanse between who I am when I'm performing and who I am in reality seems so vast that I'd once asked Ronnie if she thought I had a dual-personality disorder. She'd said we all put up facades and that if I could learn to combine both personalities, I'd be unstoppable. "Like me," she'd laughed. I think of it now. To me, Ronnie has only ever been one way: tough.

Exiting the bathroom, I pause at the bar and look in her direction. Her head is inclined like she's praying. As soon as I'd walked into the restaurant, I'd noticed she's lost weight. Her hair is the longest I've ever seen it, too, making her appear softer. Although her make-up is pristine and she's dressed in a razor-sharp trouser suit, Ronnie

132

suddenly doesn't seem so stern. In fact, she looks vulnerable. Lifting her head, she reaches for the champagne flute and takes a large gulp. As she replaces her glass, she exhales slowly, then takes a visible breath as though gasping for air. This way, Ronnie looks afraid.

###

"First things first," I begin before I've even sat back down. I sit and go in light. "Faye and Milo will not be featured. But I'll talk about motherhood in general, considering this entire business started when I was pregnant. Also, I want your word that —"

"Christ, Eve!" She rolls her eyes. "I knew you'd be laden with conditions. We'll get to them. Aren't you going to ask how I've been?"

I glare, deadpan. "How are you, Ronnie?" For one instant, I think she's about to tell me that she's sick. Perhaps this is about making amends, sorting her affairs. The idea evaporates when she begins drumming her nail extensions on the table.

"Well," she purrs, "it hasn't been easy. How is your life going?"

"It's fine." I glare at her fingers until she stops tapping.

"I've been following you closely." She scowls when my mouth drops open. "My God, your face! Online, obviously. I'm not peering through your apartment window."

I don't correct her faux pas. My studio must look like an apartment. It's what I wanted people to think. Clearly, it worked.

"I've had better things to do like saving my business," she continues. "Trying to find new clients, diversify, reinvent." She glares at me. "Your numbers are dwindling, Eve. And we all know this is a numbers game. Mind you, I noticed a slight increase since I leaked the news of the documentary, but how long will that last? You should be thanking me for throwing you a lifeline."

Over the past year, my followers had dropped slightly, along with my passion for the job. It's another reason I've agreed to do the documentary.

"Hardly surprising when your content is so poor," she says, then states the obvious, "You've gone from showing people everything about your life to standing in front of a mirror in some pokey-looking apartment looking … miserable. It's boring, Eve. People want to see you out and about like today in restaurants, having a good time. Otherwise, you'll become invisible, irrelevant, dare I say cancelled."

I roll my eyes at the woke term. "I beg to differ," I argue with little conviction.

"There's still a huge level of loyalty out there."

"And for how long?"

"Brands are still using me, and I have control over what I do now, not like before. Contrary to what you used to say, I don't have to show people where I am every minute of every day. I'm no longer your puppet." I employ Dex's word. "Anyway, I had no choice but to change the way I operated." I don't elaborate. "Now, I do everything myself."

"And whose fault is that? You're the one who left. And for what? So you could go it alone, holed up somewhere because you had a tantrum. Why haven't you signed with another management company? Have you employed someone to help out? What's with the martyr act? Why?"

"You know why!" I spit.

"Do I?"

I shake my head. "I wanted privacy … a life."

Ronnie laughs wryly. "And how's that going for you? Because it doesn't look like you have much of a life to me. Is Dex keeping you locked up someplace against your will? Did he find out what you did? Are you being punished? Should I call the police?" Her voice drips with cynicism.

I glower at her.

"So, where are you living anyway?"

I don't respond.

"I can't figure it out." She doesn't wait for me to answer. "Then again, I haven't looked very hard. I thought I'd wait it out. Let you come to me. And here you are." She looks smug.

"Do we really have to talk in sarcastic riddles?" I place both hands flat on the table and lean closer. "You obviously have something you need to get off your chest, Ronnie. So go on. If we're going to be working together again, then maybe we both have things we need to say."

She leans forwards too. "Are there things you need to say, Eve?"

I chew my lip. *Was it you, Ronnie? Were you the one trying to destroy me?*

"You ruined my business. You screwed me, Eve!" Ronnie says suddenly.

"And what about what you did to me?" I say in disbelief. "Let's talk about the photo, shall we?" Ultimately, it's the reason we're sitting opposite each other, separated by an ocean of hostility. "Are you going to try to tell me you weren't trying to ruin *me*?"

It had happened a few months after I decided to speak out about the online trolling and intimidation on *Jabber.ie*. Despite a vast difference of opinion, Ronnie and I had continued to work together. Things were strained, and I kept kicking back against almost everything Ronnie suggested. I felt so let down by her lack of support that I was being intentionally troublesome, argumentative, fussy. Ronnie made it clear that it needed to stop, or she'd make me stop.

Then came the photo.

The morning I saw it, I'd spent the previous night tossing and turning, thoughts scouring through my head, finally dropping off in the early hours. Despite barely sleeping, I woke early – wired, alert, filled with an energy I hadn't experienced in years. Dex was already up, his side of the bed smoothed down as if he hadn't been there at all, although I knew he had. Dex was already asleep when I crept into bed late the night before. Straight away, I reached for phone to text Ronnie. I'd asked her for a favour the day before and though our relationship still wasn't on the best terms, she'd agreed. There was already a text from her. Satisfied with it, I was about to get up when I mindlessly opened Instagram. That's when I wished I hadn't asked for her help. Seeing the photo posted to my account was like seeing a ghost. It took me a few moments to register that I was looking at myself.

Snaking out of bed, I crept to the top of the stairs. I could hear Dex downstairs, whistling, banging about in the kitchen. Going back to my room, I forced myself to look again. With a trembling hand, I opened Facebook, trying to understand what was happening. The two media are linked, so of course it was there too. I gasped when I read underneath that the photo had been posted from Ronnie's device the night before. Paralysed with confusion and panic, feeling violated, I struggled to delete it, suddenly unable to remember how. I could see likes and comments building. At last, I managed to coordinate my thoughts, force my finger to click the three dots next to it and follow the instructions until it vanished.

"*For the thousandth time, I didn't post that fucking photo,*" Ronnie says through gritted teeth.

"And for the thousandth time, I don't believe you." I take a breath

136

to try a different tack. "If you could just admit it, Ronnie," I plead. "Then maybe we could move on. Be accountable, just this once. You're always saying never to admit to anything, but I need you to make an exception, for me." My eyes fall for a moment.

"But it wasn't me!" Ronnie throws her hands up. "I'm not admitting to something I didn't do." She shakes her head and exhales. "Christ, I can't do this again, Eve. You know where I was that night. I was at home, asleep. My phone was next to me. All night. No one has my passcode."

"Well, then how? Explain it to me, please!" The frustration is still as raw.

"We've been through all this before. Why would I even post it in the first place? *Why?*"

I shrug helplessly. "As a warning. To reel me back in. To control me. I hadn't been playing by your rules —"

"Oh, come on!" She grits her teeth.

"Or maybe in some deluded way you were trying to protect me. Were you?"

This time, her voice soars. "*Read my lips. I didn't post that photo.*"

People turn to look.

I lower my voice. "This was a mistake," I say. "Too much has happened between us." I pause for a moment. "How did we get here? We used to be so close. We were family."

Ronnie squeezes her eyes shut. When she opens them, she appears calmer.

"I just wanted to talk about the future, Eve. I thought you were over all that other stuff. This documentary is a good opportunity for both of us." There's a pause. "What happened between us nearly broke me. You probably think I'm doing this for money, but it's not the only reason." Her voice falters. "I want to make amends. I actually sat down yesterday and tried to write down what happened between us. I still couldn't make sense of it." She shakes her head. She seems so genuine that's it hard to believe she isn't. "All I could come up with is that somewhere along the line, there was a communication breakdown – crossed wires. And yes, I was angry with you for what you were doing. But I didn't post that photo."

I drop my head. "After I spoke out about the hate and the trolling ..." I look up and point at her, "*you* stopped supporting me. After all the years together, you just stopped. I felt like such a fool. I felt really alone."

She nods. "I'm sorry for that, truly, but I knew you wouldn't be able for the backlash, and I was right. It weakened you, Eve. I mean, look where it drove you."

I look away. The feeling of shame is still so intense that I can hardly breathe. Regardless, I need to know the truth. "What about all the stuff after the photo?" Ronnie stares at me blankly.

"All those other things you did," I say.

"What other things?" She looks confused.

I narrow my gaze, testing her. "I think you know, Ronnie. You've admitted you were angry. There's no one else alive who knows that much about me. I just want to know why. Just tell me ... *please*."

Ronnie frowns deeply. "What the hell are you talking about?"

There's nothing I can do to stop it. My performance crumbles as mortifying tears flow and my shoulders convulse.

CHAPTER TWELVE

@beli'EVE

Public Figure

Mama. Wife. Model. Content Creator. Collabs. Beauty. Fashion
Interiors.

5,698	1.1M	212
Posts	Followers	Following

Ronnie has me out of the restaurant so fast that I barely notice her indicate to the waiter that we're leaving. Outside, she throws her long black coat over my shoulders. I allow my hair to fall over my face, concealing two years' worth of pent-up tears, paranoia, hurt, panic. Ronnie ushers me up South William Street, where we flit across Grafton Street to the Westbury Hotel. Barely ten minutes later, I'm sitting on the sofa in a second-floor suite. Not only does Ronnie know the staff of the upmarket hotel well, but from years of experience she understands there's nowhere more discreet than a five-star hotel.

Ronnie perches on the coffee table opposite. "I'm sorry," she says at last. "We should have met somewhere more private. I can see there's more to discuss than I'd realised."

I swallow, trying to compose myself, but my face contorts again. I release a sob, then sniff loudly. "Did anyone see?" The question throws me back to my college days. *Who saw? Who noticed? What happened?*

Ronnie shakes her head now as she did back then.

"No one saw," she assures. "Just relax for a minute. Kick off those boots. I'll order food. Maybe a bottle of wine."

"I'm driving."

"One glass won't kill you." She tilts her head and frowns. "You look exhausted. I had to pay for the room for the night anyway. Why don't we have a drink, talk. You can take the room? I'll go home later. I'm sure Dex will understand."

"Will he?" I force a smile, fix my hair and wipe at my eyes with the back of my hand. "Things are different now, you know? I don't stay out at the drop of a hat anymore. I don't put myself first anymore."

Ronnie frowns. "Well, maybe you should. *Text him, Eve.* It's one night."

Despite my doubts, I remove my phone from my bag and do as she says. I feel so shaken that the thought of getting into the car and having to drive home is making me feel sick. Composing a message, I tell Dex where I am and that there's a lot to go over. I give him my room number just in case. He reads it – three dots flash up to indicate that he's typing. It stops, starts a few times, then disappears completely. Dex must have nothing to say.

"Everything okay?" Ronnie asks.

"Fine," I lie. "He knows where I am and what room I'm in." I watch her cautiously.

"Great." Ronnie doesn't seem concerned. "At least we can talk now, safely." She gets up, walks to the hotel phone on a side table and picks up the receiver. My eyes follow. "Is it safe, though?"

She turns to me with the same bewildered look she'd had in the restaurant before I broke down.

140

"Am I safe with you, Ronnie? Because if I'm not, just tell me, will you? Put me out of my misery. I'm done playing games."

Ronnie replaces the receiver with a grimace. "What do you mean, are you safe with me?" She places her hands on the back of the armchair next to the phone. "Is this what you were talking about earlier ... the stuff I apparently did to you?"

"You tell me."

Ronnie tuts impatiently. "I can't because I have no idea what you're talking about. Now you're talking in riddles."

She looks so baffled that I begin to doubt myself. I glance nervously at the door, then back at her. "Just tell me I'm safe here."

"Oh my God!" Her disbelief is palpable. "Are you really frightened of me?"

I don't answer. Instead, my gaze falls to the patterned rug at my feet. My eyes dart back and forth, scanning the design. It's as elaborate as the twists and turns of everything that happened over the last few years. Inwardly, I answer Ronnie's question. Deep down, I know that if I were truly afraid I wouldn't have come here alone with her nor texted Dex to say I was staying the night. Do I believe that Ronnie has brought me here to spike my drink and strangle me in my sleep like some horror movie? No.

All along, I'd wanted to believe it was her – that she was the one who'd been sending me messages, messing with my life, dropping little bombs wherever I went. I'd convinced myself that it was Ronnie trying to frighten me into submission, run me out of town. Being in her company again, suddenly, I'm not so sure.

"Eve?"

Her voice disturbs my thoughts. I don't look up.

"I'm going to the bathroom, then I'm ordering food and then you need to tell me what's really going on here." I see her walk towards the bathroom and close the door in my peripheral vision. I think of what she said earlier in the restaurant about trying to piece together what happened between us. I've spent the last few years trying to forget, but now I need to remember. My eyes move from the rug until I'm staring straight ahead, blindly, hypnotised.

I rewind back to when Amber was on holiday, and I first discovered the online hatred. I visualise the confrontations afterwards with Ronnie – my idea to ask people who didn't like me to unfollow me. I'd gone against her. I see myself sitting in my bedroom, speaking out defiantly, coming clean with my followers over trolling and abuse, how it had affected my life. I'd verbally omitted what had truly affected my entire existence, but it materialised anyway through raw tears. Afterwards, I'd thought about re-recording the piece, delivering it in a calmer fashion, but I'd wanted to let people see how much it hurt. Looking back now, I allowed pent-up emotions that stretched far beyond being victimised online to get the better of me. In hindsight, I revealed too much. Even still, I'd thought people might understand. Many did. Then came the criticism. I became the laughing stock, a gif, a discussion topic on radio talk shows, likened to Gwyneth Paltrow's 1999 cringe-worthy Oscar acceptance speech. Everyone was talking about it for the wrong reasons. Instead of standing by me, all Ronnie said was "I told you so". Then she flooded my pages with quotes about mental health, making it appear like I was having a nervous breakdown. Maybe I was. But, knowing my history, it was a callous act.

I was sinking. By then, Dex and I were simply existing under one roof. He was as indifferent as Ronnie. Knowing now how angry he was with me, maybe he thought I deserved what I got. I felt empty. Hollowly craving understanding, compassion, someone to care, anything to fill the void. That's what scared me most.

I squeeze my eyelids shut at what I already know comes next.

Ronnie's words echo. "You weren't able for the backlash. It weakened you, Eve … look at where it drove you."

In reality, it came to me.

I scream internally as I put my hands to my face. When I first met Dex in New York, I told him I never wanted to feel the way I had before arriving in New York, when truthfully it was all I wanted to feel. Years later, when my chips were down and I received a message of support, I realised I'd never stopped waiting for my past to show up. Almost two decades after he discarded me like a ragdoll, there he was.

#

That first day in UCD, we'd found him in the bar after I'd nervously flashed my student card at the steward, who barely glanced at it.

Inside, Conor made his way towards us as soon as he clocked Ronnie. My entire body stiffened when he stepped in front of me, a smile spreading across his face. His green eyes twinkled, dark hair glistened, as he looked me up and down.

"Conor Malone, this is Eve. He's the guy I told you about for the house-share."

"How's it going, Eve?" The words were songful.

"Good. Fine. I was registering, and I met Ronnie, and we said we'd get a drink," I babbled, blushing to the roots of my hair.

"A first-year?" He bit the tip of his tongue. "Good for you. What's your poison? I'll buy you one to welcome you to UCD."

"Vodka," I answered fast.

Conor raised his eyebrows. "So you like the hard stuff?"

"Yeah."

His eyes flashed to Ronnie. This time, he raised one eyebrow.

Ronnie shook her head at him and rolled her eyes. It seemed like a warning.

"I'll be back. Stay there."

I watched him snake through the crowd, occasionally stopping, grasping a couple of lads by the elbow to pump their hand like a politician.

"Who's he?" I asked as Ronnie led me to a high table at the edge of the room.

"That's Conor."

I sat, craning my neck to keep him in my sight. "I got that." I tut. "How do you know him?"

Ronnie shrugged. "*Hmm.* I've just known him forever," she said nonchalantly, stopping to think. "He's a friend of a friend from home."

"What's he like?" My eyes were wide.

She shrugged again. "Conor is Conor. He's in second-year commerce. He's grand … artsy. Into music, photography, that sort of thing. The business degree is to tick the box, so he says."

"He knows everyone," I said, seeing him stop to talk to a group of girls at the bar.

"Yeah. He takes pictures at sports and social events, that sort of thing. That's how."

My eyes lit as he looked over his shoulder directly at me. He couldn't have been further from the private-school boys I knew from Dalkey in their rugby shirts and chinos. He was dressed in baggy jeans, a T-shirt, a check shirt tied around his waist, leather jacket.

"I'm going to the loo," Ronnie said suddenly.

I barely noticed her leave as I watched Conor lift two glasses from the bar, flick his fringe back then stride towards me.

"Here." He handed me a glass with a single shot of vodka – no ice, no mixer. I stared at it for a moment, then boldly lifted it and skulled the contents, convulsing slightly when it hit the back of my throat.

Conor looked stunned before breaking into a wide grin as he produced a glass bottle of coke from his back pocket and set it on the table in front of me. I bit my lip and grinned back as I stared up at him. Before I knew what was happening, he leaned forward and kissed me. It was as unexpected as everything that had already happened that day. It was the best day of my life – the first day of my life. I kissed him back, melting when I felt his arms around my waist, his hips pushing forward, separating my knees. I was his.

Days later, the three of us moved into the rented house together like a strange little family, more functional than my own in many ways. Gradually, I became someone new. Conor introduced me to a world I never knew existed. I felt powerful, energetic, free, brave, and loved by him. We mirrored each other, consumed each other, became each other. Me: waif-thin, bony hips protruding through slip-like dresses, his shirts knotted over them, his jacket over my shoulders. Him: grungy, sultry, brooding, artistic. We were always together. When he wasn't taking my photo, we spent hours smoking on the steps of the Arts block, draped over each other, whispering, laughing, kissing.

Through it all, Ronnie was there too. She looked out for me, minded me, made me feel safe in our perfect life of parties, nightclubs, staying out all night, sleeping for days, being an adult. It was fast and wild: addictive, obsessive.

It was destructive.

When it ended, I almost ended. When Conor left me, I almost left myself. When he came back all those years later, it felt like I came back with him.

###

"Eve." My eyes fly open. Ronnie is standing over me, holding out a glass of red wine. "My God, did you fall asleep?"

I land back in the room, shaking my head. "I was just thinking." I take the glass and she sits down. "I was trying to do what you said you'd done last night ... piece together what happened."

"And did you?" She pops a cracker in her mouth and chews, gesturing at the table where a selection of cheese and meats have miraculously appeared.

"No," I answer. "I got to the part where Conor contacted me out of the blue." I shrink. "It got me thinking about college and him."

Ronnie turns her nose up at the mention of his name.

"When did you start hating him?" I ask.

She finishes chewing. "When he hurt you."

"The three of us used to be so close, remember? All those plans we had ..."

Her body stiffens. "It was a long time ago."

"But we were a family."

"Families fall apart."

Before I can stop it, the memory of how broken I was after college floods me. Ronnie must have sensed it. "He wasn't good for you, Eve. What happened, it was ..." She trails off, unable to finish. Instead, she takes a sip of her wine and stares straight ahead. "In the end, you weren't good for each other," she says at last. Every person in college wanted to be like the two of you. Even before you were famous, you were like this celebrity couple off MTV swanning around. Those things always end badly."

"But you mustn't have thought that when we were planning to head to London together – when you were planning to manage him too?" I object.

"Things changed. He should never have contacted you again,

dragging up the past like that. For what?" She places her glass on the table and folds her arms.

If I told Ronnie that I believed Conor reappeared a few years ago exactly when I needed him most, she'd think I'd completely lost it.

"He's different now," I muse, shrugging.

"Is he, though?"

"Yes," I nod. "He's focused. More open. Successful." I stare into space. Since moving to Annaford to start again, I've mostly forced Conor from my mind. Just talking about him, I feel the familiar yearning. I'd felt it the other night too when I opened the picture of him on his website.

"You still love him, don't you?" Ronnie watches me.

"I'll always love him, Ronnie. You know that." I meet her gaze for a moment, before rubbing my hands down my face, sighing loudly. "It was my fault." The tears well unexpectedly. "What happened was my fault."

"It wasn't all your fault, Eve."

"But I still have to live with it. Nowadays, I also have to live with the fact that I cheated on Dex." It's the first time I've vocalised what I did to my husband not so long ago. I expect the words to release me somehow, but the guilt sits as firmly as it always does.

Ronnie bats the air. "Everyone does it, Eve. It's rife. You had countless opportunities to cheat over the years, and you never did. I'd call that a pretty successful marriage. One kiss for old time's sake up an alleyway is hardly the crime of the century."

I go to correct her, but I stop myself. Something isn't adding up here. I decide to draw her out. "That's not what you said at the time."

"I was angry at the time. I didn't think meeting him was a good idea."

I stare ahead again. "If Dex found out, he'd –"

147

"So he never found out?" She sounds surprised.

I shake my head. "But if he did …"

Ronnie tuts and bats the air again. "Dex would never leave you, Eve. You know that." She hesitates. "Did you ever think of leaving him?"

I shake my head. "For a minute, maybe, but I do love Dex. He's a good man, a great dad … the kids … and we're happy again. Really happy." I'm wondering if it sounds like I'm trying to convince myself. "It's why I want to do this documentary." I nod. "For Dex. So I have the money to walk away from the spotlight. So I can focus solely on my family – on him." I look up at Ronnie. "You don't need to blackmail me into it – threaten Dex with losing that account with the Gallagher Group. I'll do it, okay? Then I want to walk away – for good, this time."

Ronnie has the grace to look abashed. "I thought I was doing him a favour." When she sees my face, she says, "I wouldn't have that power anyway. He won it on his own." She pauses. "My work is who I am, Eve. It's my life …"

I nod. "I need you to swear to me, on your life, that nothing from college gets leaked. Even when this is done. The past stays where it is."

"I swear." There's a brief pause. "Now, can you tell me what you were talking about earlier in the restaurant – what you think I did?"

I study her cautiously, accessing her body language, trying to decipher if she's bluffing. If I can trust her. There's only one way to find out. "First, I want to talk about the photo."

In the grainy image she posted to my accounts, I'm locked in an embrace with Conor, pressed against him up the side alley of the restaurant where we'd dined after reuniting. To the untrained eye, it could be Dex. Only Dex is taller and broader. Anyone who knew us would know it wasn't him. "Only you knew where I was that night, Ronnie," I say.

Ronnie rolls her eyes at the revival of the subject, but she doesn't stop me.

"When I mentioned that Conor contacted me, you were so horrible." She purses her lips.

"It wasn't long after I spoke out online about trolling. By the time Conor contacted me, you'd been off with me for weeks, angry with me about everything. Remember?"

There's no denial. "But you still asked me for a favour, though, didn't you? Do you remember that part?" Ronnie reminds me. "I still enabled you to go and meet him. I covered for you even though I knew it was a bad idea."

"I needed answers."

"And did you get them? One meeting would hardly be enough to answer for everything he did."

Again, I try not to frown at the reference to one meeting. Is Ronnie playing me? "He admitted to making a lot of mistakes," I say, keeping my voice even. "He has a lot of regrets."

"Like what?" Ronnie interjects.

"Like how he left after college." This time, I eyeball her.

As expected, she flinches. It's slight, but I catch it. She stands up. "And what lie did he tell you?"

I stand too, so I'm looking her straight in the eye. Ronnie steps back. Her eyes widen with the same look of fear I'd clocked back in the restaurant earlier.

"Conor and I were supposed to be together." I step closer. "He loved me, Ronnie. And I loved him. It wasn't over."

When I kissed Conor the night we reunited, I knew I wasn't saying goodbye to the past. I was welcoming it back. Afterwards, I felt

149

terrible but not so bad that I didn't return for more. That's the part I'm confused about now. Ronnie seems to think I met him only once. Unless she's lying, it further confirms my earlier doubts. The truth is, once I'd realised that Dex couldn't have seen the photo, I dived in head-first.

"You told him to leave me after college, didn't you? It was you who sent him away."

Ronnie's eyes fall. I prepare for profuse denial, for her to claim that Conor was looking for someone to blame. When it doesn't come, my heart sinks. Losing Conor after college had felt like drowning. I thought I'd never resurface from the confusion of being left a note telling me to move on with my life – that he wouldn't be back, ever.

"Yes." Ronnie lifts her eyes to mine. "You were sinking, and you needed a fresh start ... I was trying to save you."

I stare at her with disbelief. "How could you?" I choke.

"I'm sorry," she whispers. "I thought I was doing the right thing. I still think it was. You're better off without him."

It's something I intend to address further later, but for now I need answers.

"One last time, Ronnie, did you post the photo of me with Conor?" I take a final step towards her, so I'm inches from her face.

She looks me straight in the eye. "On my life, I didn't. I swear to you."

I step back as I realise she's telling the truth. Fresh worry surges through me. If Ronnie didn't post it, then who the hell did? And if she didn't post the photo, I'm wrong about everything else.

"Do you remember the name of one of the trolls from before?" I deviate suddenly.

Ronnie's face is blank.

"An old friend from college," I remind her.

"I think so." Her answer is noncommittal, but her spine straightens. "Yes, I do," she corrects herself. "You were worried. I told you it was nothing, and I was right. They went away."

"Only I think they came back."

Ronnie seizes her glass of wine from the table, takes a swift gulp, sets it down, then sits into the high-back armchair. "What do you mean they came back?" She begins to play with her nails, fidgeting, then sits on her hands to stop herself.

"I'll get to it," I say, dazed as I sit back down. In an instant, everything has changed. "There's something I need to tell you first."

Ronnie leans forward.

"Do you want to know how I knew Dex hadn't seen the photo of Conor and me?"

Ronnie nods.

I explain how skittish and distracted I'd been in the days after it appeared on my social pages. Even though Dex was acting normally as if nothing had changed, I couldn't relax. When he collected Faye and Milo from school a few days later, leaving his phone on the kitchen table, I used the opportunity to sift about. Using my date of birth – his passcode – to open it, I flagrantly went through his photos, messages, recent calls, internet history as if he was the one with something to hide. There was nothing out of the ordinary. As a last resort, I clicked on Facebook, scanning his list of friends before moving to Instagram and scrolling the list of people he followed. That's when I realised that Dex couldn't have seen the photo because somewhere along the way, perhaps by my instruction, my husband had unfollowed me.

"It sounds petty, I know, but it confirmed that Dex had checked out of our marriage," I reason. "We'd become a cliché – living separate lives, ships in the night. Instead of trying to fix it, to use your words, it drove me to Conor." I close my eyes, trying to absorb the guilt, then I meet Ronnie's. "It wasn't a once-off thing, Ronnie. It was more than a kiss up in a dark alley." For good measure, I challenge her again. "But you knew that, didn't you?"

Ronnie's eyes grow round. "No … I had no idea … no." She removes her hands from under her legs and covers her open mouth. For an instant, it looks as though she's going to throw up. "I'm shocked," she says, recovering. "How long?"

"A few months."

"*Months!*" she wails. "Did he … were you … did he say anything …"

"Anything about what?" I narrow my eyes.

"Nothing. I just can't believe it. After the photo debacle, you said you were never going to see him again. You swore to me the next morning in my office."

2016

It was the second time in as many months that Eve came into Ronnie's office, holding out her phone. It was similar to the day Eve discovered Jabber.ie, only it felt worse.. As it was, they were barely speaking. When Ronnie saw her coming, she visibly blanched.

"What now?" Ronnie begrudgingly took the phone from Eve's extended hand to examine the screenshot.

"I like how you're acting as if you've never seen this before!" Eve hissed, making her way around the desk. She jabbed at the screen from behind, pointing at the words beneath the picture. "When it was posted by you."

Ronnie looked again. "What even *is* this?" Moments later, it was followed with "Oh". Then another pause before she said,

"I hate to say it, but I told you so."

"Don't you dare!" Eve grabbed the phone back and made her way back around the desk to face Ronnie. *"Where did you get it? Why? Why would you do this?"* She ran the fingers of her free hand through her hair, grabbing a tuft with frustration. "You better start talking, Ronnie. I swear I'll …"

"What?" Ronnie flung her chair back and stood. "What will you do this time, Eve? As if your last stunt wasn't enough." She looked daggers at her. "Are you going to speak out online again, tell everyone how you were caught red-handed with your ex, then look for sympathy that you've been wronged?" She slumped back into her chair, shaking her head. "I don't even know what to say to you anymore."

Eve flinched as if she'd been struck.

"Someone must have seen you, but it definitely wasn't me, and I certainly didn't post that from my phone." Ronnie exhaled slowly. "You'd better hope no one else has this picture or was quick enough to notice that it isn't Dex."

"Oh my God!" Eve said at last. "Do you think I'm completely stupid? It was from your phone. It says so under the picture. Who were you with last night? Did you have someone else over? Did they post it? Did someone send it to you?" She paced the area in front of Ronnie's desk, throwing out question after question, then stopped suddenly. "Did you follow me?"

Ronnie rolled her eyes. "No! I was at home all night. You know that, and there was no one else there."

"If Dex saw it, he'll –"

"Did you delete it?"

"Yes."

"Okay. Well, unless someone tries to post it again, you're

safe. Anyway, if Dex saw it, he'd have said something, wouldn't he?"

Eve blinked. "Yes. No. I don't know."

"We'll just have to sit back, wait and see if something else comes out. I said it over and over. Meeting Conor was a mistake. Christ!"

Eve had swallowed her pride the day before and told Ronnie that she was meeting him. Ronnie spent hours trying to convince her otherwise, then at the last minute, she appeared to have second thoughts, claiming that she'd like to hear what he had to say.

"So, what did he want anyway?" she asked.

"Nothing much. He just wanted to talk."

"About what?" Ronnie looked sceptical.

"Stuff. The past."

Ronnie sat up straight. "What stuff? Did he tell you why he left you like he did? Prick," she muttered, and then, "He did you a favour. You'd never be where you are today if he'd stuck around. Don't go there again, Eve. There's nothing he can ever say to make up for what he did to you. Walk away. Do you understand me? It will ruin everything." Her voice shook ever so slightly. "I didn't post that picture … "

"Nice try. You're the only one who knew where and when I was meeting him. This was *your* doing, and I think I know why."

Ronnie stared deadpan. "Go on. Humour me."

"To control me. Remind me what I'd be throwing away if I didn't play by your rules. If I let the squeaky-clean image slip."

"I think you did that all by yourself, Eve."

"*Don't you dare!*" She spat. "I have a right to a private life."

"As your manager, let me remind you that when you sign up

as a public figure, you give up that right for everything you gain. We have companies banging down the door to work with you. You have your own clothing line, your own range of shoes, a second make-up line coming out, and you want to throw all that away for some idiot from college? You want to sully your name by –"

"Is that why you did it?"

Ronnie tutted loudly. "*I didn't post it*. There must have been some security issue, a glitch. I'll get someone to look at it, right now – I'll call –"

"Don't bother. I've changed all the passwords and removed you as an administrator. Do you know what I think? *You're* the glitch, Ronnie. You're losing control of me, and you're afraid because you need me."

"Don't be ridiculous, Eve. We're friends."

Eve walked towards her. "We stopped being friends when I found out you were lying to me a few months back. You were so against me launching a campaign against haters, but it looks like you're the hater, Ronnie." Her hands were trembling, but she couldn't stop them.

"Eve! This is complete and utter ... *Eve!* Come back!"

Eve paused as she left, her gaze caught by Conor's original framed photo of her on the wall. She stepped towards it, noticing that the glass was cracked, the frame tilting to one side.

"What happened to that? It's cracked."

When she pointed to it, Ronnie looked utterly shocked.

"Must be a sign," Eve said. "That's not the only thing that's broken in here. I won't be seeing Conor again. You have my word, but I won't be seeing you either."

CHAPTER THIRTEEN

#morethanwords #naughtyeve #persist #whathappened

@beli'EVE
Public Figure
Mama. Wife. Model. Content Creator. Collabs. Beauty. Fashion
Interiors.

5,698	1.1M	212
Posts	Followers	Following

"We both said a lot that morning," I tell Ronnie now. "I didn't think I'd see Conor again, but then he messaged again to say he was going to stay on in Dublin for a while. Everything was falling apart: my marriage, my job, you. He was the only person who seemed to care. So, he kept texting, calling when no one else did. I answered."

Ronnie's eyes fall to the floor.

After the argument that day, I'd expected Ronnie to chase after me, call, email, text, confess, tell me she'd discovered who'd uploaded that photo or where it came from in the first place. To me, her silence was an admission of guilt. The distance between us kept growing until we found ourselves working together via stilted emails, messages passed through other staff members.

At last, I ask, "If it wasn't you who posted the photo, why did you let me go? You just allowed me to drift away."

Ronnie lifts her gaze. She shrugs. "I don't know. I was angry that you thought I might do something like that. Stubborn," she admits. "I thought you'd come around." She gives a humourless laugh. "The day you came to tell me you wanted out completely, I thought you were coming to make amends. I couldn't have had it more wrong." She pauses. "So, what happened with Conor then? Did it end badly?"

"I ended it. I had to." I swallow and glance up at the ceiling. "At first, it was exciting, if that's the word. Maybe more nerve-racking, vomit-inducing." I make a face. "Lying is a full-time job, you know? Conor took a short-term rental in Sandymount. I'd tell Dex I was going into the office to meet you, but I'd really be at Conor's. Dex didn't know we'd completely fallen out until I told you I wanted out altogether. He knew things were strained, but he didn't ask much more. I don't think he cared. So, I made up events, meetings, anything I could think of."

"Wow," Ronnie mouths. "So you were with Conor a lot."

I nod. "He asked me to leave Dex, move to London with him, and I really thought about it, but then … things started happening."

"What things?"

"An old friend from college." I look up suddenly. Ronnie is frowning. "I started getting private messages from their account. At first, it was things like, *'You're a disgrace.' 'Who are you to give out advice?' 'You're fake.'* Then it started to change to, *'I remember you in college.' 'I know who you really are.'*" I pause. *"'I know what you did.'"* I take a breath. It comes out ragged. Ronnie hasn't moved a muscle while listening. "At first, I ignored it. I even tried to channel you. I could hear you telling me the usual – that it was just some jealous, crazy person until I took a look at their Instagram page. They followed only one person: me. So, I blocked it. The next day I got a message from a new account – a different name, but it was them. That time, they sent the picture of me kissing Conor in the alley." I grimace. "I blocked it again. A few days later, there was a new account. That time, they sent a photo of me going into Conor's rental house. Then one of me in the window with him." I exhaled again. "On and on it went. Everywhere I went, I'd get photo after photo taken without me knowing – collecting the kids, at the Supermarket, hairdresser. It was relentless. I ... I was terrified."

"Jesus Christ, Eve. Why the hell didn't you tell me?"

I don't answer. Instead, I wait for it to dawn on her.

"Oh my God. Because you thought it was me."

At the look of shock on her face, it suddenly dawns on me how ridiculous it must sound. So much so that I throw my head back and suddenly start to laugh. It morphs to sobs, maybe a mix of both. When it calms, I look at Ronnie. "I honestly don't know what I thought. I was so confused, lost, terrified. But it wasn't you, was it?" A guttural noise escapes my lips as Ronnie shakes her head. "There's more ... so much more. It moved offline."

While I speak, Ronnie shakes her head vigorously in disbelief as I tell her the account of what started with cancelled hair appointments, unrequested food deliveries, letters, emails to every account I'd ever created. "They started calling out Conor by name in the messages. Telling me to end it or I'd be sorry – that everything that happened in UCD would be spread everywhere. The truth would out. Justice would be served." I stand suddenly and walk towards the hotel window. With crossed arms, I stare at the street below. When I turn to Ronnie, my eyes are filled with tears. "I was so scared that it was all going to come out. I didn't know what to do."

"Did Conor know what was happening?" Ronnie asks.

I notice her curl her fingers into the palms of her hands when I don't answer. "Eve?"

I look back outside. "He thought it was you too. He said that only you knew about the things in some of those messages. One even mentioned the house we'd rented in college. Things I used to wear. Places we'd gone." There's a pregnant pause. I turn to her again so that I'm looking her straight in the eye. "That's when he told me that you ordered him to leave after college. He told me that I didn't know what you were really capable of – that if I only knew –" I stop.

Ronnie is motionless.

"What did he mean?" I ask.

Ronnie sticks out her bottom lip. "He must mean the time I told him to leave."

"I kept asking what he meant but he'd clam up before I could get him to say. You remember what he was like? But then things got weirder again."

"How?"

"I started getting these postcards in envelopes addressed to me." I close my eyes at the memory. "They were all the same but sort of different – always images of mountains or cliffs on the front." I stop. "But the back was always the same." I open my eyes and turn to Ronnie. "There'd be this drawing of a red dress. A really childish outline in what looked like crayon."

Ronnie's eyes widen. "The photo?"

"Yes. Something about the photo, obviously, but other than that I have no clue."

"You should have told me, Eve. Why didn't you tell me? You should have told me. Did you go to the Guards?"

"How could I?" I throw my hands up in exasperation. "I was having an affair! And I didn't want them digging around into my life, into the past ..."

"What happened then?"

159

"The messages and postcards kept coming. And then –" I shudder. "Then someone started coming into the house."

I tell her how I began to get this strange feeling as if the house was haunted. I'd come home and things would be moved around – the oddest things. I'd find my moisturiser in the shower, shampoo in the fridge, washing in the bin.

"I thought I was losing my mind, imagining it. I blamed the kids, Dex ... then the postcards began appearing around the house. I'd pull back the covers at night, and there'd be one. One morning there was one on the fridge. Then I found one in my bag telling me to come clean about college." I shiver. "One day, I came home to find a note in my wardrobe telling me that I had one last chance to do the right thing, and then I was going to pay for my mistakes. The next morning there was another on my car window. I was scared to leave the house. I was scared to be in the house ... Dex didn't seem to notice ... I was out of my mind."

"Jesus, Eve. So that's why you left that house, moved to Wicklow?"

"Yes. Though there were some other reasons too . . ."

Feeling drained, I move from the window and sit back down. I touch my face. It's drenched with tears I hadn't even realised were falling.

"Ronnie, I need to ask you one more thing," I say. "Because I've been trying to remember. I've been trying so hard. I've thought of nothing else for the past two years. There must have been something – something else I've forgotten."

My voice breaks, but I manage to compose myself. Staring her straight in the eye, I ask what has permeated not only the last two years but almost my entire life. "What the fuck happened in college?"

CHAPTER FOURTEEN

#psychopath #postacardsfromtheedge #crayon #wholetyouin
#threequestion #neversleepagain

@theagency

147	6,590	89
Posts	Followers	Following

Ronnie lets herself into her apartment after leaving Eve at the hotel. She locks up and turns the lights on full. In the main living area, she flops onto the sofa, closes her eyes, inhales deeply, then blows the air out. She repeats it a few times then stares dead ahead, allowing the day's events to settle. It's late. Although exhausted, her mind buzzes with information, accusations, revelations, renewed apprehension. Earlier, they'd spoken until Eve could barely keep her eyes open. Ronnie was hardly surprised. After everything Eve revealed, Ronnie wouldn't be surprised if Eve slept for a year. Eventually, Ronnie had pointed at the king-size hotel bed through the main bedroom door, instructing Eve to get some rest – that they'd talk more tomorrow.

"Stay," Eve had suggested, yawning. "If you want. There's room."

Though Ronnie had refused, she was satisfied by how readily Eve had accepted everything she had told her, especially regarding college. That said, she had been telling Eve precisely what she wanted to hear since the day they'd met. It hadn't let her down yet.

#

"Nothing happened in college. Nothing," Ronnie responded quickly, then paused to choose her words, check her demeanour. "My God, I can't believe all that was happening to you. What an absolute psychopath! You must have been petrified. Did it stop when you left Dublin?"

Eve nodded cautiously. "Straight away. I came offline at the same time for those few months after moving to Annaford."

"Annaford?"

Realising her slip-up, Eve grimaced. "Remember my aunt's house? We took it over after she died. That's where we are."

Ronnie raised her eyebrows. She'd had no idea. "Wow. You kept that on the low-down."

Eve looked distraught. "I had to. I couldn't take much more. I had to change everything, end it with Conor, sell the house. You think I wanted to leave my life? You think I wanted to wave him off back to London again?" She shook her head, answering her own question. "I had no choice. You and I weren't talking. I couldn't tell Dex the truth." A sob caught in her throat. "Annaford was there. It made sense."

Ronnie frowned. "But you must have told Dex something."

Eve's eyes fell. "I lied." And then, "At least, I used Faye as an excuse."

"Faye?"

Tears welled as she came clean about everything that had been happening with her daughter at the same time. Ronnie could barely

believe her ears. They'd spoken at length about it before moving back
to the stalking issue. Eve maintained that the two weren't connected.

"I don't think those threads about Faye were related to my past
and what was happening to me. It was just the worst timing ever. In
a way, Faye needing me, her being unwell, was what I needed to realise
that my family comes first."

"Whoever it was obviously wanted you to think that they had
something on you. All that talk of college ... what could they possibly
mean?"

Eve tilted her head as if to say: you know what.

Ronnie batted the air. "Other than that – but I'm telling you right
now, nothing happened. *Nothing*."

They hadn't spoken about "*that*" in years, yet Eve looked as uneasy
as if it were yesterday.

Ronnie began talking fast, rushing her words. "They were messing
with your head, trying to make you think that there was something
when there wasn't. Maybe they knew you back then or knew someone
who did. Maybe they were trying to tap into some insecurity, hoping
to get lucky, and they did. Maybe they heard a rumour, but that's it,
Eve. Rumours are always more exciting than the truth, remember?"

Eve nodded. "At first, that's what I kept trying to tell myself but –"

"But nothing, Eve. You were being stalked. It happens all the time
to people in the public eye. You're a target. You should have gone to
the Guards. I understand why you didn't, but it was obviously some
weird person, utterly obsessed with you, getting some kick out of
controlling you or frightening you or something equally insane. I don't
know." She shrugged then dropped her shoulders as her brow
furrowed with concern. "I'm so sorry, Eve. I should have listened
about the trolls, about the campaign you wanted to do. I shouldn't
have shut you out. Maybe if I'd listened ..." She trailed off. "Look,

I'm not playing it down, but it sounds like the stalker's gone now. It's over. What has it been? Two years? I think you're safe."

"And what if they come back?"

"If that happens, then this time we do what you should have done before – we call the Guards. This time, you have me."

"What if it comes out about Conor – the affair? I don't want to lose Dex. I can't lose anything else." Her eyes welled.

Ronnie stood, crossed the room to sit next to her and took her hand. "It's okay. Nothing will come out. I'll make sure of it. Whoever it was is gone. Mark my words. I'll personally murder anyone who attempts to harm you." She squeezed Eve's hand, attempting a smile. "We'll hire security if needs be."

Eve stifled a sob. "I can't believe I thought it was you."

The dam broke as Ronnie enveloped her in her arms and whispered what Eve needed to hear.

"It's over."

#

Ronnie rests her head back now, pondering it all. To weather what Eve had and to still be standing was admirable. To reinvent herself under duress, adjust, conceal everything in the way she had, was monumental. Mind you, it wasn't the first time over the years that Eve had impressed, even awed Ronnie. Eve was stronger than she knew, more in control of her past demons than she realised – if only she could let them go.

Years before, Ronnie had been blown away by how Eve seamlessly evolved from model to influencer. Eve made people believe that she was someone else entirely when she was just like everyone else in reality. Struggling through life with the same doubts, fears, insecurities.

Only Eve did life looking like she'd stepped out of a magazine.

Years before, when Eve announced she was pregnant with Milo, Ronnie had panicked. Back then, the only other models she'd had on her books at The Agency were gangly teens with bad fake tans, brassy highlights, yellow teeth and eyebrows like giant black sperm swimming towards each other. None held a candle to Eve in the looks department, yet all surpassed her in terms of confidence. It was hardly surprising, considering her upbringing and her neglectful mother.

Still, when Ronnie concocted the idea for @beli'EVE out of sheer desperation, she never imagined Eve would actually pull it off. It was a gamble. Over and over, she wondered if people would like Eve – if she'd charm or intimidate them. Would she be able to handle it? Would she be able to speak without shaking like a leaf?

My God, Eve amazed her – transitioned from posing in front of a camera to leading an entire generation. First, through pregnancy and early motherhood, then beyond. People adored her, and gradually Eve grew to love being adored. Ronnie clocked it by the way Eve incessantly watched the number of followers rise from hundreds to thousands to hundreds of thousands in what still feels like the blink of an eye. But it became like an addiction, an obsession, a drug, a tangible way for Eve to finally feel accepted.

Online, she spoke like a pro. Ronnie put it down to her posh Dalkey upbringing, her private education. In interviews, she'd come across as wildly confident yet humble, generous, funny, smart. She poked fun at herself. She was driven, willing to share – passionate about providing guidance in fashion, parenting, make-up … life.

Eve became every woman's best friend but, unlike your actual best friend, she was happy for you to imitate her, wear exactly what she wore, be who she was. She even encouraged it – offered discount codes to assist. Ronnie was on the money when she told Eve that people craved direction – being told what to buy, where to socialise, have their hair done, what washing detergent smells best. Eve was the canary in the mine, eradicating the hassle of buying jeans online to discover that the waist began at your armpits or that the sizing was ideal for your ten-year-old son. Most were grateful. Most took it with a pinch of salt.

As her audience grew, some turned against Eve when she reached a certain level. When Ronnie noticed, she was flabbergasted at the hatred Eve could incite in some. In one way, it was no different to any other type of fame except that people had a way to connect directly to Eve. Just as she found her voice, so too did her followers and what they had to say wasn't always positive. Perhaps Ronnie should have been more honest with Eve from the start, but she'd wanted to protect her. That's why she began deleting comments and accounts. The reason she continued doing it was to protect herself.

Standing suddenly, Ronnie walks towards the drinks trolley, pours herself a measure of brandy from a crystal decanter into an equally decorative glass, and knocks it back. Her body vibrates. Aside from the odd one, Ronnie isn't a drinker. Even in college, she never liked the feeling of anything that altered perception. It's why her memories remain unblemished. Ronnie remembers everything, even what she'd like to forget. Lifting the decanter again, she slops another measure into the glass and skulls it, once again shivering on impact. Tonight, she wants to forget. Tonight, she wants to be just like Eve.

She sits back down, cradling the now empty glass as a thought scurries through her mind. She'd meant it earlier when she told Eve she should have listened about the online trolling. Perhaps if she had, things would be different now. Two years ago, when she'd finally read Eve's proposal for the Unfollow Me campaign, Eve had surprised her once more.

###

The internet has become a frightening place. I'm devastated to say that social media has only made it worse. It allows disgruntled bullies to have their say. It allows misfits and oddballs of the world to lurk in the dark corners of an alternate Universe – one that has the power to edge its way into reality where it can hurt people and destroy lives. It's given people a place to be hateful, racist, homophobic without accountability. I still believe that social media can be a safe place. I want to fight to make it that way by lobbying to make verified I.D a legal requirement for opening a social media account and, in doing so, prevent harmful activity and allow traceability if an offence occurs. I want to encourage people to follow only those who bring them joy. To do this, I'm asking people, if you don't like what you see, to please be kind and #unfollowme.

###

Ronnie had read it, then immediately pressed delete. It was genius, but Eve could never know that. Pursuing it would rocket Eve's profile. It would also elevate Ronnie's, but she couldn't risk it. Not when she had been targeted too. Ronnie lied to Eve today countless times but, most significant of all, she'd failed to tell Eve about the typed notes she'd received to her office, also from an old friend from college. It was nothing compared to what Eve had been through, but it had been enough to stop her in her tracks. Then came the postcards.

Eve wasn't the only one receiving scenic pictures with juvenile sketches on the back. Ronnie had too.

Whoever was doing it knew something but, by the look of it, they had their facts wrong, and Ronnie certainly wasn't going to correct them. It's why she decided not to contact Eve after they argued, why she allowed her to walk away so easily … because she, too, had been terrified.

Ronnie leans over suddenly as if she's going to be sick. She takes a few breaths, swallowing the sensation of rising bile. Standing once more, she heads towards the door. As she passes, she throws the glass she's holding into the kitchen sink, barely flinching when it smashes.

In the bedroom, she removes her phone from her pocket, throws it on the bed, and then strips haphazardly. Naked, she walks to the bathroom and runs the shower. She steps in quickly, immersing herself before the water has a chance to heat. Gasping, she allows it to swallow her until all she can hear is growling, rushing water surging in her ears. Suddenly unable to breathe, she reaches up and pushes the showerhead away, then turns so that the water runs down her back. It takes her a moment to realise that tears are streaming down her face. The truth of what she did permanently residing in the base of her throat. It releases now in the form of a sob.

Switching off the water, she steps out onto the tiled floor and stands shivering, trembling with fear and adrenaline. It feels familiar, like shock. *What the fuck happened back in college?* The words reverberate as Ronnie wraps a towel around herself then covers it with a bathrobe to get warm. What a privilege it must be not to be able to remember.

Walking to her room, she lies back on the bed, moving her mind in another direction, replaying today from the start. Back at the restaurant, she considers how quickly Eve brought up the photo of her and Conor in the alleyway. Back then, with everything else going on, the trolls, the Unfollow Me debacle, the photo seemed like the least of her worries. In light of everything else, it felt insignificant.

But what if it isn't? Even though they'd been barely speaking, Eve had still told Ronnie she was planning to meet Conor. The idea had petrified Ronnie but, intrigued, she'd facilitated the reunion. When Eve stormed into her office the following day to show her the photo, Ronnie was more concerned by what Conor had wanted with Eve than a photograph of them snogging in an alleyway.

For Ronnie, the photo almost felt like a blessing, a way that would naturally prevent Eve from seeing Conor again. She almost wished she'd had something to do with it, but she hadn't. She still has no idea where it came from. After Eve left, Ronnie's I.T. manager had investigated it. From what he could tell, there'd been no security breach on Ronnie's phone. Revealing this to Eve, at the time, would only have implicated her more, so she'd kept the information to herself. Still, he'd told her, hackers often find a way. It happened all the time.

Ronnie forces her mind to slow. As it does, it flits to Conor. Was it Conor who'd been sending the notes and postcards? Had he got someone to tail Eve? Had he been trying to frighten Eve into his arms? Ronnie is still shocked that he and Eve continued to see each other after that night. She'd had to admit to Eve that it was she who'd told Conor to leave after college. Even more surprising was that Conor hadn't taken the chance to divulge more. Then again, he had as much to hide as them all. Was that why he'd come back – to find out what Eve knew? To see if Ronnie had ever told her more?

Ronnie narrows her eyes. Indeed, if Conor had come to revisit the past, wouldn't he have sought her out rather than Eve? That said, she'd warned him in no uncertain terms that if he ever came within breathing distance of her again, he'd be sorry. And why would Conor send Eve messages telling her to end it with himself? Perhaps to pin the stalking on Ronnie? After all this time, was it possible he still wanted Eve?

Something else that strikes Ronnie as odd is how the stalking ceased as soon as Eve left Dublin. Working backwards, Ronnie also stopped receiving notes or postcards at that same time. What if it had nothing to do with Eve fleeing Dublin but everything to do with Conor leaving for London? What if it was all about Conor and Eve's affair?

Ronnie bolts upright as the idea strikes. Grabbing her phone, she holds it to her face, unlocks it, opens Instagram, types a name, and clicks search. Her mouth falls open in shock. How hadn't she thought of it before now? It's the only valid explanation, so evident that Ronnie starts to laugh. It also makes sense that the person who orchestrated and posted that photo is connected to everything that happened afterwards – a person who wanted Eve all to themselves.

Renewed energy courses her veins, followed by a sudden rush of hope. It's something she hasn't experienced in a while. She stands, moves to the side of the bed and pulls open the drawer of her bedside locker. Reaching inside, she removes a jiffy envelope and empties the contents onto the bed. Scraps of paper and postcards tumble out. Frenziedly, she reads the printed notes.

You know what Eve did. Do the right thing.
It's time for justice.
The truth will out.
Eve will pay.
It's time for Eve to take the fall.

A smile tickles Ronnie's lips. How different they now sound: somewhat ridiculous in place of menacing. It changes everything. She swipes the picturesque postcards off the bed with her free hand, watching them scatter on the floor. They land face-up except for one.

Ronnie stands over the drawing of the red dress. For an instant, rage swells, but she expels it, laughing instead. She's safe.

Initially, the documentary had been a way for Ronnie to make enough money to disappear if she needed to, but suddenly she had a better idea. Perhaps it was time for a college reunion. Poor Eve. All that consternation and she'd never been at risk at all. Neither had Ronnie, for that matter.

Along with everything Eve had told her yesterday, Ronnie can prove it with a single phone call. She has three crucial questions to ask the lucky recipient. Then, Eve can go back to fretting that no one ever finds out the two things she fell in love with in college, her two biggest weaknesses: Conor Malone and every drug known to man. Her addiction to both is why she can't recall what happened at the end of college and what she was involved in. One thing is for sure, Eve wouldn't be sound asleep right now if she knew. She'd never sleep again.

CHAPTER FIFTEEN

#thefear #coke #molly #benzos #druggie #high #low
#crazygenes #panic #relapse #anxiety #guesswhoisback

@beli'EVE
Public Figure
Mama. Wife. Model. Content Creator. Collabs. Beauty. Fashion
Interiors.

5,698	1.1M	212
Posts	Followers	Following

When I open my eyes on Friday morning, I don't know where I am.
The paranoid sensation grips fiercely until I remember. I take a breath,
reminding myself that I'm in a hotel room alone. It's seconds, but the
familiar feeling hits like a punch in the gut. Back in college, it would
have been Conor or Ronnie who'd bolster me through the fear of
irrational thoughts and overly sensitive emotions that often lingered
for days. I'd ask over and over what happened, who saw, what I did.

I exhale.

I'm not that person anymore. No one knows about her. I'm here,
I'm safe, and Ronnie is on my side again. I don't need to be afraid.
The realisation takes a moment to settle. I sit up, instinctively reach
for my phone, and open Instagram. As expected, the photos from

yesterday are already on *goss.ie* and several other sites. Using my thumb and forefinger, I enlarge the image to examine myself. No one would guess that inside I was trembling with fear. I scan the article accompanying the picture, filled with hints that the rumours of an upcoming documentary must be true. At the bottom, there's a photo of Ronnie and me, clinking champagne flutes in the restaurant and grinning at each other. Without hesitating, I share the article links to my Instagram stories, making sure I tag *@BrownThomas* Department store as promised. Then I post the picture to my grid, typing the caption: **The rumours are true. Stay tuned for more. TV, here I come!** I want to be the first to confirm the news to my followers. Within seconds, there are a string of congratulatory comments. Then, I check my messages.

Before going asleep, I'd texted Dex again to say that Ronnie had sworn that she'd had nothing to do with him winning the Gallagher Group contract, and she'd been doing him a favour by mentioning his name on the news. I'd received a terse response: **If you ever come home, you can remind me to send her a thank-you note.**

I tap out a message now, telling Dex that I miss him and the kids and that I'll be home this morning. He reads it immediately but doesn't respond. Disappointed, I drop the phone and lie back. I may as well enjoy the few moments of peace before I commence my journey back to Wicklow and what awaits me there.

Closing my eyes, I sigh. For once, I'd slept soundly, possibly aided by blackout blinds and heavy drapes. But primarily because, at last, I'd exhaled after holding my breath for a very long time. Yesterday hadn't been easy, but it had been necessary.

Not only did we speak about everything that had happened in recent years, but the past had reared its head. I wince, recollecting. Talking about my dependency and the shame of where it ultimately led isn't something I often do. If it was, I'd never get through each day. I'd buried it years before, left it behind in Annaford with Aunt Lily as its keeper while I went to New York to try and move on. Yesterday, it inched its way out after I'd admitted to using Faye as an excuse to get out of Dublin. Today, before returning to my life, I'll tuck it away once more, but I let myself go there now – to remember so that I'll never forget again.

"It was my fault," I confessed to Ronnie. "I was so involved with myself, with everything … I took my eye off the ball with Faye. She was suffering."

"Suffering?" Ronnie pushed.

I closed my eyes, struggling with the words. "I should have seen what was happening, especially with my own history." I paused. "She was self-harming, cutting herself." I opened my eyes to her reaction.

"Faye? Oh my God! How? Why?" She looked shocked.

I shook my head, thinking of it. "I walked in on her one day in her room. She was using a blade on her thigh." My head falls back to prevent fresh tears. Then the words gushed. "She tried to deny it but I could see the scars. I made her show me, and she did." I looked at Ronnie again, splaying my hands. "She just showed them to me like … like she was proud of them." A whimper escaped my lips. "She kept telling me they were nothing, but they weren't nothing, Ronnie."

Neither of us said anything for a moment.

"That's not all," I said. "She'd lost weight, *a lot* of weight. She was standing in front of me, skin and bone, blood running down her leg, cuts everywhere, and I'd missed it." My voice rose. "I missed everything. There'd been stuff online about her, on Jabber.ie – mean

174

spiteful things about her being overweight, about me not feeding my children properly. She must have seen them. It's all I can think of –"

"What?" Ronnie face altered. "When?"

"It was after we fell out."

Ronnie screwed her lips together. "If I'd known, I'd have done something."

I tilted my head sarcastically. "You mean like launch a campaign to stop it. Like you did for me?"

Ronnie flinched. "*Touché*. But I'd have ... I don't know ... helped. Spoken to Faye. Something." Ronnie glanced at her feet. "You should have come to me."

I nodded sadly. "Things were so off between us that I couldn't ask for your help. I was still seeing Conor. I didn't want the judgement. I was angry with you ... myself. All the other stuff was going on ... the stalking and I ... oh God, I was sinking ..." I trailed off before admitting, "I almost slipped up."

"What do you mean?" Ronnie's eye's shot up as my face contorted.

"I asked Conor if he could get me something."

Ronnie squeezed her eyes shut like she was in pain.

"I just needed to feel ... nothing."

Asking him had made my stomach swirl in the same way it had in college, where adrenaline would fizz until he'd produce what I craved – coke, molly, benzos, weed; I wasn't fussy. Sometimes it would be just one. Other times, a specific formula to make it endure – cocaine followed by ecstasy. By the time one wore off, the other would take effect. And I'd become Me. The Me that I longed to be – in love with everyone and everything, free from the debilitating anxiety that I'd borne since my early teens – liberated from crippling social fear, nerves, feeling like the ground was undulating beneath my feet.

As time went on, the remedy became more complex. The high

might be followed with a spliff to make coming down easier. The next day, I'd need Benzodiazepine to take the edge off the crash. It was often accompanied by panic far more extreme than the reason I'd become reliant on taking something in the first place.

This was my college experience – the reason I didn't like to speak about it. Why I clammed up when anyone ever mentioned it was because I'd been *that* person – the one with the drug problem. The one who couldn't say no. The one who'd made the type of memories she could barely remember in place of ones that most people chose not to forget.

Of course, it hadn't started that way, but then it never does. It began out of curiosity. Months after we moved in together, I'd walked into the kitchen of our musty little house to see Ronnie and Conor standing so close that at first I thought something was going on between them. I'd freaked out, accusing them of all sorts until they'd had no choice but to tell me that they'd acquired a little something extra for a party that night. They didn't think I'd be into it, they said. Even now, Ronnie's reaction, the way she'd glared at Conor, signalling him to say no, is still etched into my mind as if she didn't think I could handle it. In response, I'd stuck out my bottom lip, pouting Lolita-like until Conor agreed to let me join in. Then I'd thrown a defiant look at Ronnie to say that I'd won.

The prize was addiction.

It took maybe a year before Conor and I started mixing, testing to see what gave us the longest rush, the ultimate high on nights out. We were good at it, too, except that he could stop when he wanted, I couldn't. In my eyes, I didn't need to stop. I'd never felt so in control. I had friends. The social awkwardness disappeared. I was living again. I soon figured out why Conor was popular on campus and how there was a constant supply at our fingertips. He swore me to secrecy the night I discovered his stash at the back of the wardrobe. I wasn't to tell Ronnie. It was a short-term thing, he said. A way for him to pay his way through college. Not that Ronnie would be interested anyway. She never used again after that first time. She didn't like not feeling like herself. Instead, she watched out for me, took care of me, made sure that nothing bad happened.

Somehow, I made it to my final year before it became unmanageable. I stopped attending classes, appearing on campus, leaving the house. My only concern was my next hit. By then, even my mother had established what I was up to. Indeed, I made it evident on the last occasion I visited. Instead of her ordering me to move home, forcing me to stop, it ended with her calling me every name under the sun and telling me to never darken her door again. I sometimes wonder if what I did when I was there was my way of once again asking for help. I suppose I'll never know.

Then I made another discovery. That time, there was no option but to stop. It was far too dangerous to continue. Miraculously, I stopped ... just like that.

I made it through several months before something happened that once again made me not what to feel anything, and I caved ... just like that. Only, I went much too far. I pushed too hard. The consequences of that moment have been with me my entire life. Even after Lily nursed me back to life in her makeshift rehabilitation programme. Even after I went to New York and found fame tumbling off an album cover. Even after I met Dex, got pregnant, had our children, it still echoed deep inside, so loud that I thought I'd never use again until I found myself in my late thirties pleading with my ex-drug-dealer boyfriend for a bump of coke.

###

"He said no," I confirmed to a concerned Ronnie. "I told you he's changed. He doesn't even drink or smoke. Not since we first broke up. It was a low point, but I had to go there to pull myself back together. My family needed me, not just Faye, but she scared me most of all. I kept thinking she'd get carried away – that I'd walk into her room one morning and find her ..." I couldn't finish. Pausing, I dragged my hands down my face, pulling the skin with them. "I couldn't risk her turning out like me with my stupid, weak, crazy genes. I had to do something." My voice wobbled. "The thing is, when I saw what she was doing, I understood it." I stared straight ahead. "She was doing what I'd done to myself. Only I'd done it with drugs, but it was the same thing. She was numbing herself." I growled suddenly with frustration. "But she wouldn't tell me why. I pushed to see if she'd read those horrible things online. I thought she was being bullied at school. She kept saying it was nothing."

"But isn't that how it is sometimes? There's no one reason. It's something inside you. Some people are just made that way."

I nodded. I was one of those people.

"Do you think she picked up on something that was going on with you?" Ronnie asked.

"Maybe," I shrugged. "Either way, it was my fault."

I was fourteen when terrifying, debilitating sensations took over my life, making it seem impossible. At school, the classroom would feel like it was moving, my actions would become jerky. I was hyperaware of my body, my breathing, the blood in my veins, my pulse, my surroundings. My mind raced, my thoughts scattered. Everything buzzed. It would be that way until I'd get home. There, I'd feel exhausted from trying to hold it together all day. I started getting headaches, pains in my neck. I didn't want to leave the house. I drifted from friends. I was so petrified that I went to Mum. I tried to explain

178

what she must have encountered countless times as a woman and a doctor. She told me that life was a case of getting up, getting dressed and getting on with it. Her big solution was not to give "it" any power. She achieved this by ignoring it while I suffered in silence. I managed by becoming still, aloof even, while inside I was screaming. Then I found a new way of dealing with it at college. I fed it drugs.

"But you got her help?" Ronnie pressed.

I nodded. "I ended it with Conor, refocused, took Faye to therapy," I recapped woodenly. "Then I came to ask you to release me from the business. Then we left Dublin."

Ronnie moved her eyes side to side in thought. "You were so distant that day, so matter of fact. It makes sense now that I know you thought it was me harassing you. Christ, Eve!" she shook her head. "Is Faye okay now?"

I smiled. "Since moving away, starting again, Faye is better than ever." I repeat Joanne's words from last Saturday when we had coffee in the village. "Whatever was disturbing her thoughts is gone. And Milo is great too. I haven't even had a chance to tell you what happened with him at school but I will –"

"You did the right thing, Eve. I see that now. You did what you needed to do as a mother. They're lucky to have you. Far luckier than you were with your own mother." She raised an eyebrow. "You need to forgive yourself, Eve, for the past too." Ronnie looked at me pointedly. "What happened that time in college was … an accident."

It was the first time either of us had acknowledged my relapse in many years. The mere mention drained my mind of everything else I'd been about to tell Ronnie. Namely, what happened with Milo towards the end of our time in Dublin. How I'd almost endured every parent's worst nightmare. Instead, I'd begun to cry, momentarily permitting the pent-up horror to flow, freshly mixed with tears of regret.

I think of it now, allowing my mind to process everything that happened yesterday. I'm beginning to think Ronnie is right about what she'd said before she left – that all the madness had been conducted by some infatuated person. I almost smile – the idea is comforting compared to what I'd initially believed.

"It's over," Ronnie had repeated several times last night. The relief hits me now. The postcards were hardly surprising considering the whole world knows that I'm the girl in the red dress. The notes, too, could be read a thousand ways. Someone had been watching me, that was for sure. Someone had been in my house, but they didn't actually hurt me. They went away, and now my secrets feel safe again. No one, not Dex or my children or the public, ever need to know about that branch of my life.

Just like Ronnie said, I was a target because of my job. The amount I'd shared put me at risk – where I lived, shopped, the car I drove, where I was going out for dinner, where I got petrol, who my doctor was, where I went for coffee, the time of my next hairdresser appointment … where my kids went to school. I let whoever it was see. That was my fault, but I've learned from my mistakes just like I did before.

As I prepare to pack my history away again, my intentions are bypassed by a text: **The photos from yesterday caused a stir. Stay where you are. I've had the best idea. Keep an open mind. I'll be there by noon. We're back! Ronnie x**

Before I can stop it, adrenaline courses my veins like ice. Nervous energy builds, spinning fast to break free. For two years, I've yearned for an outlet – somewhere to place the chaos of my mind, a greater purpose. As I push the covers back, I experience a high. It feels just like old times and, oh God, it's good.

CHAPTER SIXTEEN

#lifeisarollercoaster #guilttrip #gifted #fallintooblivion
#dalailama

- -

@beli'EVE
Public Figure
Mama. Wife. Model. Content Creator. Collabs. Beauty. Fashion
Interiors.

- -

5,698	1.3M	212
Posts	Followers	Following

The high dissipates rapidly after I run to shower and dress, only to
remember that I have nothing to wear but suede shorts, pink thigh-
high boots and borderline itchy mohair knit. With three hours still to
wait, I take the bull by the horns and telephone Dex.

"You're alive." He answers on the second ring with a statement,
not a question.

I wince. "Don't be like that. You knew where I was. There was a
lot to go through."

"Like?"

"Like the past few years and what happened before that."

"And?" He sounds automated.

"And we resolved a lot." I'm not sure what else to say, especially when there's so much I haven't told him. "There were misunderstandings on both our parts, and we sorted them. Agreed to disagree in some cases. Put the past behind us." I grimace. "Move on. We're on an even keel." I finish nodding, impressed by my wholly ambiguous synopsis.

"And where's the boat destined for now?" he asks sarcastically. "Are you going to try and break Asia?"

"Nothing has changed, Dex." I roll my eyes. "My plan is still exactly the same. I'm doing the documentary, and then I'm out. By the end of June, there'll be no more @beli'EVE. It'll just be you and me, Faye and Milo, our lovely house, your business – the dream. Us." I nod again at my diplomacy. Indeed, there's nothing he can say to that.

Silence.

Eventually, he asks, "And will that honestly be enough for you?"

I assess his tone. Is he implying something more? Is he referring to my affair with Conor? *Does he know?* Even after all this time, the fear of being found out is ever-present. Even though I'd got away with it, most days it sits inside like lead alongside everything else I've hidden from Dex since we met. Only that I'm used to being a master of concealment, I might have buckled under the pressure long ago.

"What's that supposed to mean?" I ask tentatively.

"Well, it wasn't enough before. Was it? Or maybe it was me who wasn't enough," he adds bitterly.

My mouth momentarily loses all moisture, making it impossible to respond. I hold my breath, waiting for him to fill the silence.

"When you tried to quit before, it was only a couple of months before you dived straight back in," he continues.

In relief, I hold the phone away and exhale, practically panting for air. He's talking about my work. Gingerly, I put the phone back to my ear.

"It's like some form of … I don't know … drug. Like you can't get enough. Is that it?"

He's skating close to the bone. If I thought my stomach couldn't plummet any further, it does.

"It's a thing, you know, social media addiction. I looked it up. It's usually teenagers but, to be honest, Eve, I'm beginning to think that –"

"It's my job, Dex." I groan inwardly. "There's a big difference. Contrary to what you might think, I'm not sitting at home staring at my phone all day, hypnotised by the blue lights, competing with my peers, for Christ's sake. God, you never got it, did you? You just don't get it. If you could just try to understand –"

He gives a short laugh. "You know what, I used to get it. I completely understood, but then I saw what happened back in Dublin."

I'm grateful he can't see my face. This call feels like a roller-coaster ride – but not a fun one.

"You totally changed when you discovered those haters. You couldn't cope," he says. "You shut us all out. I mean, I could understand it with me. Our marriage was in the shits," his voice rises, "*but the kids?*"

I can picture him pacing his workshop, combing his hair back, gripping it with his fingers.

"*Shit,*" he exclaims, angry with himself for losing his temper. It doesn't happen often. This is the second time in a matter of days.

"I'm sorry," I whisper delicately. "A lot was going on. I was –"

"What, Eve? What were you?" His voice is quiet too. "Because I'd really like to know. I was afraid to ask back then, but now I want to know why you vanished from our marriage all those years. Even when you were with me physically, you weren't actually there. You couldn't see it, could you?"

"See what?"

"You were so obsessed with work, getting bigger and bigger like

183

you had something to prove. Nothing was enough. You know what I settled on in the end."

My eyes fill with tears before he even continues.

"That I just wasn't enough for you."

"No," I deny it. Guilt burns inside. "That's not it. You were. You are. I just … I was trying to support us. I wanted to give the kids a nice life, but it got too much. I lost my way for a while."

There's so much more to say, but I can't go there now. The moment passed the day I met him in New York. I should have told him then what he was dealing with – revealed the void in my heart that I knew nothing could ever fill. At least he could have decided for himself if he wanted to try.

"You're all I want now," I muster.

"Now?"

"That's not what I mean. I could see that I needed to change. When Faye was sick, I knew …" I trail off.

"Do you ever wonder what Faye told the Dr Robin or even Joanne for that matter?" His voice is low, gravelly.

I'm about to say that I wonder the same every single day when he announces my greatest fear for me.

"She must have spoken about you," he says cruelly. "She must have said that you were more interested in telling some woman you've never met where you got your sweater or what shade of fake tan you use or how you managed to juggle motherhood with world domination." He pauses. "Only you weren't juggling it. *I was.* You checked out." He's out of breath.

I sag into the chair, where I sit in stunned disbelief.

Dex blames me too. All this time, he must have been harbouring the condemnation. Worse still, he's right. I had checked out. It dawns on me that I've got away with nothing. The lies haven't worked. I've hurt my family – Conor, Ronnie, Mum, myself. I feel so incredibly stuck with nothing left to lose that I consider telling Dex everything, releasing myself by relaying everything about college, the demons Conor left me to deal with alone, the shame of my addiction, the constant fear I live with of slipping up, people finding out.

Would he understand? Would it help him accept what drives me and what I'm afraid of? If he knew the truth, was there a chance he'd forgive my affair? He'd said it himself. Our marriage had been in trouble. If I admitted to cheating, I could tell him about the stalking, the threats – make him see why I'd been so preoccupied, how I'd missed what was happening with Faye.

"I shouldn't have said that." His voice shatters my thoughts. He hesitates. "That was petty. I was angry you didn't come home last night. I thought it was happening again."

"You thought what was happening again?" My blood runs cold. Is this my chance to confess?

Dex clears his throat. "I thought as soon as you met Ronnie that you'd get sucked in again. That you'd be gone. Have you seen the papers?"

Although he can't see me, I shake my head.

"The story is all over them. You're everywhere, Eve. Everywhere but here. We don't want to lose you again."

I take a breath, ready to speak the truth, but it doesn't emerge. Instead, I say, "No one is losing me, and I don't care what the papers say. Dex, I understand why you're angry. Maybe we need to sit down, talk it all out, finally lay it to rest. The past few years have been pretty turbulent. Maybe we're only processing everything now, but we will sort it, Dex, I swear. A lot of what you said is right. There's –"

"I need to say something," he interrupts. His voice is more gentle. "Please."

I frown anxiously. "Okay."

"I've always had this weird feeling, Eve, even from the very start … that here's something … I dunno … like you have something you want to tell me but can't."

I swallow hard.

"Is there?" he asks. "Cos you can tell me, Eve. No matter what it is, you can tell me."

The words balance precariously on the tip of my tongue. I swallow them, then squeeze my eyes shut. I can't do it. "There's nothing." I can't revisit what I've only put away again minutes before. It's too painful. Instead, I compromise. "I mean, other than what I told you about my anxiety in school and college." I pause. "I was afraid Faye would struggle like I did. It took a lot to get over it, and it's been on my mind lately." I force a laugh. "Look at me, anxious about being anxious."

"Maybe you should go and talk to someone. I think there may be things you haven't dealt with. It might help. We could find someone together. Joanne could suggest someone."

It's not a bad idea, but not right now. I brush it off. "As soon as this is over, Dex, I'll have all the time in the world to deal with everything. I'll do whatever you want, I swear. Just, please, be behind me with this one last thing. I want to do this documentary."

There's a loud exhale at the end of the line.

"I was always behind you. You just never turned around."

"I'm turning now," I whisper.

"Are you on your way home?"

"I'll be later than I thought." I squirm, realising how it must sound. "Ronnie wanted me to hang on for the day. She's had some new, probably mad idea that she wants to run past me before I leave so I'll be home before the kids are home from school. We'll have dinner. Watch a movie." I picture him rolling his eyes. "Actually, I was going to ask Ronnie out to the house next week if that's okay."

"It's fine." Any warmth that had fleetingly returned has already vanished.

"It's just, you know ... we're going to be working with each other again, short term of course, but we're still friends, and she's still Faye's godmother, so I still –" Dex says something I miss amongst my babbling. "What's that?"

"Faye was all over the place this morning."

My head snaps up, alert. "Why?"

"I don't know."

"Is she okay?" Uneasiness swells.

"She's fine."

"Are you sure? What happened?"

"Ah, it was nothing. She was late coming downstairs, which meant the day got off to a bad start. She had a face like thunder when she finally did and then forget some permission slip."

"For what?"

"Some talk in school. I had to go in and sign a new one ... It was just a really messy morning."

"What talk was it?" I couldn't even remember signing a permission slip, but I've been so distracted again lately.

"Internet safety of something. Waste of time at her age."

"Why do you say that?"

"It doesn't matter how safe you think you are sometimes. It's not hard to get in contact with people. You can find just about anything on the internet. There's always a way – always a trail."

After he hangs up, I sit staring at the wall. Oddly, what he'd said about the internet plays on my mind. Dex is right. Nowadays, we forge a path online, even without realising it, often leading straight to our front door. We give out our email address, phone number, credit card details at the drop of a hat. We leave clues of our whereabouts and our habits on social media for the world to see. I understand this part only too well. We have websites with our photographs, our contact details ... we are reachable ... all the time. And even though we do it ourselves, we warn our children what not to post online, who not to befriend. We live in fear that teenagers' blunders will linger in the cloud for the rest of their days. I suppose in that way, I've been lucky. My mistakes took place before we became traceable.

I sit reasoning that somewhere over the last few years, unbeknownst to myself, I must have dropped hints or clues as to my whereabouts, my movements, my life. Despite being vigilant, I had to have slipped up somewhere. If my stalker was still out there, still watching, they'd have been found me by now. If they wanted to, like Dex said, there's always a way. I feel a weight lift from my chest, thinking of it. Instead of obsessing over the icy patches of the phone call with Dex, I park it, take a shower, and order room service and the newspapers. Wearing the hotel dressing gown, I pore over the photos featured from yesterday. Despite telling Dex that I didn't care what the papers said, I was elated by the accompanying headlines.

—IRELAND'S HOME-GROWN BEAUTY, TOP MODEL TURNED MEDIA STAR, EVE KELLY, SET FOR NETFLIX
—AHEAD OF HER TIME – EVE WILL MAKE YOU BELIEVE ANYTHING IS POSSIBLE
—EVE BREAKS HER BREAK. SHE'S BACK!

There's only one that jolts me. Something about me keeping my private life private no more and finally telling all. Mum will be disgusted with that one. I shake my head, muttering back, "Eve tells some, not all."

Afterwards, I set about posting some fashion "inspo" pictures to my pages. It's essential to have a certain amount of stories per day and, because of yesterday, I'm behind. I'm so engrossed that I barely hear the knock on the door. It's now well after midday.

"You're late," I say as I open the door to Ronnie, who is laden with bags, grinning broadly, sunglasses up on her head, make-up perfect. She looks more refreshed than me.

"What have you been doing all morning?" She saunters inside, looks around, nods at the papers next to a plate of half-eaten poached eggs on the round breakfast table. "You're not even dressed!" She tuts at my now air-dried fuzzy hair and dressing gown.

"I was resting for what lies ahead. Posting some fashion pics."

Ronnie makes a face. "Yes, I was watching. All excruciatingly boring if you ask me." She jabs at the papers on the table. "I think today's coverage proves that people want to see Eve out and about in all her glory."

"Maybe," I say.

As Ronnie sets down a plethora of instantly recognisable grey-and-white-striped department-store bags onto the sofa, I watch with interest.

"It won't change that in a few months I'll be falling off the radar into oblivion. Never to be seen again."

Ronnie raises her eyebrows. "So you keep saying but, before you start making jam, keeping bees and sea-swimming, I think we should pull out all the stops. One final all-singing, all-dancing production. Go out big, bigger than ever. We go out like we came in." She winks and gestures at the bags on the sofa. "Some new things for you to play with – a demonstration of how you've been sorely missed."

I can't help myself: my eyes light up.

"Brown Thomas have offered you some looks for the coming weeks. They also want to supply your wardrobe for the duration of the shoot and the promo tour. #gifted," Ronnie says, making inverted commas with her fingers.

"Promo tour?" I ask.

"Didn't you read the small print? That's part of the deal, obviously. Before and after the shoot, you'll be everywhere." She echoes Dex's earlier words.

"And then nowhere," I finish. I must sound deflated.

Ronnie flops into a chair and laughs. "You're not dying, Eve. You don't have to fall off the planet if you don't want to. In fact, if you want, this could be the start of something all over again. Something new, bigger." Ronnie waits for her words to sink in before adding, "I hardly slept last night thinking about everything we discussed. I had a brainwave."

Her eyes are dancing. I've seen this same chirpiness before.

"Should I be nervous?" I ask suspiciously.

"I'll tell you all about it soon but, first, I made a really important phone call this morning.

"Who did you call? The Dalai Lama?"

Ronnie shakes her head, looking smug. "No. I phoned Faye."

"Faye?" I repeat, taken aback.

Ronnie nods. "Don't look so shocked. She is my goddaughter. I wanted to hear her voice after what you told me last night. Make sure she's okay."

I jut out my chin, trying to decipher if Ronnie phoning Faye is strange.

"You don't mind, do you?" Ronnie asks. "I didn't mean to overstep or anything."

"No. Not at all, I just … how was she?" I ask cautiously. Then I remember what Dex said earlier about Faye coming downstairs this morning in foul form. "When was this?"

"Before she left for school," Ronnie confirms. "And she was great. My God!" Ronnie's eyes twinkle. "So grown-up, confident, assured. What a difference a few years make. She was all pissed off about attending some talk at school when she could be studying. She seems really focused."

I instantly relax. So, that's what had been wrong with her. I nod in agreement. "She sure is. And yes … very confident," I smile, glancing down to pick some fluff off my dressing gown. "Sometimes scarily so." I laugh. "You wouldn't want to get in an argument with her. You wouldn't win."

Ronnie grins. "Oh, I can imagine. Except, I always win."

I glance up, suddenly sensing a change in tone, but she's smiling brightly.

"I'm looking forward to seeing her in person."

"Well, that might be sooner than you think if you like. Will you come out next week for a visit?"

"I'd love to. I'll text Faye later and let her know. We were saying we were going to meet up soon anyway."

Then I frown. "How did you get her number? She got a new one a while back."

Ronnie stands, pours a glass of water, and takes a drink. Her back is to me. "I found her on Instagram and messaged her. She sent it to me. It really was great to chat."

I sit forward, narrowing my eyes. "But Faye's not on Instagram anymore. She hates it. I made her come off everything around the time she wasn't so well, and she never went back."

Ronnie turns to me, shrugs again. "Maybe it's new."

I shake my head. Grabbing my phone off the table, I open Instagram and type Faye's name into the search. A few options appear. Although the private profile pictures are no bigger than the top of my thumb, I can indeed make out that one of them is my daughter. I press it, and it opens. I scan the titles at the top of the page. Posts: 19. Followers: 4,567. Following: 1,089. Aside from three words, the page is blank. *"User not found,"* I read aloud as I look up at Ronnie. "What does that mean? Why can't I see it?"

Ronnie sits back down, shifting uncomfortably in the chair, purposely averting her eyes.

"Ronnie?" I force her to look up. She doesn't have to answer before it dawns on me. "She blocked me, didn't she?"

Ronnie grimaces. "What do you expect? You're her mother. No one wants Mummy poking about on their social accounts. It's like reading their diary."

"Why? What's on there? Show me." I reach my hand out for her phone.

She shakes her head. "Eve! Believe me, there's nothing to see. Just pouty selfies in the school toilet with her equally pouty friends, and it's a private account, so it's safe. She's safe. Stop worrying. This is normal."

I stare straight ahead, feeling dejected.

"Imagine if your mum could see what you were up to in our day. She might have –"

"What, Ronnie? Saved me from addiction?" I challenge, wild-eyed. "Does Faye have something to hide? Is she up to something?"

"No!" Ronnie laughs. "Don't make a thing out of this, Eve. It's normal. Faye has a right to privacy."

She sounds just like Dr Robin.

"But, honestly, Faye seems great," Ronnie assures. This time, thankfully, she sounds more like Joanne. "Faye is far more capable than you give her credit for, not to mention clever. Believe me, you have absolutely nothing to worry about when it comes to Faye. I can say that with utter certainty." She smiles reassuringly.

It's good news, but I still nod absently at the thought that I have a husband who unfollowed me, and a daughter who blocked me. At least I still have Milo.

"Now," Ronnie interrupts my thoughts, "before you get waylaid pining over your teenage daughter's social-media rejection, I want to tell you about my idea and remind you to keep an open mind."

"Yes. That's why I'm worried."

There's a pause before her mouth twitches into a smile. "I think we should revisit the Unfollow Me campaign as part of the documentary. I say we go for it this time. Talk about your experience. Your original proposal was great. I think handled correctly, it will help make some noise." Her face freezes in a wide grin.

Immediately, I shake my head. "Absolutely not. No way. I'm not doing it, Ronnie. No way." Of everything I thought she'd say, I never thought it would be this. "No," I say again for good measure. Not so long ago, it was all I'd wanted to hear, but it's too late now.

She puts her hands up to stop me. "Hear me out first. Think of the publicity. The interviews we can secure around the time the documentary launches. You have something to say, and people need to hear it. It's about timing, Eve. The timing wasn't right before, but it is now. Trolls aren't going away. In fact, it's getting worse for other people. This is –"

"First, Dex doesn't know about the stalking, remember?" My voice is flat as I interrupt. "I lied because I was cheating. Second, I don't like the idea of spinning it that way. What happened to me shouldn't be a way to get publicity. It affected me. It's not some joke. Besides, don't forget that no one cared when I talked about it before. The stalking started immediately afterwards. I'm not risking that again, Ronnie. It's too fresh. Anyway, how can I suddenly turn around and tell the world I was being stalked when my husband doesn't even know?"

Ronnie waves her hands. "You went about it wrong that time. You just started speaking about it. It should have been introduced properly. I know I wasn't there for you, and that's my stupidity, but I think now if we go about it the right way, things would be different. I'm telling you I was wrong, Eve."

I glare at her. Ronnie never admits she's wrong.

"And I've thought about the Dex thing. We can play down the stalking. Instead, we go after trolls. Dex knows about that part, right?"

I nod slowly.

"Being a victim to those comments is bad enough in itself. I get that now," Ronnie says.

"Why the change of heart?" I ask sceptically, looking toward the window.

"Listening to you yesterday, I got it, especially after hearing that they targeted Faye too. Eve, look at me!"

When I do, Ronnie looks sheepish, remorseful even.

"I think every so often, life as we know it gets thrown in a blender," she says. "You can either take it as a positive and reform another way, or you can stay a watery mess."

Though I make a face at her analogy, oddly I understand what she means. On more than one occasion, my life has ended up liquidised. Each time, I've managed to freeze it back together. Maybe I can do it again.

"And, quite frankly, I think it's a good campaign."

My chest swells with something I can't pinpoint. Before I get too carried away, another thought halts me. "Hang on, you're not suggesting that I talk about college, about the drugs, are you?" I shake my head again. "Because I can't, Ronnie. I don't want my children thinking of me that way. I'm not going there, ever again."

"No." She wags her finger. "That would be a PR nightmare, but what I am suggesting is that you open up about the other parts – the panic attacks, anxiety. I know how hard you fought to overcome it all. Feeling the way you did, after everything you'd been through, you still went to New York and became famous. You're strong, Eve."

"But New York or any of it wouldn't have happened without the other parts," I say.

"I know that, but we can alter it a little to tie in with Unfollow Me. You can say how the trolls played on your insecurities. That type of thing."

"So you want me to lie?" I don't like where this is going.

Ronnie is getting impatient. "No. I want you to do what you did with Dex – omit certain parts. Come on, Eve!" She throws her hands up. "You know how this works. Bend the truth some. It's still an important message. We just need to deliver it in a way that you can maintain some privacy."

Maybe she has a point.

"And think of it. You could be behind getting legislation passed, so people will be accountable for what they put out online, just like you said in your proposal. There'll be a way to tell who's behind fake accounts so that people aren't subjected to anonymous bullying."

I'm still not convinced.

"If you don't do it for me, do it for Faye or Milo," she says.

I hold her gaze. This time, her expression is filled with concern.

"And, remember, if it goes to plan, you might even get a chance to find out who was behind all those horrible comments about you … it might lead you to whoever was doing all those weird things. And I might get to discover who hacked my phone and posted that stupid bloody photo."

"What if they come back, Ronnie? What if it starts again?"

"It won't. I'm a hundred per cent certain."

Ronnie is transformed from the person I sat opposite yesterday in the restaurant. There, she'd seemed somewhat weakened, beaten down by the events of the last few years. Today, Ronnie's eyes glisten. She's excited, assured. It's contagious. Although I feel nervous about what she's suggesting, I'm excited too.

"I know a lot has happened, Eve," she says. "I do, and I know that you keep saying you're done with @beli'EVE, but I don't think we are, not yet, not by a long shot. After the documentary, I'd like us to work together again. Albeit with major changes, of course, but I think there's scope for us to go in other directions as partners." She gestures at the space between us. "I've missed you … and this. I think you have, too."

I press my lips together, not wanting to divulge straight away that I do miss it.

"There's something else. Open that bag." She points at the biggest one on the sofa next to us.

I stare at it with trepidation, wondering what else there could possibly be. Getting up, I remove a gift box, place it down and open the lid. Separating the tissue paper, I push it apart to reveal a swathe of crimson silk.

"What's this?" I ask, removing it from the package and shaking it open. Cautiously I appraise the full-length red gown, so light that it barely feels as if I'm holding anything at all. "Ronnie?"

"I had the idea last night." She stands and walks towards me. "It's coming up to the twentieth anniversary of the original photos – *the* photos. As part of the documentary, I'm going to suggest we recreate them."

My brow furrows. I'm astounded at her insensitivity.

I turn to stalk away, but she grabs my arm.

196

"Look at me," she orders. "It's been twenty years, Eve, and you're still here. Bigger and braver than ever before after everything you've overcome."

My shoulders heave, but I don't make a sound.

"Let yourself heal. Free yourself. For us all."

My eyes meet hers. "What do you mean for all of us?"

"I spoke to Conor."

"When?" I ask nervously.

"This morning. He said he'd do it if you will. He swore he's not going to come between you and Dex. He knows your relationship is over, but he agrees that there are things that need to be said between us all."

My stomach lurches.

"We need to sit down and get over our differences, just the three of us. If this documentary explores your past, then we all need to be singing off the same hymn sheet." Then she smiles brightly. "You know, just in case."

I nod slowly, considering her words.

"Then, even if you decide you still want to cut loose from me, then no hard feelings. I promise. We stay friends, and I revert to being Fairy Godmother to Faye." She places her hand on my shoulder. "I really did miss her. You know I was trying to remember when was the last time I saw her. It was the night I picked her up from school early, and she stayed the night with me. The night you were with —"

"Long time ago," I brush her off fast. With everything else I'm about to face, the last thing I need to be reminded of is how I'd asked Ronnie to take Faye for the night while Dex took Milo to football training and I went to meet my ex for dinner, ending up kissing him up an alleyway. Nor that I'd accused Ronnie of posting a photo of the episode as my daughter lay asleep in her spare room.

CHAPTER SEVENTEEN

#thescene #godfearingchristians #skeletons #dealmein
#guntomyhead #notagain

@beli'EVE
Public Figure
Mama. Wife. Model. Content Creator. Collabs. Beauty. Fashion
Interiors.

5,698	1.3M	212
Posts	Followers	Following

It's almost dark as I drive along the busy motorway from Dublin to
Wicklow on Friday evening. The entire time, I reflect on everything
that has happened in the last twenty-four hours and how I plan to
deal with it. I'm almost at the turn-off for Annaford when I reason
that I'm pondering what I should do instead of what I'd like to do.
Forced to answer with a gun to my head, I don't want to stop working
or retire @beli'EVE.

When Ronnie revealed her plans earlier, I'd felt excited despite
myself. It reminded me that while I feel safe in Wicklow, I'm also
somewhat inhibited – unable to fully spread my wings. As I come off
the motorway, rounding the bend to quieter roads, my mind drifts to
Conor. Much as I know seeing him again will hurt, tear open wounds

that never seem to heal, some things need to be said after our affair ended as abruptly as our first relationship. Until I address them, I suppose, I'll always wonder. Ironically, Dex telling me I should face the past, for me means facing Conor again.

#

After Ronnie dropped the bombshell about recreating the famous shoot, we'd spoken some more about our time at college. I'd highlighted my concerns that the documentary researchers might dig about into my earlier years, seek out people who knew me before I was famous – when I was into drugs. That was putting it mildly.

"All the more reason why the three of us need to have our story straight," Ronnie had agreed. "Line up our individual skeletons. Then we give people something else to think about, divert interest elsewhere." This was where revisiting the Unfollow Me campaign and divulging my mental health struggles came in. It would be enough "dirt" to satisfy the information-hungry crowd. I had to hand it to her. There was nothing Ronnie hadn't thought of.

"Everything will be fine, as long as we all stick to the same story, that we were clean-living, god-fearing Christians," she joked in a Southern accent. "Anyway, even if someone from college comes forward out of the blue, it's our word against theirs. There's no proof out there. The internet barely existed. Hospital records are confidential."

I blanched at the mention of the hospital. Ronnie was so busy talking, she didn't notice.

"No dodgy videos are circulating or photos from nights out hanging about on Facebook … it would be hearsay, and we simply deny it. All they'll remember is a confident girl who loved to party," she said brightly. "But we need to make sure that Conor's on board.

That we're all friends ... just in case."

"There's something I need to tell you about Conor," I volunteered suddenly. If we were laying out skeletons, Ronnie ought to be aware. Unless, of course, she already knew, which I strongly suspected she did.

Ronnie's eyes shot up from where she was tapping notes into her phone.

"Conor used to deal." I studied her as I said it, noticing her body stiffen.

There's a pregnant pause. "I knew," she admitted. "But I didn't think you did." She shook her head in repulsion. "To be honest, that whole scene terrified me. I didn't want to know anything about it."

There was little that terrified Ronnie.

"That way, if anyone ever asked, I'd be telling the truth when I said I knew nothing."

I nodded as my mind began to turn, reminding me of something I'd planned to raise with Ronnie. If things had ended up turning sour during our meeting, I'd been prepared to use what I knew as a threat. Sometime back, I'd concluded that Ronnie might have been involved in something during college that perhaps she shouldn't have been. I wasn't entirely sure what, but in trying to recall everything over the past few years, a memory had resurfaced. Near the end of college and shortly before Conor left for good, the Guards had called to our rented house to ask me some questions.

It was only a week or so after I'd relapsed, and I'd thought they'd come to ask me more about it. Before I'd gone downstairs to speak with them, Ronnie had pulled me aside on the landing and leaned in to whisper exactly what I should say. She'd been pretty specific, saying it related to drugs and Conor – something she'd heard and to follow the script which was essentially that I knew nothing. In an utter daze and still shook after the worst trip of my life, I'd complied. The guards had asked what they needed to, I'd answered, they'd nodded, left, and I never heard from them again. Ronnie must think I don't remember. It's hardly surprising since there was so much more that I already couldn't recall from that time.

I was about to raise it when Ronnie spoke.

"I didn't want you doing drugs in the first place, let alone have you wrapped up in the scene. There was a constant supply at Conor's fingertips, and you didn't stand a chance of staying clean around him." Her voice dropped a degree. "I confronted him about it before he left for good. He knew he was bad for you too, Eve. That's why he didn't put up much of a fight about going. I also think someone tipped off the Guards about him. It was getting risky, and I didn't want either of you to get caught."

I nodded. Maybe I'd been wrong about Ronnie being involved in something shifty. "But what if a supplier or someone who used to buy off Conor link him to me?" I asked instead.

Ronnie cut me off, smirking. "Seriously? Who in their right mind will come forward to say they sold or bought drugs from your ex-fella. They'd only be tarnishing their now middle-aged name. I think you're safe." She laughed.

"But they wouldn't have to say they bought them – just that they knew what he was doing." I wasn't convinced.

"Nah." Ronnie shook her head in earnest. "The drug scene in college was a closed one. Unless you were using, you probably wouldn't have even known it existed. Remember, there were far more people chugging pints of Bulmers, barfing them back out their nose, than doing drugs. Besides, if someone was going to be specific with a rumour, they'd have spread one before now. Not to mention that there's someone far scarier above the person selling on the street. No one would risk pissing them off, even now."

I couldn't argue with that.

Despite knowing a lot about drugs themselves, the scene, as Ronnie called it, was something I didn't. When I'd first discovered that Conor was selling after finding a sports bag filled with drugs at the back of the wardrobe, he'd seemed genuinely ashamed. Once he explained it to me, I felt sorry for him or anyone who'd have to go to such lengths to fund their education. Of course, by then, I'd also discovered that drugs were my armour. Secretly, I'd been happy that I'd never have to do without. He made me swear not to tell anyone, not even Ronnie. I'd tried to quiz him further about how it worked a few times but, like Ronnie said, he'd warned me that the less I knew, the better. Then he'd promised me that someday he'd make something better of himself, for me.

"What about Dex?" I'd asked Ronnie then.

"What about him?"

"How will I explain my ex-boyfriend retaking my photo?"

"You're overthinking again, Eve. Dex knows about the original photos, and he knows who took them. You're being paranoid because of what you did. Anyway, Conor will only be here for one day. That's all he has free."

"Will that be enough time to talk everything over?" I'd asked.

"Sure, and afterwards we'll be left with fabulous photos, clear consciences, and a bright future." Ronnie had smiled broadly.

###

It's completely dark when I press the fob on the dashboard, opening the outer gates into the complex. Passing the turn for the new houses, I can see lights on in Joanne's. It takes all my willpower not to pull into her driveway to hide out in her kitchen, so I don't have to explain

202

to Dex why I'm so late or reveal Ronnie's new plans. I make a mental note to phone her tomorrow. By the looks of the rough itinerary Ronnie showed me before we left the hotel, I'll need to accept Joanne's offer of help during filming. I hope it still stands. But first, I'll need to sit everyone down and explain that it will be a short-term thing, and once it's over, it's over for good.

I squeeze my eyes shut at the thought, grasping the steering wheel, trying to banish the idea that I don't actually want it to be over. Since dipping my toe back into my old life, I suddenly want more. I'm not addicted to it, as Dex suggested this morning, but it provides me with focus and prevents my mind from travelling to strange places that I often don't understand. It's a coping mechanism. As someone who never underwent formal rehabilitation for my dependency, I've stuck to what has worked – staying busy, barely drinking, being as clean-living as possible. Aside from my affair with Conor, I've stayed within my parameters all these years. What if I don't know how to exist without them?

Though it might seem strange to some, this job or way of life helps me stay connected, express myself away from situations that often terrify me. Behind a screen, my hands don't shake. You can't see me sweating. It has helped me cope with my anxiety and overcome panic in a way that nothing else has. Like Ronnie, I, too, rely on my career. Until someone injected fear into it, it was my comfort zone. Now, I feel safe again, but for some reason it's as though I must still pick between Annaford and @beli'EVE – that I can't have both.

I click the button to open the second set of gates. Despite my trepidation about seeing Dex, a sense of calm washes over me. I'm home. As I approach, the automatic lights at the front of the house illuminate, and I'm astounded that something so beautiful is mine.

Parking in front of the steps, I grab my bags from the boot and make my way towards the back of the house where I know my family will be. It isn't until I reach the first corner that I notice no lights on inside. I glance towards Dex's workshop. It, too, is in darkness. Craning my neck, I see his truck isn't parked outside as it usually is. Maybe it's around back. I hesitate. As I do, a feeling of unease surfaces. Fumbling in my bag, I remove my phone and check it. Other than countless social media notifications, there's nothing new. I turn to look behind as the automatic lights go off, and I'm plunged into darkness.

Using the torch on my phone, I point it ahead to guide me to the back door. The nights here are dark with no street lights and set so far back from the road. I still expect to see lights at the back of the house, but the windows are as obscured as the front when I get to the final corner.

It wasn't like Dex not to say if he was going out. Maternal dread that something has happened to one of the children rears its head before I tell myself that Dex would phone if something was wrong no matter what. I'm sure there's a perfectly reasonable explanation.

Bundling my cargo into my left hand, I try to line up the key with the lock, but when I insert it I realise that the door is already unlocked. Bewildered, I push the handle and go inside. Glancing at the monitors lining the walls, Dex's truck is nowhere to be seen on the grounds. He must be gone out. Without taking another step, I dial his number, put the phone to my ear, then switch it off when his voicemail answers. I call Faye, then Milo. They all tell me to leave a message.

I gently place my bags on the floor and pull off my boots as I listen. The house is eerily quiet. I move into the kitchen and look around. Other than it being untidy, there's nothing untoward. I glimpse a scrawled note from Dex on the back of an envelope on the counter.

Gone out with kids. Dex

I roll my eyes, then take in the array of discarded cups and plates, coats and bags on the floor – a reminder that all is not forgiven with Dex. I place my phone on the counter, feeling irritated. Leaving the door unlocked was careless, and he could have at least phoned or texted to tell me where he was going. In another way, I'm relieved that he's not here. It means I can delay the inevitable conversation, still unsure how to broach everything with him. Ronnie suggested playing into his heritage: sheer American positivity. But I feel too exhausted to be optimistic right now.

I'm about to switch on the lights when I hear a faint noise – a floorboard creak, something shifting within the house. I freeze, preparing to scold myself that I'm hearing things, when it happens again. Terror pierces my senses. I take a breath and hold it, petrified to make a sound. I experience the same sensation I'd get back in Dublin when I'd return home and get the feeling that someone had been there. I'd purposely make noise or rush outside to stay in the car until I could be sure it was safe. Surely, this can't be happening again. Can it? Only, it is. This time, my deepest fears are realised: there's someone in the house.

CHAPTER EIGHTEEN

#mattedhair #facethetruth #sorryisthehardestword #londonbaby
#cliffhanger #reckless #bang

- -

@beli'EVE
Public Figure
Mama. Wife. Model. Content Creator. Collabs. Beauty. Fashion
Interiors.

- -

5,698	1.3M	212
Posts	Followers	Following

My eyes dart from side to side, looking for an escape as footsteps draw close. As quietly as possible, I reverse into the boot room. Hooking my finger over the door handle, I slowly pull it towards me, grimacing all the while. I tell myself to get outside, call the Guards. My breathing thickens as I pat my pockets for my phone, then remember that I left it on the counter. There's a clatter inside as something smashes, a voice. There's no time now. All I can do is run. I can make it to the front gate, to Joanne's. I turn towards the back door with shaking hands. That's when I hear the footsteps approach again.

I'm still trying to catch my breath when the door flings open, and I recognise my mother's voice. "What on earth are you doing, Eve? You frightened the life out of me!"

I stand with my back against the monitors and my hand to my heart, panting.

"What's wrong with you?" Mum scowls.

I drop my hand. "I thought you were ... I thought there was someone in the house."

Mum points at the monitors behind me. "Fat lot of good they did. All you had to do was to look at ..." she squints, "that one there." She points at the one that shows the kitchen. "Look." She steps over the threshold and waves vacantly. "Can you see me?"

I grit my teeth. "Yes, Mum. I can see you, but strangely when you think there's an intruder, all sense vanishes." I walk into the kitchen and brusquely flick on the lights.

"I broke a mug." Mum bends to pick it up. "I couldn't find the switches. Everything has moved since I lived here."

"I'll do that, Mum." I bend. As I pick up one of the smaller pieces, I inhale sharply as it cuts my finger.

"Oh, Eve. Do be careful. My God, you were never careful, were you?"

I stand abruptly, put my finger in my mouth and suck the blood, willing myself not to react. "It's a scratch. It's fine. What are you doing here anyway, creeping around in the dark?" Suddenly, dealing with an intruder seems less stressful. "And where's your car?"

Mum straightens, pulling at the bottom of her jacket like she's ejecting a parachute and adjusting her skirt. For as long as I can remember, Mum has habitually worn a rigid skirt suit.

"Well, I couldn't get in the gate, could I? I left it outside one of those new houses. A nice lady saw me and telephoned up to Dex."

"Joanne?" I say.

"Blonde lady. Northern accent."

I nod.

"We need to talk." Mum's tone morphs suddenly.

"Okay," I agree warily. A sudden thought strikes. Is Mum sick? "Wait, where are Dex and the kids?"

"I sent them to the cinema," she says, matter of fact. "I've been here since lunchtime waiting for you. Dex let me in. Just." She throws me a disgruntled look. "You still weren't home when he got back with the children from school." She tuts disapprovingly three times.

I let it pass, more intrigued as to why she's here.

"I suggested that I'd wait, and they should go out," she explains. "Then I nodded off on the couch and woke up in the dark."

"That's all sounds very ominous. I'll just call Dex and see when he'll be back." I reach for my phone on the counter, but Mum places her hand over mine.

"What I need to say, I can't say in front of him."

I try to read her expression, wondering if I should be nervous. By the looks of it, I should.

"You can't do this documentary, Eve. That's why I'm here. To stop you."

Her words hang for a moment while I study her face. She looks suddenly older than I remember, as though the past few years have been unkind. I wouldn't know since I've been around for none of it. Although I know she'll have had her short grey hair set yesterday as she's done all her life, it now appears badly matted on one side where she "nodded off" on it. Today, she's worried. The skin on her face, too, looks aged and papery so that if I reached out to touch it, it might turn to dust on my fingertips. I've seldom seen my mother appear weak. This is perhaps the second time. The other was when Dad died, and she'd been made sit in the second pew of the local church behind the woman for whom he'd left her. The embarrassment of all embarrassments had left her pale and shook. She looks the same now.

Although I need this conversation like a hole in the head, I take a deep breath, forcing myself to be tolerant.

"Would you like a cup of tea?" I buy some time. "Are you hungry, Mum?" She looks as though she hasn't eaten in days. Regardless of our relationship, I experience a pang of guilt so sharp that it almost takes my breath away.

"No. I'm not hungry. Not at all." Mum swallows and blinks, seemingly surprised by my composure. She must have expected resistance. "It's just ... I've been waiting all day to talk to you, and I just need to say what I need to say. I want to ..." She exhales raggedly.

"Sit down, Mum," I suggest. "A few more minutes won't hurt. I'll make tea. Then we can talk."

I walk off to fill the kettle and turn it on. Despite her protests about not being hungry, I open the pantry, take out a fruit loaf, slice some of it, butter it and put it on a plate.

Then I glance over at Mum. She's sitting in the window seat, silently staring out into pitch darkness. It isn't until I approach, carrying two mugs and balancing a plate, that I realise she's looking at herself. When she senses me, she turns around. There are tears in her eyes.

"Mum?" I set the mugs and plate on the table in front and sit next to her. Uncharacteristically, I place my hand on hers. Her skin feels loose – pliable.

"Are you all right?" I ask.

She flashes a brief smile that fades as fast, then turns back to the window where I see her squeeze her eyes shut and take a breath.

"I let you down," she begins. "I know I did." This time, she looks at me before her eyes fall to her clasped hands. "I was ... I don't know." She makes a face, visibly struggling to find the words. "It was a different time. Even doctors weren't great at talking about mental health. The advice was always the same – put a patient on anti-

209

depressants, encourage them to get on with life. You know, exercise, eat well, cut back on stimulants." Her eyes flit to mine before she looks towards the window again, back at herself. "But you weren't my patient, Eve. You were my daughter." She shakes her head. "You were so beautiful, smart. In one way, you had everything going for you, and I thought, what could you possibly have to be sad about?" She pauses. "I wasn't that bad a mother, was I?"

Even though her back is to me, I shake my head as tears well. She hadn't been a bad mother in the greater scheme of things, not really. Nor had there been anything detrimental going on to have triggered my issues, but that wasn't the point.

"Not until you needed me, of course," she sighs, taking the words out of my mouth. "God, help me, I was so angry with you," she admits through gritted teeth, forcing herself to look at me.

I blanch at her words.

"I'm a despicable person, I know, but I'm trying to be honest, Eve. I want to face it now."

"Tell me," I encourage.

She nods once and continues, "I couldn't deal with your problems too. Not when I also was dealing with your father – the philandering fucker!"

I startle. I've never once heard Mum curse before now.

"Oh God!" Her hand flies to her mouth. "I'm sorry, but he made such a fool of me – such a fool, and everyone knew. All talking behind my back, laughing. I was … I was mortified, heartbroken, but I had no choice but to carry on with the surgery and for you. Everything you told me you were feeling, Christ, I was feeling it myself." She laughs hollowly. "Your sister and brother, well, they were already gone. It was just you and me left, and I didn't know whether I was coming or going."

"It's okay, Mum." I try to stop her – half because I've never heard her speak so openly, half because I'm terrified of where this conversation is veering. The timing couldn't be worse. "You don't need to explain."

"Eve, please. I've come to say what I need to, so let me say it."

I nod as she takes a breath.

"I was in a terrible place myself, but that's no excuse for neglecting you." A lone tear escapes her eye. She wipes at it roughly then looks directly at me. "So, I tasked your father with you." She bites her lip before she says the next part. "To punish him, to make him see that he was responsible for you too, but he was never much of a father, was he?"

The truth is, I never knew my father particularly well. Growing up, he was more an aloof presence, and later, a number to dial if I needed money. When the money stopped, I lost touch with him. After I returned from New York, Mum called out of the blue one day to tell me he'd had a massive heart attack and was dead. I felt very little.

"All he did was throw money at you. You were far too young to be left to your own devices, too vulnerable." A sob escapes. "I came here to say that everything that happened to you was my fault, Eve. I've always known it. I just couldn't admit it. If I'd been there for you … if I hadn't pushed you to go to college when you weren't ready, forcing you to move out … well … it's unforgivable." There's a pregnant pause. "You have every right to hate me. Every right."

I'm lost for words. At last, I manage, "It's okay, Mum." Everything she's said is true. I have every right to rant and rave. Instead, I say, "It was a long time ago."

"Is that it?" Mum blinks. "It's okay? But it's not okay, Eve. I let you down. I was never good at talking about my feelings – not like Lily."

I smile fondly at the mention of Lily. "You couldn't have been more different, could you?"

Mum shrugs. "I did love her, you know? Lily used to infuriate me, but I did love my sister." She stops again. "She loved you too, Eve. She was there for you when I should have been."

I nod.

"I should have been grateful, but I hated her for it. I pushed you away, and she held you tight." She tuts at herself. "Lily acted like a mother while I acted like an idiot, worried what people would think. I should have been there."

I can't argue. No matter what I did, Mum should have been there for me.

"Even when you were a child," she continues, "your eyes would light when you saw Lily. It's stupid, but I felt pushed out. Still, there's no excuse. I was so ashamed by what you were getting up to in college, but I'm more ashamed that I let my sister help you instead of doing it myself and –"

I cut across her. "I know about shame, Mum, believe me. I wasn't trying to hurt you. Or be bad. I was just so ... afraid? Is that the word? From the moment I woke up every day to the moment I went to bed at night. In between, everything was a struggle. I had to force myself to get up, force myself to breath, eat, go to class." This time I shrug. "It felt like I wasn't in my own body half the time. It was –"

"Exhausting? It sounds like it."

I agree. "And endless. The drugs gave me a break from how I was feeling." My voice breaks. "I'm not making excuses either, but it was so constant."

Mum nods knowingly. "Generalised Anxiety Disorder," she states, matter-of-fact as if she's only figured it out now.

"Complete with panic attacks." I try to smile.

"Do you still suffer?"

"Sometimes," I admit. "I've found better ways to deal with it over the years. Work mostly. My family. Keeping busy. Breathing. Getting fresh air. I manage."

"I'm so sorry, Eve. What you needed were therapy and proper medication. You needed me. Not those people."

I exhale. "I know how you feel about Ronnie, Mum, but Ronnie never did drugs. It was me and –"

"Well, then *him!*" Mum holds her up her hands. "Please, don't say his name, Eve. To this day, I don't understand how he could be so stupid as to give you what he did, knowing the state you were in."

For a moment, I shut my eyes. I'd tried to put it away again earlier, but here it was again. "I wasn't in a state, Mum. I was pregnant."

Before I can stop it, I'm back there again.

#

Twenty years ago, on the worst day of my life, I'd woken feeling better than I had done in weeks. The previous months had been hard, suffused with nausea that I'd suffered almost as soon as I took the pregnancy test. Mind you, there'd been no way of telling if the constant butterflies were attributed to pregnancy, anxiety over the same, or ceasing my drug habit.

Discovering I was pregnant in college with Conor's baby shocked me to my core, instantly taking the wind out of my already deflated sails. I'd surpassed three months when it dawned on me one day that I hadn't had a period in months. Immediately, Conor suggested going to England for an abortion, that it might be for the best. Or, in other words, best for someone like me who could barely take care of myself, let alone a baby. At the time, I was a mess. I'd stopped attending lectures months before, and I was little more than a hermit, existing off the monthly allowance that Dad dutifully provided. Each month,

I'd hand the money straight to Ronnie, who'd use it to cover my share of the bills, make sure I had food while I passed the days at home, watching day-time television, waiting for Conor or Ronnie to come back. In the darkest recesses of my mind, I knew I was in a bad place, but I was too weak to do anything about it.

By then, Mum wanted nothing more to do with me. I'd confirmed her suspicions that I was using when I came home one weekend, stole a prescription pad from her surgery to write myself a script for a twelve-month supply of Xanax and sleeping pills. When I dropped it at the local pharmacy, they asked me to come back to collect it. When I did, Mum was standing inside the door waiting for me. The pharmacist allowed Mum, not the Guards, to deal with me as a goodwill gesture. To this day, I still think I'd have preferred it if they'd phoned the Guards.

That day, Mum tried to stop me from leaving the house. I stood at the front door of our three-storey Dalkey residence, screaming at the top of my lungs that I was an adult and that she couldn't force me to do anything against my will. I caused such a scene that she finally let me go, telling me that I could fend for myself if I was so grown-up.

The following month, there was no allowance. I phoned Dad, but his new partner answered, telling me that Mum had been on and under no circumstances would they be funding my habit any longer. And so, I became Conor and Ronnie's problem. Then I got pregnant. Ronnie eventually got through to me by telling me some home truths.

#

"Did you even notice that Conor isn't using anymore? It's just you, now, Eve. College is nearly over. Your allowance is gone. You're pregnant. What are you going to do? How will you support yourself?

If you don't get a grip, you're going to lose him … and me." She'd followed it with, "Then again, that might not be a bad thing. Maybe you should contact your mum again, go home …"

It was unimaginable. I couldn't lose Conor or Ronnie nor go back to Mum.

"I've had an idea …" Ronnie began to tell me how she and Conor were already planning for the future and how she wanted to manage his career as a photographer. "He's going to be famous, Eve. He's amazingly talented." She'd revealed that while I'd been holed up inside, oblivious, he'd been working on his portfolio. Apparently, a London Agency was interested in using him for fashion editorial based on work he'd already sent.

"And you know what?" Ronnie told me. "They wanted to know who his model is."

I stared blankly.

"You, Eve! They thought you were a real model. They're interested in talking to you too."

"A model?" I frowned.

"Yes! A model," Ronnie insisted. "You've never been able to see it, have you? How beautiful you are. How everyone, except you, wants to be you." Then she'd taken my hand. "I believe in you, Eve. I know you can kick this habit. And I know that there's someone great inside you. I can see it, but you have to try to see her too. Stop being so afraid. Get yourself together. Get better." Then she'd paused for a moment. "What do you love more, Conor or drugs?"

I stared at her, round-eyed. "Conor. I love Conor." My eyes welled suddenly. "I … I don't know what happened. I don't know how I got here. I don't want to be like this."

"I know how you got here, but it ends right now this second. Do you want to come to London, Eve?"

I nodded.

"Okay. Conor's going to spend the next few months working on a portfolio. He has this great idea he keeps talking about. Something about a red dress, shot at night, nature all around." She gestured with her hands. "With editing, he can make it look really cool, apparently. He explains it better than I do." She rolled her eyes. "The whole thing is inspired by you, Eve."

"It is?"

"Yeah, you should ask him about it." She stopped to allow how absent I'd been to sink in. "Conor loves you, Eve, but not this way." She furrowed her brow. "He wants you to be a part of the photos — of his future, but the way you are at the moment, he'll have to find someone else." She shrugged. "It's such a pity because it could have been a huge opportunity for you too. Imagine getting signed with a top agency …" she'd trailed off. "Especially when you're currently out of other options. There isn't a hope in hell you're going to pass your finals unless there's a miracle, and not to keep reminding you … you're pregnant."

"You think I should get rid of it, don't you?"

"That's not up to me, Eve. That's your decision."

"They should have told me," Mum interrupts my thoughts. "They should have come to me. What sort of people let someone with a drug dependency decide? *Hmm?*" She shakes her head angrily. "Certainly not anyone who cares about you. You weren't strong enough. None of you knew what you were doing. They should have come to me for help."

"And what would you have done, Mum?" I turn to her. So far, I've

216

let her off lightly. Despite how remorseful Mum looks, I ask what I've wondered all my life. "Would you have taken me in? Or would you have shut the door in my face again?"

She stares straight ahead. "I don't know, Eve." Then she exhales loudly. "I thought I was doing the right thing. I thought you'd come to your senses and come home so I could get you the help you needed." She scratches her head suddenly. "You have to understand, I'd seen it time and time again with patients. You can only get clean if you want to. I wasn't thinking." She tuts again. "I had no one to help me either. Your father was otherwise occupied, and I was ashamed. It's not an easy thing to admit, even now."

"You're right, Mum. You can only get clean when you're ready." This time, I turn to stare at my reflection in the glass. "I did want to, though. I really did. I'd never wanted anything as much."

I think I shocked myself as much as Ronnie and Conor by how quickly I managed to turn things around, terrified at the idea of losing the only family I had left. After speaking with Ronnie that day, I'd decided to keep the baby. With her help, I'd get clean, and the four of us would go to London and start a new life. I'd be a model, Conor a photographer. Ronnie would manage us and help with the baby. It sounded so perfect that it was all I could think about. For the first time in my life, I imagined a future I'd never considered with us living together in some trendy London flat, building our careers, working hard. It was something I wanted far more than drugs, and I was determined to have it.

Ronnie and Conor were with me every step of the way while I battled those first few weeks, getting clean. They fed me, held me,

217

talked to me, sang to me, cried with me until I began to feel stronger. With my stomach churning each day, I pushed myself to put one foot in front of the other. Within a couple of months, I was back at classes, studying again, eager to attempt my finals. Slowly, I gained weight. My hair grew thicker, my skin gained colour, and I began to feel human again – a human with life inside, trying my best.

When Conor took those famous photos of me high up in the Dublin Mountains at the peak of a forest walk, I was hopeful for the future. You can't tell by looking at it, but I'm five months pregnant in the photo. To this day, the gentle curve of my stomach in the red chiffon gown – my bubble of hope – is all I see when I look at it. From below, next to the river, Conor had directed me as I lay with my hair spilling over the cliff, Ronnie holding onto my legs for dear life. It was reckless, stupid even, but I felt alive that night. I felt free, floating on air. A few weeks later, I landed with a thud.

"Who gave you the drugs, Eve? Who did it?" Mum asks urgently now as if it still matters – as it will make any difference.

I smile sadly. "No one gave them to me, Mum. I did it to myself."

"But where did you get them?" She sounds distraught. "Whoever sold them to you should be in prison. Locked up."

I shake my head, biting back tears, to this day unprepared to tell her that I'd found them in my bedroom. Conor might not have been using, but he was still dealing.

"It won't change anything," I mutter to myself. "It won't change that I killed my baby."

Mum flinches at my choice of words.

I turn to her sadly. "That's why you've always looked down on me,

Mum, isn't it? Why you disapprove. Why you can't forgive me. But what you don't realise is I've never forgiven myself either. I never hated you, Mum. There was no room to hate anyone more than I already hated myself."

CHAPTER NINETEEN

@beli'EVE

Public Figure

Mama. Wife. Model. Content Creator. Collabs. Beauty. Fashion
Interiors.

5,698	1.3M	212
Posts	Followers	Following

I must have wanted the worst day of my life to be my last. There was
no other possible explanation as to why I'd step into oncoming traffic
on the dual-carriageway at night, off my face on a self-prescribed dolly
mixture of drugs. Afterwards, Conor told me that I'd found his stash
stuffed into his sports bag which he'd carelessly relocated from the
wardrobe to under our bed. That's all I know. For twenty years, I've
attempted to piece together what happened, but the memory
evaporated with the baby I'd been carrying.

By all accounts, I hadn't seen Conor since that morning. There'd
been no argument. From the college records, I'd attended classes then
presumably returned home. I spoke to neither my parents nor Ronnie,
who'd gone back to Kildare for a few days. Apparently nothing out

of the ordinary took place until I skirted across a car bonnet.

Before that, life had been good. With my help, Conor had been busy working on his portfolio, and I'd been catching up on college work as best I could. I'd decided to wait until after my exams to contact Mum, tell her I was pregnant and that I was moving to London. As far as I was concerned, I was happy. Then something changed. Something must have made me want to feel nothing at all.

"I still can't remember." I turn to Mum now, tears streaming. "It's gone. Just like that!" I click my fingers.

Mum puts her hand on my knee. "You suffered head trauma, Eve. Not to mention a traumatic event."

I hang my head and nod. The doctors at the hospital described it as my brain being so focused on survival that it momentarily lost the ability to remember. Sometimes the memories come back. Sometimes they never do. They told the gardaí the same when they came to question me in the hospital afterwards, pushing me to recall what happened, where I got the drugs, why I was walking on my own at night, who I'd been with. Unable to answer and in no fit state, I grew distressed. It wasn't an act.

Mum was contacted after my home address was found in my wallet in the pocket of my jeans. She wasn't surprised about the drugs, but she'd been horrified to discover I was pregnant. I heard her whisper to the gardaí that we wouldn't be pressing charges against the driver and that she was willing to pay for the vehicle to be fixed. The driver wasn't injured, nor were they at fault. Commendably, they'd slowed the car to a speed that prevented killing me on impact. They were as shaken as me. All everyone wanted to do was move on from what was concluded as a tragic accident. Even the social worker seemed happy to leave me in the capable hands of my mother, who insisted she was taking me home. Only, I refused to go with her. All I wanted was to be with Conor and Ronnie.

My breath shudders in my chest. "I used to get flashbacks or nightmares, whatever you call them. Lily used to say it was my mind processing."

I explain to Mum how for months afterwards I'd wake up not knowing if what I'd seen was real or if I'd invented it. I'd imagine the lights of the car coming at me. I'd picture myself lying on the road covered in blood. Sometimes, I'd be holding a baby. By then, I was living with Aunt Lily, who'd rush to my room to comfort me.

"I'm sorry," Mum whispers. "I should have insisted you come home with me. I should have …" She trails off, squeezing her eyes tightly shut. "You were so adamant that you wanted to be with those people. I lost patience. I felt like such a failure as a mother. I thought you'd be better off without me in your life."

"That was the second time you told me never to come home," I remind her. "That's why I went to Lily, in the end."

A noise escapes Mum's throat. "You almost died, Eve. I almost lost you. Do you know how that feels? I was in total shock. As a doctor, I was supposed to be able to deal with it, but I was out of my depth."

I'm about to interrupt to tell her that I know exactly how it feels to lose something. Not only had I lost a baby, but at one time I'd been terrified that I'd lose Faye too. Instead, I allow Mum to continue.

"The doctor at the hospital kept repeating that he had no idea how you were still alive." Mum stares straight ahead. "From the drugs alone, never mind the accident. I knew what he was thinking – how could someone like me, a doctor, allow you to get into that situation." Her voice rises. "You bounced off a car –"

"And landed on my stomach," I say, but the final word morphs in my throat. My body folds in two with a sob. As well as hitting my head, I'd suffered a placental abruption, cutting off oxygen to the baby. They couldn't stop the bleeding in time.

Mum puts her hand on my back and rubs it in small circles. "You weren't well enough to have a baby, Eve. You were too young, too troubled. Maybe it was a blessing in –"

"*Don't, please.*" I manage to halt her words. "It wasn't a blessing." I sit up, suddenly stone-faced.

"I just mean –"

"I know, but I never saw it that way. I still don't. I wanted my baby. It was a girl, did you know that?" But I know she does. It was Mum who made all the arrangements afterwards. She'd dealt with everything. "I may not have deserved her, but I wanted her," I say through gritted teeth. "If I could just remember why –"

"Did you ever tell Dex? About the drugs? The baby?"

I shake my head. "No. I thought about it, but then I got pregnant with Faye so soon, and I thought if he knew he'd be afraid I'd do something like it again. I must not have trusted myself either. It's why I insisted on coming home to Ireland. I wanted to be near Lily, just in case …" I trail off. "The only people who knew were Conor, Ronnie, you, Lily."

Mum nods as I turn to her.

"When I came around a few days after surgery, she was gone. I never got to see her." Even after all these years, I still feel numb saying it. Sometimes, I wonder if it happened at all.

"You were asleep for days," Mum recalls, and then, "I saw her, Eve." Her shoulders sag with the memory. "I held her for you. She was beautiful." A sob escapes her mouth.

For a while, we sit in silence, crying, remembering, questioning how it has taken us twenty years to speak about it.

"Why today, Mum?" I ask eventually. "Is it because of the documentary?" I shake my head. "If it is, you don't need to worry. I won't be talking about the past. Not that part anyway."

Mum turns serious. "I was worried when I saw you were doing it, Eve. Things like this often find a way of wheedling their way to the surface. You said yourself that Dex doesn't know. Do you want him finding out now, like this? And what about the children? The judgement. And, at my age, I don't think I could –" She stops herself in time.

"Are you afraid people will judge you, Mum?"

"It's not that. I'm afraid for you. "

I stand and walk towards the kitchen island and lean against it, not wanting to admit that she might be right. "I have to do it."

"But why, Eve? What's to gain from telling the world more about you. You've been through enough. When I saw that Ronnie one on the news the other night, boasting about you, all I felt was rage. She was never good for you. Not one bit – hanging out of you all her life, using you whatever way she could. They were all using you. Why can't you just –"

I cut her off. "It's hard to explain, Mum. Ultimately, it's for my family."

Mum's leg jiggles nervously. "I don't want you to get hurt again. Put yourself in my shoes. If you thought something or someone could hurt Faye, would you try and stop it?"

I nod, then stuffing my hands into my pockets, I change the subject. "Talking about some of my struggles might do me good. Please don't worry, I won't be discussing us. But I will be talking about anxiety and how I learned to cope. It might even help someone else."

"How can you be sure that the rest won't come out? These shows have researchers who spend their time digging around for seedy stories. I'm just trying to warn you, protect you."

She looks so desperate that I almost feel sorry for her. I notice the same vulnerability I saw in her earlier.

"I'll be fine. I have Ronnie to protect me."

"Are you so sure you can trust her, really?"

I nod tentatively. Was I? A few days ago, I would have answered differently.

Mum studies me hesitantly. I get the impression she has more to say, but she changes the subject.

She attempts a lighter tone. "The place looks well. I had a quick look about before I nodded off."

The thought of Mum fumbling around, unable to turn on the lights, makes me sad.

"That's not what you said when we first moved in," I respond drily.

"Well, maybe I was wrong." She sucks in her cheeks. "Something I'm not always good at admitting." There's a trace of a smile.

I raise my eyebrows. "So Lily used to say."

"Of course she'd say that!" Mum bristles. "There wasn't much we agreed on, but it wasn't always that way. We were thick as thieves once upon a time, running about this house, the grounds, having adventures. I have some wonderful memories here." She stops. "And some not so great ones."

"Like?" I tilt my head with interest. Mum never had much to say about Annaford, only that she was happy to get the hell away from it.

"Well, while we're being so open, our mother was ill a lot," she says with a faraway look.

"Ill?" Lily never mentioned anything to that effect.

"She suffered," Mum states pragmatically, then stares at her feet. "Stayed in bed a lot."

"Oh," I say as it dawns on me. "You mean depression?"

Mum nods. "It was never discussed, but she spent an inordinate amount of our childhood threatening to throw herself into the valley beyond." She gestures towards the end of the garden. "You know it was Daddy who originally put the lock on that gate below in case she tried anything, not that she ever did."

225

Mum shrugs as I stare in disbelief.

"Still," she gives a hollow laugh, "it scared me until I was old enough to understand that it was a cry for help. I was good at ignoring them, it seems," she says regretfully. "I used to wonder if I'd end up like her someday." She puts her head back and swallows before meeting my eyes this time. "Then when you ... I mean ... " She falls over the words. "When you got symptoms, I assumed it was my fault. That it must have skipped a generation. It's often familial, so I just assumed ..." She trails off.

I'm stunned by the revelation. It's the same fear I have for Faye. For the first time, we have something in common.

"I understand," I say gently. "But it wasn't your fault, Mum." I absolve her, thinking that if it ever comes to it, Faye will afford me the same mercy.

She nods gratefully. "You see now why I was so eager to get away from here?" She exhales. "But Lily stayed. I suppose she deserved this house after caring for my parents, and then you when I shirked my responsibilities once more. I never got to thank her. I left it too late. In the end, there's never as much time as you think there'll be."

"I'm sure she knew, Mum."

Mum smiles absently. "Did she ever tell you how we'd sneak down to Lover's Leap on Midsummer's Eve, waiting for the ghosts to appear?" She laughs. "We never saw them, but that's how I still remember her – sitting on that rock, shivering in her nightdress, a head full of dreams."

I smile fondly. "She used to bring me there too. She told me all about the story of the woman who'd rather jump than be without the love of her life."

Mum raises her eyebrows and tuts. "Is that what she told you? Trust Lily to put her own spin on it."

226

"That's not the story?"

"Not at all. The real one is of an unfaithful woman. Because of it, her lover dies of a broken heart. She loses her mind – thinks she sees him rising from the dead. His ghost leads her to the Dargle river, where she climbs the rock, follows him over the edge and plunges to her death. It's more a tale of revenge." Mum laughs.

I shiver at the epiphany, eyes wide, trying not to think of it in terms of my own indiscretions.

Mum claps her hands. "But that was Lily. She saw the good even in those who didn't deserve it. As a woman scorned, there was a time I'd have been glad to watch your father tumble off a cliff. I might even have helped him over."

She's joking, I think, but I can't manage to muster a smile. Instead, I yawn dramatically. "Sorry, Mum, I'm exhausted."

She stands and adjusts her suit. "I'd better go."

"I'll walk you down to the road."

"Not at all. Remember, I know this place like the back of my hand." Mum heads towards the hall and returns with her coat and bag moments later. "Although, please do turn on the outside lights. The last thing I need is a broken hip." She comes towards me, hugs me fiercely, then stands back. "I am proud of you, Eve."

I put my hand out to lead her towards the back door, but she doesn't budge.

"I have to say this," she says. "Stop being oblivious. Stop letting other people control you."

My eyes narrow. "Like who?" I ask, knowing she'll say Ronnie.

"Like Dex." She stares me straight between the eyes.

"Dex?"

Mum proceeds warily. "I don't want an argument, Eve. I hadn't planned on bringing it up, but I have to." She hesitates. "Ask your

227

husband more about this house and how you came to inherit it."

It's like an unexpected wallop across the face. "Please, Mother!" I can't believe she's about to open this up again. "Lily left it to me fair and square. Conversation over."

"Just ask the question. There's something about it that still doesn't add up."

I go to interrupt, but she puts her hands up.

"I'm not trying to take it from you, Eve. I swear. The house is yours now. It always will be. But just ask. I promise I'll never mention it again, but I had to say it. That and I do believe in you, Eve, but you need to stop letting people take advantage of you. Believe in yourself! Be the leader you claim to be. Stop being a sheep and open your eyes. For once in your life, look around you. See what I see."

Faye startles when she leans over the sofa a while later to see me lying unmoving with my eyes wide open.

"I thought you were asleep. What are you doing?" she asks.

"Thinking," I say. I'd been that way since Mum left, afraid to close my eyes for fear of missing whatever it was I was meant to see. As yet, nothing further than Mum being interfering had come to me. I haul myself upright.

"How was the cinema?"

"Crap." She tucks her hands into the sleeves of her orange hoodie, balls them up and crosses her arms. "Milo's choice. I really didn't want to go, but the alternative was to stay here with Granny."

I lift my eyebrows. "Thanks for the heads-up on that, by the way. You could have texted me." I try to make light.

Faye shrugs, tucking her arms in even tighter. "You never texted me last night." I detect a hint of acid in her tone.

"It was work, Faye. Please don't give me a hard time." I rub my temples suddenly, then stand, stretching out my limbs. "Anyway, I'm home now and, thankfully, Granny is all gone." I reach my hand towards her face, cupping her cheek, but she steps back.

"Dad wasn't going to let her in," she blabs, watching how I react.

I frown. "Oh?" Though Dex and Mum aren't precisely allies, he'd never purposely have avoided her. Unless, of course, he had a reason to. The thought flashes through my mind.

She shrugs again. "Yeah. When Joanne rang, he said to say there was no one home." She looks smug. "Then Granny was extra pissy with Dad. It was all knives 'til we left. What did she want anyway? What was the big secret this time?"

"It was nothing actually," I say brightly.

"Why won't you tell me if it was nothing?" Faye narrows her eyes.

"Well, if you must know she was concerned about the documentary. That's all. You know how private Granny is. She's probably worried about the reputation of the good doctor if a photo of me in a scandalously low-cut debs dress surfaces." I finish with a high-pitched laugh.

Faye studies me so intently that I grab a cushion off the sofa and start plumping it.

"And are you worried about something surfacing?" she asks.

I glance back at her. She hasn't moved an inch.

"No. I wouldn't do it if I was." This time, my eyes narrow. "Is everything okay, Faye? You seem –"

"Sorry, I'm tired." Faye shakes her head as if snapping herself from a trance.

I try not to react, remembering what Joanne said about Faye testing boundaries, being worried about college, exam stress. "You're working so hard for these exams, but it will be worth it. We're so proud of you, and look, I know you don't want me to do this documentary but –"

"It's fine. You should do it. Ronnie said –"

"How was that, by the way?" I ask suddenly. "Was it good to talk to her?"

"Yeah. It was good. She told me more about the show, and it sounds great," she says quietly, eyes on her feet.

"Anything else?"

"Like what?" Her gaze shoots up sharply.

This time, I do react. I frown deeply.

Clocking it, Faye answers fast. "We just chatted about school, college, that sort of thing." She smiles, but it doesn't reach her eyes.

I tilt my head. "Faye, if there's anything you need to say, you can say it, you know. Right now. I'm here."

Faye looks over her shoulder towards the back door as Dex and Milo come through, then she hugs me briefly. "There's nothing. I'm tired. Night." She kisses my cheek, hesitates there for a few seconds before stepping back and walking away.

My eyes flit to Milo, and I smile. When my gaze moves to my husband. It fades as I wonder how he'll answer the exact question I've just asked Faye.

CHAPTER TWENTY

#iknowwhatyoudid #besties #masterplan #fayetotherescue
#thefirstcutisthedeepest

——————————————————————————

@Fayek_but_real

——————————————————————————

19	4,567	1,090
Posts	Followers	Following

Faye shuts her bedroom door. Leaning against it, her eyes dart from side to side as she decides what to do. Just now, when Mum asked if there was anything she needed to say, for an instant, she'd wondered, is this it? The moment she'd anticipated.

When she'd kissed her goodnight, she had visualised whispering, *"I know what you did"* just to witness her reaction. To see if she'd deny it.

Hovering by her mother's ear, she'd had to remind herself that the accusation would come straight back at her, revealing what she herself had done, opening a dialogue she was unprepared to have.

Another wave of nausea hits, so strong that she gags suddenly as something ominous swirls in the pit of her stomach. She leans over, hugging her stomach in a bid to stop it. It should have abated after her conversation with Ronnie this morning, but it's getting worse. The sensation is accompanied by an unwelcome atmosphere in the house, a waft of familiarity seeping through the walls, cutting off whatever air supply had allowed them to function as normal for the last few years.

Faye wasn't surprised when Dad put his head around her bedroom door on Thursday evening to say Mum wouldn't be home – that she was with Ronnie, working. Instantly, Faye felt sorry for him just like she used to before. When she was younger, Dad would come up with fun excuses as to why Mum was missing a hockey match, gymnastics display, storytime … dinner. Things like she was rescuing a cat from a tree or speaking with the President. When Mum got home, she'd just blame work. It was work. Work was work until Faye discovered it wasn't work – not always.

It made Faye extra-protective of her dad. But today she hadn't felt quite so watchful. When Granny marched into the kitchen, throwing Dad dagger-looks and passing snide comments, Faye felt an overwhelming urge to egg her on. She'd never had much of a relationship with her grandmother. Granny asked what felt like endless, trick questions about her interests or aspirations whenever she was with her, which wasn't often. Today, Granny seemed interested in one thing only – making Dad as uncomfortable as possible. Under normal circumstances, Faye might have defended him, but after she'd gone downstairs the night before to check if he was okay without Mum, Faye had overheard something she now wished she hadn't. She'd listened for a moment before creeping away. It's made her think that perhaps her father isn't so innocent after all. Maybe he never needed her help in the first place.

#

"You posted the photo from my phone, didn't you, Faye?"

The directness stunned Faye almost as much as receiving the message from Ronnie asking her to ring back, that they needed to talk right away.

"I know it was you. My first question is why?" Ronnie's tone was frosty.

For an instant, Faye considered throwing the phone as far as she could and running from the house, never to return. "I was trying to save my family," she choked instead. "That's all, I swear." As her greatest fear was realised, she sagged to the floor in her bedroom. "I was just saving my family," she repeated.

There was no point in denying it, especially when she had always assumed it would catch up on her eventually. Now, it had. When Mum and Ronnie first parted ways right before they'd moved to Annaford, for a while Faye allowed herself to relax, forget, move on just like Dr Robin, her therapist, had advised. Moving to Wicklow, it felt like Faye was part of one of those corny movies where the troubled teen got to start over away from whatever place or the situation had been hurting them. Perhaps it wasn't so corny after all, not when it had worked for Faye. Moving schools, forming an entirely new circle of friends solely interested in her, and not just who her mother was, was the best thing that could have happened. Not just for Faye, but for them all, even Mum.

They were a family again. Mum no longer rushed from event to event, nor was she plastered all over gossip pages. She ceased filming their lives like they were trapped in some sort of perpetual cereal commercial that Faye had never asked to be part of. Dad started a business and was happy. Milo spent his time out on his bike with his new friends, building ramps in the garden, driving in circles on the ride-on mower.

JUDITH CUFFE

Here, there was room for all their dreams, and Faye no longer felt scrutinised – never sure who her real friends were, perpetually compared to her beautiful mother. Unlike what most people thought, the perks of fame never outweighed the drawbacks. But here, they were happy. They were safe, and it was Faye who'd made it happen. Losing Ronnie from their lives gave them back Mum. But now, Ronnie was back. It was all only a matter of time before everything came crashing down again.

But that wasn't the only problem. In her gut, Faye sensed that as soon as the lights shone on Mum again, it would reawaken the person who had something on Mum that could destroy everything. Faye should know. She'd given it to them.

"It's okay, Faye," Ronnie's tone morphed, softening almost immediately. "Please don't cry. I understand. I'm not angry with you."

"You're not?"

"No. I'm just glad I finally know who did it."

"She was cheating on Dad." Faye swallowed a sob.

Ronnie exhaled. "I know, Faye. Believe me, at some point everyone discovers their mother isn't the person they thought she was. Everyone makes mistakes. Eve is no different."

"Did you know? Did you know what she was doing?" Faye sounded panicked.

"Not until you posted the photo." Ronnie paused. "I knew she was meeting him, but that was it."

"It was the photographer from college, Conor, wasn't it?" There was silence as Faye allowed her thoughts to catch up. "I thought you knew. I'm sorry, Ronnie. I don't know what I was thinking. I was angry. I wanted to hurt you both."

When she was initially sent the photo, Faye had stared at it for an age before getting angry, convincing herself that Mum and Ronnie were trying to trick her. She'd felt utterly confused, furious with Mum, devastated for Dad.

Knowing what she needed to do, she'd got out of the bed in Ronnie's spare room, ready to confront her. When she'd pushed the door to Ronnie's bedroom, saw her passed out asleep on the bed, phone next to her, something else overtook her. Taking Ronnie's phone, she'd held it to her godmother's face to unlock it. With it, she took a picture of the photo on her own phone, then posted it to the @beli'EVE account on Instagram. Finally, she went into the camera roll, deleted the picture, ensuring to also remove it from the recently deleted file. Then she'd skulked back to her own room. It felt like seconds.

Less than an hour later, Faye understood that she'd made a dreadful mistake.

"Before that night, I hadn't seen you in a while," she recalled. "You and Mum were arguing all the time, and you just stopped seeing me too … when you asked me to come for a sleepover, I was so happy. Then I found out why. Mum just wanted me out of the way."

"I never meant to shut you out, Faye, but it's okay now. It's all okay."

"Are you going to tell them what I did? Because we're happy here, Ronnie. They're happy." Faye's voice sounded flat. Indeed, from what she overheard last night, it didn't seem as if her parents were happy at all. It was still all a game, a ruse, a show.

"Your mum said the same."

"It's true," Faye blurted, trying to convince herself.

"You can relax. I'm not going to tell them, but I want you to know what you did was wrong. All that other stuff you pulled was pretty scary too, but I suppose you got what you wanted in the end – Conor gone. Your mum and dad together." Ronnie blows out. "It was quite the execution, ridiculously well thought out. I'm strangely proud. Now, before I forget –"

"But I —"

"Wait! My second question. Where did you get the photo, Faye?"

Faye hesitated. Where indeed? "A friend. A girl from my class was out for dinner with her parents, and she saw Mum. She sent it to me."

"The little interfering cow!" Ronnie issued a cold laugh. "Does she still have it?"

"No. She deleted it."

"Do you have it?"

"No."

"Good," Ronnie said. "See. There's always a simple explanation. And now for my third question."

Faye's blood ran cold.

Turning the lock on her bedroom door, Faye walks towards her wardrobe and opens it. On tip-toes, she reaches up to the top shelf and paws around until she finds the old shoebox. Taking it down, she sits on the bed and opens it. Rummaging past the old greeting cards and concert tickets, she finds the brown envelope and tips the contents of it onto the bed. One by one, she lays out the printed copies of what she'd seen in Ronnie's office that day, then stares at them, trying to understand. Like Ronnie had said, there was always a simple explanation.

"Do you remember that night you stayed with me? The night you posted the photo?" Ronnie had asked.

"*Uh huh.*" Faye attempted to sound chirpy, though she was gulping for air.

"Remember we went into work after I picked you up from school. I got called to a meeting. You stayed in my office." Ronnie always made a big deal that no one other than Faye, who'd someday be CEO, was allowed in her office alone. When Ronnie wasn't there, she'd lock the door behind her, tucking the key into the inside pocket of her giant designer bags.

"Yep." Faye's hands shook.

"While you were there … did anyone else come in?" Ronnie asked gingerly.

"Nope."

"Anything happen?"

Faye hesitated. "Like?"

"Did anything break?"

"Like?" she repeated, buying herself some time.

"It's nothing to worry about. You're not in trouble or anything. I just wondered, did you … if you came across or if you found anything or if … It's just that the next day when I came into the office, the glass was cracked on the photo of your mum."

"Oh, that." Faye seized her chance. "That was me. I was bouncing one of those stress balls. It hit the frame, and the photo fell off the wall, but I hung it back up …" She trailed off.

There's a long pause.

"Did you … when it fell, did anything fall out?" Ronnie sounded cautious.

"Fall out? What do you mean?"

"You see, I'd put something behind the photo for safekeeping."

"No," Faye said assuredly. "I don't think so anyway. The glass cracked, was all. Oh, God, did something fall out and get lost?"

"No, no – I just wondered if you'd seen it …"

Though Ronnie couldn't see her, Faye stuck her lip out, shaking her head convincingly. "I literally just hung the photo back on the wall. I didn't even look behind it."

There's a pause. "That's fine, Faye. I just wondered . . ."

"What was in there anyway?"

"Oh, just the originals of your mum's photo shoot," Ronnie said noncommittally. "Stupid place to put them, but I suspect they're worth a lot of money now, and I wanted them safe. I just want everything kept safe. One last thing, Faye. Your mum is doing this documentary, so stop giving her a hard time, yeah? You've nothing to worry about. Your secret is safe with me."

Faye sits stock still now, evaluating the photos on her bed. There'd been no stress ball thrown at the wall like she'd told Ronnie. Instead, Faye had simply reached up to touch the framed image of her mum when it dropped to the floor. The photo inside had shifted on impact. Faye had brought it over to Ronnie's desk where she'd lain it face down, eased up the metal tacks and lifted the chipboard to fix it. Her eyes grew round when she saw the envelope taped to the back. Glancing over her shoulder in the direction of the door, she pulled it off and opened it. There were four photographs inside. Staring at them open-mouthed, she'd grabbed her phone and snapped a picture of each. Then she'd replaced them, realigned her mother's photo inside the frame, putting it all back how she'd found it. Right then, she'd wondered the same as she wonders again now. What the hell did they mean?

The photos are practically identical to the one that made Mum famous, yet entirely different. In one way, it's as though Faye is viewing them how they were initially meant to be perceived – so oddly fascinating that she somehow knows she's looking at something she

238

shouldn't. Picking one up, she brings it closer to her face and squints. There's no doubt it's Mum in the photos. Faye can just make out the tattoo on her wrist. It was before she'd added their initials, but the infinity symbol is there, clear as day. Faye's stomach lurches again.

Scooping them back into the envelope, she closes the box and replaces it. Then she strips to her underwear and climbs into bed. Reaching her hand between her legs, she runs her fingers down the scars on the inside of her thigh. Mum hadn't discovered what Faye was doing until there were seven almost symmetrical rungs on her ladder of despair.

Starting at the top, she closes her eyes and presses the first one. She can't actually remember the exact reason for that one, but it had felt good. It was before she even found out Mum was cheating, and contrary to what Mum believes, it wasn't entirely to do with those assholes on Jabber.ie calling her fat. Although they hadn't helped either. Faye had listened to Ronnie enough over the years to know there were crazy people out there. Still, Faye wishes she'd listened harder.

On Rung Two, Faye squeezes her eyes shut tighter. This was the cheating one. She'd lied to Ronnie when she told her it was a friend from school who'd sent the photo of Mum. Although they never actually met in person, it was sent by a friend. At one time, Faye considered Natalie the closest person in her life. They first met on Snapchat, then followed each other on Instagram, but they mainly chatted through messages. Natalie was a boarder in a school in Kilkenny, so she had to be discreet with her phone – otherwise, it would get taken off her. Although she'd told Faye, she'd prefer not to say who, Natalie's mum was famous too – an actress. She wanted Faye to like her for who she was, not who she was related to. They literally had so much in common. Faye could tell Natalie everything she couldn't tell her friends at school, who all thought having Eve as a mum was the coolest thing ever.

Rung Three happened when Natalie started telling her rumours about Mum's past, her time in college, although she wouldn't say precisely what. Faye could find nothing online. It was all so vague that Faye began to question Natalie who said she'd get proof. That's when she sent the photo of Mum in the alleyway with her ex. In fairness, Natalie was nice about it. She said she felt awful for Faye but told her there was a way to make it all okay. She suggested Faye publicly post it to save her family and get everything out in the open. It would undoubtedly stop her mum in her tracks. At that precise moment, it made sense to Faye. So much so that in search of a second opinion, Faye decided to share the set of photos she'd found in Ronnie's office with Natalie. Natalie never answered.

Rung Four: Faye never heard from Natalie again. Her account vanished. For weeks, Faye scoured the internet, trying to find an Irish actress with a daughter named Natalie. To no avail, she phoned every boarding school in the vicinity of Kilkenny and beyond. She searched lists of followers of people Natalie claimed they had in common but found nothing.

A few weeks later, she came across a photo of "Natalie" on a mutual friend's account. Only Natalie was someone called Sophie O'Neill, a fourth year in a well-known Dublin school. Faye messaged her repeatedly, asking why she'd lied. Why she'd said her name was Natalie. Why she'd dumped her? What had she done with the photos? Eventually, the real Sophie wrote back to say she'd never once messaged Faye and that if she didn't leave her alone, her parents would call the police. Shortly afterwards, a rumour ripped through Faye's school that she was a stalker: Rung Five.

Rung Six came when she received a message on Instagram from a random account with a horrifying statement about her mother. It thanked her for her assistance in uncovering the truth. Then it vanished too.

So, Faye did the only thing she could. She saved lucky Rung Seven specially for Mum. She waited until her mother was home one day, stripped to her underwear and, as soon as she heard Mum call her name from downstairs, she cut extra deep. As Mum's footsteps approached, Faye jammed the blade in so far that she thought it might pop out the other side. Despite everything, she still loved her mother. People made mistakes. Faye already knows that. She'd made one too.

After that, things moved fast. Before she knew it, there was therapy, then a move to Wicklow. She hadn't even told the therapist much. If she had, Dr Robin would have had to tell Mum. Instead, Faye mentioned peer pressure, girls slagging off Mum at school, feeling bound to social media. It was enough. She'd told Joanne the same when Mum called to have someone assess her after the move despite her telling her mother that she didn't need to see anyone. By then, though, Faye had felt safe.

She had put the words of that final message behind her, convincing herself that it was a cruel prank. But, by the sound of it, Ronnie knows what those photos mean. The question is, is Ronnie protecting Mum or herself? Right now, Faye trusts no one. Not Ronnie. Not Mum. Not Dad. Muffling a sob into her pillow, she presses her fingernail hard into the final scar, silently repeating the words of that message, praying it isn't true: *Your mother is a murderer.*

CHAPTER TWENTY-ONE

#weneedtotalk #openyoureyes #pairoftheminit #pact
#inheritance

@beli'EVE
Public Figure
Mama. Wife. Model. Content Creator. Collabs. Beauty. Fashion
Interiors.

5,698	1.3M	212
Posts	Followers	Following

Milo is a sight for sore eyes – the balm I need before I face yet another
tricky conversation. Flushed with excitement, my gorgeous son
tumbles towards me and hurls himself over the back of the sofa, full
of uncomplicated chatter about the movie and what he ate. I sit back
down next to him, happy to listen, allowing the animated chit-chat to
rejuvenate me. He tells me about a part he needs for his bike, a new
computer game he saw, a project at school, a football match. It's light,
and it's what I need.

Dex hovers in my peripheral vision. While I'm listening, I secretly
watch him putting away some bits in the kitchen, check his phone,
unscrew a lightbulb of a lamp only to screw it straight back in again.
He's stalling, attempting to act normal. It's anything but.

By the time Milo winds down, Dex has inched closer. He must want to talk. Before he approaches, I take a breath, lean towards Milo and put my arms around his neck. Quietly I say, "Milo, I need to ask you something before you head up to bed."

He studies me. "Yeah."

"Are you one hundred per cent okay with me doing this documentary? There may be times when you're in it, or they want to interview you, and I just need to check." I'd already got my approval from Faye, however bland. I needed his, too.

"Yep. I'm totally cool with it, Mum. It'll probably make me famous enough to get sponsored for Mountain Biking or something, so yeah." He nods, raising an eyebrow. "I'm in."

I fold him into my arms. "I'll do what I can to help with that, promise," I say into his ear. How I wish everyone else was as easy to please. "Now bed, little dude. Go."

Milo swings himself back over the sofa, calls goodnight to Dex and too soon I'm alone with my husband. Without meaning to, I sigh loudly, suddenly shattered. When I glance behind, Dex is right there, and I jump.

"Do you want to sit down?" I suggest, grimacing with my back to him.

It's rare to see Dex looking awkward, but he does now as he ambles around the sofa, hands stuffed into the pockets of his jeans. He's wearing a *New York Yankees* baseball cap down low almost over his eyes. He takes his hands from his pockets when he reaches me and sits. Then he pushes the peak of his cap up with his index finger and tries to smile. It fails to meet his eyes. He looks utterly forlorn. For an instant, my heart clenches. Just a week ago, things between us were never better. Now, it's as though everything has reverted to how it was back in Dublin – stilted, forced, mechanical.

"You okay?" He struggles to meet my eyes. Briefly, he reaches over as if to take my hand, then seems to think better of it. Instead, he removes his cap and places it in the space between us.

I vacantly stare at it as I answer. "I'm not really sure."

Half of me wants to forget the final part of the conversation with Mum earlier, wipe it from my memory along with everything else I've conveniently forgotten, but I can't. Mum had had plenty more to say after she told me to open my eyes for once in my life, to look around, see what she sees.

I look up at Dex, willing him to look back and banish my fears. With one glance, he could do it, prove Mum wrong, but he won't look up, or maybe he just can't. His hands are tucked between his legs, eyes averted, shoulders slumped. My lungs deflate. I'm opening my eyes, and all I see is guilt.

"My eyes are open, Mum," I'd answered impatiently earlier.

She was standing with her coat and bag hooked over her arm in the kitchen, ready to leave, having delivered her motivational speech.

I continued, "And what I see is you planting doubts in my mind." I sighed, then changed tack. "Why don't you like Dex, Mum? What did he ever do to you?"

She refolded her coat over her arm before answering. "It's not that I don't like him … well, you know what I think …" She hesitated, but unable to stop herself said, "If he'd been able to provide properly then you wouldn't be out flaunting yourself –"

"Stop, Mum," I growled, putting my hand up in warning. "Do not go there. Not after everything we've just spoken about. It's not the time."

"He never made much of an effort to work though, did he?

Because of it, I was constantly worried that you'd fall into old ways being so under pressure to make money. It was a lot for you, all on your shoulders. I mean, he just arrived in Ireland one day and never left, expecting to put his feet up."

I throw my head back in exasperation. "I was having his baby, Mum! A saner person would say that he did the honourable thing. He didn't have me under pressure to make money. We both worked."

Mum sniffed loudly. "A man modelling for a living is not working, Eve. He needed a job! A career!"

"He laboured too."

Mum rolled her eyes. "What? On the last day of each month!" she spluttered.

I tried not to lose my cool. "He tried, Mum, and that was good enough for me. The work was sporadic." I paused. "You can be such a snob. No one but a doctor would have been good enough. Look where that got you!" I instantly regretted it when I saw her face. She looked as though I'd slapped her. "I didn't mean that, sorry," I said quietly.

Surprisingly, she shrugged it off. "I think when he saw our house in Dalkey, he thought he was on to a good thing, and then when he saw this house, he –"

"What?" I threw my hands up. "He thought he won the jackpot. This house is a money pit! It's bled us dry!"

"But you didn't know that until you moved in." Mum wagged a finger.

"What exactly do you think Dex did, Mum?"

Mum shifted from foot to foot. "Ask yourself this – why do you think Lily suddenly came up with a plan to sell to a developer? Not to mention she was sick at the time. We both know Lily was as commercially minded as a toddler. The plan came out of nowhere,

245

Eve. Thin air. And, despite our differences, I know Lily would have discussed it with me."

I'm momentarily stumped. Mum has a point about the developer. I recover, shaking my head. "She didn't need to speak to you because it was her house, and she must have known there was huge work to do. Still, where the hell does Dex come into this?"

"I swore I wasn't going to say anything," Mum muttered to herself, screwing her eyes shut for a moment, then staring at me. "It's why I was so uncomfortable here when I came to visit. I couldn't bear to be in his company. It's why I didn't want to come back." She paused, took a breath. "I assume your husband never told you that he came to me, asking for money or an advance on *your* inheritance as he put it."

My eyes narrowed suspiciously. "*What?*"

"He told me you were always away from the children, your marriage was suffering, and you were too proud to ask for my help. He wanted you to stop working. He said you *needed* to stop working."

"*What?*" I repeat. "*When?*"

"Three years ago, perhaps. Of course, I said no. That I had two other children, and you were all given the same opportunities. The others never came to me for money. Besides, it didn't look much like you were struggling, out buying all those clothes and driving a brand-new car – the children in private schools. I told him it was never too late to retrain and get himself a proper job if having you not working was so important to him."

"What? Dex would never ... yes, I was busy but ... no, " I shook my head, "he wouldn't."

"But he did, Eve." Mum fixed her coat again. "Which is why I'm saying, open your eyes." To demonstrate, she opened her eyes as wide as possible. "Think about it. I say no and soon after you get this house. I'm telling you, he came to Lily, and she must have changed her will.

He must have asked her to. He would have known she was ill, that there wasn't much time."

I shook my head, trying to think. Though I couldn't believe it, why would Mum lie? She was many things, but she wasn't a liar, more someone who buried the truth like me.

"How do you know Lily changed the will? Maybe she always intended to leave me the house."

"I just know, Eve. I just know."

"Oh my God. Are you suggesting that Dex forced Lily?"

Mum looked at the ground. "Forced is a strong word ..." She stopped and thought. "More convinced. It would have taken a lot to change our pact."

"Your pact?"

"Yes. Lily swore, promised that the house would pass back to me and, in turn, I'd pass it to my children in the hope that one of you might buy the others out. We wanted it to stay in the family, to have it there for someone who might need it. That was the plan." Mum exhaled, looking exhausted. "Look, I didn't come here to throw a grenade at your marriage, Eve, but I thought you should know." There were tears in her eyes as her voice wobbled. "Lily didn't break promises, Eve. You know that."

I was flummoxed by her words because that part was true.

"We swore we'd never sell off the land either. Come on, Eve!" Mum exclaimed suddenly. "You know how much Lily adored every inch of this place, especially the tennis courts and the woodland. Do you honestly think she would have been okay with you chopping down all those trees? Do I have to spell it out for you?"

"Yes. Spell it out."

"Lily didn't go and find a builder and have plans drawn up for four houses. You have to know that, Eve."

"I do. They came to her."

"And she'd have run them off the property!"

"But Dex was never here. He never saw Lily without me." I stared straight ahead.

"How do you know?"

I didn't want to hear any of this. "I need you to go, Mum," I managed at last. "Today was hard enough, dragging up the past, without all this," I hesitated as a thought struck. "Why is it so hard for you to believe that Lily wanted me to have this house?" I don't wait for her to answer as another idea hits. "And I *did* need this house at the time. I *did* need a fresh start. Lily made that clear too. I think she'd have wanted me to have it, more than she'd want to save the bloody tennis court."

Mum looked defeated. "I'll go so." She reached out and touched my arm gently. "I honestly didn't come to fight, and I'm glad we spoke about those other ... things." She allowed the word "things" to hang in the air. "And I am sorry for all of it, Eve." She turned towards the boot room then stopped. "Do you know what Lily said when I confronted her about encouraging you to go to New York all those years ago?"

I squeezed my eyes shut.

"She told me that she knew in her gut that you were special – that this place wasn't where –"

"Goodbye, Mum," I'd interrupted before she could repeat what Lily had once said to me too.

#

Finally, Dex looks up. His eyes snap to mine before they fall once more. "So what's going on?" he asks. "What did *she* want?" He means Mum.

"You tell me."

His eyes shoot up again. "How would I know? She walked in, giving out yards about everything, then said she needed to speak to you alone. Who was I to argue?" He shrugs then rubs his hands down his face. His frown lines are more pronounced than usual, as if he's spent the entire day pondering life like me.

I test him with a half-truth. "She came to ask me not to do the documentary."

A smile instantly flickers at the corner of his mouth. "Seriously? Is that it? Nothing else?" He frowns.

"Were you expecting something more?"

"No, but I just thought there might be. It was all so covert, and ... I was worried."

"Were you?" I raise my eyebrows. "Faye said you weren't going to let her in?"

He makes a face. "Do you blame me? She's never exactly warm and cuddly, and I know how she rubs you up the wrong way. Gwen goes to extreme lengths to hurt you or ... keep you down. Let's just say I haven't missed her." This time, he grabs my hand, raises it to his mouth and kisses it.

Despite myself, I relax.

"And are you going to listen to her?"

Without realising, Dex has asked a loaded question.

When I look at him, his eyes are full of concern.

"I still want to do it."

He looks relieved. "Well then, let's do it. Let's knock it out of the ballpark. Take a parachute and jump right in."

"You mean that?" I ask, raising my eyebrows. It's a complete turnaround from our phone conversation that morning. I wonder whether he means it. Or if his positivity is to throw me off the scent, cover up something more? Lying on the sofa earlier, I'd promised myself that I'd ask Dex if there was something he needed to tell me. It strikes me suddenly that he'd posed the same question just this morning, giving me a chance to clear my conscience. Have we both done something we shouldn't? If Dex is hiding something, so am I. Suddenly, there's a part of me that doesn't want to know the truth. What will it change anyway? Nothing can alter the past. Something else I understand is how desperation can make you do strange things.

Dex's words shatter my thoughts. "If it will piss your mother off, then yes. Let's do it. This morning, you asked me to stand behind you one last time, so I will. I'm here for you. I should have said it before now, and I know she's family, Eve, but we don't need anything from her. We never did. Not when we have each other."

Unbeknownst to Dex, I breathe an internal sigh of relief. His words are not the sentiments of an inheritance-hungry son-in-law. At the very least, Dex deserves my trust after I cheated on him. Mum is the one who was never there for me, not Dex. Today, she'd seemed older, more feeble. Maybe she was confused.

As Dex puts his arm around me, I close my eyes. For now, I need to trust that I'm in the right place, surrounded by people who have my best interests at heart. I banish Mum's final words from earlier about Lily. Indeed, Lily wasn't always right.

CHAPTER TWENTY-TWO

#eyeofthestorm #blender #hell #reeltime #darkestsecrets
#whirlwind #accepthelp

@beli'EVE

Public Figure

Mama. Wife. Model. Content Creator. Collabs. Beauty. Fashion
Interiors.

5,698	1.5M	212
Posts	Followers	Following

Trapped in the eye of a storm, most people usually forget that calmness will follow. My calm comes in the form of Heather Nolan from Reel Time Productions. As soon as I meet her, I know everything will be okay. Due to a scheduling issue with Ronnie, I get a chance to speak with Heather alone the Monday after what I can safely call my week of hell. To use Ronnie's analogy, my life had indeed been chucked in a blender. Upon sitting opposite Heather in the glass meeting room of Reel Time's Merrion Square office, things begin to solidify.

"The first thing I want to say, Eve, is that this isn't about catching you out, making you look bad, unearthing your darkest secrets," she begins.

I must shudder with relief as Heather smiles, revealing straight white teeth.

"Were you worried?" She laughs.

"Terrified." I put my hand to my heart. "Not that there's much to unearth," I lie. "But right now, I'm in control of what I put out there. This feels a little like losing control."

Heather purses her lips and nods vigorously. "I completely understand. And I'm telling you now, that's not what we're about." She tucks a strand of mousey-brown hair that has come loose from her simple plait behind her ear.

Heather, who is somewhere in her early thirties, isn't at all what I'd been expecting. She's not the usual, bubbly, hyper television type. Her clothes are plain: black jeans, grey sweatshirt, Converse runners. There's not much make-up or jewellery. The look is pure youthful, yet it makes her seem professional, as though she's too busy doing her job to be concerned with appearances.

"My job is to showcase you, your story, what makes you different, interesting." She looks at me knowingly. "Everyone has a story, Eve, and it's my job to tell it in the best way possible." Her tone is even, reassuring. She smiles again. "This will be my seventh human interest piece, and I have an excellent feeling about it. And this is our first time working with Netflix. This is huge. Before I start throwing dates at you, I will say this – take it as an opportunity, Eve."

I tilt my head. "How do you mean?"

She places her hands on the ash conference table and leans forwards. "For most people who take part in these documentaries, looking back can be a life-changing experience. They realise things about themselves, their fears. They usually have a moment of clarity, an epiphany. Life is never quite the same afterwards. Like therapy, which I'll get to." She smiles.

I can feel my eyes grow round.

"In a good way," she assures me. "I'll tell you what, on the last day of filming I'll ask you about it again. Now, are you ready to change your life?"

I nod. "I'm ready."

Heather walks me through everything involved, from seeing a therapist before and during filming to ensure I feel safe and well. I inwardly smile. Dex will be happy about that. In turn, I come clean about my struggles with anxiety and panic, describing how work is a godsend. I talk about when I first met Dex, the Calvin Klein campaign that never happened, how being featured on Timeline's album cover impacted my entire life, getting pregnant in New York. I speak about meeting Conor in college and how life and youth sent us in other directions, but the photo he'd taken means that we'll always be linked. Inwardly, I acknowledge that our baby links us far more than the photo. I speak about my friendship with Ronnie, how we grew apart for a spell. I tell Heather about the Unfollow Me campaign – how it never took off but that I'm eager to revisit it.

As she listens, intrigued, I realise that she's right. I do have a story. Even without all the parts I've chosen to exclude. By the time we finish, I feel lighter than I have done in weeks, excited about telling it my way.

"Eve!" Heather grins, shaking her head. "Wow! This is great material. I thought I knew everything from following you, but you're way more interesting in person. Now, before we wrap up here, is there anything else you're concerned about or anything you'd like to say?"

"The kids mostly, but I have an offer of help from a friend. I'm also worried about keeping on top of my work while this is happening. I've worked alone for the past few years, and I don't want to let the ball slip."

Heather narrows her eyes. "You've worked alone?"

I nod. "Ronnie and I parted company a few years back. We're only back in contact since she came up with the idea for the documentary, and brought it to you."

Heather makes a face, tilts her head then opens and closes her mouth. She thinks for a moment before answering. "There's no point in pretending it isn't going to be busy, so get your head around that now. You're going to need help with your other commitments. So, use Ronnie. Use her resources and let me look after this show. Giving away control can be a good thing sometimes. As long as you're not being controlled." She raises an eyebrow.

I wonder if she means Ronnie. She hasn't mentioned her much for the duration of the meeting. I get the impression that Ronnie isn't someone that Heather appreciates. "And get that friend on board to help with the kids. You're going to need her."

I'd planned to call over to Joanne later anyway. We've been playing phone-tag for the weekend. I hope she hasn't changed her mind.

"Also," I chance, "I'm not completely sold on the idea of a reshoot of the original photos."

Her eyes narrow ever so slightly before she smiles brightly. "Any particular reason?"

"No," I answer fast. "Just, you know, ex-boyfriend and husband in the same place." I wince.

Heather purses her lips again then rifles through the printed document in front of her. She stops, then runs her finger down a page.

"So, Conor comes in for one day, which happens to be our last day of filming. Not ideal," she says, then flicks forward a few pages. "But I think I can schedule Dex's final interview at the same time. He'd be in a different location so he wouldn't be able to attend the photo shoot." She glances up brightly. "Would that help?"

It's certainly a solution of sorts, but even better would be not doing

254

them at all. Despite what Ronnie says, I don't want to see Conor. I grimace. "Are the photos one-hundred-per-cent necessary?"

Heather leans back, moving her eyes from side to side. "In a word, yes. I know the idea only came to the table very recently, but I have to hand it to Ronnie, it's a good one. I'm sorry if that's not what you want to hear, but do you know how iconic that original photo is? It's art, Eve. Not to mention how Conor is now one of the biggest fashion photographers, and you're an entity in yourself. Can you imagine if the original shoot had been filmed? We can now do that. People want to see it."

There's nothing I can say without telling her the whole truth.

"Wherever we shoot it, it'll be safe, controlled," she says. "I'll be with you every step of the way, right to the very final second."

"It's not going to be in the same place?" I ask.

"No. Ronnie says that Conor thinks it might feel too contrived. We're looking at places at the moment, but –"

The idea hits like lightning. "I know somewhere," I say.

I explain it to her and then take out my phone and scroll through some of the pictures I've taken at Lover's Leap over the years.

Heather looks impressed. "Eve, that's amazing. This place looks even more spectacular than the original backdrop." Immediately, she jots the name beside "location" on the scheduling sheet. "I'll pop out in the coming days to see it, but it looks perfect. Great idea. And you have access from your house?"

I nod.

"That helps. We can have a place to get ready on the day. Good thinking. I'll have a new schedule drawn up and email it to you straight away."

I smile. At the very least, I'll be somewhere I feel comfortable. Somewhere I know Lily will be with me in spirit.

I leave the office with a spring in my step. Heather's final advice was to relax this week. Take long walks. Jot down ideas. Think. Get myself ready. By the time I get home, she's already sent me the schedule, including the new location. Clearly, I'm in capable hands. I immediately email it to Joanne along with Faye's exam timetable and a message emphasising to have a good think before committing – that there was absolutely no obligation.

#

By Wednesday, I still haven't heard anything back. When I see Joanne's car pull into her driveway from my studio window, I take the chance to call over.

"Eve!" She smiles broadly, standing on her doorstep. "I was hoping to see you today. Sorry, I've been up to my eyes this week. I was literally about to call you. How did it all go? I'm dying to hear."

Once inside, sitting in her lovely modern kitchen, I tell her the bones of my meeting with Ronnie the week before, and the plans ahead. Without going into too much detail, I reveal that we'd sorted our differences and would hopefully be ploughing ahead with the documentary. I don't add that it depends on her help with Faye and Milo.

"I met the producer on Monday. That's why I'm here." I hesitate, pushing the piece of paper that I've been holding across the table. It's a printed version of the revised schedule. "Did you manage to have a look at what I sent you? I marked the days when I might be a bit stuck with the kids. I emailed it to you on Monday."

She blinks, taking the page. "Oh lord, I didn't see it. Sorry, Eve. I must have missed it. It's been a heavy week, there's this case and –" She stops herself. "Heavy going. Let me look now."

While I cross my fingers, Joanne takes the page and scans it. "Wow. You're going to be busy."

I nod.

"It's a lot, I know," I say suddenly when she doesn't respond straight away.

She's frowning at the page.

"God. Sorry, Joanne. This isn't your problem at all. Come to think of it, I shouldn't even be asking you. It's too much."

I reach for the page, but she pulls it away and smiles.

"Stop, Eve. I wouldn't have offered if I didn't want to help. Actually, it all looks fine."

I exhale.

"It's really only the last couple of days here in June that are flashing at me as potential problems. Remember I said I was going away with my sister? I'll be gone by the 23rd. Is that a problem?"

"No!" I laugh with relief. "Not at all. Faye's exams finish that day too. It's the last day of filming. It'll be fine."

"I could always ask her to delay a day or two, but –"

"No way, Joanne! Any help at all will be more than appreciated. Like I said before, it's really just to keep an eye on the kids."

She nods. "I told them the same last week."

I tilt my head. "Last week?"

"When you were in town meeting Ronnie. I dropped off another package. Did you get it? Big green box?"

"Again! Sorry, Joanne. And yes, now that I think of it, it was on my desk when I went up to my studio. Dex didn't mention it was you."

"I was literally there for five minutes. I thought you'd be back by then, but Dex said you were staying in town. I just mentioned that I'd be able to help out if the show went ahead, so at least Faye wouldn't be worried about the exams. I said she was welcome to study here or whatever suited. Same with Milo."

I roll my eyes. "Thanks so much and, yes, there was a lot to discuss with Ronnie that day." Then I put my hand on hers. "Thanks again, Joanne. Honestly. Knowing that you're around to keep them out of trouble will be a huge comfort."

She brushes it off. "No problem."

"Did you see the last part there on the page?" I point at the schedule.

"What part?"

"Look again."

She reads it, and her head jerks back. "Nooo!" she mouths exaggeratedly. "A reshoot of the girl in the red dress? I missed that. I think I might need glasses." She picks up the page and holds it closer to her face while she reads. Her eyes grow round. "With Conor Malone?" She looks up at me again. "Wow! How do you feel about that?"

I make a face. "It'll certainly be a look back on my life. I haven't even told Dex yet." I wince. "Ronnie is coming out on Sunday, and we're going through everything then, but I wanted to check it all with you first. I'm also nervous about telling him for some stupid reason." Really, I know exactly why I'm nervous. "Maybe I'll let Ronnie tell him."

"Good plan. Look, it'll all be fine, Eve. The kids will be fine. Dex will be fine. I'll be fine! Try and enjoy it. You seem happy. Optimistic. Good on you. I'm delighted for you."

"I feel good, Joanne. Sorting things with Ronnie has done me more good than you could ever imagine. I even had a great chat with my mum."

"Yes. I met her briefly last week at the gate," Joanne says.

"That's a story for another day." I grin before turning serious. "I was dreading all this, but I think it will be good for me." I nod absently, then turn my attention fully to her. "I feel like I'm facing my past, mistakes and all. Like you said before, it's a chance to look back over my life, like therapy. The producer said the exact same thing to me, you know. You can't all be wrong."

CHAPTER TWENTY-THREE

#familyfirst #guccislides #surprisesurprise #drumroll

@beli'EVE

Public Figure

Mama. Wife. Model. Content Creator. Collabs. Beauty. Fashion Interiors.

5,698	1.5M	212
Posts	Followers	Following

I feel even stronger and more assured by the time the week is over, and it's Sunday once more. After talking with Joanne and ensuring my family have support during filming, I'd made the decision to also accept help with @beli'EVE, so I'd journeyed back into Dublin to meet with Ronnie and the other girls in The Agency.

Knowing I could trust her again, I'd handed over the passwords to my accounts and reinstated Amber as administrator. No one but Amber knew how to be me and talk to followers like I could, so it made utter sense. Her sheer enthusiasm abated the butterflies I felt as I passed her the reins. Amber had some great ideas. From the off, she'd gushed about brand collaborations and style files. Straight away, it halved my workload and then some, and I'd left knowing I'd made the right decision.

At home, things had settled too. Dex was up to his eyes in work, inundated with calls. Much as he didn't like to admit it, secretly we both knew it was down to Ronnie's reference in her TV interview. Either way, the phone is ringing off the hook.

Milo seems fine. Faye does, too, albeit she's a little quiet, but I put it down to exam stress. As for me, I'd vowed to try and forget everything negative. Revisiting the accident in college left me exhausted, as had the difficult conversation with Mum. All I have room to focus on now was the preparing my mind for the documentary. After that, who knows?

Underlying everything, however, is the relief that my stalking nightmare is behind me. I feel light, hopeful. The more I think of it, the more I see that Ronnie is right. Whoever had been doing it had cleverly tapped into my paranoia about the past, my affair, the lot. Ronnie claims she'd been hacked regarding the infamous alleyway photo of Conor and me. I now tend to agree.

My social pages are alight with posts of support about the documentary. Follower numbers are sky-high again, and countless brands have contacted me to be featured.

However, yesterday Ronnie told me over the phone that she had something incredibly exciting to share today.

I'm nervous about how Dex will receive her and feeling tense about finally having to tell him that Conor will be coming to Ireland to reshoot my pictures. I tell myself to relax all morning – that Dex doesn't know about the affair and that he and Conor won't even cross paths, thanks to Heather. I'd considered contacting Conor to talk it over, but Ronnie is adamant that it's not a good idea – to wait until we're together in person.

#

Any tension I feel subsides when Ronnie spills through the back door laden with bags, then skids across the tiles in her Gucci slides, shrieking, "*Holy shit!*"

Her diamanté sunglasses are lopsided on top of her head when she rights herself by gripping tightly to the edges of the island counter.

Even Dex laughs. I breathe a sigh of relief when he walks over, takes Ronnie's bags, sets them on the countertop and hugs her.

"That's what you get for trying to frighten me into submission on National television," he says, patting her on the back, chuckling.

"I was just trying to get your attention," she smirks as he releases her.

It's good to see Dex laugh. He's been quiet this week, distant. Despite vowing that I trust him, I sometimes find myself watching him curiously, reading into every word he says. I'm furious with Mum for planting a seed of doubt and even angrier with myself for allowing it to grow. Not to mention that my eyes are stinging from opening them as wide as possible to stare at my reflection in the mirror, asking myself what it is I can't see.

Unsurprisingly, I haven't heard from Mum since. I'd thought about picking up the phone to question her further, but I'm not ready to talk about it more nor challenge Dex. After my affair with Conor a few years back, I may never be. Perhaps not knowing is the price I must pay for my actions.

Next, Ronnie scoops Milo into her arms. "Shit, you're tall. It's good to see you, little man." She ruffles his hair. "That big bag is for you." She gestures to the counter.

As soon as Milo opens it, he screams. "*It's the latest Xbox, Mum!*" He high-fives Ronnie. "*Thanks. Gotta go, sorry!*" He vanishes out the door with the bag.

"And never to be seen again." I laugh, walking over to fill the kettle.

When I look back, Ronnie is staring at Faye, standing back cautiously.

"Well, knock me over with a feather. I thought your mother was the most beautiful thing in the world, but I was wrong." Ronnie whistles. "No offence, Eve."

Indeed, Faye must look entirely different from when Ronnie last saw her.

"For want of sounding like a creepy uncle at Christmas, you're a young woman!"

Faye rolls her eyes and laughs. "You look good too, Auntie Ronnie."

While I make tea, Dex moves Ronnie's bags, making room for all of us to sit down. As I put mugs out, I glance over to Faye and Ronnie chatting on the sofa. I watch Ronnie lean in and whisper something to which Faye nods in earnest. Ronnie says something more, then hugs Faye suddenly. I attempt to edge closer so I can hear.

"Now!" Ronnie says, getting up suddenly.

I startle.

"You okay, Eve?"

I nod.

"Faye, see if you can drag your brother away from the Xbox for a minute," Ronnie orders.

Faye does what she asks, and Milo appears moments later.

"Now, let's get business out of the way, shall we? Then you can open the rest of those bags I brought, full of brands who want to work with you all."

"*Yes!*" Milo punches the air.

Faye doesn't look so thrilled, nor does Dex.

"But first," Ronnie continues oblivious, "I want to run through the plans for the coming months."

I swallow as she begins, knowing somewhere amongst those plans is a photo shoot with my past.

Everyone listens intently to what is involved in a set of filmed

262

interviews – fly-on-the-wall filming, mostly involving me, in several of the hotel locations, maybe at home if I am open to it. Then she runs through timings and schedules, assuring us that it will all be finished by the end of June.

"It's now mid-April, so it's tight." She turns to Faye. "It will be tricky for you with your exams. How are we sorted for that?"

Faye jumps in. "Joanne said I could study at her house. She was here when you were in town with Ronnie, Mum."

I nod.

"Yeah, she told me the other day when I called over to her. It's a great help." I turn to Dex. "You forgot to tell me she dropped up."

He touches his hand to his head. "She was only here five minutes. Slipped my mind."

"Well, that's one thing sorted. Is that okay with you, Faye?" I ask.

She shrugs, then stares at her feet.

"Who's Joanne again?" Ronnie asks.

"Friend," I answer.

"Neighbour," Dex says simultaneously.

"Well, having neighbours and friends on board is always handy," Ronnie says.

"I texted her earlier to ask her to pop up and meet you, but she had plans," I say. "We'll do it another time."

Ronnie nods. "Okay, let's move on. This is major opportunity – for us all. You included, Dex. Like it or not, this will put your business on the map, so embrace it. Now, you've all had Eve to yourselves for the past few years, but it's time to share."

Dex glances at me and throws his eyes up to heaven, but he's smiling.

"Just for a little while," I add.

"We'll see about that," Ronnie mutters. "Currently, offers are coming in that may be a way for you to have your cake and eat it, Eve.

Bigger bucks, less time-consuming."

My eyes flash up at Dex. He's listening closely, looking surprisingly agreeable.

"I don't even know where to start," Ronnie goes on. "There are at least three book deals. Countless brand ambassador offers, only now we're talking more Dubai Air than the local supermarket. There are a few TV presenting roles, a movie cameo –"

"No!" I say, utterly astonished. Without being able to help myself, I grin from ear to ear. Perhaps this is what Heather meant by life-changing.

"And then this."

She walks over to where Dex put her bags, leans in, fishes something out, returns and places it on the counter. All our eyes settle on Timeline's original album cover. My stomach clenches.

A grin spreads across Ronnie's face. "*Timeline's Greatest Hits* is out this year. They want you for the cover, Eve. They think you're some sort of good luck charm."

I'm so shocked I don't know how to respond.

Even Dex looks impressed. "*Wow*," he mouths.

"That's not all," Ronnie goes on. "They want to shoot the video in Ireland with you as the star."

"*No!*" I shriek. It's more than I could ever have imagined. I hold my breath. I think I know what's coming.

"They want to recreate the original shoot. They even want the original photographer to do it – Conor Malone."

His name echoes as I glance at each family member in turn. All but one smiles back. One expression morphs to thunder. Strangely, it isn't who I expect.

Before anyone can say anything, Faye turns on her heel, thumps upstairs to her room, then slams the door.

Dex wears a confused expression while my stomach plummets to my feet as if I've driven over a ramp at high speed. I force myself to maintain composure.

"What was that?" Dex turns to me as I shrug.

Thankfully, the news of Conor's return hasn't appeared to faze him in the way it has Faye, but I'm as flummoxed as him at her reaction.

"I have no idea," I respond, looking at Ronnie. My back is to Dex as I widen my eyes with obvious trepidation.

She, too, makes a puzzled face before shaking her head ever so slightly, secretly warning me not to panic. "Well, that wasn't quite the reaction I was hoping for," she says. "Maybe she was hoping for Justin Bieber."

Dex laughs at the joke before turning serious. "She's in bizarre form this week," he says, then looks at me. "It's huge news."

"I'll go chat to her," Ronnie offers as she moves towards the door. "Maybe it's all a bit much with her exams. She might be worried about all the distraction."

"I'd say that's it all right," Dex agrees.

"Maybe I should go, Ronnie," I say uncertainly.

"*Nah!*" She bats the air. "Let me. I love me a bit of teenage angst." She disappears around the door.

Inwardly, I exhale with relief, far too afraid of what Faye might say to go near her. Is it possible she knows something about Conor, or is this my paranoia playing tricks on me again? Realising I'm gripping the worktop and staring into space, I snap myself back to the present, nodding absently when Milo asks if he can go and play on the Xbox again. When he's gone, I turn to Dex.

"She's fine," he promises. "Ronnie is right. I'd say she's worried how it will affect her exams."

I nod, praying he's right. "Maybe I shouldn't do it."

Dex tries to laugh, but it sounds hollow. "We both know that's not going to stop you." He begins picking up mugs, heading towards the dishwasher.

My gaze follows him. "What's that supposed to mean?"

"Nothing, honestly." He turns to face me. "But come on, music videos, album covers, presenting jobs, books deals. All suddenly happening at the end of your career?" He raises his eyebrows. "I told you Ronnie would push this to the max, didn't I?"

"I had no idea."

"Didn't you?"

I frown, unable to read his tone. I decide to give him the benefit of the doubt.

"No, I really didn't."

"And are you happy about it all?"

"I'm in shock," I say. "The documentary seemed big enough without all the rest of it." I walk towards him. "Are you mad?" I ask, taking his hands.

He lets me, but his grip feels limp.

"What's the point in being angry anymore, Eve? You are who you are. It's never going to change." He shrugs, removes his hands from mine and stuffs them in his pockets.

"Hey, just a minute ago, you were congratulating me," I say, my face falling.

"I suppose the reality of what all this means has just hit. I'll never see you again by the sound of it."

"It's temporary, Dex. When it's over, I'll book a big holiday for us all before Faye starts college, and we'll have loads of time together to –"

"Is this before or after you write a book and take on a presenting role?" This time, his tone is pure sarcasm. "I've work to do right now. It sounds like you and Ronnie have a lot to discuss, so –"

"Dex!" I move closer, but he steps back defensively, leaning against the kitchen counter.

My shoulders slump under the weight of familiar guilt. Once again, I'm torn between my family and my career. I'm so tired of all this tugging and pulling with Dex, back and forth. He gives, then grabs it away. I'm instantly reminded of what our relationship was like in Dublin, pregnant with passive-aggressive remarks and jibes.

Out of nowhere, I whisper, "I wish Lily was here." Since the conversation with Mum, I've thought about Lily a lot – the things she'd say, how she'd always know what to advise me. "I really miss her lately," I say wistfully, crossing my arms and hugging myself. "She always knew how to ease my mind or send me a sign." I look up at my husband desperately. "Everything is going too fast, Dex. I'm finding it hard to keep up too, you know?" My gaze slips to my feet.

He softens. "She's still with you, Eve. If you have doubts about all this, maybe you should just say no. Maybe Lily leaving you this place was the sign – not to work too hard, to focus on your family instead." Dex gestures towards the windows at the back of our enormous kitchen.

I follow his hand so that I'm looking straight at the vast greenery right outside. My life here is so perfect, but why do I have to pick?

"Look at what we have here," he continues. "Do you really want to give it up to be running all over the place again? Never home. Lily wanted you here, Eve. That's why she left it to you."

I'm about to agree, but instead my eyebrows knit together as a memory surfaces. It's so clear. It feels as though it's been at the edge of my subconscious all this time, waiting for me to see it. Like responding to clashing symbols, I suddenly pay attention. Come to think of it, Mum had tried to remind me of it last week too before I'd cut her off. Now, I hear Lily's words so vividly that it's as if she's standing next to me.

"I know you love it here, but it's not for you, and it never will be … if you ever end up back here, then I'll know I've failed you … this place is too small for you …"

My gaze moves from my feet to my husband's face in slow motion. He's still speaking. I stare at him as if seeing him for the first time. To my mind, his speech blurs, morphing into what sounds like a continuous drone. If Lily didn't think I should end up here, then why on earth would she leave it to me? She'd said it herself, the day she told me to go to New York, then reiterated it almost every time I saw her since. Not in so many words, but by constantly reminding me that I was still on the right path – to keep moving forward, to never look back. Lily wasn't one to change her opinions and she'd adored my success, convinced that I'd continue to grow.

I snap out of my trance. "Did you come and see her, Dex?"

"What?" His head jerks back suddenly. "Who?"

"Lily," I mouth slowly. "Did you come to see Lily here?"

"Yeah," he answers as if I'm losing my mind. "With you. A load of times."

"And what about without me?" I glare. "Did you ever come here alone?"

Dex tries to answer, but nothing leaves his mouth.

I persist, "Did you ever ask her for anything?"

I no longer feel like walking on eggshells, pandering to him because of my guilt. Lily is still with me, only until now I haven't been listening to what she's been shouting. Was it possible that on this occasion Mum was right? Had Dex somehow twisted Lily's arm?

Dex looks nervous. He puffs a few times, shrugging uncomfortably. "What the hell would make you say that?" He tries to glare back, but he can't hold my stare longer than a few seconds. "Never," he responds at last. "I never came to see her alone. Why would I? What do you think I asked her?"

"When Mum was here, she said –"

"Oh, here we go! What a surprise! Gwen is nothing but a shit-stirrer."

"Maybe." I sound calmer than him. "But I've been thinking … you know Lily never wanted me to end up here, Dex. Unlike you and my mother, Lily was the one person who thought I should actually seize every opportunity."

I take a few steps back, narrowing my eyes.

Dex's mouth opens as if he's about to object, but I stop him.

"You've always had a problem with what I do, haven't you? Why? Yes, I was gone a lot. I've admitted that, but I adore my kids. I was working to give them a better life, but you always try and make out that I'm selfish, neglectful even. Believe me, I've beat myself up about it enough without you doing it too."

He doesn't answer.

I throw my hands up then rub them down my face. "Oh, God. I'm so tired of trying to please everyone all the time, but mostly you, Dex. I'm so tired of trying not to upset you." My voice wobbles. "What about what I want?"

His jaw juts forward. "You gotta be kidding me. It's always about you, Eve. Go do your stupid documentary all about *your* life. Go do your music video and your album cover. Go upset your children like you've just done with Faye, like you've always done. *Go be everywhere but here!*"

"It hasn't always been about me, Dex. I've been here for the last two years, non-stop, trying to make up for my mistakes. It's just six weeks. I'll still be around."

"Whatever." He shakes his head.

"Fine," I say. "But first, why don't you tell me the truth. Did you ever ask my mother for money?"

His face turns red. "Never. How dare she say –"

"Did you come and see Lily?"

Silence.

"I know that you must have come to see her by the way you're acting. Now, I want to know why?"

"What exactly are you accusing me of?" He puffs his chest out.

"You tell me. What did you do?"

He doesn't respond.

I'm so angry that without thinking, I babble on, "Lily believed in me, Dex. She said I shouldn't be afraid of who I am. That I shouldn't let my past stop me –" I freeze, suddenly realising I've said too much.

"And what past would that be, Eve? Come on!" He steps closer. "What's your big secret, *huh*? Because I know there's one. Why don't you tell me?" He laughs. "You absolute hypocrite!"

It hits like a punch in the gut. Before either of us can say anything more, Ronnie sails back into the room. Innocently looking from me to Dex, she asks, "Who died?"

Neither of us answer.

The tension breaks when Faye walks through the door, straight for me, and throws her arms around me.

"Faye, if you don't want me do this, just say the word," I whisper.

"It's okay, Mum. I was worried about everything, but Ronnie said it would all be fine. I freaked out," she answers into my hair, squeezing me hard.

I squeeze back, trying to hide that I'm shaking from the argument with Dex.

It isn't the first time Dex has hinted that he suspects something happened before we met. Worse still, I know Dex is lying about Lily. Another thought strikes as I hold my daughter close. I wonder what else is right there on the periphery of my thoughts, waiting to reveal itself. When I let go of Faye, Dex is gone, and with certainty I realise I've just lived through another moment that will change everything – I just don't yet know how.

CHAPTER TWENTY-FOUR

#naturetrail #paddingtonbear #alibi #homealone #ghosts #itsokay

---

@beli'EVE

Public Figure

Mama. Wife. Model. Content Creator. Collabs. Beauty. Fashion Interiors.

5,698	1.5M	212
Posts	Followers	Following

"So, what did Faye say earlier?" I ask Ronnie as we make our way along the muddy path beyond the gate at the back of the garden.

After Dex had skulked away and Faye had gone to study, Ronnie and I had escaped to my studio to continue planning. Now, I wanted to show her the place I'd suggested to Heather at our meeting for the reshoot of the red dress photos.

"Nothing more than she said to you. It was just a lot to take in. She was worried about not seeing you, that sort of thing."

"Are you sure that's all because for a moment I really thought –"

"I know what you thought, Eve, but seriously," she grimaces, "Faye knows nothing about Conor. Christ, you're so paranoid."

I nod as we pick our way along the forest path, moving branches out of our way so we can pass. "Lately, it's hard not to be, believe me. So many things seem to be surfacing out of nowhere."

Ronnie stops abruptly as a branch suddenly flies at her face. She catches it in time, pushing it away. Then she kicks a few bigger stones out of her way with her boot.

"Where the hell are we going, Eve? Honestly, if I thought we were doing a nature trail today, I'd have dressed for the occasion or, even better, I'd have stayed the hell home." She raises her eyebrows.

She's dressed in one of her usual sharp suits, gold cuff bracelets, Versace sunglasses, and now yellow wellies. I'd forced her to replace her shoes with them before leaving the house. The rig-out is a mix between Paddington Bear and Diane Keaton.

I grin. "It's not much further. I swear."

"Go on. What were you just saying?" she prompts as we continue along the path.

"I was saying that everywhere I turn, the past is out to get me. Did I tell you Mum was here when I got home last week?"

Ronnie turns her mouth down like a fish. "No. How was that? I bet she heard about the documentary."

"Yep, and she doesn't want me to do it. She's afraid things will come out about the baby … the drugs." I meet her gaze.

"I'm surprised she even brought it up with you. I thought you never spoke about it."

"We don't," I sigh. "But we did that day. I told her not to worry, of course. Still, I suppose with regards to my mental health, she probably thinks people will accuse her of not doing anything to help me."

"Well, she didn't." Ronnie tuts.

"I know, but she did apologise."

"Too late, but I suppose it's something. Did she say anything more?"

I stop walking. "Yeah. Get this, she thinks Dex did something to convince Lily to leave me this house! I told her he didn't, but now I'm not so sure."

Ronnie listens as I tell her what just happened back in the kitchen while she was talking with Faye and what I remembered about Lily.

When I finish, Ronnie looks completely taken aback.

"I remember Lily saying that to you that day," she says. "I was here, remember? I'd come to convince you to come to New York. It was a pretty inspirational speech, to be fair. I agreed with everything she said, and I still do." She splutters dramatically as an insect flies into her mouth. "Christ, it's like being in the bloody rainforest. So what did Dex say? Did he try to deny it? Mind you, it sort of sounds like something Dex might do – the act of a desperate man, perpetually afraid of losing his wife."

I stare aghast. "Is that what you really think?"

She shrugs, but her voice is full of concern. "I like Dex. I always have, but ... I don't know ... your success or something threatens him, and he's clearly afraid of hard work."

It's similar to what Mum said. Even still, I object, "That's not true. He's never worked harder in his life than he is now."

"Now," Ronnie repeats. "What about before? It's as though he didn't want to do work unless it was his dream job, but then he didn't want you working either. And how did he get the money to start the business?" She points at me and raises her eyebrows.

I tut. "It's our money, Ronnie. Not just mine."

She shrugs.

"We don't all get to *only* work at something we love. When you have a family, surely, you'll do anything. Do you want me to be completely honest?"

My eyes pop. "Is that you not being honest?"

Ronnie has the grace to smirk. "Dex controls you by making you feel guilty about the kids. It's his little bit of power. He's been doing it for years, Eve. You're a great mum and actually an amazing example of determination to Faye and Milo, but he uses the fact that you work hard and that you like working against you." She pauses, giving me time to let it sink in. "Maybe you can't see it, but I can." This time, Ronnie's eyes fall to the ground. "My dad was the same with my mum, you know."

"You never told me that."

Ronnie walks ahead. "There was nothing to say. It was what it was. My mother had absolutely no say in her life whatsoever – no control, no power. She just accepted it, went along with what he wanted. He used to guilt her into submission. I swore to myself, I'd never become that way. But that's ancient history." She shrugs again. "So what did Dex say in the end?"

"He denied it. Then said some horrible things about me upsetting the kids. Then you walked in."

Ronnie whips around. "See, that's what he does."

It's a lot to think about. Could she be right? Is that what Mum had meant too?

"Are you going to raise it again?" she asks.

"I'm not sure."

Ronnie makes a face. "Sorry, Eve, but if Dex forced Lily's hand that's really sneaky. Not to mention weird. Why wouldn't you ask him again?"

"You know why!" I exclaim, then quieten my voice. "Because I'm a cheat, an adulterer. Whatever you want to call it. I screwed up, Ronnie. I have no voice. I lost it the day I started screwing Conor. Maybe even long before that . . ." I say the last bit to myself. "Not to mention all the other things I never told him. Maybe this is the price."

Ronnie shakes her head. "Oh, for fuck sake, Eve! Don't tell me, you're never going to question Dex about anything ever again because you made one mistake?"

"Yeah … I mean no. I don't know."

"What's your gut saying?"

"He's lying," I admit. "Ugh, why is everything happening all at once? It's because of the documentary, isn't it?"

Ronnie tuts again. "No, Eve. It's because you're thinking about the past. That's it." She puts her arm around my shoulder. "I've been thinking about stuff too, you know."

"Like what?"

"Like the weekend you lost the baby. Maybe if I'd been there … maybe I could have stopped it. I shouldn't have gone home that weekend. I thought you were better. I really did."

"It wasn't your fault, Ronnie. It was mine."

"No, Eve. It was an accident."

I stare off into space for a moment. "Something made me do it, Ronnie. I just know it."

"Did you remember something?" Ronnie looks anxious. She hasn't asked me that question in years. When it first happened, she'd ask all the time.

I shake my head. "No."

"Maybe it's for the best. I know I asked before, but when you were with Conor a few years back, did he manage to shed any further light on it?"

"No." I shake my head again. "He still says he left me at home that morning. The next thing he heard, I was in the hospital. I don't think he's ever forgiven me for what I did, for losing the baby. He's kind enough to still say he bolted because the police were closing in on him for dealing, but I don't think that's true. I think he used it as an excuse," I pause, frowning. "You know what's weird, though?" I stare straight ahead. "When the police came to the house, that time near the end of college, they never mentioned anything about drugs. Nothing at all …" I trail off. This was what I'd thought about mentioning to Ronnie the day we were in town talking about the past.

Ronnie studies me carefully. "But they must have." She smiles gently. "It was so soon after you got out of the hospital. Maybe you don't remember. You could still barely walk. I was so worried about you."

But it was something I did remember. I was afraid that the Guards had come to speak to me about the accident again, but instead they'd asked where I'd been two nights before. Exactly like Ronnie said, I could hardly stand, let alone walk.

I told them I was recovering from surgery and hadn't left the house in days. One asked me what hospital, then jotted it into his notebook to check later. It was clear from my weakened state that I'd been nowhere. Then they'd asked where Conor had been. I'd repeated exactly what Ronnie had told me to say before I'd come downstairs. I told them he'd been with me all night, Ronnie too. I said we'd all been at home, together. No one had left the house.

I look back at Ronnie now, trying to read her expression. It's blank.

"But Conor wasn't home that night," I say as I stare into space again, travelling back there. "The last thing I remember from that night was being on the sofa. Conor was there, and you. I was so tired that I could barely keep my eyes open."

"That's right. You passed out cold. We stayed with you," Ronnie recalls.

"But I woke up. I must have needed the toilet or something, so I went upstairs, but Conor wasn't there. I checked every room."

Ronnie says nothing.

"I told the police Conor never left my side, but that a lie." I pause.

"The funny thing is, I put my head around your door that night too."
My gaze moves back to her. "You weren't there either. Neither of you
were."

Ronnie grimaces sympathetically. "But I was there, Eve. I was in
bed. Conor was home too."

I eyeball her. "I need you to tell me the truth, Ronnie. Was Conor
involved in more than drugs? Did I find out something that frightened
me? Maybe that's the reason I relapsed."

Ronnie immediately shakes her head, dismissing it. "Ah, come on,
Eve! Like what? Honestly, I think you're clutching at straws. I'd say
some asshole mentioned Conor's name for dealing, and they were
checking up on him. That's it. And we were there that night, Eve.
You're mistaken about that part. It's completely standard to be
confused after what happened."

I nod absently. Maybe Ronnie is right, and I am clutching at straws.
It was such a long time ago my memory is bound to be hazy. "It was
just something that came to me, that's all. I remember the Guards
made me sign something to say that Conor had been home all night
like I was his alibi or something. Maybe they think Conor was involved
in something he wasn't?"

"Nah," Ronnie reassures me. "That's just protocol for their files.
Nothing happened, Eve. They were ticking him off about the drugs,
that's it. Warning him."

"And that's why he vanished a few days later leaving that vague note?"

Ronnie nods. "Exactly. It was better that he left, Eve. I'm still not
sorry I asked him to go. With him around, the way he was, you might
have slipped up again."

I nod, exhaling loudly as we amble on.

With all the stopping and starting, it's taken us longer than usual
to reach our destination. When we do, I apologise.

"I'm sorry, Ronnie. I don't know where all the ghosts from the past are coming from. Anyway, this is what I wanted to show you, right through here." I gesture towards the clearing in the shrubbery. "In summer, it's even nicer."

Ronnie makes her way under the natural arch.

We walk to the huge boulder that is Lover's Leap and she steps up on it. I follow.

Behind her, I close my eyes, listening to the sound of the river rushing below. I open them when I hear Ronnie gasp. She stands stock-still, staring ahead.

"I'd like to reshoot the photos here," I tell her. "Heather is going to come and look at it, but I already showed her pictures. She agrees it's even more impressive than the original Dublin location. If I have to do the photos, I'd like to do them somewhere that means something to me, here, in Wicklow."

When Ronnie turns, she looks dazed. Staring beyond me, she mutters, "It's practically identical."

"I know. That's why I suggested it." I pause. "Ronnie, are you okay?"

"Fine." She staggers down, rushing past me back onto the path. "I'm not great with heights anymore. I never was."

"I can see that." My gaze follows her.

Ronnie looks as though she's seen a ghost. Then again, lately, there are ghosts everywhere I turn. Unlike Mum and Lily, I don't need to wait for Midsummer's Eve for mine to appear. Mine are ever-present, so much so that I'm beginning to come to terms with them.

I glance towards Lover's Leap. As clear as day, I can picture Lily sitting there, watching me. I nod at the figment of my imagination, then turn back to Ronnie. She smiles, but I can't help but wonder what Ronnie just saw when she looked out over the valley. Whatever it was, it has turned her face a shade paler, making her hand tremble when she reaches up to flick her hair.

Whatever it was makes Ronnie say, "It's going to okay. It's all okay. Just relax."

I nod. It certainly feels like everything is moving in the right direction, as though the smoke is clearing. I'd felt it once before standing on a similar cliff, twenty years before. This next phase isn't going to be easy. I take a breath, filling my lungs as deep as I can, but I feel suddenly stronger – ready to face what needs to be faced, stop hiding, admit some home truths, change my life.

CHAPTER TWENTY-FIVE

Two Months Later – Midsummer's Day

#whenpushcomestoshove #afterthought #instahubby #idiot
#taxbreak #plastic

@wood4lifedesign

65	3,545	598
Posts	Followers	Following

"It's going to be okay. It's all okay. Just relax." Ronnie appears to be speaking to herself when she rushes past Dex, grabs her handbag off a chair, then reverses to take her car keys off the counter.

What used to be their kitchen now looks like the set of a television sitcom – one that isn't all that funny.

Ronnie turns at the door. "I'll get Milo. We'll be back in a flash. Everything is fine."

Dex rolls his eyes. Nothing was fine. It hadn't been since the day this production was conceived. Once again, everything ran over schedule this morning, meaning he is still waiting like an afterthought, wearing a stiff shirt, trousers erring on too tight, and a face-full of heavy make-up when he should be collecting his son from football camp.

Joanne is packing for her holiday, otherwise he might have asked her to do it. She'd helped out with Faye and Milo a little, but she's leaving later today. Faye is currently sitting her final exam, and Eve, as usual, is nowhere to be seen.

The last couple of months of filming had been a complete fiasco, peppered with constant delays, electrical faults, location setbacks, a bout of food poisoning amongst the crew, permit problems, you name it.

"All part of it," the producer, Heather, constantly reassures everyone.

Nothing fazes Heather with her clipboard, neat hair, high-vis jacket, comfortable hiking boots. She is ridiculously capable, making Ronnie appear amateur.

Watching Ronnie slowly come undone of late has been the only saving grace for Dex. From the off, it's been clear that Ronnie is in over her head, sinking almost as fast as him. Never more evident than when the Gallagher Group pulled out of the location deal at the last minute, claiming filming would prove too inconvenient for their guests. Apparently, they'd received several concerned emails. Dex enjoyed that particular shot across Ronnie's bow. Especially when he was pretty confident Ronnie had cut a deal for a percentage of what the hotel would have been paid.

In the end, Heather had suggested shooting much of the documentary here in the house and gardens after she scouted Lover's Leap for the photo shoot. Ronnie grew pale when she heard how much Dex and Eve would receive for the disruption. Come to think of it, now that he knew what was involved, they weren't paying them enough.

"Any idea when they'll be ready for me?" Dex calls to a man hovering by their kitchen door.

Wearing headphones pushed up on his forehead, simultaneously speaking into a walkie-talkie, the man ignores Dex.

Today is Dex's turn to be interviewed, probed about what it's really like being married to the great Eve Kelly. On his way downstairs this morning, stepping over electrical wires, pushing past strangers in the hallway, he'd noticed that someone had scrawled "Insta-hubby" into the very last section on the schedule board. Dex wanted to pull the sleeve of his long-sleeved T-shirt over his wrist and rub it out. He hadn't dared, for fear he'd be left waiting for the rest of his days.

"Any idea when they'll be ready for me?" he repeats as a make-up artist saunters past.

She stops, narrows her eyes, then practically mounts him to press a make-up sponge across his nose. He flinches at the unexpected assault.

"Sorry, love. You're a bit shiny on your T-zone." She steps back, squints again. "They shouldn't be too much longer." This time, she blots his forehead.

"Any idea how much longer that is?" he asks hopefully.

She wrinkles her nose. "I'd say you won't be too much longer than not too much longer." Her shoulders heave at the joke. When Dex doesn't return her enthusiasm, she says, "Eve's almost ready for the shoot. I'd say once she's at the location, they might start on you." She smiles brightly. "I just heard that the photographer has arrived." She pauses, folding her arms. "I'm actually a huge fan."

Dex is unimpressed.

Oblivious, she goes on. "Honestly, this whole thing has been a dream come true, hasn't it? Can you believe Timeline are playing here later? Like right out there." She gestures towards the back garden where the stage is being set. Tonight, Dex's all-time favourite band will perform live in his back garden while Eve is filmed amongst the crowd as part of the music video. Shooting the video here in their garden was just one more surprise that materialized over the last two months.

Under normal circumstances, it should be one of the most incredible days of his life. Dex is dreading every single moment.

She interrupts his thoughts. "I've followed Eve for years like, and now I get to meet Conor Malone too. Have you ever met him?"

Dex exhales slowly. "*Nope!*" he mouths, making a popping noise at the end of the word.

"Eve was just telling me they were a couple in college," she prattles on unaware.

"So I believe."

"Sweet, isn't it? How they created something so beautiful and now they get to do it again after years apart." She opens her eyes wide. "It's making me well up." Realising her error, she claps a hand over the mouth. "Jesus! Sorry. I forgot who I was talking to there for a minute." Yet still she continues. "Wait 'til you see Eve. She looks *stunning*. I'm gonna miss her so much. She's been such an inspiration. Literally, my hero. You're a lucky guy!" She winks, then walks away.

Dex clenches his jaw. Right now, he feels like the unluckiest man alive. A part of him would like to call her back and tell her that Eve isn't quite so perfect in reality. Not that anyone would believe him. Not when every person here has fallen madly in love with his wife in one way or another.

Dex stands, picks the constrictive fabric of his trousers out from between his legs and walks towards the window. Spectating the activity at the end of the garden is like watching worker bees in a hive. No surprise who is Queen Bee. Lately, Eve has been thriving like she's woken from a bad dream. She's changed, blossomed somehow, in what appears to be her natural environment of being around people. She starved herself of company for two years, but Eve is a people person. Dex doesn't necessarily like it, but he can admit it. Eve is calm and dedicated when everyone else is frantic. Not once has she complained or moaned throughout the oft gruelling schedule. Instead, she has put her head down to get the work done, and spend time with Faye and Milo any minute she has free. She remembers every crew member's name, making sure everyone feels appreciated. Everyone that is, but Dex.

If he wasn't so agitated about what will happen when this is all over, Dex might admit that he's equally impressed by Eve. A few times he's found himself standing mesmerised, staring at the monitor during her interviews, filled with impactful opinions regarding social media, people, how the world works, her experiences, her struggles. Even knowing that Eve is holding back, not delivering the whole story, she still sounds genuine. Eve is a star – one destined for far greater things than creating content, influencing … being married to someone like him, and Dex is petrified. Clearly, filming isn't the only thing that will end today. Tugging at the collar of his shirt, he swallows the lump of impending doom in his throat.

Just that morning, he'd hopefully asked Heather if she thought they might need more time, a few more days to wrap everything up.

She'd laughed heartily before issuing a strangely ominous response. "It ends tonight." Then she'd followed it brightly with, "Then life can go back to how it was before."

"I think we both know that's not true," Dex had muttered to himself, trying to smile when he saw Heather watching. He'd pointed to the acrylic clapper board, lying on the chair displaying the show's title: *Unfollow Me – The Fall and Rise of Eve.* "I think the rise has only just begun."

"I think you might be right," Heather responded, patting his shoulder in what felt very much like sympathy.

#

Eve knows what he did with this house. Dex is sure of that. What he doesn't know is what she intends to do about it. After she'd confronted him in the kitchen that day when Ronnie came to visit two months before, she had mentioned it again that same evening.

"When this is all over," she'd stated in no uncertain terms, "there are things that need to be said. I want it to be you who tells me, Dex. I can easily go rooting for the truth, but I want you to tell me."

She hasn't mentioned it since, nor has Dex managed to fabricate a way to explain it away. Certainly not one that doesn't make him sound like a greedy, manipulative, controlling liar. If anything, he's only gone and made everything a million times worse. Now, he can't see a way out.

Right on cue, his shirt collar tightens further as his mind flits to the text he received just that morning. He can't ignore it for much longer, not when time isn't on their side. His stomach somersaults at the idea that Eve isn't the only one who wants answers.

Hands on his hips, he shakes his head at the extreme lengths he'd taken to fix his marriage. All for Eve, he'd attempted to manufacture a perfect life – one where she didn't need to work and she could be at home with them. He'd been wrong to even try. Work is who Eve is. Her success isn't a fluke as she sometimes claims. *She* is a success. She'd made the business work even without Ronnie, and now her voice is more robust than ever. He was an idiot to think he could control her, shut her in a box. Now, she was about to break free, soar even, and it was all his fault.

He should never have gone to his mother-in-law asking for money, in hindsight. He'd thought Gwen would understand, given that she despised what Eve did for a living. In his mind, if they had a sum of money in the bank, it would give Eve freedom. Dex presented it to his mother-in-law from a place of concern, labelling it an advance of

Eve's inheritance. He'd even gone so far as to say that gifting the money would act as a tax break – a way to stop the government from getting their hands on Gwen's hard-earned cash after she was gone. He'd honestly believed she'd appreciate that part.

Gwen had glared at him like he was the stupidest man on earth. "And why on earth would that make me happy? I'll be *dead!*"

She'd spat the last word, then humiliated him with further titbits of advice from going back to college, getting a proper job, to growing a spine.

"You know I've just found out my only sister is gravely ill, and you're here pleading for money. Do you know what you are, Dex? Lazy." She'd slowly looked him up and down before muttering that it was all Lily's fault for telling Eve to go to New York in the first place.

It was only after he left, tail between his legs, that he realised what she'd meant – if Eve had never gone to New York, she'd never have met him.

Still, the reference to Lily planted a new seed. Eve often spoke about living with her aunt after college. Although she'd admitted to suffering with her mental health at the time, she still cited it as the fondest time of her life. The idea had hit like lightning. Lily already considered Eve a daughter. It made sense that one day Lily might leave Eve her house, which was even more grandiose than the familial home in Dalkey. For all Dex knew, it was already the plan. There'd been only one way to find out.

Dex lied when he told Eve he'd never come to visit Lily alone. In truth, he'd come many times, gradually building up to what he wanted to say. Thankfully, Lily proved far more amenable than her sister. With only minor probing, she'd revealed more than Dex had hoped for, all the parts Eve had conveniently omitted in the past. All Dex had to do was mention that Eve was under tremendous pressure and that he was fearful she'd crack. It wasn't entirely true. What was actually about to crack was their marriage, and him.

"You will look after her, won't you, Dex?" Worry flashed in Lily's eyes. "Eve is so strong, but I worry. How could I not?"

"Exactly." Dex went with it. "She's achieved so much. I'd just like her to have time for herself now, but you know Eve." He grimaced. "It's my fault, really. If I'd been able to provide like your sister has always said, then . . ."

"Don't you mind Gwen," Lily tutted, taking the bait. "Eve adores you."

"I'm just so worried," Dex went on. "She's not herself, so agitated and . . ."

Lily's hand flew to her mouth. "Is she using?" she whispered with a look of trepidation.

Uncomprehending, Dex nodded anyway.

"It's so easy to fall back into bad habits," Lily began before highlighting the state Eve was in when she'd first arrived in Annaford all those years before. Lily told Dex everything – how Gwen hadn't wanted to know, how it took Lily months to restore Eve back to health, how the grief of losing her baby almost tore Eve in two. A few times, Dex almost had to manually reach up to close his gaping mouth while pretending to already know.

It all made sense. Straight away, Dex understood everything he never had – Eve's struggle for approval, her drive to succeed, her addiction to work, how protective Ronnie was over her. Worst of all, it explained why Eve had been so adamant about keeping their baby after getting pregnant so soon after arriving in New York. Dex hadn't been part of some great love story. All he'd ever been was the supporting role in a tragedy.

"How can I help?" Lily had demanded. "Just say the word."

So he had. Dex used the newly acquired information about his wife and said that Annaford was where Eve needed to be.

"On two conditions," Lily set out. "One. I need you to swear that this place stays in one piece. I promised my sister, and I must keep my promise. And two, Eve must never know that I thought she needed my help. You cannot tell her that you came to see me or that I was worried she'd slip up."

One condition proved far more straightforward to keep than the other.

After giving it some thought, Lily had phoned Dex, asking him to take her to the local Annaford solicitor to amend her will. Dex ended up having a great chat with the solicitor afterwards. When Dex showed up a few months later to explain that Lily asked him to drop off a personal letter to be given to Eve in the event of her selling the property, the solicitor greeted him like a long-lost friend. To make it all the more authentic, he'd got Lily to write Eve's name personally on the front of the envelope and on a card for Eve's upcoming birthday. Dex kept the envelope, put the typed letter inside, and threw the card in the bin.

Of course, Dex sought advice regarding the house and land from his old developer boss between both meetings. He quickly discovered that the easiest way to hang on to a property of this ilk was to sell some land. Luckily, the same developer was interested. They started scratching each other's backs and managed to pull some strings to get in an initial planning application before Lily sadly passed away. Once again, the poor dear had no idea what she was putting her name to.

Then all Dex had to do was stand back, feign ignorance, and allow Eve to come to the conclusion that Annaford was where they all needed to be. That part had been excruciating for him. His mother-in-law did exactly what Dex thought she might – tried to convince

Eve to sell so she could include the siblings she barely knew in her good fortune. It resulted in a trip to the solicitor who produced the carefully forged letter from Lily, and Eve changed her mind. After all, Lily knew best.

When Faye became unwell and Eve fell out with Ronnie, the stars aligned in a manner of speaking. Dex distanced himself as much as possible. Eve acted so peculiarly during that time that Dex genuinely wondered if she had fallen off the wagon and was using again. Until one day, Eve came home pleading with him to move to Annaford, where Dex would have everything he'd ever wanted. Namely, Eve, all to himself.

He thought he'd left no stone unturned. It came as a surprise when his mother-in-law began glaring at him suspiciously. Since Eve had practically no relationship with her mother, Dex thought he'd have nothing to worry about. Apparently, he'd been mistaken. Dex also overlooked how much the house would cost to renovate. When the bills began to mount, edging their way through the already patchy roof, Eve used it as an excuse to promptly return to work.

And now, here they were.

Catching a glimpse of his reflection in the window, Dex is startled. With the make-up, he appears plastic, fake.

"They're ready for you now," a woman's voice breaks into his reverie.

Looking beyond himself, Dex sees Eve appear on the other side of the glass, making her way, barefoot, towards the granite steps. Until recently, they were where she'd sip coffee each morning wearing his old wax coat. He wonders now what she'd really been thinking while she sat there, longing for more.

If he'd thought her beautiful then, now she's almost ethereal in her red gown, her back bare, save two thin red straps running down her skin. She pauses as one of the team reaches up to adjust her hair. Someone produces a pair of Ugg Boots for her to wear on the way to the location. Eve says something, and they laugh. Dex has a sudden urge to bang on the glass in the hope she turns around. He lifts his hand before noticing someone else has caught her attention. Even from here, Dex can tell who it must be. Although Eve's back is to the window, he somehow knows his wife is smiling at the man at the end of their garden – the same one who'd once shattered his wife's heart into a million irreparable pieces. That man captured Eve for eternity. Now, he was about to do it again.

"*You fucking idiot,*" Dex mutters suddenly.

"What's that?" the woman behind asks.

He turns to face her. "I'm a fucking idiot."

"That's great," she smiles woodenly. "This way, please."

Dex follows just as he'd once followed Eve halfway around the world. Only this time, he's gone a step too far. Now, there was only one thing to do. He stops suddenly.

"Are you okay?" the woman asks. But she's already speaking to his back.

#

Before the door closes behind them, her arms are around him, her lips heading for his mouth. For one moment, he finds himself responding before he remembers why he's come. She'd texted that morning to say she needed to speak with him urgently – that before she left, they had decisions to make.

"Wait!" Dex removes his arms from around her body. "Joanne, wait, please."

Joanne stands back, staring up at him intently, just as she had the night she'd called around when Eve stayed in town after meeting

Ronnie. She'd stayed far longer than the five minutes she'd told Eve.

"We need to halt everything right now," he pleads. "I don't even know how it's got this far." But of course Dex knew. He remembers now how he'd seen red when Eve texted to say she wouldn't be home that night. Later that evening, when Milo went to his room, Joanne was suddenly knocking at the back door then sitting on the sofa next to him and Faye, offering Faye a place to study during her exams. When Faye, too, went to her room, Joanne stayed on.

They chatted for hours and, for the first time possibly ever, Dex felt he was heard. As a counsellor, he'd wanted her advice. Maybe she could recommend someone for Eve to talk to. He wasn't the problem, was he? Surely it was Eve. Joanne understood everything, agreed with him, so much so that he ended up revealing more than he intended – things like how he secretly believed his wife enjoyed the drama, liked being controlled, and how he knew something that could seriously damage Eve's reputation. Instead of being appalled, Joanne lent him her ear, encouraging him to open up. When tea transformed to red wine, Dex was sure he felt something stir between them. Joanne must have thought it too because she'd excused herself fast. Nothing happened, but it had been enough for him to lie to Eve about it.

After that, Dex avoided Joanne until Eve started asking questions about the house and Lily. When Dex slunk away after Faye reappeared in the kitchen, instead of going to his workshop, automatically he'd headed for Joanne's door. Once again, he'd ended up telling her more than necessary. That time, she'd pulled the curtains in the front room, pushed him onto the sofa and climbed on top of him.

Afterwards, although riddled with guilt, Joanne revealed how she'd come to care for him, believe in him, recognise he deserved more than being second best. She was lonely. He knew how it felt. It's been going on ever since.

While Eve has been otherwise occupied, Dex has spent more time here with Joanne than with his wife. Repeatedly, he finds himself picturing how simple life would be with someone like Joanne – someone who wants him that little bit more than he wants her.

"I can't go through with it," Dex says desperately now. "I can't do it. I think I still love her."

Joanne nods once, pivots, and disappears into the living room without a word. Moments later, she returns and hands him a piece of paper, then asks, "And what about now, Dex? Do you still love her now?"

He stares at it.

"Where did you get this?"

"A friend," she answers.

His blood runs cold as guilt morphs to palpable rage. The palms of his hands tingle as he pictures placing them on Eve's bare back, tensing his biceps and pushing her off the cliff where she must now stand.

It would certainly solve everything.

CHAPTER TWENTY-SIX

#coattails #heathershimmer #criminaloffence #orginalplan
#ohshit

@theagency

147	6,590	89
Posts	Followers	Following

Ronnie is growing impatient. She grabs her phone off the passenger seat, looks at the time, curses, and throws it back down. Conor must already be at the house by now. The shoot is probably happening without her. This isn't how it was supposed to be. If everything had gone to plan, Ronnie would have driven to the office, picked up the envelope that she'd moved from its original hiding place to the newly installed safe, then gone directly to the airport to collect him. They'd have had plenty of time to set things straight in the car on the way to Annaford when Ronnie handed over the envelope containing the photos and negatives. Then Conor would shoot the new pictures, and Ronnie would send him on his way with a similar warning as before. Only this time, he wouldn't be back.

Instead, Ronnie is now sitting outside Annaford Football Club, waiting on Eve's son due to the usual delays. Taking a deep breath and exhaling slowly, Ronnie closes her eyes. Immediately, she finds herself fantasising about Eve tripping on the skirt of her red dress and tragically tumbling off Lover's Leap. Now, that would be an ironic twist to *Unfollow Me – the Fall and Rise of Eve.* Ronnie growls at the thought. Even the name of the documentary makes her want to scream. It was Heather's idea, of course. Everything is bloody Heather's idea. In fact, ever since Heather of the sensible shoes arrived on the scene, Ronnie has found herself pushed to the periphery, relegated to holding Eve's coat between outdoor takes. Most days, Ronnie hasn't even bothered to show up since she's clearly not needed. She has a good mind to remind everyone that if it wasn't for her, there wouldn't be an Eve in the first place.

Heather has had it in for her from the moment the contracts were signed – all but ignoring her at every turn, leaving her out of decisions, forgetting to tell her schedule changes. Ronnie suspects she found out that Eve and her had already parted ways by the time Heather contacted her about the documentary. She probably knows now that she could have bypassed Ronnie altogether and gone directly to Eve, which she could have, of course. It wasn't her fault that Heather hadn't done her homework properly. Only now, instead of being at the helm, she has somehow morphed into a general dogsbody, a runner. It's no wonder Dex gets frustrated. Not that she has that much sympathy for him either. Dex has been noticeably absent lately. Whenever he's needed, he's nowhere to be found.

If forced to pick, Ronnie isn't sure who she hates more: Eve or Heather. But then, she also hates Dex and Faye, for that matter. Faye has proved to be nothing more than a sneaky little manipulative troublemaker. Yes. Ronnie hates them all, equally, even Milo. By default, he, too, is screwing up her plans.

She almost jumps out of her skin when her phone pings beside her. Gritting her teeth, she flares her nostrils. This morning, she'd received yet another message from a vague Instagram account. It made five in total over the last couple of months. Word for word, they were identical to the ones she'd received three years before. It removed the element of surprise when you already knew what was coming and when you knew precisely who was behind them.

The four messages said:

You know what Eve did. Do the right thing.

It's time for justice.

The truth will out.

Eve will pay.

Ronnie had known what today's would read before she'd even opened it.

It's time for Eve to take the fall.

She'd got the first one the evening after coming to Annaford to speak with Eve and her family about the documentary. All in all that had been quite a memorable day. It was the same day Eve brought her to Lover's Leap, where she'd stood on the rock feeling the past tighten like a noose around her neck. It was also the day Ronnie had threatened Faye in her bedroom after she'd stormed out of the kitchen upon hearing about the reshoot with Conor. And therein lay the problem.

It has taken all Ronnie's resolve not to text Faye directly, telling her to cop on or at least get some new material instead of sending the exact same messages she had three years before. Only Ronnie doesn't even want to acknowledge its stupidity. Faye is far too old to be playing the same mind games, especially when she'd already admitted to causing all the trouble three years back. Luckily, Ronnie has barely laid eyes on Faye during filming. If she had, she'd probably have strangled her with her bare hands, but her goddaughter has been holed up in the neighbour's house, busy studying or indeed hiding from her. Now that the exams are finished, Ronnie will be sure to tell Faye later that she's done taking crap from a psychotic teenager. This time, she will be even clearer than before.

"How could you?" Faye had looked up from where she was sitting on her bed when Ronnie barged into her bedroom that day. "Why would you want that man to photograph Mum again? How could you bring him back into our lives?" Her face was wet with frustrated tears.

Ronnie approached. "This is work, Faye. It's different. That other stuff is in the past. Your mum and dad are happy again and –"

"Not now they won't be. I'm going to stop it." Faye went to stand, but Ronnie pushed her back down.

"Don't you dare! You started this mess. If you say anything, I'll tell them everything you did, breaking into my phone and posting that photo …" Ronnie stalled, grappling for something more. "That's a criminal offence," she said at last. She had no idea if it was, but Faye looked suitably frightened. "Not to mention everything else you pulled," she went on. "Now, if saving your parents' marriage is what you actually intended to do, then pull yourself together. You are making it so obvious that you know something. Wipe your face, get down there, and apologise, because if you don't, you're about to ruin more than you realise. If you care about your mother, fix it, now."

###

Exhaling, Ronnie reaches for her phone. Thankfully, it's just a message from Amber in the office. Ronnie reads it and shakes her head. While Eve was shooting the documentary, Amber and the team were holding the fort.

Reached 2 mil followers! Ordered balloons! Please ask Eve to do a little thank-you video for followers if possible. I know she's probably way too busy but gotta keep them happy.

Again, Ronnie throws the phone onto the passenger seat, puts her face in her hands and groans. She's had enough of everything. With the help of the documentary, @beli'EVE has ballooned even further. It should be great news, only when it's all over tonight she will no longer have Eve. Eve has come into her own during this entire process, so much so that she no longer needs her. In fact, she is starting to believe Eve never did. Worse still, Eve is beginning to remember.

"Sit. Have a coffee with me. You look wrecked."

Eve had been getting her make-up done when she'd summoned Ronnie the other day, patting the seat beside her.

It had been on the tip of Ronnie's tongue to answer that she was wrecked from running around after her, but she was grateful for the break.

"We've barely had a chance to speak lately." Eve's eyes danced. Her hair was waved, clipped back off her face with tissue so as not to disrupt the curl. "What about all this?" She nudged Ronnie's arm and glanced around. "It's been crazy, hasn't it?"

Ronnie nodded.

"I was with the therapist again yesterday," Eve began.

Much to Ronnie's aggravation, Heather had insisted that Eve be assessed before and during the show.

"Anyway, something came to me out of the blue, and I asked him what he thought it meant." Eve paused again as Ronnie's back straightened. "Actually, a lot of mad stuff has been coming back to me lately."

"Really? Like what?" Ronnie swallowed nervously while Eve considered the question.

"It's hard to explain. Nothing terribly concrete, more bits of conversations, weird flashes, that kind of thing." Eve stared straight ahead, narrowing her eyes as if trying to picture them, then turned to Ronnie. "Do you remember the original plan?"

"What plan?" Ronnie's insides quivered.

Eve placed her hand on Ronnie's forearm. "Wasn't Conor meant to use other models too? Weren't the original photos meant to be a series?"

Ronnie stuck her bottom lip out and frowned. "Were they?" Her voice sounded painfully high.

"Yeah." Eve nodded assuredly. "I'm almost sure. There were meant to be all different girls, all wearing the same dress." She tilted her head and bit her lip. "It was meant to mean something along the line that no matter who we are, we all end up the same. We all fall together. Something like that."

Ronnie rolled her eyes. "*Hah!* Sounds like Conor's typical artsy-fartsy mumbo-jumbo!" She attempted to laugh.

Eve laughed too, then grew serious again. "What's weird is I keep picturing this other girl. I see her for a second, then she's gone." She growled with frustration. "It's just really annoying. It's right there ..." She tapped her forehead with her finger then looked at Ronnie. "What do you think it means?"

Ronnie grimaced. "How would I know? What did the therapist say?"

"He said that it could be my mind processing what's going on right now, appreciating that all this is happening to me." Eve paused. "Imagine if Conor had taken more pictures – it could just as well be someone else here, in my shoes." She shrugged. "I suppose I'm lucky it never happened."

"Very," Ronnie agreed.

Eve nodded philosophically. "Life is so strange, isn't it? A few years ago, something like this would have been my worst nightmare, but I've found talking about the past, my anxiety, really cathartic." She had stared ahead again. "Why didn't I go and talk to someone years ago?" She mused. "I have no idea what will happen after all this, but for once I'm not frightened anymore. I feel in control."

Ronnie was a fool to think she could mend things with Eve, work together again as if nothing ever happened. There were far too many secrets, too many lies, gallons of water under the bridge. Besides, Ronnie had already played her trump card with this documentary. All it had done was catapult Eve into another stratosphere, leaving Ronnie firmly behind. It should be Ronnie being interviewed, fawned over, adored. She'd be able to tell people what it really took to make it in life, to progress. For it was Ronnie who'd journeyed farther than them all, starting at the very bottom of the pile, clawing her way through mud, doing whatever it took. It was Ronnie who'd come from nothing, who'd escaped her controlling drunk of a father, and found a way to fund her education.

Ronnie may not have taken drugs, but she'd undoubtedly sold

enough of them in college to pay her way, even supporting Eve when her parents cut her off. Dealing was a temporary solution for more extraordinary things. It was how Ronnie first met Conor. A dealer from home had put her in touch. It didn't take Ronnie long to move up the command chain, so soon enough Conor was the one working for Ronnie. Eve was so caught up in herself that she never even noticed. All the while, Ronnie cleverly concealed herself behind both Conor and Eve so that no one was ever watching her. It worked.

Someone like Eve shot straight out of a perfect life would never understand that success wasn't always pretty. It meant doing what needed to be done, especially when someone threatened your future. To this day, Ronnie is still cleaning up the mess. If only Eve knew what Ronnie really did for her that night twenty years before – the one Eve recalled recently that the Guards came to question her about in college.

Eve was right. Conor and Ronnie did go out that night, leaving Eve asleep on the sofa – they'd be back by the time she woke. In the end, it took far longer than they could ever have imagined. It was only fair that Eve provided them with an alibi for what they did for her.

Everything would have been fine if Conor hadn't gone to pieces. That's the real reason Ronnie banished him. He couldn't be trusted. In truth, Conor never wanted to leave Eve. She meant the world to him, except he didn't deserve her. He fought Ronnie on it for days until she threatened to develop the roll of film he had given her for safekeeping. He was gone the next day. Now, he's back and deep down Ronnie knows he still can't be trusted. This time, she'll have to give him what he wants.

Ronnie's stomach clenches suddenly. Now, Eve's memories are resurfacing almost as rapidly as her confidence is growing. If her interviews are anything to go by, it shouldn't be much longer before she remembers the lot. Last week, Ronnie stood in stunned silence during filming, listening to Eve speak.

#

"At first, social media was like a new drug that no one knew the side effects of yet. It was exciting. I can admit that." Eve nodded. "The attention was nice, as was watching it grow, seeing people respond. For a while, it felt great. I really loved it. I still do, in many ways, but like everything in life, there's another side – one where people rip you apart and tear you down. Not only have I seen it, but I've been subjected to it." She paused. "I've had people say things online about me and my family that you wouldn't say to your worst enemy, but it stops here." Eve had stared straight at the camera.

To Ronnie, it seemed as though Eve was looking directly at her.

"Social media should be social. *Full Stop*. When it stops being social, when it starts encouraging behaviour or speech that you wouldn't be willing to say to another person's face, there's a problem. No one should have to experience that hatred. It's simple. If you don't like someone, press unfollow." She'd paused. "There's always a door, so leave, walk away, unfollow."

There'd been awed silence before the place erupted in applause, and Ronnie turned to walk away. Moments later, she'd spied Dex slinking out the front door, heading for the gate. It looked like he'd got the message too.

#

Ronnie is jolted back to reality by a sharp knock on the window.

"You have to sign me out." It's Milo, looking hot, his fringe spiked up with sweat.

Ronnie puts the window down. "But you're already out. You're standing right there."

"But you still have to come in. It's a safety thing." He splays his hands. "You could be a kidnapper like before. Only I'd beat the shit out of them this time." Milo makes a karate-chop gesture.

Ronnie's eyes narrow. "What do you mean 'like before'?"

Milo looks uncertain, then shrugs. "Just some weird thing at school once." He stops. "Actually, I'm not meant to say anything. Mum said not to tell anyone, not even Dad, cos she didn't want him to worry." He grimaces. "Now, I've told you. In my defence, it was ages ago."

"When?" Ronnie demands suddenly. Her entire demeanour changes as a memory of something Eve had said in the hotel room months back hits. She'd mentioned something about Milo and school, but the conversation had swept in another direction for some reason. They never got around to discussing it again.

"It was before we moved here," Milo answers.

"I need you to tell me about it, Milo. I won't say anything to your dad, I swear, but it's important."

Milo looks puzzled but nods and begins. "So, Mum was late one day to collect me. Someone cancelled her hair appointment or something, but this woman came instead. She walked up to me in the yard and said Mum had sent her from the hairdresser's, which was weird cos she had this mad curly red hair. She didn't look like a hairdresser to me, so I went up to my teacher and we went back inside to phone Mum, but Mum said she didn't know what the teacher was talking about – that she was already on her way and was just a bit late. The woman was gone when we came back out."

Ronnie feels the blood drain from her face. "Did they call the Guards?"

"No. Mum told the teacher it was just a mistake or something.

302

Then she told me we had to be super-careful from now on and not to tell anyone."

"Did the woman say anything else to you, Milo, anything at all?"

"Yeah, she told me her name. It was something beginning with N – beginning with 'Na' I think."

Ronnie whispered, "*Natalie.*"

"That's it. Good one, Auntie Ronnie. You know her?"

"No, Milo." Ronnie stared straight ahead, feeling bile rise in her throat. "Go back inside, okay? I'll be there in a sec. I just need to make a call."

Milo nods and turns. With a trembling hand, Ronnie reaches for her phone.

#

"What do you want?" Faye answers the call almost instantly.

"Where are you?"

"I'm walking back from the village. I got the bus after my last exam. Why?"

"I need you to stop, Faye. This has gone far enough," Ronnie begins, still praying there's some other explanation. "I know you're not happy with me about inviting Conor back, but this isn't funny anymore."

"What the hell are you talking about?"

"I think you know, Faye. Sending me creepy messages again. It's pathetic, psychotic actually, you need help," Ronnie's voice shook. "And what you did to your mother –"

"*I don't know what you're talking about!*" Faye shouts. "*What messages?*"

"Eh, try today's one – '*It's time for Eve to take the fall*'? Honestly, I haven't got time for this, Faye. Just –"

"*Ronnie!*" Faye shrieks. "*I swear! Wait. Someone sent you that?*"

Ronnie feels the air leave her lungs. "Please, Faye. I'm here collecting Milo, but you're scaring me –"

"I didn't send any messages. You have to listen to me, I think –"

Ronnie cuts her off. "But they're exactly the same as last time, Faye. It could only be you."

"*What last time?*"

"It was all you, Faye. You posted the photo. You sent Eve and me the threatening messages, the postcards. It was you. You followed Eve to Conor's house. You cancelled appointments. You moved things around the house. You were stalking your own mother. *It was you!*" Even as she speaks, Ronnie knows she was wrong. Unless Faye also tried to abduct her brother, she has been wrong about everything.

"All I did was post the photo!" Faye says down the line. "I thought that's what you meant." Then she starts blurting, "There was a girl … she sent me the photo of Mum. She pretended to be my friend but then she dumped me. I never met her. She called herself Natalie … Ronnie? Are you there? Ronnie? There's more. I need to tell you –"

Ronnie drops the phone. She drives away fast. In the rear-view mirror, she glimpses Milo waving for her to stop, but she can't. Ronnie needs to get that envelope from her office, and do what she needs to do, one last time. If it wasn't Faye, then there's someone else out there who believes Eve was someplace other than asleep at home twenty years before. Someone who thinks it's time for Eve to take the fall – accept the blame. Ronnie slams on the brakes suddenly as a thought crosses her mind. Then again, maybe that would solve everything.

CHAPTER TWENTY-SEVEN

#rockband #shinebright #innocent #samebutdiffernt
#whatdotheymean #oh

@Fayek_but_real

19	4,567	1090
Posts	Followers	Following

Faye has solved nothing. She gets up from her bed and walks towards
the window. Outside, the garden is transformed into what looks like
a movie set, paper lanterns hanging from every conceivable branch,
fairy lights strung like a canopy. There are industrial-looking lights as
tall as the trees pointed at a full-on stage ready for Timeline to perform
later. Faye gasps at what they've achieved since she'd escaped to her
room to think. Her mind has been heavy under the weight of the
earlier phone conversation with Ronnie and what happened next.

Her bedroom is one of the only places in the house yet unscathed
with electrical tape, complicated equipment, people milling past.
Securing the door, Faye had once again gone to her wardrobe, taken
out the photographs she'd found before in Ronnie's office and laid

them on the bed, but it was still no use. She had no idea what they meant.

Faye's eyes drift back to the stage where crew members, mostly dressed in identical black jeans and T-shirts, commence the sound-check. The sun is beginning to fade. Faye had been told earlier that they'd start shooting as soon as it's dark. By the looks of it, that will be in a few short hours. Momentarily distracted by the activity, she almost smiles. It wasn't every day a famous rock band shot their video in your back garden, featuring your mum. If she wasn't feeling so afflicted, she'd be out of her mind with excitement. But since speaking with Ronnie and then seeing her father how she had, Faye feels far too nervous to think of anything else.

She grabs her phone off the bed and tries Ronnie's number for what feels like the hundredth time, groaning with irritation when it goes straight to voicemail. Pressing end before leaving a message, Faye tucks the phone into her pocket. What she needs to tell her must be done in person.

Sitting back onto the bed, Faye gives herself one last chance to figure it out. She doesn't have much time before the friends she'd invited from school arrive for the after-party. It had been Mum's idea to ask them. Mum had also extended the invitation to their neighbours when she'd finally dropped by to introduce herself. It was only Joanne who couldn't make it. She'd left earlier this afternoon for a holiday in Tenerife with her sister. Joanne was gutted when she discovered that Timeline would be performing here. She'd even tried to convince her sister to delay by a few days to no avail.

The other neighbours all accepted. Though Heather had said she'd get someone to do it for her, Mum had insisted on calling to each of the four houses to tell the neighbours about upcoming filming and to warn them of any disruptions. Faye had gone along with her. Mum profusely apologised for not coming before then to welcome them to the neighbourhood, explaining that she'd been up to her eyes herself since moving in. She'd had to ask them to sign a confidentiality agreement until the programme was aired.

Mum had charmed them all – particularly the couple in the farthest house – especially Eoghan. He'd almost fainted when he clocked Mum on his doorstep. He's been utterly oblivious that he was living next to Eve all this time. To their amusement, he'd run to fetch his bottle of Holiday Feels and asked Mum to sign it. Apparently, he only used it in summer and just on his legs which simply refused to take a tan. He confessed to naming a character in one of his books after Mum. When one of their Ridgeback dogs sauntered over, stuffing its long snout between Mum's legs and almost lifting her off the ground, Eoghan had blushed deeper than any fake tan, exclaiming, "See, Coco's a huge fan too!"

Faye had mocked her mum the whole way home, saying that the experience had felt more like "Stalker Feels" than Holiday Feels. Suddenly it doesn't seem so funny.

Ronnie's earlier words ring in Faye's ears again now. "You were stalking your own mother. It was you!" What had Ronnie meant? Taking another breath, her thoughts return to their neighbours. Being with Mum that day, chatting happily, had reminded her of how Mum was back in Dublin before everything turned weird. Back then, Mum was always inviting people into the house, sitting them down at the kitchen table, offering them tea. She'd known all the delivery drivers, all about their families, often giving things she'd been sent to pass on to their wives and girlfriends. Whenever Mum was out and about, she'd chat with people in shopping centres and cafés – have her picture taken.

When they'd moved here, everything changed, including Mum.

Here, there were security gates and cameras, only one delivery man who was barely allowed in the gate. Mum filmed solely in her studio instead of showing her followers everything, as she once had. Here, Mum had practically no life, no friends. She rarely left the house. There were rarely other people in the house. Faye had believed that Mum was happy here, content to be home all the time, not as interested in work.

Now, it seems her mother had been hiding. Something must have happened in Dublin to change her – something other than an affair with her ex. Forcing herself to think, Faye tries to remember everything Ronnie had said earlier – "You sent Eve and me the threatening messages, the postcards. It was you, Faye. You followed Eve to Conor's house. You cancelled appointments. You moved things around the house."

Chills run up Faye's spine. Faye hadn't been the only one receiving messages. Mum and Ronnie must have been getting them too. Mum was being stalked. Worse still, Ronnie believed it was Faye.

"Oh my God," Faye whispers, finally comprehending.

When Ronnie deciphered that she had posted the photo, she must have assumed that she was behind everything else too – acting out like a baby because Mummy was cheating on Daddy. And if it was Faye, Ronnie must have concluded that they had nothing to worry about. Her mouth turns dry as realisation dawns even further. Earlier, Ronnie had said there'd been more messages – something about it being time for Eve to take the fall.

She stands suddenly, glancing back at the photos strewn across her bed.

She's sure it has something to do with those photos and "Natalie". Whoever Natalie is, she believes Mum is a murderer, and she must be planning to finally point the finger at Mum.

Right before Ronnie had hung up earlier, Faye had been about to confess to finding the photos in Ronnie's office, but the phone had gone dead. Does Ronnie know who Natalie is? Had she even heard Faye say the name?

Faye begins to panic. Reminding herself to breathe, she gulps for air. Whoever is behind it is mistaken about Mum. Deep down, Faye knows her mother would never do anything to hurt anyone. Indeed, Mum must be hiding something from her past, but it isn't murder — Faye is sure of that.

Going to the window, Faye peers out. She sees her mum standing in her red dress on the patio below, a coat over her shoulders, speaking with Heather, the producer. The photo shoot must already be over. Conor Malone must already be gone. Apparently, he isn't staying for the party. Faye had been glad to hear it at the time. Only now, she wishes he was. Conor must know what the photos mean. After all, he took them. Now she's missed her chance to ask.

For an instant, she considers going outside, walking up to Mum, and asking straight out. Only, she would need hours to explain it all. If she is wrong, she'd end up ruining the most important day of her mother's career. No. She can do this herself, prove Mum is innocent before anyone accuses her of anything. Removing her phone from her pocket, she tries Ronnie again. When there's no answer, Faye snaps a picture of the photos on the bed, opens Instagram, searches for the correct account, then sends the images in a message. As fast as she can, she taps out an explanation below, then sends that too.

It's her fault that the photos may have fallen into the wrong hands, so now she must fix it. Once again, without being able to stop it, her mind veers in a direction she can no longer avoid — a path that's far too close to home for her liking.

Pulling on her runners, she grabs her hoodie, opens her bedroom door, and makes for the stairs. Slipping out the front door to avoid the activity around the back, she glances right. Dad and Milo are standing to the side of the house, talking to some crew members. She half-smiles at Milo, wearing a high-vis jacket with a walkie-talkie tucked into the pocket, so invested in his temporary security position that he fails to notice her. For a moment, Faye pauses, half considering approaching her father, but she doesn't. Instead, she glares at the back of his head. Her father isn't the man she thought he was. Then again, he isn't the only person she has lost faith in today.

For the second time today, Faye approaches Joanne's house. She had called in earlier after her cryptic phone call with Ronnie. Feeling muddled, as out of her depth as she had done in Dublin, she'd found herself outside the house. Joanne was always saying to come to her if she ever needed to talk. Now, she did.

Knocking at the front door, Faye had stood back, still so dazed that she barely noticed how long it took for Joanne to come to the door. In hindsight, she understood why.

"Faye! How are you?" Joanne spoke loudly, flinging open the front door. Accustomed to being there, Faye strolled past her straight into the hall.

"Well, I'm done my exams, at least," she'd said with a shrug.

"What can I do for you?" Joanne smiled broadly, keeping the door open.

"I was just passing. Thought I'd call in," Faye began. "Actually, can I use the loo?" She winced, suddenly feeling the urge.

She stepped towards the downstairs toilet door, but Joanne flew in front of her, standing with her back to it. "No!"

Faye froze.

"I'm in here, Faye!" Dad's voice unexpectedly called from the other side of the door.

"Oh, hi," Faye said, startled. "Any chance you could hurry, Dad? I'm dying out here."

"Eh, I'll be a minute. Go upstairs," the muffled voice came.

Faye made a face at the entirely awkward situation.

"Your dad just dropped in to thank me for loaning you a place to study. I'm heading off soon. How's your mum?" Joanne smiled. "Star of the show is too busy for the likes of us, *huh*?"

"Good, I think. I haven't seen her yet." Faye winced again, jiggling. "Sorry, could I use upstairs?"

Joanne hesitated. "Sure. It's the door right opposite the stairs."

Faye climbed the steps, realising she'd never actually been upstairs before. Glancing briefly at the four other closed doors on the landing, she walked straight for the bathroom and shut the door. Sitting there, she wondered if it was strange that Dad was here. Indeed, he and Joanne appeared to be friends. Certainly, the night Mum had stayed over in town with Ronnie, Joanne had stayed chatting even after Faye went to her room. She had actually felt sorry for Dad that night. Before turning out her light, she'd gone back down to check on him. Realising Joanne was still there, Faye had stood outside, listening. She'd overheard Dad saying things that had shocked her – something on the lines that Mum wasn't so squeaky clean – that he knew stuff that could destroy her reputation. Then he'd said something odd about Mum liking to be controlled. It had turned Faye's stomach, making Dad sound like a jealous, chauvinistic pig. Then he lied to Mum about it, saying Joanne had just popped up for five minutes. Afterwards, Faye tried to put it out of her mind, dismissing it as Dad being angry with Mum – venting.

Faye flushed the loo, washed her hands, and quietly opened the

311

door. Downstairs, she could just make out the sound of Dad and Joanne talking. She stepped out of the bathroom and looked at the other doors, wondering which room was Joanne's. It was likely the one to the right, over the living room. Come to think of it, you could probably see their house from the window. Without thinking, Faye walked towards it, turned the door handle and peered inside. There was an old-fashioned vanity screen immediately in front of her, blocking her view around the corner into the room. Faye was about to leave when something caught her attention. Although the room was dark, she noticed a framed picture on the far wall so familiar that it almost didn't register. Not quite able to make it out, she was about to go in for a closer look when she heard Dad call her name from downstairs. Already uneasy, she startled, quickly closed the door and ran back downstairs to where Dad was waiting.

"Come on, Faye! I just got a call to collect Milo and several more from Heather." He shook his head and rolled his eyes.

Faye stared at his rubbery-looking face until she remembered today was his interview, but even with the thick layer of foundation, Dad seemed pale.

She smiled brightly at Joanne. "Have an amazing holiday, and thanks again!"

"Tell your mum good luck from me. I'll text her later anyway," Joanne said.

Faye stepped outside and began to walk towards the gate. Turning briefly, she saw something pass between Joanne and her father – a brief touch of hands, a hesitation, a look. Joanne leaned close to whisper something to him then stopped, whipping her hand away when she saw that Faye was watching. Oddly, the corner of Joanne's mouth had lifted into a smile. When he'd turned to Faye, Dad's face was a mix of emotions that no amount of make-up could conceal.

#

Standing outside Joanne's driveway now, Faye looks around. Joanne has already left. The car is gone, the blinds are all pulled down in all the windows. Tugging on her hoodie, Faye zips it, pulls the hood up, glances around cautiously, then heads up the driveway. Kneeling near the shrubbery, she reaches her hand between a mound of rocks, searching around. She'd seen Joanne do it once when she'd locked herself out by accident. She wasn't sure it would still be there, but it was. She exhales raggedly when she finds it, pulling out a key wrapped inside a plastic bag.

Her heart hammers in her chest as she approaches the front door. Once more, she looks nervously over her shoulder. Inserting the key into the lock, she quietly recalls the alarm number Joanne had told her, praying that it hadn't been changed since then. If it has, Faye's plan is to run as fast as she can out the gate onto the road, then cut back up through the fields to the back of Lover's Leap, where she can get back to her own house safely.

Inside, panting with fear, Faye reaches up and taps the code into the alarm pad, almost passing out with relief when it works. Though still light out, the house is in darkness with the blinds and drapes all shut.

Faye listens for a moment. When all she can hear is her own breath, she takes her phone from her pocket, opens the camera, so she's ready, then takes the stairs two at a time.

She heads straight for the door she'd opened earlier. Opening it again, she flicks on the light and steps around the screen. This time, her mouth hits the floor.

Faye stares in shock at the floor-to-ceiling rails of clothes – shelf upon shelf filled with bottles, boxes, packages from practically every brand her mother has ever worked with. Every dress she has worn, every single item of clothing, every pair of shoes, earrings, every product she has ever used or put her name to is right here in one room, like a shrine to Eve.

She stands mesmerised, trying to understand, attempting to find sense, an explanation, anything. But she already knows that what she sees before her is no coincidence. Earlier today, when Faye had noticed the framed picture of a girl in the red dress hanging on the wall, she'd known that something was off.

It instantly slots into place.

Over the last few months, spending time at Joanne's, Faye had noticed other things too that now make sense. For a start, Faye had glimpsed something on Joanne's phone one day when she'd gone to the bathroom. Before the screen faded to black, Faye noticed the Instagram app logo. It had struck Faye as odd for someone who claimed to be anti-social-media.

Joanne had also begun to ask a lot of questions about Mum. More than a few times, she'd passed some snide remarks to Dad about her, then tried to pass them off as a joke. Clearly, from what Faye had seen today, it seemed as though Joanne and Dad were more than friends.

Faye needed to find Mum or Ronnie and tell them what she's discovered. She removes her phone from her pocket to call Ronnie. When she doesn't answer, she tries Mum. It goes to voicemail. It's okay, Faye tells herself. Once she gets out of here, she can find them in person. Opening her camera quickly, she snaps a few pictures of the clothes and products as proof, then she walks towards the picture on the wall to do the same. It's almost identical to the famous photo of Mum that everyone knows – the girl in the red dress falling. Only Mum isn't the girl in this one. Instead, this picture is of a different girl in a red dress with a head of red spiral curls. This is one of the photos that Faye stole from Ronnie's office.

Faye's eyes settle on another large picture frame on the floor, propped up against the wall. Inside are the three other duplicate images also featuring the girl with curly red hair, except Mum features in these ones too. You can just make out Mum's hand with the tattoo on her wrist in the very corner. The photos are identical to the pictures that still lie on Faye's bed at home – the ones she has pondered over so often.

Seeing them arranged this way, framed in sequence, it clicks with Faye what they mean. This was no trick of the light or creative photography or editing. Like Eve, this girl had hung off a cliff. Only this girl fell. This girl hit the ground.

Faye jumps suddenly as she hears a sound behind her.

"It was you." The words float from Faye's lips as she turns.

"And it was you who sent me the photos. You provided the evidence I've been missing all these years. I did say thank you, remember?"

"Natalie?"

"No. Faye. As you can see, Natalie's dead. I'm her sister," Joanne says. "I'm the invisible one."

Then everything goes black.

1999

"What about *her*?" Eve asked as Conor shook his head. They were sitting on the steps of the Arts building, watching other students pass by. It was a change from how they usually sat, staring into each other's eyes. It was days after the photo shoot on the cliff, and Eve was on a mission.

"*Her?*" Eve gestured at a small blonde girl. "She's pretty."

Conor shook his head again.

"Not as pretty as you," he took her hand, kissed it and then tucked it into the crook of his arm.

She smiled. She was feeling better today.

"But they're not supposed to be me. Isn't that the point? They're meant to be different," she said.

"Yes, but she's not different enough. I'll know the right person when I see her."

Eve leaned her head against his shoulder, exhausted. Yesterday hadn't been a good day. Her stomach had felt crampy on and off and, from the moment she'd woken up, she'd felt anxious and dizzy, completely exhausted. Ronnie had insisted that she go to the doctor, but they'd told her it was all par for the course. Cramps were a sign that her uterus was expanding. Exhaustion was normal in pregnancy. It should have made her relax, but she'd still felt jumpy.

"It's to be expected, Eve," Ronnie had reassured her. "You're also learning to cope with your anxiety without, you know ... medication," she said diplomatically instead of "drugs". "Give in to the tiredness. You just need to breathe, rest."

Eve had nodded.

She'd been about to joke that what she actually needed was a line of coke to give her some energy, then a spliff to chill her out, but it wouldn't be funny. Not when the last few months of going cold turkey had been so tough and not when she was determined to leave that part of her life behind for the baby.

She supposed that being worried about becoming a mother was also normal. Only Eve was also concerned about her exams, moving to London, not being able to find work, telling her

UNFOLLOW ME

mother she was pregnant … relapsing. She was also worried about Conor. He seemed under as much pressure as her, if not more.

"I think I'll just develop the photos of you that we took the other day and send what we have," Conor said. "I might go and book the darkroom now." There was one on campus that he used.

Eve lifted her head to look at him. He looked tired, grey in the face, defeated. "But you said it was a photo series? It's what Ronnie promised the agency in London. If you don't deliver, they mightn't sign you!"

He tutted, then ran his hands down his face.

"I know. I know. Don't hassle me. There's enough going on."

Eve removed his hand from his arm. "Sorry, I just meant –"

His shoulders slumped. "No. I'm sorry. I'm just having second thoughts about the photos. Maybe it's the wrong idea altogether." He exhaled raggedly.

"*No*." Eve sat up. "I don't know how but I know those photos are going to be amazing, Conor. The other night felt special. Something happened up there when you were taking those photos. I could feel it."

Eve was right. Something had happened. She'd looked like a goddess while he photographed her, but he'd also put her at risk by asking her to pose off a cliff, hanging backwards with his unborn child inside her. Afterwards, it hit him like a tonne of bricks. What if something had happened? It had made him realise how afraid he was – how unprepared he felt to be a father. Ever since he'd felt sick. What if he couldn't provide for Eve and the baby? What if the agency said no? What if Eve relapsed? He knew he loved Eve, but he'd started to question

317

if he loved her enough to be tied down so young ... for the rest of his life. Was this it? Was he ready? Would he fail her?

"Do you not think the photos will be okay?" she asked, sounding worried.

Conor had been distant since the shoot. Perhaps she'd messed it up. After it, they'd gone home and feeling elated, she'd reached for him in bed, kissing him hungrily, but he hadn't responded. Lately, he seemed almost afraid of her, terrified that he'd hurt her by touching her.

"I already know they'll be beautiful," he said at last.

Eve relaxed.

"Then, you can do this. I believe in you. We'll find the right person. What about *her*?"

Their eyes moved to the concrete canopy beyond the steps to where a tall girl, with curly red hair twisting down her back, was standing talking to another girl. As if on cue, the girl's eyes flashed towards them. She smiled, looked away then said something to the other girl. Seconds later, she looked back again. The other girl turned to look at them too, but she pivoted back quickly, said something, and headed in the direction of the lake. The girl with the red hair remained.

"I've seen her before," Eve said out of the corner of her mouth. "A good few times, actually. She's always around the Arts steps. Look, we have the same shoes." She tilted her head. "That's mad," she said with a laugh. "Do you recognise her too?"

"I think so. Now that you say it, she looks familiar," Conor squinted. "She's the same build as you. The hair colour is good."

"Oh my God, look at her stomach," Eve said enviously as the girl turned to lean against the canopy pillar. She was wearing low-cut hipster jeans and a cropped T-shirt under a leather jacket.

"She dresses like you too. Well, like you used to," he teased.

Eve smiled back, sensing his mood lift.

"Wait there," she said.

Before he could stop her, Eve was on her feet, heading towards her. Conor sat back to watch. He saw the girl smiling, nodding along while Eve spoke. The girl jerked her head back in surprise, putting her hand to her chest as if she was flattered. Then she opened her bag. She took out a camera, waved it in Conor's direction, and smiled. Her smile was stunning. Conor laughed, waved back. She was a knockout. In another lifetime, perhaps, he smirked to himself.

Eve held the camera while the girl took out a notepad and pen. While Eve spoke, the girl jotted down what she was saying. When she was finished, she glanced up at Conor, smiled again, waved, and walked away.

Eve ran back to him and sat down.

"Done," she said, clapping her hands together. "You won't believe it. She's one of you."

"One of me?"

"From Belfast, *and* she loves photography. What are the odds?"

Conor raised his eyebrows. "I saw the camera all right."

"She's in. She said she'd do it. Her schedule is a bit tight. She's free a week from Saturday. I told her where to buy the dress, the place, the time, everything. I'll come too. All the same as last time. She has a class now, but I told her you'd meet her after, so you can run through everything again. Tell her more about it. Talk photo stuff. She was really interested. I, on the other hand, am wrecked. I'm going home to sleep. Apparently, I'm in a growth spurt. Her name is Natalie, by the way. Natalie from Belfast."

"You're amazing."

"One more thing. Why don't you wait and develop all the photos together? It'll give us something to aim for."

CHAPTER TWENTY-EIGHT

#showtime #bigrevelation #youcameback #momentoftruth

@beli'EVE

Public Figure

Mama. Wife. Model. Content Creator. Collabs. Beauty. Fashion
Interiors.

5,698	2M	212
Posts	Followers	Following

I search the crowd hopelessly. Barefoot, my dress flows behind as I
meander, this way and that, captivated by the lights, the music – my
face filled with anticipation.

"*And cut!*" the director calls over the loudspeaker.

The pre-recorded music ceases immediately, and the crowd relaxes.

"That was great, guys. Good job, Eve!" The director gestures to
me. "We're close now."

He turns to his assistant, describes something. I see them nod.
"Let's reset and go from the top."

I catch Heather's eye and grimace. I'm tired and she knows it. She
must be too. She raises her eyebrows, gives me a thumbs-up, and
mouths, "*Ten more minutes.*"

I show her my crossed fingers in response and take my place near the front of the stage once more. I think I'm still shocked that Timeline is in my back garden. If I wasn't so exhausted, I'd probably label tonight the most exciting of my life.

It's impossible to get my head around everything that's happened over the last couple of months. Heather was right. The entire experience has proved life-changing, but this final part is taking longer than expected. It's late, and I'm starting to fade. Refocusing, I shake out my hands, jump up and down a few times, take a few breaths, pep-talk myself that I can do this. While make-up retouches my face and the crew reset, I take the opportunity to glance around the sea of unfamiliar faces.

The garden is filled with strangers: extras, crew, security, sound technicians, you name it. Amidst the circus, I've barely laid eyes on my family all day. Craving a familiar face, I spy Milo at the very back, waving frantically from where he sits on scaffolding for a bird's-eye view. I gesture for him to be careful until I notice a crew member standing right behind him, holding on tightly. I sigh with relief, give Milo a big wave, then stand on tip-toes, hoping to catch a glimpse of Faye. She's probably off enjoying herself with her friends but, wherever she is, I know she's somewhere close by. I can catch up with them both as soon as I'm finished here.

Tonight feels like the end of an era. I've had the same bittersweet feeling all-day – anticipation, nerves, regret. I glance about, trying to locate my husband. I haven't seen him much either. Thanks to Heather, he was otherwise occupied while Conor was here. Later, I'd spied Dex once or twice in the distance, possibly avoiding me. I'm hardly surprised. We both know that there will be difficult conversations after tonight. I wonder what he plans to say. Will he continue to lie or come clean about convincing Lily to leave me the house? Either way, I already know the truth. Though I said I'd let him tell me, curiosity got the better of me, and I'd recently paid a quick visit to Lily's solicitor. He confirmed that a lovely American man had indeed accompanied Lily on her visit. When I showed him a picture of Dex, he'd nodded, adding that he'd come back a second time to deliver Lily's letter to accompany the will. I asked if he'd ever confirmed that the letter was actual from Lily, but he'd grown defensive, stumbling over his words. I'd let it pass. What did it matter anymore? The damage was already done.

Since then, I've rationalised that in a very strange way Dex did what he did to save our marriage. At least, I hope that's it. Either way, I'm not faultless. I had an affair. I also failed to tell Dex about my past. I've decided to tell him everything after tonight. I don't know if it will save our marriage but, for the sake of our family, I need to try. I can only do so with honesty. Let's hope he feels the same.

Turning to my left, I notice Ronnie scuttle across the patio and disappear inside the house. I get the impression she'd dodging me too. Considering that the documentary, the photo shoot, everything for that matter, was her idea, she's really failed to turn up, seeming generally disinterested most of the time. She's been standoffish, even rude, to Heather and the crew on several occasions. She'd been let down by the hotel group over the location, which meant using here as a base. Today, she'd gone to collect Milo and somehow driven off without him. But, most surprising of all, she never bothered to make the photo shoot with Conor – after all chat about making sure the past was in order. Now, it seems that whatever she needed to get in order didn't involve me at all. What Conor told me earlier is still playing heavily on my mind. I have some questions that I need to ask Ronnie later. This time, I hope she stops lying to me.

As I glanced up at the stage just over my head, the lead singer of

Timeline winks down at me. It's so surreal that despite my obscure thoughts, I laugh. For now, at least, I should try and enjoy this once-in-a-lifetime experience. It's undoubtedly proving far more uplifting than the photo shoot had been.

"Can we have a minute, please?" I'd asked Heather earlier when I came outside ready for the shoot to see Conor waiting at the end of the garden next to his assistant. He stood expressionless for a moment until a smile broke across his face, twisting my insides like only he could. I grinned back.

At Heather's command, the crew dispersed as we made our way towards each other. It felt as though it were just two of us alone. Though Conor had never been here before in person, in spirit he'd been present with me more than he could ever know.

Instinctively, I threw my arms around him and rested my head on his shoulder. "It's good to see you!" I exhaled in relief. When I lifted my face, there were already tears.

He studied me for a moment, searching my eyes.

"Don't cry, Eve." He tilted his head to one side.

"I'm sorry. I just … I missed you …" I tried to smile. "Look at us." I gestured down at my dress, pointed to the camera around his neck. "Same but different."

"You look better. I don't know about me." He half-laughed in his songful tone before turning serious. "Why did you agree to this?" It sounded almost like an accusation. "After everything … and then what happened a few years back. Wasn't it enough?"

I frowned. "I didn't want to do it. Not at first, but Ronnie said you did … I was worried Dex would …"

324

"And yet here we are," he interrupted, then tutted. "So, where is she? Where's the puppeteer?" He looked around. His northern accent was more pronounced than usual. "I thought she'd be the first one here, standing over us, having the last laugh."

My head snapped back. "Ronnie?"

He squeezed his eyes shut, growled, then bit his lip before he spoke. "I told you a few years back that Ronnie is dangerous, but you wouldn't listen, would you? Well, you did for a while, it seems." He took a step closer until his lips were next to my ear. Despite myself, something stirred inside. "Why did you go back for more?" His breath tickled my skin. He stepped back again.

I stared at him, bewildered. "If you feel that way, why did you say yes?" I asked.

"I'm here because I had no choice. When it comes to Ronnie, there's never a bloody choice. She controls everything. It's why I –" He stopped abruptly, glancing around to make sure no one listening. "Those original photos of you were never meant to go public, Eve. Ronnie had no right to sell them or put my name to them. She used me." He shook his head. "Can't you see, Eve? She used us both. Ronnie sold those photos without my permission. I never wanted to see them again after I left. I didn't want to be reminded of any of it."

I stepped back, hurt. He must mean the accident, the baby? I'd been right. Conor hadn't forgiven me. Even worse, Ronnie had always maintained that Conor had given her the photos to sell.

I felt winded. "Why does it always feel like there's some big mystery when it comes to you and Ronnie? Why didn't you tell me all this two years ago?"

"Because two years ago, I was so happy to have you back in my life, Eve, that I didn't want to raise the past. I loved you. I still do." Conor kicked the ground. "But she couldn't leave us be, could she?

Stalking us and whatever the hell she was doing."

I shook my head. "But it wasn't her, Conor. I know that now, and it all stopped. They went away. It's over."

He didn't look convinced. "And are we over, Eve? Because I still don't think we are." He eyeballed me. "Three years ago you told me you'd never stopped loving me, next you asked me to leave."

I shook my head. "There was so much going on back then. I had to say goodbye. For my family. I ..."

I faltered when I saw tears in his eyes.

"Why did you contact me back then at all?" he asked. "After all that time, why?"

My eyes were suddenly round. "But you contacted me."

Conor shook his head. "You contacted me."

My insides churned. "Yes, after you sent me a message."

"No, Eve." Conor's demeanour changed. "You emailed me asking me to contact you on Instagram."

Everything slowed while I listened, trying to read his face.

"I thought it was someone messing with me but, when I messaged you, you answered." He shrugged. "What does it matter anyway?"

It mattered so much I could barely speak. *"Where's Ronnie?"* I suddenly shouted behind me, needing to talk to her.

Instead, Heather appeared, making an urgent face, tapping her watch with her finger. "I'm really sorry, guys," she called. "We need to get moving."

"Two minutes!" I shouted, then turned back to Conor, panicked. Over the weeks of therapy, I'd been encouraged to face things head-on. It was now or never. "I need to ask you some things." I spoke fast. "I didn't the last time because ... I was also so happy to be with you again, but lately ..." I paused to gather myself. "I've started to remember things. Like memories or flashes. But before I can tell what

they mean, they vanish. Conor, I think there's something or even someone I've blocked out. I need you to tell me if it's real –"

"Someone?" Conor stared at me like I'd lost my mind.

"I'm not sure. That's what I'm trying to say – a girl, I think, or –"

Conor rolled his eyes, then ran his face down his hands. "You're talking gibberish, Eve. Honestly, this is just too much. I don't know if I can do this –"

"Please, Conor. I just –"

"*Guys!*" Heather shouted. "*We're running out of time here!*"

"Can we talk after?" I pleaded.

Conor shook his head. I could already tell he'd shut down. "I won't be here, Eve. I've a flight to catch. The sooner I go, the better." Then he gently placed his hand on my arm. "Do one last thing for me, will you?"

I nodded, utterly forlorn.

"Get the hell away from Ronnie. Open your eyes."

I baulked at the familiar words, but he'd already turned to where his assistant had reappeared to lead him to Lover's Leap.

For the duration of the shoot, I somehow managed to pull myself together to play my role. The grief etched into my face was genuine, but it was nothing like before – nothing like the night we shot the original photos twenty years before when we all believed our lives were already mapped out. That night, we'd made magic.

Conor had immediately switched into professional mode. Watching him work, it was plain to see how he'd climbed to the peak of his career. As I lay there on the cold slab of rock, my hair loose over the edge, my arms over my head, inside it felt like I was actually falling. Instead of Ronnie gripping tight to my legs, this time there was safety equipment. The valley was too low for Conor to climb down, so he'd been lowered over the side with safety ropes. Nothing was the same.

327

When it was over, Conor briefly hugged me. "You're still a star, Eve Kelly. If you're ever free, you call me. Until then, stay safe, okay?" Then he leaned forward and kissed me on the lips. "I'd follow you to the ends of the earth," he whispered and walked away.

Moments later, Heather appeared, slipping a coat over my shoulders.

"Can I have a minute alone?" I'd asked as the crew tidied up.

Heather agreed to meet me back at the house.

I made my way back onto Lover's Leap to sit, hugging my knees, trying to make sense of it all, pondering how everything always seemed to come back to Ronnie.

Still no clearer, I ambled back along the path. As I got to the gate, I stopped suddenly. Peering around it, I could see Conor and Ronnie standing amongst the trees. I was about to approach, but they looked deep into what appeared to be a heated conversation. Conor was speaking animatedly while Ronnie shook her head with her arms crossed. Tucking myself close to the entrance, I watched as Ronnie took a brown envelope from under her arm and smacked it into Conor's hand. Briefly, he opened it and glanced at the contents. Afterwards, he grimaced and rubbed his hand across his forehead. Was Ronnie paying him? The scene felt familiar – Ronnie and Conor huddled together whispering, passing each other envelopes. I squeezed my eyes shut, trying to force a memory, but nothing emerged. When I opened my eyes, I saw Conor step close to Ronnie and grab her arm. With his forehead practically against hers, he'd said something. When he let her go, she'd rubbed at her arm like he'd hurt it. Then Conor stalked away. I'd waited until Ronnie went too before emerging, more confused than ever.

###

I listen now as the music begins to play once more. I take another breath, ready to give it my all this time, watching for my cue. When I see the director nod, I start to move. As instructed, I look up at the band and sway from side to side before turning. Like I've been told to, I imagine I've just seen "the person you want more than anyone else in the world – someone you'd die for, but you can't get to them". Thus far, I've stared into the crowd, selecting any random face. Only this time a face finds me first. Conor is right there. He's come back, and all of a sudden I think I understand what Heather meant earlier when I'd met her back in my bedroom to get ready one final time.

###

"So, has it happened yet?" Heather had asked, smiling.

Immediately, I knew what she was talking about. On the day I first met her, Heather told me that the subject usually experiences clarity, a life epiphany during these pieces. She'd promised to ask me about it on the last day of filming.

"Have you had your moment?" she'd continued, plonking onto the bed and rubbing the back of her neck. "Faced your biggest fear, overcome it?"

"Other than being cancelled," I'd joked, drawing a blank. "I think I missed my moment. Or maybe I'm overthinking it."

"There's still time," she'd mused before getting up to answer a knock on the door. She gasped as a crew member held up what looked like a hundred red roses. Opening the envelope, Heather had held the card under my nose for me to read.

I'd wrinkled my nose in confusion, then showed it to her.

"Good God! I hope that's not the revelation," she'd said with a laugh.

#

Now, Conor stands motionless, watching me, the connection between us so magnetic that I try to push forward through the crowd. My gaze fixes on him as I attempt to plough ahead. My God, it's so clear. Conor is all I want. I'm not afraid anymore – not of the past or the future. Desperately, I glance around, searching for a way to him, only this time when I look back I see Dex. He stares at me, then he looks behind him. I watch it happen in slow motion – Dex on top of Conor, pushing, shoving, limbs flailing. I see Ronnie appear, then security, but before they drag Dex away he glares back at me.

"*And cut! That's it, people!*"

The director's voice startles me.

"*Congratulations, guys! That is a wrap!*"

There's raucous applause as the lead singer of Timeline shouts into the microphone, "*Let's get this party started!*"

As the music commences and the crowd lunges for real, I force my way out. I lose sight of Conor for a moment, looking about until I see him with Ronnie near the fountain. They're speaking frantically. Conor holds his phone up to her face, and Ronnie shakes her head in what looks like disbelief. I was wrong. Conor isn't here for me. Clearly, there's some unfinished business between them.

"*What's the hell is going on?*" I hiss as I approach. "*What the hell was that with Dex?*" I turn to Conor, who doesn't respond. "Ronnie?"

Ronnie's gaze drops. "Faye is missing," she says.

It's so far from what I'm expecting to hear that I laugh. "Eh, no, she's not. She's right over there." I search the sea of strangers. "There, look!" I point to where her friends are standing by the back door of the house. I nod at Ronnie, but I see that Faye's not there, and her friends appear utterly lost when I look back. I start to panic.

"They haven't seen her since they arrived," Ronnie says. "She's not in her room. I've been looking for her, but … no one has seen her."

"*Since when?*" I demand.

"Since early this evening." Once again, Ronnie looks at her feet.

"No. Faye's here." I shake my head, gripping my hair. "*Dex? Dex?*" I shout anxiously over my shoulder.

Heather appears instead.

"Tell me," she says calmly.

"It's Faye. We can't find Faye!" I swallow. It's all I can manage.

For Heather, it's enough. She takes a step away. Immediately, I see her speaking into her walkie-talkie.

"*My phone. Where's my phone?*" I shout.

Heather places it into my hand. I immediately see a missed call from Faye. From nowhere, Dex appears, and I see Heather fill him in as I try to phone her. There's no answer. My hand starts trembling as I try again.

"Maybe she phoned me. I'll get my phone too," Dex says. Before he moves, he turns to me. Stepping closer to my ear, he whispers, "You were fucking him. I know." Then he strides away, followed by Heather.

My legs give way. Ronnie grabs one arm, and Conor takes the other. They ease me towards the fountain, so I'm leaning against it. Everything reels. I don't know how long I'm there before Conor speaks.

"*Tell her!*" I hear him hiss over my head.

"Tell me what?" I look up.

Ronnie hesitates. "Faye knows," she says. "She knows you had an affair with Conor. She posted the photo from my phone, Eve. She was with me that night, remember? It was her."

"*No,*" I whisper, breaking away from them, but this time Conor grips both my arms tight.

"Faye sent me a message earlier on Instagram, Eve," he says. "I only saw it after I left. It's why I came back. She has something she isn't meant to have."

"*What?*" I'm practically screaming. "*What does she have?*"

"Someone was contacting her, Eve," Ronnie says. "I think it was the same person who was following you. I think –"

I jolt as my phone pings. I open it and read, barely breathing.

"*It's okay!*" I gasp. "*Faye's okay!*" I look from Ronnie to Conor. "She's with Dex. I have to go to her." I take a few steps, then stop. Turning, I ask, "Where did Faye get the picture of me and Conor from, Ronnie?"

She doesn't answer.

Then I glare at Conor. "I didn't send you an email two years ago. I didn't contact you first, *and it does matter*. Because if I didn't, who did? You're hiding something, both of you. I know it in here!" I thump my chest. "Unless you're willing to tell me right now, you can both get the hell out of my life."

Neither replies.

"*Go!*" I order.

I'm a fool. Conor returning isn't my moment of clarity. Realising nothing matters but my children, is. I get it now – my greatest fear is them seeing me how I've spent half my life seeing myself – a failure. As I turn, running as fast as my feet can carry me towards the gate at the end of the garden, it dawns on me that my greatest fear may already be realised.

CHAPTER TWENTY-NINE

Joanne

#invisible #irishtwins #destroyedevidence #watching #cliché

- -

@anoldfriendfromcollege

- -

0	0	1
Posts	Followers	Following

Joanne is out of breath when she arrives at the meeting point, concealing herself behind thick foliage as planned. She can hear Timeline performing from here – loud, chaotic, and distracting. It's perfect. Inhaling deeply, she smiles.

She'd passed the last hours tucked behind dense bushes at the bottom of Eve's garden, directing the soap opera. When the drama commenced, Joanne waited for Dex to storm off searching for Faye and texted Eve from his phone. After getting inside the house earlier undetected, Joanne had noticed it, idle on the kitchen counter, and swiped it, confident it would come in handy tonight. She'd been right.

She's waited a long time for this day – twenty years in total. Finally, it's here, and it's going to be beautiful. And to think, in the end, it was

Eve who invited Joanne right into their lives. Honestly, people will believe anything you tell them. Joanne isn't even a counsellor. Mind you, she had studied psychology at university. She's an office temp mostly. She likes her freedom.

She'd followed Eve the day she'd curiously picked Faye up early from school and driven her to the medical centre in Sandyford Industrial Estate. It's one of those larger ones, home to several different practices with administrative staff buzzing about like flies. She'd followed Eve and Faye right into reception and stood close behind them to hear the good news – a recurring appointment for Faye with Dr Robin every Friday at 1 p.m. Joanne was glad Eve was getting poor Faye help. She hadn't liked doing what she'd had to do to her when she was being Natalie.

After they took their seats, Joanne approached one of the receptionists, looking for an appointment with the adjoining physiotherapist. She chatted for as long as she could with the receptionist until Faye and Eve were ushered away, then she, too, made a recurring appointment with the physio for her back – every Friday at 1 p.m. Week after week, she learned something more while they waited for their respective appointments. With headphones on but nothing playing, Joanne listened as carefully as possible.

By the time Faye had undergone eight sessions, Joanne had hit the jackpot. Eve announced to the receptionist that there was only one more session – they were moving to Wicklow.

"We have a sister practice in Wicklow if you need it. The details are all online." the receptionist offered.

Right then, an idea formed.

The following week, Joanne hung back near the bathroom until she saw Eve settle the bill with the receptionist and leave. Joanne dumped her bag and coat in a stall, pulled off her baseball cap and made her way through the reception. When Eve was out the first set of doors, Joanne called, just inside the large foyer, *"Ms Kelly! Excuse me!"*

Eve turned. Faye carried on out to the car.

Joanne extended her hand with a card in it. She'd had them made that week, connected to her phone number.

"Sincere apologies, but Mandy at the desk was to give you the card for the Wicklow practice. Dr Robin asked her to pass it on. We sometimes recommend a follow-up session after a couple of months. There's no rush at all. She's delighted with Faye."

Eve took it and smiled. "Oh, of course, thank you."

"I'm one of the counsellors in Wicklow. I'm just covering here, so I might see you again sometime. Take care." Joanne went to turn.

Eve looked anxious. "Thanks again. Did Dr Robin say when – it's just we're about to move and –"

Joanne placed her hand on her arm. "Whenever you're ready. Six to eight weeks usually, but you know best for your daughter. You can also come back here if you prefer."

Eve thought for a moment and shook her head. "It'll be a bit far to come in."

"Don't I know?" Joanne laughed. "I've spent a lot of time in the car this week. Anyway, mind yourself during the move. It can be stressful. We'll chat soon." She smiled warmly and walked away.

The rest is history.

Joanne allowed Eve to rebuild her life, helped her even, then when she heard about the documentary, she saw her opportunity to pick it apart once and for all. Starting with Dex.

At her house earlier, when Joanne disclosed the photo of Eve kissing Conor, it took all her reserve not to reach up and smack Dex across the face in a bid to make him understand that Eve doesn't love

335

him. It's so obvious, it hurts. Nor does she herself love him, for that matter. Still, she'd enjoyed seducing him, finding it reassuring that someone like her could turn the eye of someone like Eve's husband, proving she is no longer invisible.

Although she can still make herself so when necessary. During filming, she'd been able to access the set under the guise of keeping an eye on Faye and Milo. It enabled her to come and go, cut wires, hide things, move equipment, change schedules, slip contaminated meat into a catering truck, anything to wreak havoc, cause delays, make sure the final day of production proved as frantic as possible.

When Joanne first opened the email that Eve sent disclosing that Conor would be reshooting the original photos at Lover's Leap, she could barely believe her luck. When Eve showed her the printed version in Joanne's kitchen later that week, she'd pretended she hadn't yet seen it. In truth, she'd already examined it and began to make plans before Eve called over. Immediately, she'd bombarded the Gallagher Group with complaint emails from concerned guests about filming. It was so late in the game that there'd been no other choice but to move the entire production here. It was perfect.

Glancing at Dex's phone, she can see that the text to Eve has been read. By now, she should be on her way. Bending, Joanne feels around for the bag she'd hidden there early this morning. Picking it up, she removes the incriminating photos of her sister that Faye had kindly sent "Natalie" years before and another photo of Natalie taken in a restaurant shortly before she'd died. She tucks them into the back pocket of her jeans then reaches for the gun.

Joanne is still flabbergasted at how easy it is to get your hands on a gun. On a few occasions, going over the plan in the privacy of her home, she'd practised pulling it fast from her waistband and aiming it like an American cop. Holding it now, her hand trembles. Rallying herself, she tucks it into the waistband of her jeans, feeling the cool metal against her skin. She doubts she'll need to use it. Hopefully, Eve will go over without a fight. Joanne doesn't like violence. She'd found having to hit Faye earlier horribly disturbing.

Running over her lines quickly, Joanne nods, satisfied. Once Eve gets here, she'll need to be brief. She won't have much time to explain before people come looking.

Joanne also has the added problem of Faye, unconscious in her house, to deal with. Although, a solution has already dawned. Once she gets back to the house, Joanne intends to plug in the faulty charger and connect her iPod. She was glad she'd hung on to it now. Weeks ago, she'd come home to find the wire omitting smoke where she'd left it plugged in. Googling it, Joanne had been shocked to discover how many house fires began that way. It was nearly as disconcerting as the gun.

When that was done, Joanne needed to get back to the airport, where she'd apparently been waiting all day after stupidly muddling her flight times. In reality, after driving there earlier, she'd parked in the long-term car park, then caught a taxi back to Annaford. Faye wasn't part of the plan. Joanne liked Faye. Faye had already done enough for her – given her the proof she'd always needed in the form of Natalie's photos. Teenagers were clueless when it came to safety, constantly glued to their phones, snapping their location every few seconds. Back then, posing as "Natalie", Joanne learned so much from Faye – everything from where they hid the front-door key in Ranelagh, how to get into the house, their schedules, who'd be home when. Gradually, a fuller picture formed far beyond what Eve shared online. Soon Joanne knew more about them than they knew about themselves.

Faye turning up today to break in almost ruined everything. Hiding out in her own kitchen, Joanne nearly died when she heard someone enter the house, turn off the alarm and go upstairs.

It had momentarily thrown her, especially when the original plan was far less complicated. It had involved sending a message to Eve from Conor's assistant, Nina. Weeks before, Joanne had phoned her, under the guise of finding out numbers for the after-party. Conor wouldn't be there. With them out of the way, Joanne intended to text Eve as Nina – a number Eve indeed wouldn't have, to say Conor had misplaced his phone, was on his way back, and needed to speak with her at Lover's Leap. When Faye showed up, Joanne had to come up with a new plan.

Hearing twigs snap, leaves rustle, Joanne freezes. This is it. Peering out, she sees Eve. Alone.

"*Dex? Faye? Where are you?*"

"Eve?" Slowly, Joanne emerges.

Eve whips around, holding her phone up for light, squinting. "Joanne?" She sounds shocked. "Is that you? I thought you were … where's Faye?" Surprise turns to concern.

Joanne steps closer, hands outstretched as if Eve is about to bolt. "Faye is okay. My flight got cancelled. When I got back, Faye was at my house. She's fine, Eve … upset. I walked her back to your house just now and met Dex. She's with him. He said he texted you to let you know."

Eve nods uncertainly. "He asked me to meet him here so we could talk, away from the chaos, but –" Confused, Eve glances at her phone.

"Faye wouldn't come," Joanne says. "She was in such a state. Dex asked me to find you, tell you. He seemed angry. He said things … " She trails off as Eve goes to leave. "Wait, Eve. He asked if you'd give him a minute." She hesitates, then asks, "Were you really having an affair? It's what Faye said, but I –" Her face fills with concern. "Were you? With the photographer?"

Eve's eyes drop. Tears pooling, she says, "I need to talk to Faye."

"I think they need a wee bit of time, Eve. Why don't we give them a few minutes, and we can go back together. Sit." She gestures at Lover's Leap. Digging deep, she says. "You said it always worked for you and Lily. It might be the same now."

Eve sighs, then obediently clambers onto the stage. Sitting, she sets her phone down beside her.

Joanne goes and sits next to Eve, keeping her back to the valley, facing the path. "Sorry. I'm not great with heights," she apologises. Deliberately, she places her hand over Eve's phone, concealing it, then tucking it quickly under her leg.

Eve stares ahead, shoulder slumped. "Strange, it's the one thing I don't mind. It's everything else I struggle with."

"We all struggle," Joanne says.

"Me more than most," Eve continues, deflated, then throws her head back. "*Ugh.* What have I done? I'm an idiot. I came here to get away from everything, but I'm still a mess. Still trapped in the past. I should have just been honest."

Now that she has the phone, Joanne stands slowly, manoeuvring herself towards the path. Noticing, Eve turns her head.

"Sorry," Joanne peers up the path, "I thought I heard someone coming. It must be the music. Go on with what you were saying."

Eve turns back to look out over the valley again. Joanne remains standing behind her.

"I didn't mean for it to happen," Eve says. "It just did. It was a mistake."

"Talking of mistakes," Joanne cuts across her. "That's not the only one you made, is it, Eve?"

Eve pivots her entire body this time, staring nervously at Joanne. "What do you mean?"

Joanne smiles brightly, counting on her fingers. "Well, there was the drugs, then the baby, then throwing yourself in front of a car, then having an affair."

With each statement, Eve's mouth gapes open further. Fear and disbelief form on her face. She goes to stand, but Joanna advances fast.

"*Sit the hell down! I'm speaking now – you'd better listen,*" she threatens through gritted teeth, then brightens as quickly. "I'm sure I'm forgetting something …"

Eve starts breathing heavily. "How do you know those things?"

"Well, it was Dex who told me about the baby and the drugs, but I already knew about the drugs from college. Everyone knew about the drugs. I'm so surprised no one from UCD has outed you before now." She shakes her head in disbelief. "I should have done a wee thread about it on Jabber.ie." She tuts again. "But then life is full of missed opportunities, isn't it?"

"You weren't in UCD. You said –"

"I lied. I've been with you for a long time, Eve. I know everything about you." She frowns. "Although I must admit, I never knew you were pregnant in college. That's sad. Dex thought so too." She sticks her bottom lip out.

"Dex doesn't know … I never …" The colour drains further from Eve's face.

"But he does know, Eve. Dex knows everything, well, almost everything. He'll know the rest soon. The whole world will too. They'll know exactly what you did to succeed." Her northern accent is thicker than usual. "Tell me, did Conor know that you were going to push her? I've always wondered. Or was it a surprise?"

Eve is paralysed with fear.

Joanne's eyes light. "Wasn't it great to see him after all those years back in Dublin?" She wags her finger at a petrified Eve. "Although

340

maybe I'm a wee bit to blame for that. Hands up, it was me who emailed Conor pretending to be you!" Joanne slapped her own hand, then grimaced. "Silly of him to fall for it, wasn't it?"

It was child's play creating an email address using someone else's name. Joanne had done it for fun, to toy with them, see if they'd start communicating, if it might lead to something emerging about the past. Eve hadn't been online that much after telling people to unfollow her like some sort of victim, and Joanne had been growing bored. Not for one moment did she think that Conor and Eve would actually meet up, and she certainly never believed they'd rekindle their romance. After what they'd done, it was disgusting.

"I'm a bit of a photographer too," Joanne muses. "Nothing like Conor, of course, but I dabble. I took the photo of you two that night after the restaurant." She smiles smugly.

"Who are you?" Eve asks quietly. "Why were you following me?"

Joanne laughs. "Mainly because you told me not to, but let's stay on track. It was also me who sent it to Faye. I've been friends with her for years, too, even back in Dublin. Online only, of course. No need to worry. I'm not some sicko. And alas, I'm not a counsellor. Tricked you."

Eve scrambles to her feet. *"You crazy bitch!"*

Joanne pulls the gun and aims it at Eve. This time her hand is steady. Eve puts her hands up and stumbles backwards, shaking.

Undeterred, Joanne goes on. "I never thought Faye would manage to post it, but she's a real go-getter, our Faye. You'll be happy to hear, she understands the fundamental concept of business – nothing for nothing. In exchange, she gave me something invaluable." She patted her pocket then shook her head in wonder. In one swoop, it proved precisely what she'd tried to tell her parents and the Guards twenty years before. It changed everything.

"*It was all you?*" It dawns on Eve. "You did all those things. You were in our house, following me. It was you ..." She snivels, her body convulsing with fear.

Joanne claps slowly. "*Bravo!*"

"I don't care," Eve pleads. "Just let me go. I won't tell anyone what you did, please."

Joanne laughs. "That's funny, especially when I'm about to tell people what you did to Natalie."

Twenty years ago, the pathologist said it was likely Natalie died on impact. In the unlikely case that she hadn't, she'd have been killed through drowning or frostbite and exposure. Not to mention the myriad of drugs found in her system.

Oddly, their parents seemed more shocked about the drugs than learning that Natalie had driven alone to a forest in the Dublin Mountains, left a practically illegible suicide note, then flung herself off a cliff in a flimsy red dress.

Only ten months younger than Joanne, they were in same class at school. Natalie was the beautiful one, who had their parents wrapped around their little finger with her head of red curls. She had Joanne wrapped around her finger too for that matter. Joanne adored her, almost couldn't exist without her. She'd get to sit in the front seat of the car, stand ahead of Joanne in a queue. Because Natalie was taller, Joanne got handed-down clothes instead of the other way around. Natalie always got what she wanted. When she wanted to leave Belfast to study in UCD, Joanne went too. Their parents rented them a tiny house, and they headed off for Natalie to steal the show with her figure to die for, her feline face, and her alluring presence.

Eve's head jerks up. "Who's Natalie? Please, you've made a mistake."

Joanne exhales impatiently. "Stop the games, Eve. You may not have noticed me in college, but you noticed my sister. You picked her out for Conor yourself – for the photo shoot. The one just likes yours."

Eve's eyes narrow. "Natalie," she whispers the name this time, trying to remember. "I don't know what you're talking about. Please … where's my phone?"

Removing the phone from her pocket, Joanne throws it onto the path behind. As if by magic, it starts to light. Someone is calling. "*Whoops*, we'd better hurry." She aims the gun again. "You gave Natalie the drugs. Was it to help her relax before you pushed her over the edge?" Joanne's voice soars: "*Was it so you could get the perfect picture, or was it because she was screwing your boyfriend?*"

Eve jolts as if she's been electrocuted.

Keeping the gun pointed at her, Joanne pulls out the photograph of Natalie smiling in a restaurant and pushes it at Eve. "The total opposite of you, wasn't she? You told her that it's what Conor wanted for his series."

Eve stares ahead in a trance, realisation dawning. "I saw them together," she whispers to herself, eyes wild. "I saw them together the day I lost the baby. They were …" She's talking to herself. "I went home, and I …" Eve's features twist further as she remembers. "Conor came after me. I did see him that day. He lied. He said it only happened once –"

Joanne holds up another photo of Natalie, this time on the cliff. Then she shows her the next photo.

Eve shakes her head. Over and over, repeating, "I wasn't there."

"But you were, Eve. You were on the cliff with her. Then you pushed her. You did it on purpose. Then you left her there, wrote a note to make it look like suicide." Joanne holds up the last two photos.

Eve flinches at the broken-looking body swathed in red, then covers her eyes with her hands. "I wasn't there ... It wasn't me."

But she doesn't look convinced. Even less when Joanne points to her tattooed wrist that appears in the corner of the photo.

#

Natalie was found by a group of well-meaning walkers the next day. Apparently, they'd all gathered around the river in their heavy hiking boots, and one of the men had waded in to fish her out. They'd then covered her body with a blanket until the police arrived. Any evidence that may have been there was disturbed through kindness and the heavy rain the night before.

Joanne screamed and shouted, trying to tell her parents again and again what had really happened, but they wouldn't listen. Instead, they repeated that it was a cry for help gone wrong. Next, Joanne went to the Guards. They looked at her like she was crazy, patted her hand in sympathy and told her they'd look into it. Days later, they called to the house in Dublin where her parents were still staying with her. They asked to speak with them alone. When they emerged from the other room, they gave Joanne the same look of pity they had at the station.

Her parents ordered her to stop whatever she doing, wasting police time, creating stories. Seemingly, the Guards had asked around campus, and several students reported that Joanne used to follow Natalie about endlessly. Apparently, Natalie's friends also reported that she'd recently become distant, refusing to go out, not turning up for classes, preoccupied. The guards claimed it was all standard behaviour.

Her mother placed her hand over Joanne's. "Natalie told us the same thing a while back. She came home for the weekend, especially to tell us that she was worried about you, Joanne. That you wouldn't give her an inch of space. You were upsetting her terribly. She said you were obsessed with this one boy – a fellow from Belfast. Natalie said you used to follow him, watch him. Is it true, Joanne?"

Joanne raged. "She's a liar." It was Natalie who'd been obsessed with Conor. Not her.

They demanded she stop the wild accusations of photo shoots and a girl called Eve who'd orchestrated it all.

"The Guards told us she's this boy's girlfriend," her dad said. "They questioned them. Those young people were home all night. There was no photo shoot, Joanne. It never happened." He broke down suddenly. "Please, stop this now. Let Natalie rest in peace."

There was nothing she could do to convince them, especially since Joanne had already destroyed Natalie's diary after she'd read it the night the photo shoot took place. After Natalie had left the house that evening, refusing to tell Joanne where she was going, Joanne had searched her room for a clue. It came in the form of a crudely hidden diary left out on Natalie's desk, just waiting to be found. Natalie had written down every shred of evidence Joanne could ever need – a detailed description of the day Eve first came to her outside the Arts building, explaining the photo series and asking her to take part. Where and when she was to meet Eve and Conor a few weeks later. Where Natalie was to buy the dress ... everything.

Joanne read accounts of how Natalie had met Conor on the steps after her class to discuss it more. How they'd ended up talking about Belfast. The places they knew from childhood. How good it was to be around someone from home. How she'd noticed him months before and decided to go after him if only she could get him away from his clingy girlfriend. She'd made sure to be around them as much as possible so he'd eventually notice her. She'd even started dressing like Eve, wearing things she'd seen on her, carrying a camera even though she didn't know the first thing about photography, hoping it might impress Conor. It detailed how she'd brought him back to the house, ended up sleeping together. How it had happened almost every day since.

Then Natalie wrote about Joanne. It went on and on – describing Joanne as the bane of her life. How she was sick of having to mind her. How she couldn't make a life with her always being around. How she wished she'd go back to Belfast. How she'd probably be stuck with her for the rest of her life. Humiliated, Joanne had thrown it straight into the fire, watching the evidence burn before her eyes. The next day, she'd never regretted anything so much. Despite everything, she'd loved her sister. She's spent the last twenty years utterly lost without her. Ever since, she's been waiting for her moment to make Eve pay.

#

Joanne flies fast at Eve – years of agony erupting. *"You took her life, and you ruined mine!"* she spits as Eve flinches.

"I don't remember doing it, I swear. I remember Natalie now, but I don't remember the rest. I swear," Eve sobs. "I'm sorry. I would never … I didn't mean it … please let me go, please." Frantically, Eve attempts to rush past Joanne, but she pushes her back.

"There's no way out, Eve."

Eve sinks to her knees as Joanne takes Dex's phone out, cruelly snapping photos while Eve sobs. Eventually, Eve grows quiet as she stares into the distance, shivering.

Joanne points the gun at Eve's temple. "It's over. Eve. Your career … your marriage … Conor … your children … everyone will know what you did. If you don't cooperate now, one by one I'll destroy their lives like you destroyed mine, starting with Faye. Faye isn't with Dex."

She waves his phone at Eve. "That was me too. Right now. Faye is locked in my house. No one knows where she is, but if you do what I say I can save her."

Eve issues a guttural moan as Joanne nudges the side of her head with the gun.

"*It's time to fall.*"

Joanne watches reality shadow Eve's face, resignation settle. On cue, the river below rumbles, growling like a hungry dog. Eve grips the edges of her dress as if it will somehow save her. This time, there'll be no hope of rising, no second chances. She'll be dead on impact. As she turns towards the edge, Joanne sees her take a final breath.

It's over.

CHAPTER THIRTY

#itsover #itsover #itsover #itsallover

@theagency

147	6,590	89
Posts	Followers	Following

Still standing next to the fountain, Ronnie can hear Conor talking, asking her what they should do. The words blur in her ears. Eventually, she turns to him in a daze. "Go home, Conor."

Eve would find out soon enough what they'd done. Faye would tell. Conor would come clean. Whoever wanted justice would finally get it.

Conor is still speaking, but Ronnie can no longer hear the words. She reaches both hands into the fountain, scoops out some water and splashes her face. Then, she sinks to the ground allowing the years flash before her eyes.

It's all over.

It's what she should have told Conor twenty years before at the hospital after Eve lost the baby. Back then, Conor had been devastated, angry, crying, pulling his hair out with remorse, repeating how he'd messed up by cheating on her, it was his fault she'd taken the drugs, but he loved Eve. Ronnie hadn't been all that surprised that he'd cheated. Eve had had them all under immense stress for a long time with her addiction, discovering she was pregnant, getting clean, and final exams looming. They were still only kids.

"Ronnie?" Conor calls her name again.

She looks up. Despite it being too late, she says it anyway, "It's over."

Conor stomps away, and she stares ahead again. To have got this far is a miracle, she supposes, especially when the warning signs had been flashing all day.

First, when Faye said Natalie's name earlier on the phone. That time, Ronnie had ended the call and sped off. It was only when she'd turned her car onto the motorway that it dawned on her that perhaps all was not lost. So, it hadn't been Faye stalking them, and there was someone out there who knew about Natalie – but without proof, what could they do? Ronnie still had the photos. Without them, no one could prove a thing. Better yet, as soon as she handed them to Conor as agreed, he'd destroy them. It was how she'd got him to agree to the reshoot in the first place.

Right then, she'd come up with a new plan. She'd wrap up her life in Dublin and move to France or Spain, anywhere for some peace, a fresh start. Ronnie had made her fortune off Eve. With her cut from production, the reshoot, the music video, coupled with the sale of her apartment, she'd have enough to start again without Eve. All Ronnie had to do was get the photos, get back to the house, give them to Conor and then she was free.

By the time she did, she'd already missed the photo shoot, running

349

into Conor in the garden as he made his way back from it. Conor walked straight for her, opening the exchange with, *"You bitch!* You ruined my life!"

Ronnie rolled her eyes. "Oh, get over yourself, Conor. You should be thanking me. I made you famous."

"You forced me to leave. Then used the photos, knowing I couldn't stop you. You used us all. I want to tell Eve the truth, so badly ..." He'd growled with frustration.

"But you can't, can you? Because you're nothing but a cheat. You and Natalie are the reason Eve relapsed, took all those drugs, walked out in front of a car. You're the reason she lost the baby."

"I fucked up," Conor admitted, hanging his head. "I made a mistake. To this day, I don't know what I was thinking. It was only a couple of weeks, but – *she* got clingy," he said, unable to utter Natalie's name. "The day Eve saw us, I was trying to end it with her ..." He paused, ran his fingers through his hair. "I wanted Eve. I wanted to go to London." His voice wavered. "I was scared. When Eve didn't remember it, I thought maybe ..."

Ronnie and Conor made a vow not to remind her. When Eve wouldn't go home with her mother, they took her home to nurse her back to health. They'd still go to London.

That's when Natalie showed up at their front door late one evening. She hadn't heard anything from Conor, she'd said, was the photo shoot still happening? Conor tried to send her away, close the door in her face, but Ronnie stopped him. She'd leaned in to whisper that the photos were exactly what he needed, to think of his portfolio – to do it for Eve. Ronnie would go in her place. They'd be back before she woke.

"I didn't want to do it," Conor said to Ronnie. "One minute she was up there with you. The next, she was falling." His face contorted.

"It was an accident. She was off her face on drugs … she wouldn't stop moving. *You* gave her the drugs."

Conor squeezed his eyes shut. "She wouldn't shut up. She just wouldn't stop. You heard her."

Yes. Ronnie had heard her. They'd driven there separately, and from the moment they got out of their cars, Ronnie knew it was a mistake. Natalie was hyper, obsessed with Conor, wouldn't stop talking. Conor would give her something to relax, he'd suggested. Instead of calming her, it had the opposite effect, leaving her manic, wired, loud. All the while, Natalie endlessly babbled about how she wanted to be a model, how gorgeous Conor was, how this was the best night of her life.

When Conor climbed down the cliff to shoot from below, leaving Natalie alone with Ronnie, Natalie began spouting about Eve, going on that she was crazy, a druggie, that Conor was tired of her. She revealed how she'd been hanging around all year near the Arts steps, trying to get Conor to notice her, how she'd bought a camera so he would. At last, he had, she'd said. Now, she wanted him for herself. She'd go to London too, she told Ronnie. She'd do anything to be with him. She knew everything about them – where they lived, places they went. She'd clearly been following them, waiting for her moment. Then she said she'd heard on the grapevine that Ronnie was a dealer. On and on, she went about how Conor would be hers, that Eve would be nothing without him, neither would Ronnie. Ronnie saw red. One minute her hands were around Natalie's ankles holding her, and the next they weren't.

Leaving a note in Natalie's car along with a decent smattering of cocaine had been Ronnie's idea. It started raining heavily when they got into the car to drive away, then she'd made Conor give her the film so she could destroy it. Only she never did.

Within hours, it dawned on Ronnie that Conor couldn't cope. He was a liability, fretting that Natalie might have told someone where she'd been going that night. When the police finally came to question them days later, and Eve said they'd been home all night, they left satisfied. They never even mentioned Natalie. The entire visit was as though they were simply ticking a box. When Conor started acting strange, suggesting they come clean, go the Guards, confess, Ronnie used the film and the fact he'd cheated on Eve to get rid of him for good.

When Ronnie developed the film in the college darkroom, she discovered Conor must have been clicking automatically as Natalie drifted to the river below. He'd captured it all. On the same roll of film, he'd also captured Eve looking like an angel.

When she'd handed Conor the photos earlier in the garden twenty years too late, he'd grabbed her arm, came close to her face and said, "How do you live with yourself?"

Sitting here now, slumped on the ground in Eve's garden, Ronnie recognises only now that she doesn't live with herself. She's had the steadfast company of Natalie on her mind for twenty years.

Once again, Ronnie had got back in her car and driven away. That time, she was almost far as her apartment in town before her conscience got the better of her. She couldn't do it – leave for good without saying goodbye, offering some form of explanation to Eve, an apology to Faye, who'd been frantically calling all day. So, she'd come back because, in her way, Ronnie loved them all. She'd hurt enough people.

Immediately, she'd gone to find Faye. Taking a deep breath, still not knowing how she'd explain it, she'd knocked tentatively on the bedroom door. When there was no answer, she'd peered around the door before going in. Faye wasn't there. Glancing out the window, Ronnie had watched the activity. It was almost dark. Everything was ready. Eve would be in her room, prepping for the pinnacle moment of her career. Ronnie would go to her next.

Turning, her eyes had settled on the photographs of Natalie strewn across Faye's bed. Realising that Faye must have found them that day in her office, Ronnie sank to the floor and sobbed for everything she'd done. She'd stayed that way for a long time before deciding she still needed to find Faye. Folding the photos into her pocket, she'd left the room. While the video shoot was happening, Ronnie, trying to remain calm, had searched the house, the garden, everywhere, endlessly trying Faye's phone. When her friends revealed that they hadn't seen her either, nor anyone for that matter, Ronnie began to worry that Faye might be in trouble.

When Ronnie rounded the corner onto the patio and saw Conor standing staring at Eve being filmed, she almost died. She didn't have a chance to think before he was hissing that he was almost on the plane when he noticed a message from Faye who'd sent him a message along with Natalie's photos, asking for an explanation or she would go to Eve. He barely got time to finish what he was saying before Dex was on top of him. Then Eve was there, and Faye was missing, and Ronnie was still trying to explain, to lie.

She is done now. She's had enough with the lies, the pain, the secrets. Hoisting herself up, she removes her phone from her pocket and throws it into the fountain. Then she staggers towards the driveway. She walks past her car, out the gate, heading for the road, blindly passing Dex, Heather and another man in a huddle. Ronnie stops when she hears Dex call after her, asking if she has seen Faye.

She turns in a daze. "But you found her. You texted Eve to say you found her. She said so."

Dex looks alert. "No, I didn't. How could I when I can't even find my phone?"

"*Will one of you listen to me!*" the other man says urgently. "I saw Faye go into that house earlier this evening." He points. "I was walking the dogs. I thought it was strange since Joanne is away, but then I thought I saw Joanne earlier, so I must have got it wrong. But I saw your daughter go in there, Dex. I'm certain."

Dex takes off. The man follows, leaving Ronnie and Heather staring after them.

"There were flowers," Heather says absently. "A huge bunch of red roses delivered earlier." She looked puzzled. "And a good-luck note ..." She frowns. "But it had the name of the show wrong. It said – *The Rise and Fall of Eve.*"

"Give me your phone," Ronnie orders suddenly. "Please, Heather. Trust me."

Heather takes her phone from her breast pocket, unlocks it and hands it to Ronnie. "Get someone to call the police," Ronnie adds, then takes off in the direction of Lover's Leap.

It was time to confront a ghost.

It was over.

ONE YEAR LATER

#epiphany #unfollow #theend

@producergirl

325	1,875	606
Posts	Followers	Following

Heather had heard talk of cursed productions plagued by strange occurrences where people died. She'd always believed they were fabrications to boost sales of horror movies. Producing documentaries, she never thought she'd encounter anything akin to the making of *Unfollow Me – The Fall and Rise of Eve*. It was no horror story, albeit, in the end, it proved just as unbelievable.

Heather pauses the final segment in her home office and leans back, sighing deeply. After months of post-production, editing, watching it endlessly, she still finds it chilling.

Meeting Eve that first day, Heather never imagined that a show about an influencer would strike so many chords, yet it plucks at every emotion known to man. Even more so since she has included the

355

newer segments, filmed months after they wrapped.

Everyone is saying she'll win an award for it when it eventually airs.

"If it airs" has become her go-to response. With all the legalities surrounding it, it's been impossible to secure a release date. Mind you, they're getting closer. Especially now that the court case is almost over. In her heart, Heather believes the real story deserves to be told. It's what Eve would want.

Whenever Heather thinks of the wrap night, she still finds herself shaking her head in disbelief. The idea that one woman orchestrated such a bizarre string of events, set a scene, controlled them like puppets is almost admirable if that's the word, which it isn't, of course. Years and years of planning, waiting, toying. It was unimaginable, so far-fetched it barely seemed real. Heather sincerely hopes they lock Joanne up and throw away the key. Apparently, she'd pleaded insanity to both counts: attempted murder and manslaughter. Of course she had! The rest of it – accounts of stalking, intimidation, breaking and entering, were all entered into evidence but weren't charged. Heather still finds that part outrageous. Almost as outrageous as what she witnessed the night she arrived on the scene at Lover's Leap, followed by two security men. Heather was already on her way there when she heard the shot fired. For that, her husband has castigated her ever since, insisting she should have run in the opposite direction. Instead, Heather ran towards the sound, then came to an abrupt halt as she tried to take in the scene before her.

It was Ronnie who'd taken the bullet. Apparently, she'd charged Joanne, who fired the gun. Undeterred, Ronnie managed to grab it, throw it at Eve, and kick Joanne to the ground. Then she'd ran to Eve and stepped up onto Lover's Leap beside her. When Heather got there, Eve was quivering like a leaf, a gun in her hand aimed at Joanne on the path. Beside her, Ronnie stood, clutching her upper arm where she'd been shot, silently convulsing. When Eve saw Heather and the men appear, she called out like a maimed animal. Sobbing, she let the gun slip and clatter off the rock as if she no longer had the strength to hold it. Then she pointed a violently shaking hand at Joanne. Joanne scrambled to her feet, eyes darting. She tried to bolt, but the security men forced her to the ground, clamping her arms behind her back.

When Heather looked up, Eve was holding on to Ronnie, nodding while Ronnie spoke. Still unsure what was happening, Heather approached cautiously, stretching a hand up to help Eve down. Eve stooped to take it, then turned back to get Ronnie. What Heather saw next will remain imprinted in her mind for the rest of her days.

Ronnie smiled once, took a deep breath, then stepped backwards off the cliff.

If Heather hadn't jumped up to grab Eve and pull her to the ground, she still maintains that Eve might have gone over after her with shock.

Immediately, one of the security men had leapt up, peering over, already knowing the outcome. Hunched over on the path, Heather held Eve until her screams turned to weeping and her body ceased convulsing.

Although she'd had the culprit wrong all along, Joanne still got what she wanted – a life for life.

They'd found Faye tied up, locked into the room in Joanne's house after Dex broke the door down. Thankfully, she survived what could have been a fatal blow to the head with a rock.

If she'd wanted to, Ronnie too would have survived the gunshot wound, but from the video she'd left on Heather's phone, it was clear Ronnie hadn't wanted to survive. She'd gone there with intent – to save her friend, to make it right.

At first, they'd thought Heather's phone had gone over with Ronnie, until Heather had used *Find my iPhone* to uncover it inside the gate to

Lover's Leap. On it, Ronnie had recorded her free will confession, clearing both Eve and Conor and accepting all blame for Natalie's death.

Heather thought she'd never hear from Eve again until Eve contacted her several weeks later, looking for a favour. They'd met in Eve's mother's house in Dalkey where she and the children were staying. Dex had remained on in Annaford. "For the time being," Eve said. "We're in therapy."

To Heather's surprise, Eve had wanted to see Ronnie's interviews. Apparently, when Eve went to identify her body, without the gold cuffs on Ronnie's wrists, she'd noted that Ronnie had had their matching tattoo removed. All along, it had been Ronnie's hand in the corner of Natalie's photos, not Eve's. Ever since, Eve had questioned if Ronnie, at one time, had intended to condemn her. "But then she did what she did," Eve had reasoned. "I don't know how I'm meant to feel about her. If she was using me or protecting me ..."

It was something Heather, too, had pondered. Opening her laptop, she'd pressed play. In silence, they watched Ronnie speak. When it got to the final part, Heather casts a glance at Eve. Tears were rolling down her face.

"Some people are just special." Ronnie is smiling. *"For a start, Eve is ridiculously humble. I mean, no one with a body like hers should be humble, right?"* She laughs into the camera before wrinkling her nose. *"But she's also kind, funny, ridiculously hard on herself, and strong. Much stronger than I used to think."* Ronnie shakes her head and grins, *"In truth, it was never just about how Eve looked. She's so much more."* She'd leaned closer to the camera. *"Eve has a lot to say. You should listen ..."*

Heather pressed pause on the video and then asked what she'd wondered for months, "What did she say to you up there before ... ?"

"She said she did it for me. Then she told me not to follow her. I didn't know what she meant until she was gone."

After that, Eve had one more favour to ask.

#

They'd shot it with minimal fuss with just Heather and a cameraman. It took one take. After it, Eve entrusted Heather to do with it what she saw fit. Heather was moved by Eve's frankness regarding addiction, tragedy, loss, life, mistakes – how she no longer wanted to be a prisoner to her past, how she wanted her children to know the truth, and that having their understanding and acceptance was the only thing in the world that mattered. It was raw honesty, and it deserved to be seen.

It was as painfully beautiful as how Timeline's album cover turned out. Out of respect for Natalie, Eve had requested they didn't use the new photos that Conor had shot, considering the revelation that there had once been another girl in a red dress – a girl who'd never had a chance to rise after she fell. The new album cover is a striking image of Eve in a black dress standing against a stark white background. They used a new photographer. Her vision of Eve twenty years later is powerful.

"I almost gave up," Eve admitted to Heather off camera. "Before Ronnie showed up, I nearly stepped off the cliff. I'd forgotten so much of that time that for a moment, I thought maybe I had done what Joanne claimed. I thought I'd pushed Natalie." She'd paused to stare out the window. "I'd spent two decades stuck inside that photograph, and I just wanted to be free. But I've faced the truth now. I've made my mistakes, kept going, and now I'll keep on going." Then she'd added, brighter. "I've decided to keep working. Although, I'm looking for new management." She'd grimaced.

Heather leans forward again and presses play, watching Eve fill the screen. "*Social media is meant to be social!*" Eve nods her head. "*It's what*

I'd like it to be anyway. It's what I'll keep calling for until I'm heard, until it's a safe place to interact, meet people, find support, be heard. Of course, there are risks." She frowns. *"I know that first-hand, and we're still only learning, but I believe in us."* She smiles.

While Eve speaks, Heather grabs her phone from the desk, opens Instagram, and clicks on her profile. She scrolls down the following list, one by one, deleting those she no longer enjoys watching or people she hasn't seen in years – people, if she is honest, she'd probably avoid. After all, what right does she have to watch their lives unless she chooses to be a part of them, or at the very least interact with them online?

Like it or not, we are all part of a culture of stalkers, she thinks, all guilty to some degree. Right then, Heather considers how often she has leaned over to show her husband a post or a photograph, raising her eyebrows or making a face. Or the number of times she has mindlessly scrolled past people's real-life triumphs or challenges and read them without an acknowledgement, a like, a comment, anything. In the privacy of her office, she contemplates how she's taken countless screenshots of something she finds ridiculous, an outlandish filter, an unflattering outfit, a rant, and sent it to a friend.

"No matter how many followers we have. We're real people with feelings. We're all the same," Eve says into the camera. *"Truly, there's nothing special about me. I've made mistakes, broken my own heart, failed, let people down. It could just as easily be someone else sitting here in my place, more than anything. I know that now."* She looks down at her clasped hands. *"I'm delighted people do, but honestly, I have no idea why they follow me."*

Then Eve opens her eyes wide and flashes a smile – an honest, flawed, humble, vulnerable, heartfelt smile, making it clear to Heather why they do.

The End

Acknowledgements

My sincere thanks, as always, to Paula Campbell and all at Poolbeg Press. To Gaye Shortland for what was the most challenging edit yet, thank you for pushing me that bit further. I am once again astounded by your attention to detail. A good team are akin to friends who won't allow you to walk out of the bathroom with your skirt tucked into your tights. I am fortunate to have these people behind me. To the typesetters, designers, and proofers, thank you.

Unfollow Me was conceived during yet another lockdown. Within a five-mile radius, I concocted the story on my daily (sometimes more – what else did we have?!) walk. Lover's Leap is a real place in Enniskerry, Co. Wicklow. If I weren't so afraid of heights, I might, too, sit upon the rock to look across the Dargle valley and marvel at the view. Instead, I gaze from a safe distance. I wrote with poetic license about the village I named Annaford. It is loosely based on my hometown of Enniskerry. All characters are entirely fictional.

As a social media enthusiast, I dipped my toe into chatting online with my small number of followers for the duration of the writing of this book. What I discovered was a fantastic community of supportive people. Alas, another side of social media is the not-so-nice part that this book addresses. Thank you to Yvonne @ystyleireland and Gina

@accessoryfairy for kindly giving me some insights into the daily life of content creation. You are incredible women far beyond your impeccable style.

Thank you also to my sister-in-law, Jennifer Drew, for her legal advice. How I love when you text your associates with questions that must make them very concerned about your intentions!

Yvonne Treacy @downdogstudio.ie for being the most positive person on earth. Thank you for keeping my body and mind relaxed during the writing process.

Joe @consistent_performance, for getting me media-ready by filling me with turkey burgers and string beans, sort of thank you!

As always, immense gratitude for my family and friends. My exceptional children: Martha, Bruce, and Gertie – to the moon and back stuff. To my husband, Malcolm, for his steadfast belief in me, us, and them. Wilbur and Blue – the boys – you guys are the best colleagues.

To Yvonne Gunne (Close), to whom I dedicate this book, for the laughs, encouragement, and lifelong friendship. Our phone calls are hilarious stuff.

To my parents, John and Amy Small. Without them, sure, I wouldn't even be here!

To my readers who have cheered me along to get me to this stage, we did it!

You can follow me on Instagram and Facebook at @judithcuffeauthor to hear me chat about life, writing, and a bit of fashion. Sure, why not! Please, no stalkers! And, finally, to anyone who puts themselves out there, creatively, online, or otherwise, I have nothing but admiration for you. Live and learn, take chances, and be honest. Like it or not, social media is here to stay. Used positively, it has the power to bring us closer together. Everyone has a voice – use it wisely.